TRACEY MARTIN

DIRTY LITTLE MISERY

MISS MISERY

BOOK TWO

DIRTY LITTLE MISERY

TRACEY MARTIN

CITY OWL
PRESS

DIRTY LITTLE MISERY
Miss Misery, Book 2

CITY OWL PRESS
www.cityowlpress.com

Cover Design by MiblArt. All stock photos licensed appropriately.

Edited by Danielle DeVor.

For information on subsidiary rights, please contact the publisher at info@cityowlpress.com.

Print Edition ISBN: 978-1-64898-179-1

Digital Edition ISBN: 978-1-64898-178-4

Printed in the United States of America

To my family, who insist I have a weird imagination. Just remember who I inherited it from.

PRAISE FOR TRACEY MARTIN

"The action in *Wicked Misery* was great, as was the suspense. Each character felt authentic, and the dialogue had me laughing. I definitely want to continue this series."
– *Bad Bird Reads*

"Readers of *Wicked Misery*…will surely be turned into fans, and will find themselves eager for the next installment."
– *RT Book Reviews*

"*Darkest Misery* is recommended for paranormal romance readers who enjoy a high-stakes story."
– *Library Journal*

"This world is rich, it has a lot of non-human, mystical elements in a human setting… I also loved the plot. A nice murder mystery with twist after twist."
– *Fangs for the Fantasy*

"Jess is finding out it's not so easy to let go of her past as she discovers the terrifying truth behind the Gryphons' treachery in this riveting urban fantasy romance, *Misery Loves Company*."
– *Evampire*

"The action was intense and the danger and mystery behind Jess's case brought along lots of drama and suspense in *Dirty Little Misery*."
– *Urban Fantasy Investigations*

ONE

Be careful what you wish for.

Ever since the day I first stepped foot on the marble floor of Gryphon Headquarters in Boston, I'd dreamed of strolling through the massive lobby with a purpose. And by purpose, I didn't mean because I was visiting my father's office, or as part of a school tour. I meant *purpose*. As in, I was there because I was supposed to be there. I was there because I was someone important.

I should have been more specific in my daydreams about what "supposed to be" and "important" entailed.

In the past week, I'd been in Gryphon Headquarters because I was supposed to be and because I was someone important an awful lot, and neither reason was good. In fact, as of today, I had a feeling those reasons would prove to be very bad indeed.

My stomach knotted as I joined the line of people waiting to get through security, and tension put an extra spring in my step. Such was the joy of being a misery junkie and getting high off my own suffering. Being nervous made me peppy.

I emptied my pockets and stepped through the metal detector, eyeing security round two—the magic detectors—that hung just ahead. Brand-new charms twinkled under the overhead lights, ready to turn from green to red if someone tried sneaking by them with something they shouldn't. The display was almost pretty, and the charms showed no signs of imp damage.

Funnily enough, the memory of releasing a minor swarm of the nasty magical insects in here brought a smile to my lips. My best friend, Steph, and I had unleashed the imps in order to take out the magic detectors, part of a hastily thought-out plan to hack into Gryphon Headquarters' servers a couple weeks ago. At the time, it had been one of the scariest things I'd ever done. But hey, when you were framed for murder, you got desperate.

The guard handed me back my ID as I exited the metal detector. "You again? What are you here for this time?"

I stuck my ID in my wallet. "I have a meeting with Olivia Lee."

"The Director, eh? You're moving up in the ranks." The guard looked me up and down, no doubt thinking I was underdressed for the occasion. Despite the heat, I wore a light jacket, my favorite jeans, and my most badass pair of combat boots. I didn't know how long it took to get arrested and arraigned, or whether I'd have to spend the night in a jail cell, and I wanted to be comfortable for the ordeal.

Did I mention that sometimes having a purpose for meeting law enforcement was bad? I suspected I'd have a lot of time to contemplate my poor life choices and even poorer wishful-thinking skills soon enough.

"Yeah, I'm moving up." I slapped on a fake smile for the guard and attached my visitor's ID badge to my jacket. "Lucky me."

I passed through the magic-screening station next with no issues and no more conversation, then checked the clock near the elevators. It was five minutes to four. I was going to be disgustingly punctual for my shakedown and arrest. Maybe my public defender could use that as a point in my favor.

"Well, yes, Your Honor, Jessica did run the first time the Gryphons tried to arrest her. And yes, she did mug people for their blood. And yes, she has used pred-like magic to bend humans to her will. But she was courteous enough to arrive on time for the second attempt to arrest her. We think that ought to count for something."

Or maybe not.

Squaring my shoulders, I checked the office directory and pushed the elevator's up button. To my right, a huge reproduction of Michelangelo's *Triumph* dominated the lobby wall. It was a gorgeous but completely ridiculous painting of Gryphons slaying a bunch of preds, mostly furies and satyrs. I was all for killing furies, seeing as a couple of them were the culprits who'd framed me for murder, but part of me took offense at the ugly portrayal of the satyrs.

It wasn't that satyrs were better in the way they treated humans. Like the furies and other pred races—goblins, harpies, and sylphs—satyrs used their magic to enslave humans by "addicting" them to their power. But having recently discovered I was part satyr, the painting left me uneasy. Although I'd been using my satyr-like power for years without understanding where it came from, I didn't want to identify with that piece of myself.

My only saving grace was that the Gryphons didn't know I wasn't entirely human. No one did except me and the goblins' Dom who'd told me the bad news, and I didn't think Gunthra intended to spread the word any more than I did, though for very different reasons.

As a hybrid, I could reverse a pred's addictive magical bond and feed on the power of any pred clueless enough to screw with my soul. That made me a threat. Or in Gunthra's words, an abomination.

I was about to jab the elevator button a second time when a familiar voice spoke my name. I turned, forcing another fake smile as Gryphon Agent Bridget Nelson strolled up to me.

A couple weeks ago, Bridget had been the lone person from my days at the New England Academy for the Magically Gifted—aka, the Gryphon pre-training school—whom I'd counted as a friend. These days, I wasn't certain where we stood. She'd tried to arrest me. I'd resisted and had beaten up a couple of her coworkers in the process. I wasn't sure if the fact that it had all been a giant misunderstanding could atone for my actions. Nor was I sure I wanted it to, seeing as I was still feeling kind of sore about the whole ordeal.

Bridget was dolled up in the Gryphons' dress uniform, and I guessed she'd come from court. I knew she was working on the case against Victor Aubrey, a former fury addict and the guy who'd worked with his evil masters to frame me for his murders.

The elevator door opened as if on cue when Bridget stepped up to it. "How's your wrist? You're here to meet with the director, aren't you?"

I clasped my hands behind my back to hide my nerves, a move made more difficult by the brace on my sprained left wrist. "Wrist is healing, and yes. I don't suppose you know why the director herself wants to see me?"

Bridget pressed a button for the third floor, then helpfully pushed the fifth floor for me. "Not a clue, actually. If it had something to do with the Aubrey case, I'm sure I'd know."

That was probably true. Although my quasi-crimes had only been exposed thanks to Victor Aubrey's totally real and disgusting crimes, it was likely they would be handled separately from the Aubrey case.

"Whatever it is, let me know," Bridget said as the elevator arrived on the third floor. "I'm working late tonight, but we could grab a coffee across the street after your meeting's over."

"Whatever it is, I'm sure you'll find out. I have to go to work later, but we can get coffee soon." Maybe she could bring me some in my jail cell. I had a feeling prison coffee would not be up to my standards.

On that thought, my insides squirmed like a salamander caught in the rain. It took me so long to move when the elevator doors opened on the fifth floor that they almost shut again with me still inside.

Courage, I told myself. How was it I'd had the guts to face down some of the nastiest preds in town, but walking down the industrial-carpeted floor of Gryphon Headquarters was a battle for each step?

Oh, right. Because I was reckless but not stupid. I could practically hear Lucen's voice in my head. My satyr friend with benefits had been saying that a lot lately. He believed I usually knew exactly what I was doing, but showed way too little regard for my health.

I couldn't get over the idea that he cared. A satyr giving a damn for a human was unheard of, and since Lucen didn't know my secret, that's all I was in his eyes—a human with a freaky gift.

The sooner I get this over with, the sooner I can see him again. Lucen had promised he'd spring for my bail if he could. I looked forward to owing him for it.

The thought of what owing him might entail hurried my steps. I needed to walk off the heat that came over me as my imagination ran wild.

Headquarters' fifth floor housed offices for all the truly important Gryphons, and it wasn't long before someone's secretary or assistant intercepted me. I was led down a couple generically beige hallways and deposited in front of a desk containing yet another secretary.

"I'm Jessica Moore," I said to the inquiring gaze behind the desk. "I have an appointment with Director Lee."

"Yes, you do." She pressed a button on her phone. "Director, Jessica Moore is here. Should I send her in?"

I couldn't hear the response because I was too busy willing my stomach to stop its flailing. It must have been a yes, however, because the secretary smiled up at me. "You can go ahead."

Awesome. Here went just about everything. Trying not to look as anxious as I felt, I opened the highly polished wood door.

Olivia Lee, director of the Boston Regional Office of the Angelic Order of the Gryphon, the hallowed international magical law enforcement agency, stood as I entered. Since my unfortunate role in Victor Aubrey's murders had made me one of the case's most important witnesses, I'd seen the director around on several occasions. On a first impression, she didn't scream badass, pred-killing, crime-buster. She was several inches shorter than me with a slight build, gray threaded through her tidy, black hair, and a face that had probably turned heads a couple decades ago.

But as I knew better than most, looks could be deceiving. If you listened to Olivia Lee speak for long enough, you could tell that not only did this disarming woman pack a powerful magical punch, she also wasn't afraid to use it. I could respect her even though I assumed we weren't going to be best buds.

Director Lee held out a hand. "Afternoon, Jessica. Our paths have crossed several times lately, but we haven't actually been introduced. It's nice to meet you. You're an interesting person."

I took her hand, which was as calloused as my own. Proof that working one's way up the Gryphon ranks was hard. "I get that a lot."

"I imagine you do from those who are aware of your gift." From her tone, the implication was clear—she wanted to know why she hadn't been made aware of it sooner. She motioned to the chair in front of me. "Have a seat. I've been reviewing the information you've given us with regards to the Aubrey case, but I wanted the chance to talk to you personally about your unique abilities."

I shifted in the leather seat, searching her for signs of deception. How long until we got to the now-I'm-going-to-arrest-you part? Although I could sense something deceptive in her, it was faint. No doubt the good director had several motives and schemes. No doubt someone like her had many she was hiding from someone like me.

I wet my lips. "I explained everything. It should be in the reports." Everything, that was, except my freakish and previously unheard-of biology. "I'm not sure what else you want to know."

Olivia—if she was going to refer to me by my first name, I was going to take the same liberty—picked up one of the papers on her desk. "I know, but I'd like to hear it from you. You're quite something."

There are ways of saying that phrase that make it sound like a compliment. This wasn't one of them.

"So the reason we found a vial of blood in your apartment," Olivia continued, "is because you'd obtained the blood from someone in order to trade it to a pred? Did you do this a lot?"

"I did it when it came to my attention that someone needed help getting out of a pred contract." I had no idea exactly how many people's souls I'd traded over the ten years since I'd begun my hobby business. A lot was probably an understatement.

Olivia leaned back in her chair, scanning the paper. "Explain the process for me."

I sighed, wondering if she was hoping to trip me up by making me repeat myself. "Someone would come to me with a sob story about how they traded their soul to a pred. I'd use my gift to find someone evil, take a bit of their blood, then trade their blood to the pred to get the first person's soul back."

To say I traded in actual souls was a bit of a misnomer. I traded in blood. The preds would use the blood to find the person it belonged to, then use it again to bind that person to them. Blood made it easier for preds to break a person's soul and turn them into an addict.

Addicts, or blood contracts to turn people into addicts, were like currency to the preds who needed addicts to live. The older, more powerful ones could be discerning about whom they addicted, choosing humans who were valuable for reasons other than the emotional meal they provided. But younger and less powerful preds had to take what they could get.

Although preds claimed differently, there wasn't much good in the bargain for the addict except whatever had been so necessary that they'd willingly agreed to become one for it in the first place. Usually what drove people to such desperate measures was an extremely powerful spell. Often it was an illegal one. Preds owned plenty of legitimate businesses and worked in totally mundane professions, but those who created charms for a living did most of it on the black market.

That bit aside, addict contracts were legal so long as they weren't coerced. What I'd done was coerced—as were most pred contracts in reality—and it was most definitely of questionable legal status.

Olivia set the paper down and regarded me, her fingers pressed together beneath her chin. "So you admit you traded innocent people's lives away to preds in exchange for money?"

"I went after violent criminals—murderers, rapists, child molesters. Not exactly upstanding citizens."

"And that gave you the right to decide they should become addicts rather than people who knowingly entered into a legal contract?"

I shrugged. "Maybe, maybe not. But most of the people who came to me for help didn't deserve their fate either. Anyway, I didn't always do it for the money. Some people I helped on principle."

"So very kind of you."

Given the danger often involved in hunting those murderers and rapists, I thought the director's sarcasm was misplaced.

She answered my unimpressed stare with a sigh of her own. "So according to your earlier statement, you chased these criminals down because you could sense the evil in them and knew they were about to act on it. This is because you have a pred-like ability to feed on negative emotions."

"I prefer to think of myself as a misery junkie."

Olivia's smile was thin. "Can you sense what I'm feeling now?"

I raised an eyebrow. "Annoyed at me? No special talent required to notice that."

"Why didn't you tell any of your instructors at the Academy about this?"

Speaking of things that ought to be obvious. But Olivia seemed genuinely perplexed. I could taste her butterscotch confusion. "First, this ability didn't come around until I'd been kicked out of the program. Second, it's not something I'm proud of or happy about. And it's not like anyone could have done something about it. What was there to tell?"

"It would have been good for us to know. We could have helped you find a way to put those talents to better use. An ethical one."

Would they have? It had never occurred to me that the Gryphons would think my gift was anything other than evil. At best, I figured they'd turn me into a lab rat. At worst, they'd label me a danger to humanity and lock me up. Unlike a full-blooded pred, I had no Dom to watch out for me.

I frowned at the large seal hanging behind the Director's desk. The lion-tailed, eagle-winged gryphon in the center clutched a sword in each talon. Encircling it was the Gryphons' motto: For the Gifted Have a Duty to Protect Mankind.

Ignoring the old-fashioned, sexist language, the message was clear. The Gryphons had always been a humans-only and humans-first organization. They often allied themselves with the magi, a race of bird shapeshifters, but there were no magi in the Gryphon organization.

So despite what Olivia Lee said, it had never been obvious to me that a human with a non-human power should turn to them for help, and I said as much.

"That's unfortunate, because I think this organization could have benefitted from your talents." Olivia absently moved some of the files around on her desk. From beneath one of them, she produced a paper and slid it toward me. "However, now that we know what you can do, I'd like to rectify the situation. I want you to come work for us."

I froze, certain I'd heard incorrectly. "You what?"

"Given your past activities, we'd have to consider this on a trial basis, and you'd only have limited clearance, but I'd like to bring you in as a special consultant on cases where you'd be useful."

I gaped at her. All my life, I'd longed to be a Gryphon like my father had been. The pain of my gift turning rogue, the bitterness of getting kicked out of the Academy and watching my friends graduate—those things had haunted me like a curse for the past ten years.

Until two weeks ago. Until I'd been framed for a series of gruesome murders and the Gryphons had become obstacles to clearing my name. And until I'd learned the truth about my biology and the Gryphons had become, by their very ideals, potential enemies.

I glanced down at the paper, which appeared to be some sort of hiring agreement, but I didn't take it. "You want to give me a job?"

Olivia's dark eyes bore into me. "Let me be frank. I'm not sure 'want' is the most apt word, but I think you could be useful. I've been over your records from your time at the Academy, and I have to admit I was surprised to discover how highly your teachers regarded you. You had a very powerful gift, and you were at the top of your class academically. It's impressive."

Now *that* I was sure I'd heard right. "You're surprised I wasn't failing out?"

"Considering what you've done."

"You mean help people?"

Olivia pursed her lips. "I mean trading away innocent people's souls."

"I explained that. I think we have a very different definition of innocent. Those people were evil. I would know."

Olivia's face filled with disdain. "That's precisely the problem. Did you never think? The only thing worse than a truly innocent person being enslaved to a pred is a pred enslaving a violent criminal—the sort of person who might enjoy carrying out whatever horrible demands they're ordered to do. Who might go above and beyond for the sheer joy of it, or to please their master."

My rebuttal died on my tongue, recognizing it had lost the argument before it could begin. Well, damn. Actually, I hadn't thought about it that way. I wasn't certain most preds engaged in illegal activities any more than most humans, but they definitely didn't hold much regard for the human laws they ostensibly obeyed.

This realization must have shown on my face, judging by Olivia's triumphant expression. "Without your former academic record to go by, I'd have thought you were very stupid. Instead, it appears you're just reckless, mercenary, and shortsighted."

Scowling, I flung her hiring agreement away. "I concede the point, but you're not exactly doing a good job of convincing me to come work for you."

"That's unfortunate, because my good will and willingness to give you a second chance are all that stand between you and a prison cell. Endangering humans is only the beginning of what I could charge you with if I chose."

My heartbeat stuttered.

Was it? I always assumed I was keeping a toe on the line that separated the questionably ethical from the flat-out illegal. As a result, I'd gone into this appointment figuring there were a dozen minor laws I could be accused of breaking, but any decent lawyer could get me a livable deal. Probably the sort that involved mandatory community service.

But endangering humans? That was a felony, and way more than a couple toes over the line. More like an entire foot.

Damn. I hated being a gracious loser, and I hated even more that she'd gotten the upper hand on me so easily. But Olivia Lee was right about two things. I wasn't stupid. And I didn't want to go to jail.

"Well, then, you should have said so," I said, adopting my sweetest voice as I picked up the agreement. "That's so much more persuasive."

In the future, I was going to have to be way more careful about what I wished for.

TWO

I LEFT THE DIRECTOR'S OFFICE IN A DAZE AND FOUND MY WAY back to the lobby. There, standing among the commotion with dozens of voices echoing off the marble floor, I paused. Conscious of a stress headache forming behind my eyes, I staked out an empty but friendly-looking patch of wall to mentally regroup.

Finally, I was living my dream, only the dream had become a nightmare. The Gryphons were blackmailing me. Blackmailing me! Weren't they supposed to be the good guys?

Okay, fine—I suppose the legal phrase would be they were "cutting me a deal," but that was merely a euphemism. It still amounted to "work for them or go to jail."

Sounded like blackmail to me.

To be fair, it was a sweet blackmail-like offer. The Gryphons were going to pay me for this consulting gig, and the money Olivia Lee had offered was nothing to whine about. I didn't know what the going rate for a Gryphon consultant was—I didn't even think there was such a thing until today—but if I only ended up working part-time, I'd still be making more than I had full-time at my last job. Besides, considering how the whole being-framed-for-murder ordeal had cost me my last job, I'd have had a strong inducement to take the offer anyway.

To be more than fair to the Gryphons, it would probably be fascinating work too. That said, I was so over wanting to be a Gryphon. But what choice did I have? I didn't want to end up in a jail cell next to Victor Aubrey either.

I pushed my hair behind my ears, breathing deeply and focusing on a woman in the far corner of the lobby. She was on the phone, and though I couldn't hear her conversation, something upset her. I sucked on the sweet vanilla sadness she emanated, hoping the energy hit would clear my head and ease the headache away before it could take over.

It worked. Mostly. Feeling more focused, I checked the time. I hadn't been in the director's office long, which meant if I hurried, I could stop at my apartment before heading to Lucen's.

A surprisingly short time later, I opened my apartment door and reached out with my gift, searching the place for signs of emotion. All I got back was emptiness. Excellent. I rushed down the short hallway and frowned when I encountered my bedroom door. Someone had taped a note to it. Not so excellent. I ripped it off as I entered my room.

In the days immediately following Victor's arrest, my roommates Geoff and Valerie had done their best to avoid me. Bruised and beaten, mentally and emotionally, I'd been thankful for that as I recovered. But my reprieve from their curiosity hadn't lasted long.

Once the news spread that I was a key witness in Victor's murders and that I'd resisted arrest by the Gryphons in connection with his crimes, I suddenly became very interesting. Not just to my roommates, but to the press.

The latter was easy enough to ignore, particularly since I'd been legally forbidden from speaking. But for a few days, Geoff and Val had begged me for details. After they got as many from me as I was willing and able to provide, they'd started avoiding me again. I wasn't sure how much of my non-human magical skills they'd discovered, but it must have been enough.

I opened the note, scanned it, and dumped it in the trash. They wanted to talk. Whatever. I'd already suffered through one unpleasant conversation today. I wasn't hanging around for another. If it was important, they had my cell number.

Throwing my jacket on the bed, I examined myself in the mirror and decided I needed to change. My jeans and shirt were fine for working at a bar, but I assumed I'd be spending the night at Lucen's once it closed. That required less practical, more attractive underwear. I took care of that, then stuck a set of clean clothes in my duffel bag for tomorrow and added my most important accessory to my outfit.

Once upon a time, that would have been a protective charm, but I no longer felt the need for one of those. My current accessory, which I'd named Misery, was one of several reasons why.

Misery was a sleek, nicely balanced knife I'd stolen from a fury bar. The black blade announced to the world it had been forged in salamander fire, which, besides making it extremely expensive, meant it was the only type of weapon capable of killing a pred. As a bonus, the single word engraved on the hilt—*souffrance*—announced to me that we were made for each other.

This was the main reason I'd wanted to stop at home before heading to Lucen's. Although I trusted him and no longer had reason to fear a pred's attempts to addict me, I'd made lots of enemies in the preds' neighborhood during the past few weeks. Being visibly armed with a lethal weapon just made good sense.

With the knife strapped to my hip and my hair pulled off my neck in a ponytail, I was ready. I grabbed my bag and left before Geoff or Val showed up.

Not surprisingly for a Friday evening, the trains were packed, and a large group of humans got off at the Shadowtown T station with me. For many, particularly barely legal college students and recent grads, going to a pred-owned bar was simply another type of thrill-seeking behavior. Much like doing a hundred miles per hour on the Mass Pike without a seat belt or skydiving without a parachute.

Some people made *me* look cautious.

Those dipshits, however, made up a large portion of the clientele for Lucen's bar, The Lair, so I wasn't surprised when several of them trailed after me. Located a short block from the T stop, The Lair was an easy to get to, easy to get out of location for stupid humans. It was also the unofficial gathering spot for Boston's most powerful satyrs—possibly the result of Lucen being the third on his Dom's council.

Speaking of powerful satyrs, a familiar one was sitting at one of The Lair's few outside tables. Devon raised his beer to me as I walked down the four steps onto the sunken patio. He was the first—the lieutenant—on the satyr's council, and a good friend of Lucen's. Perhaps because of that, he was nice to me. I almost liked him, though I trusted him as much as any other pred. Which was to say not even half as far as I could throw him.

My muscles tensed, waiting for intense lust to come over me like it used to every time I was surrounded by satyrs, but it never arrived. During my final confrontation with the furies, I'd used my power to reverse the bond on the one who'd addicted me. That act seemed to have fried my emotional nerve endings. I no longer felt much of any pred's power—no harpy jealousy, no fury anger, no sylph self-doubt, no goblin greed, and no satyr lust. It was like wearing the ultimate protective charm.

And it was fabulous.

It was also one of those secrets I was keeping close to my chest. Like the Gryphons, the less the preds knew about my abilities, the better.

But immunity to pred magic aside, I had to admit something about Devon's voice made my body a little hotter. I blamed it on his faint British accent. "Lucen mentioned where you were. So I see you're still a free woman? Good to know."

I threw him a sarcastic smile. "Not that free."

"One day I'll change your mind." He lowered his sunglasses, and his mischievous blue eyes traveled the length of my body. "You should know, Jess, I had my lawyer on speed dial for you."

I stepped out of the way as the humans who'd been behind me entered the bar. The other satyrs at Devon's table were checking me out too. I recognized a couple of them but didn't know their names. "I'm betting you always have your lawyer on speed dial."

"Okay, yes, that's true. But for you, I'd have used it." His oh-so-earnest tone got a laugh out of me, and Devon grinned.

Leaving him behind, I entered the bar, and my eyes adjusted to the dim light. The Lair was nice, not what most people would expect from a satyr-owned bar. Dark red walls. Dark wood tables and booths. Understated décor. Lucen had taste, and I liked to believe the fact he found me interesting was proof of such.

Predictably, the bar was packed. Satyrs and the occasional harpy mingled with the reckless humans, who were clearly infected with the preds' power. I tried to ignore them. All that unrequited lust should be boosting my energy levels and leaving a distinctly delicious taste in my mouth, but the satyrs lapped it up before I could.

"Jess!" Lucen darted out from behind the bar, and now the only lust that mattered was my own.

As far as I was concerned, Lucen was exactly what a creature of lust should look like, and I wasn't referring to the small horns all satyrs had. From his honey-blond waves, to his broad shoulders, to the six-pack he hid beneath his tight T-shirt, he made my mouth water—and he had, like no other satyr could, since the day we met.

Even with my increased resistance to pred magic, my heartbeat quickened and my blood grew hot. He was the only one of his race who retained that effect on me.

I dropped my bag as he wrapped his arms around me, and though I tried to feel merely relieved and comforted by his presence, that didn't work out so well. I mean, I did feel relieved, but that was far from all. As usual, his magic smelled lightly of cinnamon, and as I breathed it in, it took all my willpower not to start undressing him right here. But damn, I wanted nothing more than to run my hands beneath his shirt, feel the heat of skin, and taste his tongue in my mouth.

He fed off my lust too. I could feel him growing hard as he pressed more tightly against me. Unfortunately, the bar was busy, which meant I had to settle for one long, slow kiss. Still, it was enough to make my skin tingle from my neck to my toes.

Lucen ran his thumb down my cheek, and my eyes closed involuntarily. "I got your text. Since they didn't arrest you, what was the meeting about?"

I backed away and picked up my bag, my nerves almost past the point of no return. The last thing I wanted was to become one of those humans driven to doing sociably questionable things in public because of satyr magic. "Long story. I'll explain later. Let me dump this, and I'll make myself useful."

Lucen shook his head like I was crazy, but he let me pass. "If you insist, little siren."

"I insist."

Yes, it was true that a cocktail waitress with a sprained wrist was not the most useful employee. Apparently, Lucen hadn't expected me to actually work when he'd offered me the job. His reason for doing so, he'd claimed, was simply because he liked having me here—a phrase he'd clarified in multiple positions and in multiple places around the bar ever since, including on top of the bar itself, on several tables, and in the kitchen.

But as much as I'd enjoyed his employee benefits package, I also had pride, and I intended to work for the cash I was supposed to be earning. As long as I could pour beers and serve drinks, albeit with less grace than I might like, then I would.

And so I did over the next eight hours. The satyrs and harpies thinned out soon after I arrived. Most probably had to head to their own jobs, since for preds the setting sun meant their day was just beginning. But the human crowd didn't let up until around midnight, denying me time to ruminate over my situation with the Gryphons. When Lucen hung up the closed sign at 2:00 a.m., he looked at me expectantly, but I pressed my lips together. His other bartender, Paulius, was wiping down the last of the glasses, and this was a conversation best had in private.

While they finished the cleanup, I traipsed up the back stairs. Lucen lived above The Lair in an airy apartment that was roomier, cleaner, and way better furnished than my own. By the fireplace, his pet dragon, Sweetpea, snorted at me from within his cage. He was a young dragon and every bit as antisocial as the worst of his species, but he couldn't breathe true fire yet. A puff of smoke dissipated into the air as I passed.

"Oh, give it up," I told him, flopping on the sofa and grasping a cushion to my chest. "You should be used to me by now."

Sweetpea snorted again and raked a claw against the cage floor in a gesture I took to mean, *Come closer you stinky magical mammal so I can bite you.*

I declined the offer.

The door at the top of the back stairs creaked, and I tossed the pillow away. A tiny entryway joined the kitchen to the living room, and craning my neck, I could see straight into the far side of the apartment. A moment later Lucen appeared in the kitchen. He looked tired as he pushed sweaty hair off his face. Even with the door propped open and ceiling fans going, the number of bodies packed into the bar had made it hot. A thin layer of sweat coated my skin, and I gave my arm a covert sniff. On Lucen, sweat looked good. On me, not so much.

"I saw that, little siren." He grabbed two cans of soda, opened them, and handed one to me.

I took a long sip. "Maybe I should go shower."

"Only if I can join you."

"When have I ever objected to that?"

Lucen set his soda down and bent over me. "I don't know? The better part of the past decade?"

I slipped my hands under his shirt, my heart beating faster. His closeness was like the sun burning off my sleepiness. It also relieved the aches in my feet and drove away my anger at the Gryphons. Being on fire had never felt better. "Okay, true. But I've been making up for it lately."

Lucen climbed onto the sofa next to me. Smiling, he tugged me on top of him. "Prove it."

Like I needed the challenge. Was there any better form of stress relief than a beautiful, adoring man offering himself up to you?

I pulled my shirt off, then ran my fingers over his stomach until he took off his own. The line of blond hairs that ran from his chest into his waistband called to me, and I set my lips to them, slowly kissing my way down. As he was a pred, I couldn't taste Lucen's emotions, but I could hear the way his breathing changed and could feel his body shifting beneath mine, and it was as heady a rush as anything I'd ever experienced.

My own body ached with desire as I grazed my teeth over each hard ab. His skin was slightly salty with sweat, and the scent of it mixed with his cinnamon. Gently, I dropped each kiss deliberately lower until I reached his waistband. The bulge in his jeans pressed against my cheek, making me acutely aware of the emptiness between my legs pleading to be filled.

Lucen tangled his hands in my hair, and I closed my eyes, relishing the way his fingertips caressed my scalp, the way they sent tendrils of magic down my nerves and explosions along my tender skin.

"I can't believe you made me wait ten years." His voice was low, his breathing heavy.

Neither could I, and I had to fight the longing to go faster. To reclaim our lost time.

Wetting my lips, I undid his button. Then his zipper. He stared down at me, a fierce glow in his eyes that urged me on and heated my blood. My fingers trembled as I resisted the itch to quicken my pace, then I wrapped them around his length, so silky sweet and hard, and eased him free of his jeans. My body clenched in time with his.

His breath hitched as I leaned over to taste him once, a single lick to hear him moan and stoke my hunger. His grip on me tightened. "Jess."

I teased us both with my lips, letting them brush against his wet tip while my free hand reached lower to cup the rest of him. I wasn't sure who wanted the next part more, but my body screamed with a throbbing need. To hold his powerful erection in my hands, to watch his naked chest rising and falling, to meet the intensity in his eyes—to know I was the one stirring this reaction in him—pitched my own desires to levels I'd never experienced before.

I couldn't believe I'd managed to hold out for *ten years*.

TWENTY MINUTES LATER I WAS ON MY HANDS AND KNEES, retrieving my pants from beneath the table and even more in need of a shower. My hair stuck to my neck, but my body was languid with fulfillment and my mind at peace. It didn't hurt that Lucen hadn't bothered to put his shirt back on either. Half-dressed myself, I watched him head into the kitchen, admiring the muscles in his back.

"Ready to shower?" I asked, amused at my own licentiousness. Satyrs could turn anyone into a sex fiend. I'd practically been a nun before this. After all, it was hard to maintain any sort of relationship when you got a high off ruining them, and I'd never been the sort who was comfortable jumping into bed with someone I didn't know well. Thus, my sex life had been almost as nonexistent as my dating life.

Lucen laughed, and I could hear him rummaging around in his cabinets. It was dinnertime for him, but past bedtime for me. "Soon, but first I want to hear what happened today."

Shit. The Gryphons. My post-sex contentment died a painful death. Groaning, I climbed to my feet and padded over to the stairs in the center of the apartment so I could see him while we talked. I dropped off my jeans on the bottom step. Knowing Lucen, he'd probably wash them while I was sleeping.

I cleared my throat. "Right, the Gryphons." I dragged out the word, wrapping my arms around the baluster. Lucen glanced my way, his eyebrows raised while he waited. "They offered me a job."

"A job?" I imagined my expression earlier in the day had been an awful lot like his was now.

"A job."

His blue-green eyes filled with disbelief. "The kind that comes with a uniform and badge, or the kind that involves cleaning out their salamander cages with your bare hands?"

"The director made no mention of a uniform or a badge, but given what they offered to pay me, I'm assuming it's not cage duty."

"Interesting and unexpected, but I hope you told them where they could stick that job."

I bit my lip, grasping the baluster for all it was worth. "I'll only be a consultant, not a real Gryphon."

Lucen threw the bread he'd been slicing on the counter. "You already said yes?"

"Yeah. As much as I joked about how I'd enjoy owing you for bail money, I really didn't want to go to prison." I released the railing and frowned down at myself, thinking how bizarre my life was that I was having this conversation in my underwear. "That was my choice—take their offer or go to prison. Tell me I should have chosen differently."

"So they threatened you."

"Basically. You blame me for saying yes?"

He brushed crumbs off his hands and sighed. "No, I don't. But damn it. Did they tell you what they wanted you to do?"

Gryphons had specializations, just like any law enforcement organization. While the stereotype of a Gryphon was the ass-kicking warrior who could stand up to and fight law-breaking preds, the truth was more complicated—as truth usually was.

Some Gryphons specialized in healing addicts, others in making charms, and there were still others in jobs I knew less about. I had a feeling none of those specialties were what Olivia Lee had in mind for me though.

"The director said they'd call me in on cases where they thought I'd be useful."

Lucen rolled his eyes. "That's unhelpfully vague."

I didn't bother responding. Tiredness was overcoming me again, and my annoyance with the Gryphons killed off any remaining desire I had for Lucen. Instead of sex, I wanted to hit someone.

Lucen must have sensed what I was feeling because his hands appeared on my arms as I started to put on my jeans. Hello, lust, again. That didn't take much. "I'm not mad at you, Jess. I'm furious at them."

"So am I, as you can obviously tell. Olivia—Director Lee—said they could charge me with endangering humanity. You think they can?"

"They can charge you with anything. Making it stick is another matter, but I doubt any jury of your peers is going to be too sympathetic. They'll hear you traded souls, and it won't matter what the details are."

A jury of my peers. For the hundredth time, I considered telling Lucen the truth about me. That I was a freak who didn't have any peers. But something stopped me. While I didn't believe he'd call me an abomination like the goblin Dom had, I wasn't eager to find out.

"So I'll do this," I said. "How bad can it be? I used to want to be a Gryphon."

Lucen wrapped his arms around me and kissed my neck, and I was so done thinking about Gryphons. "I was very happy the day you realized they don't deserve you, little siren. Don't let them change your mind. I waited ten years for you. I refuse to let them turn you into my enemy."

"Believe me, I know who my enemies are." I touched my lips to his.

Every nerve from my tongue to my feet came to attention. "Look on the bright side. Isn't it every satyr's dream to bed a Gryphon?"

Lucen laughed, though the lines around his eyes made it clear he was not entirely amused by the situation. "I hope you get a uniform. Because you will definitely need to wear it for me if you do."

THREE

I wasn't sure what time Lucen joined me in his bed, but it was well after I fell asleep. So when a god-awful noise woke me up, I had a momentary panic attack. His arm was over me and I couldn't move.

"Is that your phone?" Lucen murmured into my hair.

Mentally half asleep, I had to think about it. "Shit. Yes." I slid over to the edge of the bed and nearly tumbled onto the floor in an effort to reach it in time.

The clock on the nightstand told me it was only nine in the morning. In other words, way too early to be awakened when I hadn't gotten to sleep until almost four.

I swore at the number on my caller ID and picked up right before the phone switched over to voicemail. "Yeah?"

"Jessica, good morning. I hope I didn't wake you."

If I'd wanted to punch Olivia Lee yesterday, it was nothing compared to what I wanted to do to her now. I wasn't supposed to report in to Headquarters for my orientation until this afternoon.

Rubbing my tired eyes, I pulled my bare legs underneath me. "Nope, you didn't wake me. I always sound this groggy before noon."

Lucen raised his head from the pillow, cursed silently, and flopped back down. I envied him the luxury.

"Good." I couldn't sense emotions over the phone, but I swore I could hear her smirking. "Something came up this morning. We've been called in to a case by local PD. I'd like you to get to Newton as soon as possible. I already have a team on the way, and I want you on it. You can come by the office afterward to take care of your paperwork. Can you do that?"

I gritted my teeth, considering whether I ought to say no and tell her I had another obligation. Said obligation was watching me from under a set of cool cotton sheets, his hair tousled, his eyes sleepy, and his body naked.

On the other hand, I was wide awake and I knew there'd be no falling back asleep.

I yawned. "It might take a while. I don't have car." I had a motorcycle, but it was parked at my apartment complex.

"Take a cab. We'll reimburse you for the expense. When you get there, find Agent Andre Pagan. I'll text you the address."

"I'll be there."

I didn't say how fast. With a second yawn, I hung up and began putting on my clothes, which Lucen had left folded on a chair after I'd gone to bed.

He watched me as I changed. "I thought I had you for five more hours."

"So did I, but apparently something happened in Newton."

Lucen buried himself under the sheet. "Great. If this is how it's going to be..."

I bent over the sheet-covered lump and kissed him through the cloth. "I seriously doubt this is going to be normal. But I'm awake, so I might as well go. Can I make some coffee?"

He lowered the sheet, grabbed my hand, and pulled me closer for a real kiss. If he was hoping to make it difficult for me to leave, he was succeeding. "Of course you can make coffee."

When he didn't let go right away, I knew he was more than hoping. He was trying quite blatantly to change my mind. The heat of his magic was slipping its way up arm. "Nice trick."

I yanked my hand away, and he smiled sheepishly. "I had to try."

"Yeah, yeah. I'll see you later."

He muttered something as I left the bedroom, but it was muffled beneath the sheets.

———

"YOU KNOW WHICH HOUSE?" MY UBER DRIVER ASKED ME SOME time later. "Something's going on over there."

I pressed my head against the window. Something was indeed going on several houses down on the right. I couldn't see a street number, but we'd clearly arrived at my destination. "That's it. You can pull over."

Stuffing my hands in my jeans pockets, I stood for a moment, taking in the scene as the car drove off. Three cop cars, plus possibly another unmarked one, and two Gryphon SUVs were parked in front of a huge yellow colonial. As I watched, a van from the coroner's office squeezed into the driveway alongside a BMW. Given the house had a three-car garage, I assumed the BMW and the other expensive cars in the driveway belonged to guests.

As I headed toward the commotion, I breathed in the smell of exhaust mingled with freshly cut grass and sneezed. Allergies. Just one of the many reasons I preferred living in the city to living in the suburbs.

"Hey!"

Recognizing the sound of authority, I tore my eyes away from what was no doubt at least a million dollars worth of house. A uniformed police officer was waving me away. "You can't come any closer."

A slight breeze blew my hair in my mouth, and I fought to remove it so I could speak. "I'm supposed to meet Andre Pagan. He's with the Gryphons."

The cop gave me a once-over, and I could taste his suspicion. It was a bitter film over the rest of his emotions. Whatever was in that house had freaked the shit out of him.

Peachy. I didn't really want to find out what that was. Damn the Gryphons. "Look, tell him Jessica Moore is here. Please. I'm new—first day on the job and no badge. But he's expecting me."

The cop raised a hand toward me. "Wait here." He got on his walkie-talkie and wandered away. A minute later, he beckoned me forward.

With a deep breath, I walked up the brick path to the front door. Before I could climb the portico's stairs, the door opened and a man in a Gryphon uniform smiled warmly at me. "You must be the infamous Jessica Moore."

Despite my anger at the Gryphons as an organization, I took an instant liking to this particular member of it. Unlike a true pred, sensing positive emotions was beyond my meager abilities, but he had a friendly face. His black hair was only a shadow on his shaved scalp, and there were amber tones in his brown eyes. He was tall too. Close to Lucen's height if I had to guess.

"I'm infamous? Excellent. But you can call me Jess. Are you Agent Pagan?"

"I am, and you can call me Andre. I'd shake your hand and all that, but as you can see…" He held up hands covered in gloves. "Come on in, and let's find a pair for you."

I followed him into a high-ceilinged foyer and wrinkled my nose. Alcohol, stale sweat maybe, and something fouler lurked in this house. "Please tell me that's not the smell of dead bodies."

Andre handed me a pair of gloves from a box by the door. "No, decomposing bodies smell much worse. Trust me. I think you're sniffing the food the owners had sitting out all night. You been briefed on what the cops found?"

I wiggled my fingers around in the gloves. They were way too big. "I've been briefed on precisely nothing."

"Fantastic. And you've never done anything like this before?"

"Nope. But I read a lot of mysteries. I suppose that doesn't count, huh?"

He snorted. "You're in for some fun then. Come watch, learn, and don't touch anything. They haven't taken the bodies away yet because we're still collecting evidence, so you'll get to see this insanity for all it's worth. Just try to stay out of the way."

I'd have done a much better job of staying out of the way if I could have been brought in later and allowed to sleep, but I kept the thought to myself.

Andre led me through one enormous room after another until we reached a blindingly stainless steel kitchen. The source of the house's odor was plain, and as Andre had indicated. A couple pizza boxes, ripe with garlic and sausage, sat on the center island next to several wine and liquor bottles. The booze was gone, but the pizza was untouched.

Another cop was holding a door open as a photographer came up a set of stairs. The officer gave me a curious glance.

"Basement?" I asked.

"Yes, and what a basement it is." Andre paused, taking the door from the cop. "You are going to be okay seeing dead bodies, right?"

I swallowed and adopted my best nonchalant expression. Judging by the undercurrent of anxiety I picked up from the more seasoned people here, this was one hell of a group of dead bodies. Then again, I'd experienced some truly awful stuff thanks to Victor Aubrey and the furies, like people whose hearts had been removed. My stomach was tougher than I'd have thought. "I'll be okay. How many bodies are we talking?"

Andre seemed to consider the truthfulness of my response, then shrugged. "Nine."

"Damn. Did someone slaughter a party? What was going on here?"

He started down the stairs. "Something like that. Come see for yourself."

A bit lightheaded from all the diffuse anxiety I was sucking in—and probably a lack of breakfast—I headed downstairs. Something told me I was just as well-off not having eaten. Andre might have been right about the smell of decomposing bodies, but the stench down here was nonetheless worse than the kitchen reek. And decidedly different.

He stopped on the landing at the bottom of the stairs and held up a hand. "Whatever jokes you want to make about stiffs? Don't. I've heard them all from the cops, and once is enough."

"I think I'm too much of a newb to make jokes about—" My words died on my tongue and my brain seized up. Andre had stepped aside, revealing a scene that was nothing like my imagination would have conjured if given a hundred years.

I'd expected something horrific given the way everyone was feeling—blood everywhere, hacked-up limbs, stab wounds. You know, your typical gruesome murder scene. But that's not what I found. And while not finding something that could have come from a B-slasher flick was a relief, my brain had a hard time understanding what I did find because it was so not right.

"Tell me I am not looking at some kind of dead people orgy."

My eyes didn't know what to take in first. There were nine naked people, and given their positioning, they hadn't died in some peaceful post-coital state. They'd died right in the middle of having a good time. Either that or some creep had positioned them so it looked like they had.

I asked which of the two it was.

Andre coughed. "Medical examiner's got to give the final word, but me and the homicide detective are both putting our money on them being alive when the debauchery started. It appears they died the way you're seeing them. *In flagrante delicto*—or however that phrase goes."

I put my hand on the stairwell wall for support. If the cops thought that, no wonder they'd called the Gryphons in for a second opinion. We'd clearly entered fucked-up territory. So far as I could see, there was nothing wrong with these people other than them being dead. No blood, no wounds, no weird skin discolorations. They were simply dead. While having sex. "I suppose there's got to be worse ways to go."

"Remember—no stiff jokes."

"Promise." Cynical as I was, I pitied anyone jaded enough to make jokes about nine dead people. Even if they were naked and in some, uh, interesting positions.

Andre patted my arm. "You all right? You look pale."

I glanced down at his tan hand contrasting against my pasty skin. No kidding. "I'm fine. I've seen worse. What should I do again?"

"Stand back and observe."

"Got it."

There were four other living people in the room. Two uniformed police officers, a man who I assumed was the police detective, and a second Gryphon. The cops appeared to be searching for clues, and the Gryphon had a portable magic scanner she was using on one of the bodies.

"Have you found traces of magic?" I asked.

Andre cast a glance at the other Gryphon, and she raised a finger in a give-me-another-minute gesture. "No overt signs, but we're checking. The

Newton police called us because the scene seemed off, if you know what I mean. No noticeable causes of death."

I nodded. "Looks like a lot is off. Um, no pun intended."

Andre shot me a dirty look and went to consult with the detective.

While he did whatever trained Gryphons did in these situations, I took in the rest of the scene. Dead bodies aside, the basement wasn't a bad place in a brothel kind of way. The carpet beneath my boots was thick, three of the walls were painted black and red while the fourth was entirely mirrored, and the furniture appeared every bit as expensive as the stuff upstairs. There was also a high-end sound system.

Minus the dead people, the swing, and the manacles bolted to one of the walls, this place was in better shape than my apartment.

The superfluousness of my presence was sinking in when Andre returned to my side. "This house belongs to Michael and Shannon Stacy, twenty-eight and twenty-six years old, respectively."

So the guy was my age. "Nice digs for such a young couple."

"Yeah, apparently he's a corporate lawyer in daddy's firm. That's all I know so far." Andre pointed to one of the dead men. His wrists were bound over his head with fluffy red handcuffs. I didn't think the crime-scene photos were going to help the firm's PR.

"I suppose the woman on top of him isn't his wife?"

"Not based on the wedding pictures upstairs." Andre gestured to a lifeless threesome by the mirrors. "She's over there."

Right. Well, that wasn't a surprise.

"Hey, Andre." The other Gryphon finished her scanning. "We got something."

Andre motioned between us. "Anna Scott, meet Jess Moore."

Anna's brown eyes opened wide in way of greeting. She was cute and looked way too young to be here, although in reality I suspected she wasn't much younger than me. "The infamous one? Is it true what they're saying about you?"

"Depends on what they're saying."

"That you can suck on emotions like a pred."

I winced. "Yeah, sort of."

Her eyes widened farther. "Wicked. Hope I get to test your blood later.

Anyway." She showed her scan to Andre. "There are strong levels of insoluble magic in all the victims' blood. I won't know for sure until I can take it back to the lab, but these markers are a pretty good indication of what we're dealing with. Just as a guess—I'd say these people were all sky-high on F when they died."

I tried to hide my reaction, but mentally I swore. It figured that this would be the case the Gryphons were bringing me in on. F was a potent and highly illegal aphrodisiac produced and sold by satyrs. And if satyrs were involved, then my new consulting job with the Gryphons had just gone from being a minor annoyance to a major relationship disaster.

I stood around some more while Andre and Anna related their discovery to the detective, then called it in to their supervisor at Headquarters. From the sound of it, the Newton police would officially have to turn the case over to the Gryphons later, but unofficially it was theirs already. All the evidence they'd collected would be passed along, and whatever the autopsies uncovered would be reported to them as well.

In fact, once the words "magic" and "F" were mentioned, the cops became even more jittery, which naturally made me jittery too. With only a single cup of coffee and no breakfast in my stomach, their emotional buffet was all that was keeping me awake. Alas, this sort of anxiety made me feel like I'd OD'd on sugar instead of anything nutritious. I bounced on my toes, trying to keep focused.

I soon learned Anna was basically a magic analyst, and her super-sensitive charms detected a couple empty envelopes in the Stacys' trash that showed faint traces of F in them. She left soon after the bodies were taken away, not having discovered anything else.

I shadowed Andre around the house for another hour while he explained what he was searching for and answered my questions with surprisingly good patience. If he was annoyed at being stuck with giving me on-the-job training, I couldn't detect it.

We finally got to leave when a second team of Gryphons arrived to secure the place. By then I was yawning, since the jittery cops had long disappeared, and my stomach was begging for food.

"So no car?" Andre asked, unlocking the Gryphon-issued SUV.

"Who needs a car? I live right near a T stop and I have my Dragon'sWing if I need to get really far away."

Andre whistled. "You have a Dragon'sWing? Those are nice bikes."

I grinned. "Very nice. I got it from one of the people I used to work with, for probably half of what it should have cost. Only reason I could afford it."

"How did you manage that?"

I put my sunglasses on as Andre pulled out onto the street. "She seemed to think she owed me. Plus it was her soon-to-be ex-husband's, and I think she was trying to get rid of it cheap to piss him off. I'm the one who got her proof of his cheating. Detecting deception is easy when you can taste it."

I figured Andre would want to talk about the case on the way downtown, but he kept things more personal, asking about my family and where I'd grown up. Not once did he steer the conversation toward my unusual abilities, the Aubrey case, or why a certain satyr had been willing to help me hide out during it. I couldn't decide if he was avoiding the topic because he knew too much already, or if he simply wanted to get off to a good start while working with me. Either way, I appreciated that he was smart enough to avoid those topics.

"Lunch?" Andre asked as we slowed to a stop for a red light. "Like Chinese? I know this great hole-in-the-wall place. It's a quick detour through Chinatown."

I didn't see how any detour through Chinatown could be considered quick, but I was hungry and in no rush to get to Headquarters. "Starving, and sure."

As it turned out, Andre wasn't kidding with his description of the restaurant. If he hadn't sworn he'd eaten there on several occasions, I wouldn't have trusted it. My plate of fried squid and hot peppers, however, was amazingly good. Just not my usual breakfast food.

Across the tiny table, Andre dug into his beef and broccoli. "So what do you know about F?"

Finally, it appeared we were going to talk about the case. "Only what most people know. It's an aphrodisiac, usually, if not always, made by satyrs. Some people call it the worst of the date-rape drugs because it makes people crave sex even if they'd never have wanted sex without being drugged, so it's a great and terrible way to overpower someone's will. I've never heard of it killing anyone though."

Andre swept some rice around on his plate. "You never tried it?"

"Are you, a magical law enforcement officer, really asking me if I've ever done any illegal drugs?" I hadn't tried F, but I sure wouldn't admit it if I had.

He chuckled. "Half the people I know tried it at one point. Physiologically, I'd say it's far less harmful than alcohol. But it's not an aphrodisiac in the usual sense."

I took a long swallow of water, my mouth burning. "No?"

"That's too mild a term. It's like calling a Lamborghini a car. It's true, but it's not in the same class as my busted-up Focus. F—pure F anyway— is powerful stuff. You've been around satyrs. It's like their ability to mess with your head all distilled into a nice white powder."

I hadn't heard anyone describe F that way before, but it made sense. If satyrs made it, odds were it did have some of their magic in it. Andre was almost making me curious to try it, if only to see if it had any effect on me since satyr magic in general didn't. "So you're saying it's an instant orgy."

"Just add people." Andre started to say something else, but his phone rang. "Work. Got to take this, sorry."

I went back to my food, pondering what Andre had told me. Everything he described coincided with what I'd heard. F wasn't harmful as long as it wasn't used in a deceptive or cruel way. All it did was make people horny. So just because those people in Newton probably had F in their systems when they died, didn't mean that F had anything to do with their deaths. Right?

Then again, under normal circumstances, people didn't die for no apparent reason in the middle of getting their freak on. I couldn't think of a way F wouldn't be a contributing factor.

Dragon shit on toast. If F was involved and I was expected to investigate, it wasn't only my relationship with Lucen that was going to feel the strain. My friendly relationship with the satyrs as a whole—and their Dom, Dezzi, in particular—was going to go downhill fast. Why couldn't I have gotten brought in on a case involving a magi selling bad charms or something?

I stabbed another hot pepper. Obviously because Olivia Lee had called me in specifically, because she knew about my relationship with the satyrs and had thought death by sex would be a case I could be useful on.

Between the super spicy food and the tension in my muscles, my stomach didn't feel so good.

Andre hung up the phone and returned to the table. "Sorry about that. Another case I'm working on. Where were we?"

"F. It's not dangerous, but it's not surprising that people having a sex party would be taking it. So it's possible something else killed them, right?" I wasn't sure who I was trying to convince—me or him.

"Possible, sure. Anything is right now."

"Also, if this had anything to do with F, then wouldn't there be other cases? Other victims? Have you heard of anything like this before?"

Andre captured the last piece of his broccoli but didn't eat it. He seemed to consider me instead. "You're friends with some satyrs, aren't you? They were the ones helping you during the Aubrey stuff."

I pushed my plate aside. "I'm friends with *a* satyr, and I'm just trying to think this through. F isn't an uncommon street drug. Seems like there'd be other incidents if it was involved."

"The day is young, and there's always a first. But we will be looking into other cases for similarities, so don't worry. We won't know more until we get the full analysis done on the victims' blood and the autopsy reports come in. Speaking of which, we should get to the office. You've got to give some blood too, I think."

We'd paid when we ordered, so I finished my water and got up. "Wait, Anna was being serious? You want my blood?"

"It's standard procedure. They take a bit of blood from all of us from time to time to keep in storage. You never know when you're going to get blasted by a nasty spell, and it helps the lab techs develop counter-charms if you have an untainted blood sample for comparison."

Great. Lucen and I had once wondered what the Gryphons would find if they did a full analysis of my blood. Now that I knew I was part satyr, I was even less thrilled at the possibilities of what they might discover.

FOUR

When we got to the Gryphons' building, Andre went to file his report and I was dumped at HR. Apparently I'd been right to think that the Gryphons didn't hire consultants very often, because the HR woman who was stuck with me didn't know what to do until several phone calls clarified the situation.

Unfortunately, the clarification left me with a mountain of paperwork I had to fill out for her. After that, a photo was required so I could get my own spiffy ID badge with Special Consultant printed on it. My photo was awful, but the badge meant I wouldn't have to go through normal security checks again, and I could carry charms into the building. My knife, however, remained off-limits. Only Gryphon-issued weapons were permitted, and I was not permitted a Gryphon-issued weapon.

From HR, I was shuffled to another section of the building where I was made to endure a physical, followed by the promised blood-drawing. I was poking at the bandage taped over my stab wound when Bridget entered the exam room.

She was wearing her regular uniform today, and her light brown hair was pulled into a ponytail. "Coffee? I thought it was time to have the one we didn't have yesterday."

"That depends." I adjusted my shirt. "Am I allowed to leave yet, or is there more of my brain to pick and my body to poke?"

She didn't even smile at my quip. Typical Bridget. "I meant I brought you some coffee. And, no. Or, yes. I get to take you to your last stop for the day."

I joined her in the hallway where she handed me the promised cup of coffee. "I need this. Thanks."

"I thought you might. Andre said you were yawning a lot earlier."

"Yeah, I had to work late last night and was not expecting a call this morning. Speaking of which, what are you doing working on a Saturday? Don't you get time off?"

Bridget rubbed her eyes. "It's the Aubrey case. The furies aren't cooperating—big surprise—but neither are the sylphs. You'd think they'd want justice, but they trust us so little that they'd rather stew."

The sylphs probably didn't consider Victor going to jail to be justice. Neither did I for that matter, since Victor had merely been the murderous puppet. His fury master needed to be brought in too. But I also knew firsthand the sylphs wouldn't be satisfied until all involved were dead, and they'd prefer to handle that business on their own. As any pred would.

"Any leads on the fury who was pulling Victor's strings?" I asked as we turned a corner. I knew which fury had addicted Victor, but only by sight. I didn't have a name, and Raj—the furies' Dom—was playing ignorant, protecting his own.

Bridget wrinkled her nose in disgust. "Nothing yet, and Aubrey isn't being helpful. He knows that given how many people he killed, he's not going to get much for himself by cooperating, but I don't understand why he'd protect the fury."

I suspected I did. Victor had liked being the thing's addict. He got a high off misery, like I did, but unlike me, he'd never wanted to use his freakish ability for good. He'd wanted an excuse to chase the high, and the fury gave that to him. On his master's orders, Victor got to torture and kill, and soak up all the suffering he caused. He'd loathed himself for it, but being an addict meant he didn't have to take responsibility, at least internally. It was the perfect fucked-up relationship.

"Where are we going by the way?" I asked. We'd been walking with a purpose, but since I had no idea where anything was on this floor, I was totally turned around.

"Right here actually." Bridget opened a door to a long room similar to the one we'd left, only this one, instead of being decked out with a blood pressure monitor, scale, and other basic medical equipment, contained what I thought might be charm-making supplies.

A couple obsidian bowls sat on a stone counter that spanned the length of the room, along with an assortment of knives, several mortars and pestles, and multiple sinks. One of the shorter walls was lined with locked cabinets. The room's only living occupant was a white-haired man who was reading a magazine.

Bridget pulled a chair over for me. "Andre said you're supposed to get protective charms."

Before I could respond, the man set down his magazine. "Yes, if you're Jessica. I've been waiting for you to arrive."

I started to say I didn't need any protective charms, then caught myself. If I said it, I'd have to explain why I felt that way, and I wasn't willing to enlighten the Gryphons yet.

So what the hell. I might as well take advantage of what they could do, seeing as I didn't have a choice about working for them. After all, a protective glyph or two wasn't going to hurt me. Not too long ago, I'd have needed to pay a lot of money for such a thing. It was kind of satisfying to be given this sort of charm for free.

I'd learned a bit about magic during my time at the Academy. Enough to realize I didn't know salamander spit about how to do anything, and enough to appreciate why high-quality charms cost so much. On one hand, magic was an awful lot like chemistry, but grosser given what went into making many spells. On the other hand, there was a certain art to it that required the person creating the spell to be able to sense the magical properties of every ingredient and adjust them on the fly. As such, even though all Gryphons had to learn basic spells, only certain ones specialized in magic.

Bridget introduced the new Gryphon as Mike, and fascinated, I watched him combine the charm components into a paste.

Once the paste was ready, Mike rolled a wooden dowel through it until it was coated. Then, with a pair of tweezers, he took a tiny red salamander egg from a spelled container, set it in a large obsidian bowl and dropped a lit match on it.

The fiery creature burst from the egg and scampered around the edges of the bowl, unable to get out. In its baby state, it was almost cute. Flaming, but cute. The ones that had not so long ago destroyed a good chunk of the city, courtesy of Victor, had been huge and anything but.

Mike stuck the paste-covered dowel over the bowl, and the salamander obliged, chomping down on it with burning teeth. As the magical fire cooked the paste, it turned from brown to bright blue, and the salamander grew bigger.

I'd owned protective charms before, but nothing like this. The more you used charms, the faster you used them up. I'd bought cheap ones, which were nonetheless expensive. They'd come in refillable charm vials, and I'd only worn them when I was going into Shadowtown. Such was my best effort to help them maintain their potency as long as possible.

But spells could be worked in several ways. One of them involved a complicated series of glyphs, almost like a spell-caster's alphabet. A glyph, or several, applied directly to the skin and made of the correct ingredients, could produce far more potent effects than my vials. They would also be used up much faster, but I supposed that didn't matter to the Gryphons.

The paste had turned a bright cobalt blue by the time Mike removed it from the salamander. He waved the dowel a few times, as if trying to cool it down. "We put these as close to your heart as possible. Most women prefer their backs to their chests though. Up to you."

Looked like this would be the second time today I would be taking my shirt off without anything fun to show for it. "My back is fine."

I sat on the stool Mike indicated and pulled up my hair and shirt. The paste was warm on my skin, and I wondered how many glyphs he was drawing because it felt like a lot of writing.

"The standard is two glyphs," Bridget said, as if reading my thoughts. "One is for all-purpose protection. The other is specific to countering the effects of pred magic. That one should make it a lot easier for you to go into Shadowtown without having your soul violated."

"Sounds good." Or it would if I had to deal with that problem.

The pressure on my back ceased, and I let go of my hair and shirt as Mike dumped the improvised pen on the counter. "You're all set. Those should last between two to four weeks, depending on how much trouble you get in, or how many preds try working their magic on you."

"This is great," Bridget said as we left the lab room. "We're finally getting to work together, although we won't be working on the same case."

I forced a smile because "great" didn't quite describe it for me. I got what Bridget was saying, and it sure beat fighting with her, but no matter how many friendly people I met around this place, I had to consider the Gryphons a threat. And that wasn't even getting at the blackmailing bit.

Anyway, I'd see soon enough if Bridget still thought this arrangement was great when my blood analysis came back. Just what would she—and everyone else in my life—think if she discovered that the human with the cursed gift was not so human at all?

The question made my stomach turn, so I pushed the thought aside and finished my coffee. There was nothing to be done about it. I was what I was, and as far as I knew that couldn't be changed. It was best, therefore, not to think about it until I was forced to.

"So am I free to go, and how do I leave?"

"You are free." Bridget dumped our empty coffee cups in the trash. "Andre will call you when the analysis is done. I can walk you out."

"Actually," came a new voice from behind me, "I'd be happy to do that. I'd very much like a chance to meet Ms. Moore."

Bridget and I had entered a busier part of the floor, and I turned around. The man who'd spoken acknowledged Bridget with a slight tilt of his head before facing me.

He smiled and held out a hand toward me, but something in that smile didn't quite reach his eyes. "Tom Kassin."

Confused by my immediate distrust of him, I took it. "Nice to meet you." Or not.

No, probably not. I wished I knew why.

Tom Kassin was my height, and with his round face, pale blond hair, and blue eyes he was almost cherubic. Almost. Because something about him got my hackles up, and I couldn't figure out what. Thanks to my misery-sucking abilities, I was usually a very good judge of character, and this new Gryphon was setting off all my alarms. Yet when I stretched out my gift toward him, I got nothing. That disconnect left me uneasy. For humans anyway, I always had a good reason if I distrusted someone.

Bridget didn't seem to share my strange antipathy toward Tom Kassin. She merely shrugged at his request. "Sure. I'll talk to you later, Jess."

"Yeah, okay." I returned my attention to Tom, half wondering if I was ever going to get out of this building today.

He began walking. "I've read a lot about you in the files from the Victor Aubrey case. The gift you described is quite unusual."

I was beyond sick of hearing that or similar phrases. "So it seems."

We reached the elevators, and Tom pressed the down button, making a few more vacuous comments about my gift as we waited. He had a faint accent, British of some sort, only it wasn't the same accent as Devon's. In fact, it didn't sound quite right. Some of Tom's words almost had a southern twang to them, as well.

That wasn't the only odd thing about him either. He had a red-and-gold pin on his uniform collar, something I'd never seen before. Gryphons gave out medals for extraordinary service, but they weren't the sort of decorations that were worn.

"You look puzzled," he said as we stepped into the elevator.

"I'm trying to piece together your accent."

He smiled again, and again something about it didn't sit right on his face. Bridget never appeared truly happy when she smiled either, but this wasn't the same thing. Tom's smile was patronizing. Smug. "I'm originally from Savannah, and I worked out of the Atlanta office for several years before transferring to London and eventually to World in Grenoble."

I blinked. "You're from World Headquarters?" Maybe the pin on his uniform had something to do with that.

"I am." The elevator arrived on the ground floor, and Tom waited for me to step out. "I'm here on a special assignment. People are very interested in what the furies were up to. While Agent Nelson works on the Aubrey end of the case, I'm doing some investigating for a commission that was formed regarding the furies' actions."

I paused. We were in the lobby, and freedom wasn't so far away. Yet

Tom had gotten my full attention at last. "What is it about the furies that's so curious?"

"Surely you realize how unusual their behavior was. Furies thrive on rage and chaos, but to attempt what they did here, instigating fights among various pred races and the magi, that's not normal."

I swallowed, remembering something Lucen had said during the Aubrey business. He and Dezzi had worried that the furies were trying to start a war. It might have been for kicks, which was entirely possible given the furies, but it also might have been for something worse. Lucen had suggested that the power the furies would raise by feeding off so much suffering could be used for a variety of nefarious purposes.

"You think they're up to something more than just starting fights?" I asked.

Tom's face was perfectly neutral, and his emotions didn't give anything away. He was like a block of ice—cold, hard, and unpleasant. "That's part of what I'm here to find out. It was nice to meet you, Jessica."

Only once he left did I realize he'd said that was part of what he was here to find out. I had a feeling if I'd probed about the other part, I'd finally have gotten a good taste of deception and lies from him.

FIVE

I WENT STRAIGHT TO THE LAIR AFTER LEAVING GRYPHON Headquarters. Not only could I use a drink, but my shift would be starting in a couple hours. I figured I could have that drink, borrow Lucen's shower, then come back to the bar ready to push liquor.

Strangely enough, these day when I needed normality in my life, Lucen was the person I thought of. It wasn't too long ago that I'd have viewed him as proof of the lack of normality in my life, but I'd known Lucen for ten years, and I'd finally had to accept that he'd always been there for me.

Before everything that happened with Victor, I'd assumed Lucen took an interest in my life because he was toying with me like a cat playing with a mouse before biting the poor creature's head off. But apparently not. Lucen had taken me in when I was hiding from the Gryphons, risked his standing with the satyrs to protect me, and still had the nerve to get pissed off at me when I'd tried to protect him in return.

Much as I liked to think of him only as my satyr-with-benefits, or blame my attraction to him on his lusty magic, I knew better. I just hated to admit it. When I was feeling beaten down, I wanted him there to talk sense into me. And when I was angry and looking for a fight, I wanted him to help me work out my aggression in a less violent, more naked manner.

And when I needed to talk about weird shit with someone who understood, he was a good option.

Steph was the only human who knew about my abilities, and she tolerated a lot of weirdness from me, but she didn't have the knowledge of magic or the loathing for the Gryphons that Lucen did. She also wouldn't understand the significance of what Tom had told me about his investigation of the furies. If I wanted to discuss that and my unpleasant vibe about Tom himself, Lucen was the person I needed.

More to the point, I also craved reassurance that being brought into an investigation that could potentially involve illegal activity on the satyrs' behalf wasn't going to destroy this unusual relationship of ours. I mean, it probably would, but I wanted Lucen to lie to me and tell me it wouldn't. Since I couldn't sense preds' emotions, I could pretend to believe him.

Did I say I needed a drink? I needed more like several.

Saturday's crowd didn't get thick until around seven, so Lucen saw me right away as I entered the bar. I took my favorite stool near the end and rested my head on my arms until he made his way over.

"Do you need some coffee, little siren? You've been gone a long time."

I raised my head, and some of my tension lifted as I saw the concern in his eyes. How did I end up making a satyr care about me, and why couldn't I simply feel better knowing he did care? Why did it also make me long for his touch?

Damn his magic. Sometimes a girl wanted comfort without sex. But with satyrs, that was as likely as finding chocolate without calories.

"How about something more alcoholic than coffee," I said, sitting up. "I'm awake but stressed. The investigation took a while, then I had to do all this paperwork and other crap at the office."

Lucen smirked. "'At the office.' You sound so professional."

"Please. How should I refer to it?"

He poured me a shot of Jameson. "When we want to get all literary, we call it Mount Doom. Mostly, though, it's The Fucking Gryphon Building."

The whiskey burned my throat, but settled in my stomach just right. "You're so eloquent."

"I can be, but I've known you long enough to know you're not the type to get hot from me quoting Shakespeare. So on that thought…" He leaned over the bar and winked. "Got a uniform?"

"Alas, no. Got a shiny ID badge, but no uniform and no weapons."

"Damn."

I sighed dramatically. "I know, and I look so good in black too."

Lucen topped off my drink. "Actually, I prefer you in as little as possible, but if we're talking about your underwear, the red lacey ones are my favorite."

"Good to know." I put a hand over the glass. "Hey there, go easy on the booze. I need to work soon."

"Don't be absurd. Of course you don't."

I narrowed my eyes at him. "Don't start. I'm not letting you pay me to hang around this place and pretty it up."

He stuck the bottle back on the shelf. "I'm not paying you at all anymore, and I've got your shift for tonight covered. Caroline had asked for more hours, so this worked out about as well as Gryphon shit can."

"Wait, what about Caroline? Did you just fire me? And for one of your addicts?"

Lucen's face tightened, no doubt picking up on the disdain I had for his Caroline.

Addicts who were driven to deals by desperation earned my pity, but Lucen wasn't one of those preds selling hope by the charm vial-full. He got his addicts by preying on their lust. I had a harder time feeling sorry for them, especially because he had to sleep with them every now and then to keep them healthy.

"I didn't fire you, Jess. You got another job. That's called quitting."

"It's not a job I asked for or wanted."

He took my hand, but my annoyance was too great to be overcome by his power this time. "No, but be reasonable. It's one that's paying you a lot more than I can pay you, and it might—and is likely to—interfere with your ability to work here. I have to make sure I have my shifts covered, and you have to make sure you have money and don't go to jail. So we'll both make do."

I scowled. Lucen had a point, but I didn't like it. "You'd better get me another drink then. Yesterday, I was blackmailed. Today, I was fired, and that's after I was probed and saw some really twisted stuff this morning."

Lucen kissed my hand, and my bitterness relented a touch. "You'll have to tell me about it later."

"Yeah, I've got a few things to tell you."

Lucen had to go back to work, so I sat and texted with Steph while nursing a beer. We hadn't gone out in a while because I'd been working nights, and the few evenings I'd had free Steph had been hanging out with Jim, her boyfriend. I liked Jim and approved of their relationship. That was no small thing given Steph's history of dating guys who were either in serious need of therapy or borderline psychos, so I did all I could to encourage them.

Absorbed as I was in my conversation, I didn't notice the bar's atmosphere had changed until a familiar voice spoke my name. "Ah, there she is. I'd thought I might find you here."

I put my phone down as Dezzi, the satyrs' Dom, swept through The Lair. As the most powerful satyr in Boston, Lucen—and all the other satyrs in the bar—answered to her, and their deference was quiet though noticeable. Dezzi was tall and voluptuous with pheromones that smelled vaguely like coconut. I could recognize their traces even if they weren't making me squirm in my seat with lust.

As usual, Dezzi had piled her black braids around her head to a height that obscured her horns, and her silver jewelry gleamed against her dark skin. Even in jeans and a simple peasant blouse, she looked regal. Lucen seemed to adore her too. I didn't know much about pred hierarchy, but when it came to Doms, I assumed they could be every bit as loved or loathed as any leader.

Dezzi could have thrown me out on my ass when I'd tried hiding from the Gryphons with Lucen, and she could have demoted him from his position as her third for daring to take me in. Instead, she'd heard us both out, and though saying she wasn't pleased would have been an understatement, she'd given us a chance to make things right. And when we'd needed her support to follow through in the end, she'd given it.

Although once she'd kind of terrified me, these days I had no problems with Dezzi.

Now the satyr who was walking with Dezzi, however... I'd have been happy never running into her again. Lucrezia was Dezzi's second, and although I had to admit she was gorgeous, I didn't find her personality nearly as attractive. To Lucrezia, I was merely human cattle, and she didn't understand why Lucen kept me around as a nonaddict fuck-buddy—her words, not mine.

I pushed my empty glass away. "Hi, Dezzi. Lucrezia."

Lucrezia sat on the stool next to me, crossing her long, barely covered legs. "Pet, I'm surprised you're hanging out here, all things considered."

Behind Lucrezia, Lucen said something to the other bartender and wandered over. He took my empty glass away but continued to hover protectively.

Dezzi looked me up and down. "Rumor around Shadowtown is that the human with a satyr's gift has become a Gryphon. I assume the rumor refers to you. Is it true?"

"That's a rumor?" I cast a glance in Lucen's direction.

He shrugged, setting two glasses of wine on the bar for the other women. "Don't look at me. I haven't said anything. I'd have told you eventually, Dez, but I was waiting to see what it meant myself."

"So it is true?" Dezzi said again.

I didn't know why, but I was feeling defensive all of a sudden. Maybe it was because I was surrounded by three powerful satyrs and feeling very human as a result. "It's not like I went and applied for a job. I'm being blackmailed into working for them." I gave Dezzi the briefest of rundowns about what happened between me and the director.

"Nasty thing, isn't she?" Lucrezia said, referring to Olivia Lee. "And you were so busy trying to defend them recently too."

"Well congratulations, I'm over it. But that doesn't mean I want to help you destroy them."

Dezzi ran a finger over her full lips. "Do you know what they want you to work on?"

I hesitated a second. There was no use in lying. She'd know. "Yes, I was brought in on a case this morning."

"This wouldn't have something to do with the murders in Newton, would it?" Lucrezia asked, picking up her wineglass.

I tensed. "Actually, yes. How did you know that?"

She gave me a pitying look. "Pet, don't you check the news? They said there were Gryphons on the scene."

"Oh. Well, I haven't exactly had time to read the news. The Gryphons have sucked away my entire day. Believe me—I'm not happy about this."

"No, I can tell you're not." Dezzi finally took a sip of wine. "But it doesn't change the fact that you're now working for our enemy."

I jumped off my stool in disgust. It was clear where this conversation was going, and the worst wasn't even public knowledge yet. If the news had mentioned anything about F, surely Lucrezia or Dezzi would have brought it up, and this chat would be less friendly than it already was. "Give me a break. I just got done being enemies with the sylphs. Can't I go a month without people picking fights with me?"

"Dezz, she doesn't have a choice," Lucen said.

"To work for them? No." Dezzi crossed her arms. "Perhaps not. I am not suggesting Jess should go to prison. But if the time ever comes when Jess's involvement requires that she make certain difficult choices, I do hope she remembers what we've done for her."

Although she was speaking of me in the third person, Dezzi watched me as she talked. I managed not to flinch, but internally my mind and emotions raced as I considered what Dezzi might know about the Newton case.

Yes, I appreciated that Dezzi hadn't kicked me out when Lucen offered me the satyrs' protection, but it wasn't like Dezzi would have provided it herself. I thought she was fair, but she wasn't a saint, and I didn't owe her anything. Finding Victor and bringing him to justice hadn't benefited me alone. It had benefited everyone in Dezzi's domus, all of Shadowtown, and the greater Boston area alike—preds, humans, and magi. Therefore, as far as I was concerned, any debts I'd accrued to the satyrs had been paid.

Especially if one of them was responsible for killing nine humans.

"Nothing's changed," I said. "As long as you don't do anything to hurt people, we're good. If you'll excuse me."

"Jess, where are you going?" Lucen asked as I wormed between Dezzi and Lucrezia.

"To meet Steph. I've got the night off, right?" Thanks to this brief interlude, I really, really wanted to be around humans. My people. Even if that wasn't one-hundred-percent biologically accurate of me, I knew who I identified with.

The absurdity of coming here dawned on me as I stepped onto The Lair's patio and breathed in the evening air. As much as I wanted him to be, I'd just gotten a very clear reminder about why it was a bad idea to let myself fall into the trap of letting Lucen become my normality.

WHEN I'D SAID I WAS OFF TO MEET STEPH, IT HAD BEEN A LIE. But as it turned out, the hospital where Jim worked as a nurse asked him to take a second shift when someone called out sick, and Steph was all dressed up with nowhere to go. One text from me changed that.

Half an hour after leaving The Lair, I was holed up at another bar. Kilpatrick's Nutty Irishman Pub wasn't just any bar either. Like The Lair, we had history. Steph and I had been hanging out here for years thanks to the discounted beer we got from her cousin who owned the bar. For that reason, it had also become soul-swapping headquarters for me.

Steph hadn't arrived by the time I got there, so I immediately headed for the right-hand bathroom. After locking the door, I climbed on the toilet, moved a ceiling tile aside, and took down the Rubbermaid container in which I'd hidden a notebook and pen.

This was how Boston's mysterious vigilante known as the "soul-swapper" communicated. It wasn't exactly secure or high tech, and it definitely wasn't flashy, but it had served me well over the years.

Emphasis on the "had." Since I was working for the Gryphons, I should be putting this part of my life behind me. Actually, to be more precise, since I was being blackmailed into working for the Gryphons because this whole soul-swapping thing could get me in an assload of legal pain, I should definitely, absolutely, and irrevocably put this part of my life behind me.

Funny, though, how that didn't make me want to put this behind me. It made me want to step up my efforts for no other reason than to piss off the Gryphons.

Maturity—I had it. Right along with a serious chip on my shoulder and a sense of spite that ought to make my nose quiver in fear every time my face itched.

I also had a message. Setting the container on the sink, I opened the lid. The writing on the paper inside was simple and direct, if not a touch more dramatic than what I usually found.

Dear soul swapper, I'm in desperate need of help. Please respond. I can pay.

The writer hadn't signed the note, but she—a guess based on the flowing handwriting—had left the date. It was written two days ago.

Peachy. I'd come to remove the container for good, before it got me in more trouble. But now... I debated for less than a minute before writing a response.

Regardless of my feelings about Caroline or any of Lucen's addicts, I didn't like to see people suffer. And I was intensely aware, all day long, of how much suffering there was around me. I couldn't shut off my ability to sense it. I could only intensify my ability to feel and identify its particular flavor if I concentrated. So if I had a chance to prevent more suffering before it began, then I should.

Then I would.

After all, it had taken years for word to spread about my ability to help those in need. How could I be so callous as to cut that off? Even tonight, someone was hoping for my help, believing in my ability to provide it.

Did that make me sound self-important? I didn't care. I wielded a pred's power because I was part pred. I liked being able to use that evil power for good. It had taken me a long time to realize I controlled my gift and that it didn't define me.

After sticking the container back in the ceiling, I returned to the main room. Steph was at the bar talking to her cousin, and I joined her. A few musings about politics and the Red Sox later, we ordered.

Kilpatrick's had to make some of the greasiest fish and chips in New England, but they paired well with a Guinness, and it was dinnertime. Good thing I'd skipped breakfast, given the way I was eating today. As it was, my pants probably wouldn't button tomorrow. We took our beers to a corner away from the pool tables while we waited for our food.

Steph tossed her hair over her shoulders. "What do you think?"

I assumed she was asking about the new wig she was wearing. "It's a lot less red."

"It is, but I thought the blonde in this one was more summery."

True, and it was summer, but I didn't usually think "summery" when I thought of Steph. Five foot ten—and that's when she wasn't in heels—with a wardrobe that consisted of blacks, grays, and more blacks, and an attitude to match, Steph was more of a winter sort of girl.

I sipped my beer, searching for a polite but truthful response. "It's not bad, but not what I'd expect from you. Honestly, I'm going to have to get used to it."

"Don't bother. It's not me. I just wanted to see if you'd lie like everyone else. But never mind that. I'm waiting to hear what went down with you and the Gryphons yesterday. Learn anything new about Victor?"

"No, but look at this." I pulled my ID badge out of my bag. "Impressed?"

Steph choked on her beer, then grabbed the badge. "Is this real, or did one of your satyr friends forge it?"

"It's real. I'm an honest-to-goodness special consultant for the Gryphons." For the second time in almost as many hours, I related what happened yesterday.

Our food had arrived as I finished, and I picked at my French fries while Steph processed my story by ordering a second beer. "This is awesome."

"Sorry? Did you miss the part about me being blackmailed into working for them?"

Steph gave me her best *oh, please* look. Some people would cower from that, but I knew her too well to take her seriously. "You're overreacting, and that's something coming from this self-acknowledged drama queen."

"They tried to arrest me for murder."

"Yeah, because Victor did a damn good job of framing you, and you had a bit of bad luck." Steph paused her rebuke as she squeezed a lemon wedge all over her fish. "Look, we always knew the soul-swapping thing was sketchy, so that's beside the point. Clearly the Gryphons recognize you have an amazing—if somewhat creepy—gift, and some kickass skills to go with it, and they want to see you do some good with them. It's an opportunity to do what you've always deserved to do."

I crushed a fry between my fingers in annoyance. "I'm not being given a choice."

"What would there be to choose? Would you actually have turned them down? You always said you wanted to help humanity. This is your chance."

"I've been helping humanity just fine without the Gryphons. In spite of the Gryphons even."

"Come on, Jess. Yes, you've helped people, but now you get to take a bigger role and earn real money for doing it. I can't believe you're upset about this."

"And I can't believe you're not indignant on my behalf. Do I have to remind you about what you helped me do recently?"

Apparently not. Judging from Steph's sour surge of fear and anxiety, she knew I was referring to how she'd helped me hack into the Gryphons' servers. "No, but that was done for a specific cause—you. Not because I have something against the Gryphons. I like knowing there are people out there risking their lives to watch over my soul. I like it even more knowing someone smart, capable, and dedicated—aka, you—will be one of them."

There wasn't much I could say to that. Steph's feelings were genuine, including the flattery. She didn't know that a big part of the reason I was bothered was because I was part satyr, and the reason she didn't know was because I couldn't bring myself to tell her. Steph, like most sane people, lived in fear of preds. She disliked them, distrusted them, and disapproved of me having anything to do with them. Even my gift pushed her squick buttons too far on occasion. Sometimes I wondered if she'd be my friend at all if she hadn't met me before my gift had turned me from normal to pred, and she hadn't seen the way I'd freaked out when it did.

"I take it your satyr friend isn't too happy about this?" Steph asked. "At least you don't have to work for him anymore."

I stabbed my fish. "No, he's not happy, but I didn't mind working for him."

"I don't understand why not. I know you basically wrap your soul in dragon hide when going into Shadowtown, but I can't imagine working for a guy who could hurt you that way. Friend or not." She sounded dubious about whether Lucen could be a friend.

Again, I couldn't blame her. Most of my life, I'd felt the same, and I'd sure never told her how my relationship with Lucen had recently changed.

"I trust him," I said. "But speaking of trust and people I don't trust, what's up with those files you got from the Gryphons?"

After Steph had hacked into their servers to get me the information I'd needed on Victor Aubrey, she'd done a bit more poking around. I supposed her appreciation of the Gryphons and all they did for humanity couldn't overcome her curiosity. The Gryphons had patched the security hole she'd created, but before they did, Steph had discovered a file with my name on it, and four other similar files. One of those other files had Victor's name on it. Given what I knew about our magical similarities, this was interesting.

To put it very, very mildly.

Alas, our names and "Philadelphia" were the only readable parts of the files. Steph had tried to decrypt them with no luck.

She chewed her fry slowly. "I might have gotten the name of someone who could help, but I've been warned he's not necessarily trustworthy."

"I'm looking for someone to break the encryption on what are stolen, probably top-secret Gryphon files. Anyone willing to do that is unlikely to be trustworthy by definition."

She made a face. "True. But you're working for them, so don't you think—"

"No."

"But you might be able to find out more by poking around."

I threw my lemon wedge at her. "How? Poking around, asking about information I'm not supposed to know in the first place?" When Steph didn't answer right away, I went on. "If you don't trust this guy enough, I can ask Lucen. I'm sure there's someone among the satyrs who can do it."

That got her back up. "Forget I said anything. I'll set up a time to talk to my guy. Just consider this a warning. We don't have any idea what dirt those files might have on you, and if he can decrypt them, he'll be the first to find out. If it's something you'd rather not be shared..."

"Point taken." I drained my beer and tucked into my fish. "And don't worry. I have an idea for how to deal with the lack-of-trust situation."

Steph gave me a wry look. "Why doesn't that make me feel any better?"

SIX

For the second day in a row, I woke up to my cell phone's ringtone. This time, however, I was in my own bed, which cut down on the disorientation. Rubbing my eyes, I checked the caller ID.

Also, for the second day in a row, it was the Gryphons. "Yeah?"

"Jess, it's Andre. Sorry for the lack of notice, but the lab finished analyzing the Newton blood samples an hour ago. Can you come in to talk about it?"

I rolled onto my side and sat up. Sunlight glowed around the edges of my curtains. It was almost noon. Apparently, I'd really needed to catch up on my sleep. "Yeah, sure."

"Great. Can you get here by two? We're pulling together an official team meeting."

Beyond my door, I heard one of my roommates thudding about in the hallway. That's when it dawned on me. "It's Sunday. Don't you people get any time off?"

Andre laughed, but it sounded humorless. "Occasionally they let us out of the cage, yeah. But seriously, we got nine dead people in Newton. Time off will be in short supply for a while."

"Yeah, right. Nine dead people." And a possible connection to the satyrs. I swung my legs over the side of the bed and stood, wishing I could crawl back under the blanket. "I can be there."

Two hours was plenty of time to shower, eat, and hope the magic analysis had discovered something totally different than what I feared. It was also, as it turned out, a long time to try to dodge my roommates. Geoff cornered me while I was in the kitchen settling down with the egg white omelet I'd made myself.

"Where have you been?" Geoff stretched out his hairy arms and took a soda from the fridge.

"Busy." I dumped salsa on the eggs, silently cursing myself for not taking breakfast into my bedroom.

Geoff rested his elbows on the tiny counter. His casual stance was a total cover-up. Inside, he was a jumble of discomfort, and the taste of it did not mesh well with my breakfast. "Val ran to the store. If you have a minute, we should talk when she gets back."

In an effort to leave before that happened, I shoveled egg in my mouth. "No minutes, sorry. I'm running late and need to get to work."

"Already? I thought you worked at a bar these days."

"Quit." I still felt like Lucen had fired me, but I'd gotten fired from my last job thanks to my inability to get to work while hiding from the Gryphons, and I didn't feel like saying I'd been fired a second time. It sounded pathetic. "I got a better paying job, and I'm running late on my second day. Sorry."

I dumped my plate and coffee mug in the dishwasher, and hurried to my room to put on my shoes.

"Can we talk later today?" Geoff called after me. Some of his anxiety had lifted, which suggested he didn't want to have this conversation any more than I did. His reluctance didn't bode well. I had a feeling we weren't going to be discussing the electric bill or who kept leaving their hair in the shower drain.

I grabbed my bag. "Yeah, sure. Later is good." Then I dashed out the door before he could say anything else.

Thanks to my roommate-avoidance efforts, I got to the Gryphon's building twenty minutes early. I bought a large latte at the shop across the street, then called Andre because I didn't know where to go. A few minutes later he met me in the lobby.

"This is great that you're early," he said as we approached the elevators. "I can show you your desk."

"I get a desk? Fancy." And here I'd been feeling special for simply being able to flash my shiny new ID badge at security.

Maybe Steph was right. Maybe I was looking at this blackmail thing the wrong way. I could stew over it, or I could embrace what I couldn't change. Throw myself into this opportunity and take some pride in what I was doing. Olivia Lee might have forced my hand, but that was no reason this wouldn't necessarily work out for the best.

Such cheery thoughts lasted about thirty seconds. That's when I caught a glimpse of the painting in the lobby and remembered what I was. Besides, me plus bright-siding went together about as well as peanut butter and salsa.

Nope, Little Miss Misery—that was me.

"What was that?" Andre had been talking, and I hadn't been paying attention.

"I was saying most of the meeting rooms are on the fourth floor. Your desk is on the third. IT should have your computer set up for you to use today."

Andre gave me a quick tour that included a stop at my new quasi-office. It wasn't much of one—a space partitioned off with a half-wall along a mostly empty corridor, no window, and barely enough room for both of us and the desk—but I was impressed in spite of myself since I hadn't expected as much. After that and a tutorial on how to use my badge to unlock the interior doors, we reached the meeting room.

Two other people were already in it—Anna, who I'd met yesterday, and one of the assistant directors named Brian, who I was told would be supervising our work. We sat around a long conference table while Anna brought some data up on the screen in the front of the room.

Brian regarded me with some suspicion but was otherwise cordial. I didn't sense any true negativity from him. My gift merely confused him, and that wasn't something I could hold against anyone.

After the introductions were over, he shut the door. "Anna, walk us through what the analysis found."

With a press of a button, Anna dimmed the lights, then presented slide after slide detailing the magical components found in each of the victims' blood. Without any background in magical chemistry beyond the very basics, most of what she showed was lost on me, but I got the gist.

There were two types of magical debris, or dust—for lack of a better word—that could show up in blood. That debris was called natural magic if the person had a gift themselves, like I or any of the Gryphons did. It was called unnatural if the person had no gift, and the debris had been left by someone or something else. In the Newton victims' case, the debris left a signature behind that resembled the signature left by F.

I balled my hands into fists, wishing there was a better way to release my tension. Punching someone would be nice, and Olivia Lee's face came to mind for having dragged me into this mess.

"All that means is the people had F in them when they died, right?" I asked. "That's not exactly shocking."

Anna brought up another slide, this one covered with the complex lines created by another type of scan. "Maybe."

"Maybe?"

She looked extremely pleased about something, bouncing on the balls of her feet. "See, here's where it gets interesting. See this and this?" She pointed at various spots on the scan that meant nothing to me. "All the victims showed this same pattern, but I've never seen magic like that associated with F before. I don't know what it is, but it was something seriously strong."

I hoped my sigh of relief wasn't too obvious. "So the F didn't kill them?"

"I wouldn't make that assumption at this point." Anna turned off the slides and turned the lights back on.

Andre had a laptop open and was taking notes. "What about the envelopes you found in the trash? They had F in them."

"Yeah, but just residue." Anna sat down. "There wasn't enough to get a clear reading off them."

Brian rubbed his hands together. "And no other evidence of magic was found on the bodies or at the scene?"

Andre shook his head. "Nothing, but those people had been dead for at least six hours before we got called in. If there was another weak source of magic around them, it could have dissipated before we got there."

"Or been removed." Brian paged through his papers. "Who found them again?"

"Michael Stacy's father. According to his statement, he was dropping off his son's golf bag that he'd borrowed. Newton PD claims he was in serious shock."

"No wonder," Brian said. "It seems unlikely he'd have tampered with anything if he didn't try to cover up the scene itself. But it can't hurt to do some digging at this stage. You might turn up more ideas. In the meantime, the most likely explanation is that additional magic trace Anna found came in on the F. There's a good chance we're dealing with someone selling contaminated drugs."

I frowned. "Contaminated? Why would someone purposely add extra magic to them?"

"Could be a lot of reasons," Andre said. "Preds will often throw extras into the charms they sell to humans, or outright lie about what they're selling. It's no different when the charm comes in the form of a magical drug."

Anna yawned, stretching out on her chair. "Nope. It's actually not that different than a human dealer cutting their non-magical drugs with cheaper drugs or other chemicals. Sometimes it's harmless. Sometimes it's not."

Great. I had heard about that sort of thing happening, and Andre was right. It wasn't uncommon at all. The Gryphons, as well as various government agencies, often put out PSAs, reminding people why they should only buy charms from trustworthy sellers. Of course, such sellers never included preds, and F wasn't a legally produced spell in the first place.

Brian cleared his throat. "All right, here's how I'm suggesting you approach this. Andre, you should do some digging into the victims' backgrounds. We need to rule out other motives or possible causes for their deaths. Jess, this case is going to exemplify why Director Lee thought you'd make a valuable consultant. You're going to need to use your connections in Shadowtown to help us find out about the F."

I shifted in my seat. "I don't exactly have connections in Shadowtown."

Brian appraised me, his gray eyes hard through his glasses. "You have stronger inroads there than we do, as evidenced by the satyrs helping to protect you. The satyrs—or certain satyrs—will be the ones who produce F."

"I'm aware of that."

"Then I need you to use your connections with them to see what you can find out about the producers, or who their dealers are."

"There are a few hundred satyrs in Boston," I said, pulling a number out of the air. I didn't actually know, but it seemed like a reasonable guess. "The ones I'm on friendly terms with all work at or own legitimate, legal businesses. They're not drug dealers or F producers."

"You sure about that?" Andre asked. "You're friends with Lucen, aren't you?"

I spun my chair to face Andre, my stomach twisting unpleasantly. "Yeah, but he owns a bar."

Andre raised an acutely skeptical eyebrow. "We can't keep track of all council members, but we do our best with the inner triads. We know Lucen is number three on their Dom's council. How does a bar owner legally get enough powerful addicts to bump him to that sort of position?"

Obviously, the answer was he didn't. I'd pretty much known that, but I didn't think Lucen's not-legal methods included making or selling drugs. I'd have seen evidence of that by now, given all the time I'd been spending in his company recently.

Saying as much, however, would lead to more uncomfortable conversations. These people didn't need to know how long I'd known Lucen or how close we were.

If we were. After all, I'd only discovered Lucen was Dezzi's number three a few weeks ago. I was out of my depth with Lucen, the satyrs, and the Gryphons. The more I learned on all ends, the more I realized I didn't know.

So instead of admitting anything, I deflected. "That's a good question, and I'm not friendly enough with Lucen to know the answer. But it also means he's not exactly going to share whatever information he has with me."

"That's why we want you to do some digging," Brian said. "You're obviously a clever woman. I'm sure you'll think of something. If nothing else, you can ask questions and see what sort of answers you get. You're more likely to get their cooperation than we are."

I raised my hands in defeat. "Fine. I'll see what I can do, but I can't make promises. I assume you have some leads on dealers or something I can use to get a start?"

Brian, Andre, and Anna all looked at each other, and it was Andre who responded. "Not really. Busting an illegal magic operation is tricky. When it comes to F, we can pick up the lowest of the low-level dealers, but working up the chain is problematic unless we're dealing with stupid preds."

"And whoever produces F within Boston," Anna added, "isn't stupid."

"How so?"

"They use a variation on a compulsion spell," Andre explained. "It's not uncommon in this type of situation. Any time we reach a human dealer who might know something, we find they've had the compulsion put on them. They can't tell us anything about the F or who they get it from."

Interesting, and nope, definitely not stupid. Compulsion spells didn't wear off the way charms did. I'd only had a single experience with one, and its effects lingered.

Devon, or one of his employees, had set one up at the club Devon owned, and I'd tripped it. The spell had tried to prevent me from entering the club's basement. Possibly because I was part satyr and the spell had been intended for a full-blooded human, I'd managed to overcome it. Yet despite my ability to fight off part of the spell, I'd been unable to talk about it afterward, even to Devon himself. In fact, that I remembered what I'd seen at all had seriously confused Devon.

But just because a spell didn't wear off, didn't mean it couldn't be broken, and I asked about that.

"We can't break the compulsions on the dealers," Andre said.

"Why not?" The satyrs had given me a crash course on charm-breaking once. I was no expert, but I figured a Gryphon ought to be.

"Well, 'can't' might not be the best word, but it's tricky. If the person who put the spell on the dealers knows what they're doing, they could tie their spell to another spell that would cause serious harm to the person. There have been cases when the compulsion spell is rigged in such a way as to destroy memories rather than block them if attempts are made to break it. In most cases, we've been unwilling to take the risk. Frankly, when it comes to search-and-destroy missions for dangerous magic, F is very low on our priority list. There are far worse charms and curses being peddled."

"The bigger dealers are usually lust addicts, as well," Brian said. "That adds another layer of complications when breaking spells because addicts have so much pred magic in their blood. This is why your role is going to be important, Jess. We're glad to have you on board."

Three faces looked at me expectantly. Andre smiled.

Crap.

The meeting broke up soon after, but I continued to talk to Andre for a while. He filled me in on more of what to expect with the case and simply more in general about work schedules and my day-to-day activities. He also promised he'd send me files on everything they knew about F dealings in the area, although he wasn't hopeful I'd get anything useful out of them.

I tucked my notes from the meeting in a drawer in my new desk and stared at the computer. Since I'd yet to log on, someone from IT had helpfully left me instructions and a temporary password to use my first time. I considered trying it out, but as curious I was about the limited access I'd been given, I wasn't in the mood to poke around. To go "digging," as Brian had phrased it.

The one thing I wanted from the Gryphons—knowledge about what was in those stolen files—I was unlikely to have access to. Nonetheless, Steph's comment about seeing what I could find out on my own had stuck with me. Was there a way?

Footsteps approached from behind me, and I set IT's instructions down.

Olivia Lee clasped her hands behind her back. "I was in the office and wanted to check in to see how you're faring."

I wanted to ask her how she expected me to be faring. "Okay, I guess. Nice case to ease me in on. Nine dead people in a creepy situation? Very gentle on the newbie."

Her smile might have tightened a touch. "Considering the nature of their deaths and your relationship with a certain pred race, it made sense. I didn't doubt you could handle it."

"I like to think there's not much I can't handle." Except, maybe, coming to terms with what I was and telling the truth about it to the people I cared about. But that went above normal day-to-day kinds of situations and into the territory of the absurd. It shouldn't count.

"I'm sure there isn't." Olivia nodded in a satisfied way. "Good then. If you have questions about getting settled, make sure you talk to Agent Pagan. He's been instructed to help you in any way necessary."

She'd started walking away when a new idea came to me, and I decided to seize the opening I'd been left. "Actually, there's something I was hoping you could help me with. It's not related to this case specifically, but I've been thinking it would be a good idea if I could get a better grasp on my abilities. You know, it might help me handle things that could come up while working here."

I could taste the director's suspicion. "Yes, I suppose that makes sense. I'm not sure how we can help though. Perhaps once we get your analysis back from the lab we'll know more."

I'd bet they would, and I didn't want to dwell on that. Nor did I want to bring up the stolen files. I'd had another idea. "I'd like a chance to talk to Victor Aubrey."

Olivia had stepped away again, but my comment froze her mid-stride. "Why would you want to talk to Aubrey?"

"Well, we do have a similar ability." Actually, we might have several similar abilities, but I honestly didn't know if that was the case. Victor had claimed to feed on negativity like I did, but whether he could also create addict-like bonds with humans, or reverse a pred's bond remained to be determined.

Those talents aside, we also had one more thing in common—our names on the stolen files. That was what I really wanted to talk to him about.

Olivia was sucking on her bottom lip, and although she hid it well, I sensed she felt foolish for not seeing the connection immediately. "Yes, of course you do. But I'm not sure how useful you'd find talking to him to be."

"Just because we used our gifts for different purposes doesn't mean he might not know things I don't. He was a fury addict for a while. It's possible his master told him things."

Olivia smoothed her black hair. "Aubrey is going through withdrawal. I'm not sure how cooperative he'll be with you. He's not cooperating with us."

"I've heard, but I'd like to try. In the beginning, before he framed me, he was very interested in meeting someone else with his ability. He might be open to talking."

I could taste Olivia's emotions churning inside her. She was a soup of anxiety, suspicion, and dislike in my mouth. I wondered who the latter was for—me or Victor or both. "I'll look into it," she said at last. "Because you're one of the witnesses, getting in to see him might be problematic. You know what happens once lawyers get involved."

I'd figured that might be a problem, so I tried not to be disappointed. "Thanks."

"Anything else?"

I ran a hand over the computer. "Actually, since you asked. I get this and a desk. How about a uniform for when I'm out on Gryphon business? The cops were suspicious of me yesterday. It would make things easier if I looked official."

Most importantly, I could wave the uniform in front of Lucen. He was not going to be any more pleased by my first assignment than I was, but maybe I could lessen the sting. Or at least distract him temporarily.

Olivia's phone buzzed. She checked it then stuck it away. "We might be able to supply you with a jacket to wear on official business, yes. That makes sense."

I grinned as she left, but the expression faded quickly as the floor descended into silence. Sitting at my desk, I replayed my meeting and the conversation with Olivia in my head. Uncovering information about F would require subtlety. As my talk with Olivia made abundantly clear, subtlety wasn't one of my strengths.

Even armed with a Gryphon jacket, how in the world did the Gryphons think I'd learn anything useful from the satyrs?

SEVEN

I was not the only person to suffer from a lack of subtlety. With my head full of everything I'd learned this afternoon, I'd forgotten all about my roommates' request to talk.

Alas, they hadn't, and they'd given up on vague notes and cryptic conversations in the kitchen. No sooner than I'd shut the apartment door behind me, Val darted out from the living room and Geoff from his bedroom. I was trapped.

Geoff positioned himself in the middle of the narrow hallway. "Jess, we need—"

"To talk. Yeah, I know." Resigned, I dropped my bag to the floor. "Were you waiting for me this whole time?"

Geoff stared at his bare feet, and Val tucked her hair behind her ears. I didn't need to taste their emotions to see how uncomfortable they were. Also, nervous. This was going to be bad.

Valerie slinked back into the living room and moved her knitting off the sofa as if inviting me to sit there. I didn't. "It's Sunday afternoon," she said. "It's not like we had anywhere else to go."

I let the comment pass though I knew it wasn't true. Geoff spent most of his weekends with his girlfriend, and Val enjoyed the sort of social life

I'd never had even before my gift had turned me into poor company. She was always out and about, either with friends or her guy of the month.

So yeah, this was a total ambush, and that meant it was time to rip off the bandage and get the unpleasantness over with. I collapsed on a chair. "This is about me and what went down with the Aubrey murders, right?"

I didn't see what else it could be. None of us were exactly friends, but friends didn't always make the best roommates in spite of what TV claimed. We were three people who'd managed to tolerate each other, and that was a lot. Or it had been until recently.

Val put her knitting on her lap like the yarn brought her comfort. "We just don't really understand the part you played in all of that, and…" And? I waited, but Val had run out of words.

"I know you'd like me to tell you more about what happened, but legally I can't talk about a lot of it." That was partially true. Mostly, though, it was simply none of their business, and I wasn't about to share with them the things I wasn't ready to share with actual friends. "You know I had nothing to do with the murders. I didn't even know Victor Aubrey until he decided I'd make an excellent patsy."

"What I don't get is why," Val said. "Why you?"

There was no way to explain that without explaining more than she should know. So I shrugged. "Bad luck. Look, you've already grilled me on this. What else do you want me to say?"

Val resumed knitting, presumably so she didn't have to meet my eyes.

Geoff paced in front of the window, obviously realizing it was up to him. "We don't need you to say anything, Jess. But when the lease is up next month, we'd like you to move out."

I stared at him, air sticking in my lungs. "What?"

Val's face crumpled. "Jess, we're sorry, but everything that's happened…it's making us uncomfortable."

I bolted to my feet, shock turning to anger. It blocked out whatever Geoff and Val were feeling and made my bones buzz with excess energy. "You're uncomfortable because I was framed for murder? For the love of dragons, do you have any idea how stupid that is?"

"Jess." They said my name in unison.

"I was living here before either of you moved in."

Geoff quit his pacing. "That's hardly fair. All three of us have our names on the lease. You don't get special privileges for that."

Val pulled her knees to her chest. "It's nothing personal. You're a nice person. But if you've been targeted once, you could be again."

"Seriously? Being framed once was like getting hit by lightning. Random bad luck." Except it wasn't, and I knew better.

Also, as I defended myself, it occurred to me they might have a valid concern. In a way, I had been putting them at risk because of my soul-swapping. At any time I could have brought serious trouble down on myself or those around me.

But that was beside the point. Val had no clue what she was talking about, and shit. I was pissed off and didn't feel like being reasonable.

"Fine. Whatever. If you want me to go, I'll start looking for a new place. Since I'm consulting for the Gryphons now, I'm sure I can afford something nicer."

"You're consulting for the Gryphons?" Geoff called after me as I stormed out of the room. "Doing what?"

I threw open my bedroom door. "Catching bad guys, obviously. Apparently I have a knack for it."

I could hear them talking in low voices in the living room, and worse, taste their conflict. I'd caught them off guard with the Gryphon thing, and I wouldn't be half surprised if Val changed her mind. She was one of those people who thought Gryphons walked on water. But even if she did reconsider, I didn't care. They wanted me out? I was so gone.

Taking a deep breath, I sent Lucen a text asking if I could come over. I had to leave the apartment, and he closed The Lair on Sundays, so I couldn't just pop in there to hang out.

Pity too, because I could use a drink. My anger was fading to annoyance and no small amount of feeling abused. It kept me wired, but not in a good way.

Only what I thought of as the major emotions gave me a smooth burst of energy: anger, sadness, fear, and hatred. Lust worked pretty well on me too, although that didn't fall into the same category, and I assumed it was only because I was part satyr. All the other negativity people carried around—anxiety, embarrassment, frustration, and more—made me jittery.

On that thought, maybe it was time to get rid of roommates entirely if I could afford it. I'd never had much choice before. Boston rents were high, and even with soul-swapping on the side, I could never have managed a place on my own on my old salary. But with what the Gryphons were paying me, maybe I could at last. If I were willing to look in Shadowtown...

It wasn't something I'd ever considered before, but since I no longer had to fear preds any more than I feared strange and violent humans, it was worth considering. Shadowtown rents were cheaper because places weren't in as high demand. Humans had to be pretty desperate to live there in spite of the prime downtown real estate. It was worth asking Lucen about it.

On cue, my phone signaled the arrival of a text. *Come on over. I'll make you dinner.*

My shoulders sagged in relief. Until that moment I hadn't realized how uncertain I'd been about his answer. It was good to know he wasn't upset about me stomping out of the bar yesterday. Or, if he was, he was willing to talk about it.

I grabbed my belongings, and after checking that the path between my bedroom door and the apartment door was clear, got the hell out of Dodge.

I MUST HAVE BEEN THROWING OFF A BLACK-ENOUGH CLOUD that Lucen could sense my arrival. His door swung open before I could knock. He'd just showered, judging by his wet hair, and he smelled like soap mixed with his usual satyr cinnamon.

"Hey." God, I loved the devious gleam he got in his eyes sometimes. I was relaxing already.

"Hey." He shut the door and pulled me close.

I buried my head against him, inhaling deeply, letting the magic I'd once feared do a glorious job of chasing away more of my tension. One by one my muscles relaxed while my hunger for his body grew. Satyr pheromones were better than any massage or drug.

Drug. F. Damn. Some of that tension returned to my shoulders.

I pressed myself closer as he kissed me, but he pulled away. "What's wrong, little siren? You're really stressed."

I grabbed his shirt, sliding it up his stomach. "I know. I'm trying to destress. Work with me."

He laughed and removed my hands. "How about something to eat and drink first? I think you should start slowly and tell me what's up. You ran away so fast yesterday that I was wondering when I'd hear from you again."

Groaning, I followed him into the kitchen. "Aha. This is punishment for me running out, is it?"

"Yes, I always punish people by pouring them wine and cooking them dinner. You know how evil I am."

I pouted, watching him get out the glasses. "Sorry. I *am* feeling irritable. You just happen to make me hot and irritable."

Lucen grinned and handed me a glass of merlot. "Little siren, much as I enjoy toying with your desire—and yes, I do, can't help that—it costs me something not to touch you too. I'd just like us to have a normal conversation first. We haven't done that in a while."

"Does it? Cost you something, I mean?" I sipped the wine and had to admit it was very good, though not as good as he'd have been. "I always figured satyrs could flip the sex thing on and off on command. It's how you torment people."

"Not exactly...no." A flicker of some emotion passed over his face. "It's actually more complicated than that."

I wasn't sure I'd ever heard him hedge so much on anything. It was very un-Lucen-like. "Meaning?"

"I can explain another time. Drink your wine and tell me what's bothering you."

Okay then. Shut down twice in five minutes. That certainly necessitated drinking. "My roommates are kicking me out."

He pulled out one of the kitchen chairs and sat backward on it. "What the hell? Is this because of what happened with Aubrey?"

"Yup. Apparently, I make them uncomfortable. But it's fine. I'm getting too old for this roommate crap, and I was thinking I might be able to find a one-bedroom or a studio in Shadowtown I could afford on my own. I want to stay close to a T line."

"You know, I distinctly remember a time not that long ago when you were afraid of being an outcast among humans and forced to live with us."

"Yes, but I'm more practical these days."

He pointed to my knife. "And armed."

In more ways than he knew. "Yeah. So do you know of any decent landlords who lease to humans around here?"

Lucen nodded. "I can help you there. Would be convenient having you closer by. In fact..." He swung himself off the chair. "If you don't feel like dealing with your roommates until you move out, you can stay here more often."

"You wouldn't mind?" I'd been staying over several nights a week, but only when he asked. Lucen had other things going on in his life besides me. To be specific, he had other people in his bed. Keeping his addicts healthy meant satiating their needs every now and then, and I didn't care to be around for that. The less I remembered he had to do that at all, the happier I was.

On the other hand, my indignation simmered, and I really wanted to get away from Geoff and Val. If there was a way we could schedule this living thing temporarily so that I could keep pretending Lucen wasn't preying on or screwing other people, it might be worth it to me.

"I've got the extra bedroom," Lucen said. "You're welcome to it. You don't make me uncomfortable. I like having you here."

I rolled my eyes at the ongoing joke. "Except when you're making me wait."

"Anticipation, little siren. You have to let the rush build." He raised his glass to me. "So what else is bothering you? I don't think that's the only thing."

"No, it's not. I had to go in to work today."

"And?"

"And." I set my glass down and wrapped my arms around myself. Since I wasn't sure how much had been in the news or what he might know from other sources, I gave Lucen a brief rundown of what had been discovered in Newton. "The Gryphons did some magical analyses on the victims' blood. They found what they think is contaminated F."

It was my turn to wait and watch. Lucen was quiet for a second, then his face turned to surprise. Whether it was genuine, however... Who knew? My job would have been a whole lot easier if I could read preds the way I read humans.

"That's odd," he said finally.

I wasn't sure what sort of reaction would have been useful, but I knew I wasn't getting it. "That was our thought too. Satyrs make F, right?" As far as attempts at subtlety went, that was pathetic. It was also the best I had.

Lucen raised an eyebrow and took another drink. "Usually."

"Usually?"

"F is usually produced by satyrs because you'd need satyr cooperation to make it. It doesn't have to be made by satyrs though. Theoretically, anyone magically skilled could do it if they could get the ingredients."

I picked up my wine, trying to get a better look at his face as he opened the fridge. "Because one of those ingredients happens to be satyr pheromones?"

"That's part of it, but you know enough about magic to know it's more complicated than that. I was going to suggest spaghetti Bolognese for dinner, but I know you're not a fan of pasta. Burgers on the grill okay?"

"Fine. Go back to the magic thing. How is it produced?"

"Did you come over here for my company or to question me?"

"I thought I'd made it pretty clear before that it was for your company."

The suspicious expression on his face turned to amusement. "Company? I thought you'd made it pretty clear it was for sex."

"Which is something I prefer in your company. You're the one who wanted to talk first."

"I did, didn't I?" He was against me in a second, his hands on my arms and his mouth on mine. I sank into the kiss even as my brain screamed he was trying to distract me. It was working too. I was slowly becoming less concerned with everything except the feel of his body, and if he hadn't pinned my arms to my sides, the ploy might have worked. But Lucen had pressed me against the cabinets, and I couldn't touch him. As hot as it could be when he restrained me on occasion, this time my inability to move left me with enough brainpower to stay focused.

I pulled my head away, gasping for breath. "Nope. You chose to talk. I want to talk."

"I changed my mind." He reached for my mouth again, and when I dodged, he went for my neck, trailing kisses down my skin. Releasing my arms at last, his hands slipped under my shirt and cupped my breasts.

It was difficult enough to breathe, never mind think with his thumbs teasing my nipples, and the scent of his skin was stronger than ever. He had to be hitting me with everything he had. I was moaning against my will, aching, and the part of me that could think straight was getting annoyed.

Recognition of such was all it took. The protective glyphs the Gryphons had drawn on my back grew warm. I focused on that heat which was so unlike the heat the rest of me was feeling, and pulled the power in deeper. I hadn't thought I'd need to use their magic at all, but I guess it could be handy.

With the protective magic dulling my senses to Lucen's power, I pushed him backward and extricated myself from the cabinet. "You don't get to do that. You know I want you, but I'm not an addict you get to fuck into submission."

Lucen flinched. Then he ran a hand through his drying hair with an apologetic expression. "Sorry, Jess. You haven't minded when I've used my magic on you before."

"No, but that's not the point, and you know it." I wanted to stay angry at him, but the chagrin on his face was softening me. Damn him. "You were using it to try to distract me. That's what I object to."

I didn't expect him to deny it, and he didn't. But then, I suspected that Lucen didn't lie to me often, if at all. If he didn't want to tell me something, he was upfront about it—maddening, but honest.

He was quiet a moment longer while I fixed my clothes. "You're right, and I'm sorry." He kissed me on the forehead. "I'm going to go light the grill."

I collapsed at the table with my wine as he stepped onto his tiny deck off the kitchen. Well, this had gotten off to a great start. The Gryphons thought I was going to dig out information? The only satyr I could actually call a friend was not merely clamming up on me, but being dickish and manipulative about it. Lucen must know something about F that he didn't want to tell me.

I wasn't going to get answers. Just frustrated in a variety of ways.

I was mostly through with my wine when Lucen returned. He opened the fridge and took out the food. "Come on outside. It's cooling off."

I eyed him warily from where my head rested on my arm, then took the remains of my wine and joined him. It had indeed cooled off, but the setting sun continued to throw off an orange-gold heat that illuminated the deck. It was toasty, especially with the grill going.

Lucen's deck was barely big enough for the two of us and the table of charm-making supplies he had out here. There were glass jars filled with clear liquid that could have been water but probably wasn't, and a variety of substances of even less certain origin. Some required time to soak in the sun, others the moon. Hence, their positions on the table. I didn't touch them, but I examined them.

"They're mostly for making some basic healing aids," Lucen said, putting the burgers on the grill. "Can't be too careful when you're friends with a woman who carries a salamander-forged knife around at all times."

He smiled, and I returned the gesture. *Mostly* for making healing aids. Got it. He wasn't about to say what the rest were for. "Maybe I should take the knife off before I try jumping on you next time? Is that what you're suggesting?"

"Maybe not a bad idea. It's all fun and games until one of us bleeds to death."

His tone was joking, but I'd seen what those blades did. Lucen had only been nicked by one once. If it weren't for having a magical remedy quickly on hand, he might well have bled out from the injury. The memory of seeing so much of his blood everywhere still horrified me.

He probably noticed my anxiety because he kissed me again, less chastely this time, but with none of his magic behind it. "So you want to know about how F is made?"

I almost knocked my wineglass into one of his jars in surprise. He was going to talk after all? "I'd appreciate learning whatever you're willing to share."

"Honestly, little siren, I don't make it, so I can only tell you in the most general of general senses. So back to your first question—yes, it's usually made by satyrs because it requires certain bodily fluids that would be challenging to get without our cooperation."

I choked on the wine. "Really? That's what goes into it?"

He laughed. "Sweat. It's a potent source of pheromones. Get your mind out of the gutter."

"Ah, okay. I mean, not that I'd have been shocked or anything if it were something else."

Lucen continued to silently chuckle as he finished his wine. "In the future, keep in mind that you never want to ask what the goblins put in their fertility charms."

I shuddered. "Thanks for the warning. So anything else you can tell me about F?"

"Don't know. You tell me—what was the F contaminated with? Magic or mundane?"

"Magic."

He flipped the burgers thoughtfully. "Then I can't tell you much except if it's being cut with something, it's probably happening with one of the dealers."

"That doesn't make sense. Dealers are usually addicts. They'd have to be buying charms or curses off another pred to mix in. Why would they do that?"

"I have no idea, but she—" He swore and shut the grill.

"She? It's a 'she' who produces F? Just one person?"

Lucen opened the deck's screen door with unnecessary force. "Jess, if you want me to ask some questions for you, I can. But you're on the wrong trail, and you're just going to have to take my word on that and any answers I get."

"Not good enough. Nine people are dead, and you know who produces our best lead."

He returned to the deck a moment later, carrying a plate and some cheese. "Nine people are dead, and it has nothing to do with us. Why is everyone so eager to blame us for murder these days? First it was the sylphs. Now it's you. I think you'd have learned. It's probably the furies again. We're the least violent of your so-called pred races."

Generally speaking, that was true. "Well, it would be convenient if it were the furies, since they already hate me. This doesn't seem like their MO though."

Lucen handed me the burger plate. "Nor ours, little siren. Don't forget that."

EIGHT

I SCORED A SECOND GOOD NIGHT'S REST IN A ROW, THEN snuck out of bed Monday morning while Lucen slept. After a quick trip to my apartment so I could refill my overnight bag, I headed into work.

There was something thrillingly strange about being around so many Gryphons and clipping an ID badge to my shirt while knowing that last night I'd been sleeping with the so-called enemy. Badge or no badge, I didn't fit in around this place for a multitude of reasons.

That didn't affect my enthusiasm, however, when I saw what was hanging on the back of my desk chair. "Sweet."

Someone had dropped off an official windbreaker. Black with gold lettering and the winged insignia on the back, it was the sort of jacket Gryphons wore over their uniforms in chillier weather. Although this wasn't the sort of weather that called for jackets, I'd take it. Honestly, I hadn't expected Olivia would give me one.

I left the windbreaker on the chair and checked the new pile of notes that had been left for me. One was from Andre, telling me to email him once I got in and set up.

IT's instructions for getting on the computer worked fine, and I found Andre's address in my email program, along with those of the rest of the Boston office employees. While I waited to see what he wanted, I explored the file access I'd been given. There was a document left on the computer desktop for me, explaining my access allowances, though it was only a rehash of what Olivia and Andre had explained. Basically, my access was seriously limited. I'd have to ask for anything I wanted.

Next, I went through the files on F that Andre had given me. I was halfway finished when he tapped on my cube wall. "Afternoon, partner."

"Afternoon?" I checked the computer's clock. "Oh, so it is."

"So it is indeed." He bumped his knuckles together.

"You're perky. I hope you're not expecting me to have already cracked this case and discovered who's producing F."

"You haven't? Slacker." He shook his head, feigning disappointment. "Actually, I'm here because we've got another lead. Well, maybe we got another lead. Come on, we get to go meet him."

I got up and stretched my back. "Our lead is a 'him'?"

Andre consulted a notepad he was carrying. "It is, and he has a name too: Curt Murphy. He came forward to the Newton PD, and they turned him over to us. He just got here, and we get to question him. Aren't you excited?" He punched me lightly on the arm.

I punched him back. "I can barely contain myself. Suspect, witness, or something else?"

Andre scratched his head, his expression turning serious. "Something else from the sound of it. He's a friend of the Stacys who wanted to give a statement. He thinks he might know something."

Down on the first floor, we passed through a cluster of rooms I'd gotten very familiar with during my own questioning. Those few days after Victor Aubrey had been arrested, I'd been forced to tell my story over and over again to multiple Gryphons while sitting in one of these bland little rooms with their bland little furniture, often while drinking bland little cups of coffee. I shuddered to see them again.

We entered one such gray-walled room, and its sole occupant checked us out expectantly. Curt Murphy appeared to be in his late twenties and was in every way as bland as the room, from his khaki pants to his blue button-down office shirt. His hands fidgeted with his phone, and a thin sheen of sweat clung to his face. It was over air-conditioned in here, so that had to be the result of nerves. Beneath his not-so-calm exterior, he was filled with indecision, fear, and no small degree of boredom. None of that was surprising under the circumstances.

Andre held out a hand and did the introductions. "I hope you haven't been waiting long."

Curt shook his head. "Not long. I'm just... I'm not sure I can help, but Mike was a good friend. I want to do whatever I can."

"Michael Stacy?" Andre confirmed. "Did you know his wife too?"

"I knew them both, yeah." Curt spun his phone around on the table. "The thing is, the police aren't saying exactly what happened, but it sounds like everyone at their party on Friday was murdered. Is that true?"

I took a seat and waited for Andre. He'd told me on the way over to let him do the questioning, and I was fine with that. This was another watch-and-learn session.

Andre laid his notepad and pen neatly out on the table while he assessed Curt. If I could have, I'd have told him there wasn't much to assess. Curt's anxiety spiked when he mentioned the party, but I didn't sense anything malicious in it. It was a good bet Curt knew what went on at those parties and was feeling awkward discussing it with strangers.

"The people at the party died," Andre said. "Whether it was murder, an accident, or some other cause remains to be determined."

"So it wasn't necessarily foul play, or whatever the reporters are calling it?"

Andre picked up the pen. "Nine apparently healthy people dying in one place for no clear reason is suspicious. Let's go with that. So what do you know that might be helpful?"

Curt squirmed in his seat. "I was supposed to be at the party, but I backed out last minute. I got sick Friday afternoon, half of my office did. Anyway, I was feeling it Friday night, so I stayed home."

"Good call," I muttered.

Curt's attention shifted to me, maybe hoping I'd be more sympathetic. "Come on, tell me. What happened to them? It wasn't just Mike and Shannon that I knew. I had a few friends there."

Andre cleared his throat. "What happened is something or someone killed your friends. Can you tell me about them? Start with the Stacys. Did they throw these sorts of parties often?"

Curt must have figured out what Andre meant by "these sorts" because his cheeks burned and the vinegar-like taste of his embarrassment flooded my mouth.

I supposed I was spending so much time around satyrs that other people's sex lives no longer seemed weird. I'd witnessed too many dipshit humans driven to all sorts of public displays of depravity at The Lair. At least these people had been having fun behind closed doors and not in a place where I'd have to be an unwilling witness.

Curt talked a bit about the Stacys before finally coming around to Andre's question about the party. "They had parties about once a month or so."

"How long had that been going on for?"

Curt twisted his fingers together. "A year, maybe more?"

"And did you know everybody who was supposed to attend Friday's party?"

Curt took a deep breath, and his body sagged. "Yes. I wasn't close with everyone. But Mike and Shannon were careful, you know? They didn't just invite anyone. You had to be vetted, so I'd gotten to know everyone there at least casually."

I bit my tongue because I wanted to make an inappropriate comment about our differing definitions of casual. Andre caught my eye, apparently sensing my childish behavior.

"But that's actually..." Curt cringed. "That's what made me think I needed to come talk to you about it. Something was supposed to be different this time."

I leaned forward. "Different how?"

"Mike said something about a surprise. I don't know what he meant by that." Curt rested his face on his hands. "I was super pissed off to not be able to go, because whatever it was, he was very excited about it."

Well, that was ominous. I looked at Andre, figuring I should keep my mouth shut.

Andre seemed to be debating something. "When your friends died, they all had F in their systems."

Curt's icy surprise and fear peaked then dimmed like a melting sour orange popsicle. "Did they?" Curt glanced between us. "I wouldn't have thought..."

And now he was lying. The burnt-toast taste of that sort of anxiety was unmistakable.

"Sure, you would have. I mean, that wasn't the surprise, was it?" I asked, taking a stab at what I was sensing. "They've had F at their parties before."

It was Andre whose surprise I noticed this time, but the corners of his lips twitched, so I thought he was pleased. "Mr. Murphy, we're only interested in the F if it relates to why your friends died. So you need to be honest. You came to us because you had information and wanted to help."

"I know. Sorry." Curt rubbed his stubble. "Yeah, that wouldn't have been the surprise. They used to get F occasionally."

"Do you know from who or where?"

"Only that it was at some club."

"What kind of club?"

Curt stared at his phone as though he wanted to hide behind it. "A dance club. That's all I know. I never went with them. The noise and the crowds—not my thing. But I guess this club did some fetish thing every now and then that they liked. That's all I can say."

Dance club. Fetish thing. F. Checkmate. I knew our club, and it wasn't a surprise considering it was owned by a satyr. Damn it.

Andre probed Curt with a few more questions, but the guy didn't seem to have much else of use to share. He was feeling survivor's guilt and thus felt obligated to tell us what he knew. His problem was that he felt stupid doing it. Stupid and embarrassed.

Andre got Curt's contact information then walked him to the lobby. I was still sitting in the room, silently cursing what the next item on my to-do list was likely to be, when he returned and collapsed into the chair across from mine. "That explains why there were ten wineglasses sitting out at the party, but only nine used. Makes sense, doesn't it? Even numbers?"

"You're asking me?"

"Sure. What do I know about swingers' parties? Handcuffs and blindfolds and whips, oh my."

I snorted, grateful to Andre for relieving some of my tension. "What? You've never been to that sort of shindig?"

"I've never been that cool." He narrowed his eyes at me. "You?"

"Closest I've ever gotten was working at a satyr bar." It was a risky thing to admit, but not like my very temporary stint as one of Lucen's servers would be difficult to uncover. Besides, I'd rather these people know as much of the publicly strange parts of my life as possible. It might keep them so distracted that they wouldn't think to search for all the truly important strangeness I was hiding.

A smile slowly crept over Andre's face. "You did what? I have to hear about this someday. I could tell you were wild."

"Oh, come on. Anyone who knows how I got drafted into working here knows I have to have led an interesting life."

Andre laughed. "True enough. Okay, so back to the case. Curt Murphy's information about a surprise at the party is interesting, but not illuminating. We'll have to keep digging. And that reminds me—nice job catching him on the F. I forget sometimes I'm working with an empath."

"A very limited-in-her-scope empath."

"Limited or not, it's plenty useful in this line of work. We've got all kinds of tricks for detecting lies, plus regular old polygraphs, but I'm going to guess you're just as efficient and accurate. And best of all, I don't need permission to use you."

"I'm probably more accurate." I slid off the chair, frowning. Might as well bring up the next point. "The club he was talking about—I think I know which one it is."

Andre picked up his pen and paper. "Now see, that also surprises me because you don't seem like the clubbing type."

"I liked to go dancing when I was younger." Actually, I'd liked to go dancing at that club in particular. Fetish Fridays—which I guessed was what Curt was talking about—wasn't my favorite event, but in general the place had been a haven for dark, angry dance music. I'd had a lot of angst to work out of my system back then.

Hell, I still did.

Andre seemed amused by my comment as he chewed on the pen cap.

"Okay then, clubbing queen, what place do you think he's talking about? I think I know too. It would be good if we were thinking of the same place."

I sat on the table. "Purgatory."

"Purgatory, it is."

"Damn. And how did you know the club?"

"We keep a list of all the businesses in the area that are owned by preds, especially the ones that are pred-owned but not obvious about the fact."

I squeezed the table edge. "Like Purgatory." As with so many things, I'd had no idea the club was owned by a satyr until recently. "So are we going to go there?"

"Do dragons bite? We just got a tip that F is being dealt out of Purgatory. This means we can be thorough and professional about it."

I got off the table and followed Andre out of the room. "And thorough and professional—what does that mean?"

"It means if someone's dealing F out of Purgatory, and satyrs produce F, and satyrs own Purgatory… Then you add it all up, throw in nine dead humans for extra credit, and we can get a warrant to search the premises."

I paused in the hall, my stomach sinking to my boots. "Do I really have to go with you?"

Andre threw me a funny look. "You're my partner-in-training. This is our case. Of course you're coming with me. Just hang on because it could take a couple hours to get the warrant. I have to do the dreaded deed called 'paperwork.'"

"Got it."

I took several deep breaths as he walked away. It wasn't just satyrs who owned Purgatory. It was Devon. Which meant in a couple hours I was going to be pissing off Dezzi's lieutenant.

Fucking awesome.

While Andre obtained the warrant, I returned to my desk. Though I tried reading the files on F, I wasn't comprehending much.

Showing up at Purgatory with a warrant, getting on Devon's bad side—these things didn't leave me with lots of good feelings.

I looked up at the sound of someone approaching, and Tom Kassin gave me one of his strained smiles as he stopped at my cube. "Ms. Moore, I'm glad to find you here. Would you mind coming to my office with me so we can talk?"

Actually, I would mind. The unsettled feeling I got around him hadn't subsided since Saturday.

I made a show of checking the time. "I'm waiting for Agent Pagan to let me know—"

"Yes, I know about the warrant, but that's going to take a while. This won't." He stepped back and gestured into the hall. "Please."

"Of course." What else could I say?

Tom's office was down the hall, a weirdly shaped interior room that was covered in boxes. I supposed even Gryphons from World Headquarters didn't have the seniority to bump someone out of an office with a window. Some of his boxes were unpacked, and the contents—or so I assumed—were sitting on one of the several bookshelves behind his desk. The books themselves appeared gravely old. Many were leather-bound, and the writing on the spines of several had worn away to the point where I couldn't read it.

Spell books? Pred lore? I wondered what was in them, why he needed them, and if I could take a look.

Tom moved a box off one of the room's two chairs so I could sit. "I apologize for the mess. I needed to bring some resources with me, and it's amazing how few of our old texts have been digitized yet."

"I remember hearing there are storerooms full of interesting old books and artifacts at World," I said, thinking about the stuff I'd learned at the Academy.

Tom closed the office door most of the way. "There are, all meticulously catalogued, yet not easily accessible despite that. So." He sat across from me and folded his hands.

"So?" I raised my eyebrows. He was the one who'd requested this meeting, after all.

"I understand you asked to speak to Victor Aubrey."

A small drape or flag in the same red and gold colors as Tom's pin sat in a crumpled ball on one of the bookshelves. I pondered it and the pin as I responded. "I did."

"I'm curious about why."

Dragging my eyes away from the cloth, I gave him my full attention. It wasn't his fault, but his baby face made every question from him sound condescending. Maybe that was why I didn't care for him. When he spoke, it felt like a child was lecturing me.

I tried to hide my annoyance. "As I explained to Director Lee, Victor and I have the same weird ability, and I thought his fury master might have told him a few things about it that would be useful for me to know too."

It was clear from Tom's face he didn't quite buy my reasoning, and the bitter chocolate of his suspicion confirmed it. It was muted though. Watered-down chocolate. I wondered if he were truly uninterested, or if he had some seriously powerful magic protecting him. "I would think it's unlikely that anything Victor Aubrey tells you could be trusted. He might tell you what he believes is the truth, though I doubt it. But even so, if anything was told to him by a fury, I'd say it's unlikely to be true. If you want to know more, you should turn to us for answers."

"No one around here has heard of anyone with a gift like mine. That doesn't bode well for discovering answers."

Not unless someone had the clearance to decrypt my stolen files, but yeah, I wasn't about to bring those up.

"We have all kinds of resources at World. For example..." Tom picked up one of the books on his desk and read the title. "Well, this wouldn't be of use, but I can help you access a lot of information. All you have to do is let me know what it is you want to find out."

The falseness of his sincerity made me want to smack him. "The problem is I don't know what I want to find out. All I know is I want to know more. Anyway, I thought you were here because of the furies. You probably shouldn't be wasting time helping me."

"You're connected to the furies. I can't imagine helping you would ever be a waste of my time."

"That's nice, but you've read the reports on me. You know what I know. If you have any suggestions for where to look for more information, I'd be happy to hear them. Meantime, I think it's worthwhile to talk to Victor."

Tom sighed. "That can't happen because of the case."

Shit. I'd expected as much, but still.

"I know you're disappointed," he continued, reading my face, "but trust me, you're better off. He's not a pleasant person, and he's less so going through withdrawal."

"Yeah, I'm very aware of Victor's personality flaws, having been on the receiving end of a few. Was that all then?" *Or did you want more time to dig for information?*

"That's all. I just wanted you to know that I'm available as a resource and a friend, and I'd be very interested in helping you answer any questions you might have about your unusual situation. I realize you might feel a bit concerned after what happened, but we're here to help. I hope you feel you can trust us."

Uh-huh. Trust me, said the scorpion to the frog, the pred to the human, and the mysterious Gryphon to the woman with something to hide. No thanks.

"I appreciate the offer, and actually I do have a question." I pointed to his pin. "I haven't seen any other Gryphons with one of those. Does it have something to do with being stationed at World?"

My question caught Tom off guard, and finally I could taste some real emotion from him. Surprise and disappointment that I wasn't asking about something important.

He touched the pin. "This? Oh, no. It marks me as a member of the Brotherhood of the Wing. It's a kind of Gryphon fraternity."

"Oh." I'd never heard of it, but then, why would I have? "Interesting. I didn't know there were fraternities in the Gryphons."

His face was a curious mix of pride and tension. "I'm not sure there are fraternities, plural."

"I see." Actually, I didn't. Why did the Gryphons need a fraternity? But whatever. I had real issues to ponder. "Thanks for your concern, by the way. If I think of any specific questions, I'll be sure to let you know."

Not.

I beat it out of Tom's office, my head filled with two more worries. One, how was I going to get to talk to Victor? And two, what was with Tom's prying into my life? The latter could simply be because he found me interesting, like so many others, or because he thought my gift might be related to the furies' interest in me somehow. But the bad feeling I had about him stuck with me. I couldn't shake the idea there was something more sinister in his attempt to "help" me.

The first thing I did when I got back to my desk was text Steph to see if she'd managed to talk to her contact about breaking the file encryption. Tom probably did have access to a lot of potentially useful information, but I didn't want to go through him to get it. I didn't want the Gryphons to know anything until I knew more myself, particularly more about what they were doing with files on me and Victor. I had to get those things cracked.

My phone rang shortly after. "I've got the warrant," Andre said. "I'm pulling together a team to do the search. Meet me downstairs in five?"

"Sure." I hung up and put on my new jacket for the first time. If I was going to piss off the satyrs' lieutenant, then I might as well look official doing it.

NINE

Purgatory was located among a row of clubs in a just-this-side-of-seedy neighborhood. At night, especially on the weekends, it was a safe area, flooded with twenty-something-year-old partiers and overflowing with booming bass and expensive cars. During the day, all was silent and sunlight exposed every crack in the sidewalk and splotch of graffiti along the ugly façades of the trendy nightclubs.

Andre cursed as he parked the SUV. "I don't believe this. How did he get here first?"

I adjusted my sunglasses as I got out of the car and held in a groan. I'd known it was inevitable that Devon would discover my involvement in the search today, but I hadn't actually expected to run into him during it.

Yet here he was, standing in the building's shade, impeccably dressed in a crisp dark shirt, sports jacket, and tie as always. A woman was with him, also dressed to kill in a sleek suit and pissy expression. She was probably in her forties, and she was definitely a lust addict. Whether she was one of his, I couldn't tell, but it stood to reason.

"How *did* he get here?" I muttered.

Andre squared his shoulders as he locked the car. "Tipped off to the warrant. Every pred race in this city has people placed in strategic positions around town to keep them informed. It's why we need you to be our strategic person."

Great. Because I was off to such a good start there.

The two other Gryphons who came with us to conduct the search wore grim faces as we approached the club entrance. Afternoon sun bore down on us, but I wanted to hide inside my jacket regardless. I couldn't tell where Devon was looking beneath his sunglasses, but I swore I could feel the weight of his gaze on me as we approached.

He stuck his hands in his pockets as he stepped into the sun to meet us. Partly it was meant to be rude, I was sure. But it was also practical. Preds didn't like the sun. Their skin and eyes were very sensitive to it.

"You must be Devon, the owner of this fine establishment?" Andre pulled a copy of the warrant from his pocket, and my respect for him increased. I could taste his annoyance and anxiety, but he kept the latter out of his speech and manners.

Of course, if I could sense it, Devon could too. But it was a good showing.

Devon smiled coldly. "I am. And you must be the Gryphon who's confused as to the nature of my business."

Oddly, I could feel Devon's annoyance too, at least in the sense he was throwing off a lot of power. Preds tended to do that when they were feeling particularly aggressive, and I didn't think it was something they necessarily could control. In this case, Devon's voice melted on me like butter, smooth and sweet. And oh, somewhat disconcerting. It had been a while since I'd been able to sense pred power other than Lucen's, and I wasn't prepared for it.

Devon caught me staring at him in surprise, and he silently shook his head as though disappointed. Then he motioned for Andre to hand the warrant to the woman with him. "I'll go unlock the building so you don't feel the need to break down my door in your zealous but misplaced quest for justice."

I followed the others into the club as the woman scanned the document then handed it back to Andre without comment.

I'd been in Purgatory on many occasions, the most recent of which was a few weeks ago, but the club was an entirely different place while empty.

As sunlight had changed the nature of the street outside, lights and a lack of crowds showed me the club for all it was—the smudges on the walls, the exposed scaffolding in the ceiling, the dirt ground into the dance floor. In the harshness of the day, the black upholstery looked tacky and the chrome cheap. Darkness and smoke machines covered a variety of sins.

Speaking quietly with his companion, Devon led us into the middle of the main room. Once there he stopped and spread his arms. "Enjoy yourselves. I'll be in my office. Any questions should be directed to my lawyer."

"Actually," Andre said, "your office is the place I thought we'd start."

As this was mostly another watch-and-learn trip for me, I stayed close to Andre during the search. He'd explained the procedure and legal technicalities to me on the drive, but my cluelessness couldn't be cured in a mere twenty minutes.

Devon's office was large but sparsely furnished, and one wall consisted entirely of one-way glass that overlooked the main dance floor. The Gryphons were able to make quick work of the place without discovering anything questionable. While they fanned out afterward, the memory of what I'd done the last time I'd been in Purgatory weighed on me.

That was the night I'd discovered cocoon-like things in the club's basement. Would the compulsions Devon had placed around that floor be enough to keep the Gryphons out? They hadn't worked on me, but they had silenced me from speaking about them.

I tried again, now, to bring up the topic, but I could barely get the word "basement" to cross my lips. The Gryphon I was speaking to regarded me like I was choking.

"Never mind." I wandered away and half-heartedly began poking around at the main bar.

Devon sidled up to me. "I promise you, Jess, there's no F down there."

Aha. He must have seen me trying and failing to talk to the other Gryphon. I adopted an innocent voice. "No F down where?"

He rolled his eyes. "There's none anywhere around here, and you're wasting your time. But you know what I store in the basement, and it's not drugs. So do me a favor and pretend you're normal and affected by the compulsion like the rest of them."

"Really? I don't know what you store in that place I can't name because you won't tell me anything, remember?"

"And why should I? Here you are, wearing the opposing team's colors and snooping through my club on some misguided crusade. It hurts." He put his hand to his heart, but I got the distinct sense that Devon's ability to make light of the situation was running thin.

"Opposing team's colors? I'm glad everything's a joke to you. People are dead."

He frowned. "Yes, and I find it a bit insulting that you assume I might have something to do with it. I thought we were friends."

"Friends implies a degree of trust I'm not sure is possible. I was settling for friendly."

"Keep this up and even that will be uncharacteristically optimistic of you."

Peachy.

I started to say something else, but across the room Andre had gotten into a heated discussion with Devon's lawyer, and Devon was eyeing them with great interest. Taking a last scan of the bar, I moved closer to Devon. "You know what? Maybe that's as it should be. I'm not exactly comfortable being friends or friendly with people who go around ruining other people's lives."

"How have I ruined anyone's life?"

I nodded toward his lawyer. "Seriously? Is this the woman you keep on speed dial? You made your lawyer into an addict."

That earned me one of Devon's smirks. "Lydia Cordero is one of the best criminal defense attorneys in the Greater Boston area. How else do you expect me to be able to afford her rates?"

"I don't care if that was a joke." And I wasn't sure it was a joke. "Sometimes you disgust me."

"I'm well aware of it, although it's disappointing." He smoothed the wrinkles on his sleeves, and I might have been imagining it, but his eyes seemed to harden. "I'm not about to hold you up as a paragon of moral virtue, Jess. Let's remember—you're working for the Gryphons only because it's keeping your own ass out of prison. Or isn't that what you told Dezzi the other day?"

"I'm being blackmailed." I lowered my voice as Andre and the lawyer stopped arguing. "How does that make what you do okay? So the Gryphons aren't perfect. So what?"

"So that's my point. You're not a great defender of humanity, that's all. And you were perfectly fine accepting our help when you needed it. Hypocrisy is unattractive, even in you."

I clenched my jaw. "I'm not being hypocritical. Accepting your help isn't the same thing as condoning your actions."

"Nor is fucking Lucen, I suppose?"

Alas, I didn't have a good retort to that. Although Devon's assessment of my relationship with Lucen was a lot baser than mine would have been, he did have a point. I counted Lucen as a friend, and it was hard to argue that wasn't condoning his behavior.

Dragon shit on toast. There was a difference here, but this wasn't the time to try to explain it. The more he talked to me, the more irritated Devon was getting. The rise in his emotions was having a noticeable effect on his power and thus on me, and that was uncomfortable. I didn't understand why I could sense his magic, but my body was flush from the heat of it.

Was my numbness wearing off? That would be horribly disappointing.

Devon straightened, no doubt well aware he'd gotten to me. My silence likely only proved the point. "It must be uncomfortable having your knickers twisted up your ass the way you do. If Lucen's not doing a good enough job of removing them, let me know. I'd be happy to try, and you don't need to call me a friend unless you want to."

WE LEFT PURGATORY WITH NOTHING. NOTHING TO HELP THE case, and nothing to atone for the fact that I was now in even deeper salamander shit with the satyrs than I'd been this morning.

Andre was annoyed, and so were the other Gryphons. I was more like livid, although I didn't have anyone to direct my anger toward. I was simply mad at the universe for dumping on me.

When Andre declared it quitting time later, I was only too happy to hightail it out of the office. I had one thing to look forward to this evening —my meeting with my soul-swapping client. I clung to that single act of defiance against the Gryphons to potentially make up for my shitty day. This was who I was. This was what defined me. And damn Olivia Lee's rationale for why it was a bad idea.

But in the meantime, I had to pass several hours. Once I'd have gone home or maybe to The Lair, but under the circumstances neither appealed. Instead I bought some dinner to go and headed over to the Esplanade to watch the runners and rollerbladers sweep past the Charles River.

When I finished eating, I got some exercise of my own, meandering through the brick sidewalks of Beacon Hill and wandering the paths in Boston Garden. Even though this area hadn't been hit the worst, the damage from the salamander fires was nonetheless apparent everywhere I turned. But Bostonians were nothing if not resilient. Already, the smoke-blackened buildings and rubble that scarred downtown were being healed by a massive recovery effort.

Around ten, with the sky dark and a chill rolling off the river, I headed back toward the Esplanade and the Hatch Shell Amphitheater where I'd told my potential client I'd meet her. Since I didn't have anything with me to obscure my face, I hung out among the trees some distance away.

Behind me, the street noise was a constant din, punctuated by the occasional siren as ambulances came and went from nearby Mass General. But in the lulls between the noise, it was just me and the rush of the river. My thoughts drifted as if carried on the current, recalling that day Lucen had found me here. The day I'd met him. The day he'd stopped me from doing something overly dramatic and put me—inadvertently—on the path I now walked.

I knew why he'd intervened. He'd found my emerging pred-like talent fascinating because he didn't understand it any more than I did. But when did his fascination with my gift turn into something more? He claimed he cared about me, and I was starting to accept that might be possible, but what did it mean for us? How could this relationship work?

Much as I hated to admit it, Devon had brought up a good point at Purgatory. In a way, I was condoning what Lucen did by being friends with him. I made excuses for him I didn't make for other preds. He needed addicts to live. He took good care of his addicts. It wasn't his fault.

But I didn't even know if that last one were true. Maybe Lucen had wanted to become a satyr. There was no reason I couldn't ask except one. If I learned he had chosen this life for himself, then what did I do?

I shivered and blamed it on the breeze.

A blast of fear dragged me from my gloomy thoughts, melting on my tongue like lemon sherbet. I adjusted my stance and traced the emotion to a small figure heading my way from the opposite side of the amphitheater. Her size gave me pause. Her form was no bigger than a child's.

Pulling my hood on, I inched closer, keeping to the shadows. The stranger noticed my movement immediately and stopped right in front of the amphitheater itself. The stonework reflected the scant light, and I could tell that her face wasn't a girl's after all. She was just a slightly built woman wearing a short dress over a pair of leggings.

"Are you...?" She raised a hand to her lips as if surprised she'd spoken.

I took a step backward, closer to the trees, and silently cursed myself for forgetting the scarf I usually wore to cover my face. "If you're supposed to be meeting someone, then I'm the one you're supposed to be meeting. Come forward so we can talk, but don't step onto the grass."

She wrapped her arms around herself and stopped at the edge of the walk so that the toes of her ballet flats skimmed the dirt. Either she was quite literal or a perfectionist. "I've heard you can help. It's true?"

"I can, depending on your situation. Tell me your story, and I'll tell you what I can do." Technically, I didn't need her story. All I had to know was who she'd sold her soul to, but details helped me decide what I wanted to charge. Like I'd told Olivia, sometimes I helped for free, but that was rare. Most people offered to pay. With my old job, I was often in need of money, so unless it seemed like too much of a hardship, I took payment even if it was nothing more than ten dollars. Preds typically demanded a cut of my fee to do the soul exchange, and ten percent or ten dollars at a minimum was what I offered them.

My would-be client tucked stray strands of her long brown hair behind her ears. "My name's... Do I need to tell you my name?"

"You don't need to tell me your real name unless you want to, but it might be nice to have something to call you."

Her right hand absently tugged at the earrings she wore. "Okay, right. I guess you can call me Bee. I'm a dancer with the...with a local group. We have a new production coming up, and I was competing for the lead role with another dancer, and..." She took a deep breath. "The director favors her even though she's not as good. So I did something horrible." Her voice cracked.

"You bought a curse and used it on her." It wasn't the first time I'd heard this sort of story, although it was the first time I'd heard it from a dancer. Musicians rigging auditions, grad students fighting for scholarship money, athletes taking down rivals—I got them all. Hell, I'd gotten lawyers so desperate to win a case that they'd torpedoed other lawyers or even clients and judges. Justice might be blind, but She wasn't immune to a powerful curse or two. There were a thousand types of curses out there, ranging from generic bad luck to all sorts of unspeakably specific evils. If you could imagine it, there was probably a pred who could conjure it up for the right price. And it was all highly illegal.

It was also highly frustrating. Cases like this were never ones I took for free. While there were always worse people out there than my client, I had a hard time pitying them.

This time, at least, my would-be client seemed to have remorse for what she'd done, which was more than I could say for many. Beneath her fear, I could sense her sadness and self-disgust. That softened my feelings for her a bit. Everyone made mistakes.

Bee covered her mouth with her hands again as if trying to hide her face from me. "I feel horrible, and I wish I hadn't done it. And what's worse is that it hasn't changed anything. I'm still jealous of her. I still hate that she's perceived as being better than me. And if it's this bad now, these feelings, I can't imagine what it's going to be like if I'm an addict. You have to help me, please. If I could take back what I did, I would."

It's easy to believe someone's being sincere when you could taste deception. In her case, I didn't. "I can help you, I hope. Tell me who you bought the curse from." And please let it be from someone I'd done business with before. That always made my life easier.

"He's a harpy. I was told his name is Rich, or it might have been Rick. I met him at a bakery in Shadowtown."

It was Rik, not Rick, but they sounded close enough. My shoulders relaxed. I'd dealt with him before. Rik thought of himself as an artist with sugar, but he wasn't averse to making money on the side by selling illegal charms. His MO was to work them into his confections.

"I know who that is. Check back at the bar in a week. I'll either have straightened this out for you, or I'll leave you a message with an update."

The taste of lemon sherbet lightened on my tongue. "I don't know how to thank you. How much do I owe you for this?"

I hesitated. Maybe it was because my new job meant I wasn't hard up for money, or because I was taking more pleasure than usual in helping this woman since I was metaphorically spitting on the Gryphons. Or maybe I was trying to make myself feel better after a crappy day.

Or maybe I was getting soft. Could happen.

"We'll worry about that later, after we know I can complete the job. When it's done, you can decide how much it was worth to you."

Bee nodded vigorously. "Okay, that seems more than fair."

It was more than fair. The dangerous part of my job was tracking down someone else's soul to trade away. She'd have no idea what I'd need to go through to do that, and at this point, neither did I.

Regardless, I took great satisfaction in watching her leave. I could do good deeds, damn it. It might not make up for condoning what Lucen did, but it might alleviate my conscience for a while.

WHEN I GOT TO THE LAIR, IT WAS CLOSING IN ON MIDNIGHT. Shadowtown was bustling with activity, but the bar itself was emptying out. No one felt much like enjoying themselves on a Monday, no matter what race they were.

I didn't see Lucen right away, but Paulius nodded at me in greeting as he dried a shot glass. Wondering if I should have gone straight to Lucen's apartment, I wandered deeper into the bar. Since I was here, I might as well go up the back stairs.

I'd just opened the kitchen door when Lucrezia's voice stilled my stride. "You invited her to stay with you again?"

Slowly, I lowered my hand and let the door close all but a crack. Standing utterly motionless, I strained to hear the response.

"What I do or don't do with Jess isn't your business." Lucen sounded angry, which I expected him to be after what happened this afternoon, but Lucrezia sounded far more pissed off.

"I can't believe you said that. As Dezzi's second, it is very much my business to be monitoring what you do because what you do reflects on all of us. Last week, I wouldn't have cared. But you heard about the Gryphons searching Purgatory today, and Jessica was there. She's not just a human snack for you anymore. She's a Gryphon."

Something went bang inside the kitchen. "If Dezzi has a problem with it, she'll make it known. Until Dezzi has a problem, you don't have a problem."

"No, that is the problem, Lucen. Dezzi has her hands full, so she's turning a blind eye to too many things lately. First it was Angelia, then it was you taking Jessica under our protection during the murders. If Dezzi's overlooking that, then she'll overlook this. But others won't. What if the Upper Council finds out? It's my job, and Devon's job, and your job too, which I shouldn't have to remind you, to help Dezzi out—not to make things worse. We have a responsibility to every satyr in this domus."

Lucen must have started pacing because I could see his body flash by the crack in the doorway. I held my breath. "I'm not getting into the Angelia situation again, but protecting Jess worked out in our favor in the long run. So let Dezzi handle this too. If something is going on with the F supply, then she has bigger problems than me letting Jess sleep over a few extra nights a week."

Who the hell was Angelia?

Lucrezia clicked her tongue. "Yes, and if something is going on with the F supply, then sharing your bed with a Gryphon is such a smart move. You're proving my point. She's a threat to us."

I winced because Lucrezia's argument wasn't without merit. If someone in the satyrs was killing humans via F, I'd have no qualms busting them for it. Looking past Lucen's addicts was one thing. Condoning murder was something else.

Dragon shit on toast. What was it with satyrs pointing out things I didn't want to hear today?

I missed half of Lucen's response, and just in time caught him telling Lucrezia he needed to go back to work.

I stepped away from the door, wondering if I should bother pretending I hadn't heard anything. Lucen and Lucrezia might have been too busy arguing to sense my presence, but Paulius had probably noticed me listening at the door.

Speaking of which, said door swung open and Lucrezia swept by me without a word. I thought I'd gotten lucky, but she seemed to reconsider a moment later. Before I could dart into the kitchen, she'd grabbed my arm.

She was made-up and dressed as stylish as always, but beneath her carefully put-together appearance, I could detect a weariness in her face. Lucrezia was more stressed than I'd ever seen her.

She bent her head toward me. "If you cared about him, you'd stay away. You're not doing him any favors."

I flailed for an acerbic retort, but Lucrezia didn't give me the chance. She released me and left in a cloud of pheromones.

Regaining my composure, I stepped into the bar's kitchen and coughed loudly to get Lucen's attention. His forehead was pressed against the fridge, and he seemed surprised to see me.

"I think I arrived at a bad time."

Lucen shook off his daze, but his smile was thin. "Never a bad time for you, little siren."

"I'm getting you in trouble again, aren't I? If it's not a good idea to have me stay here, just say so. I still have an apartment."

"What? No. It's fine."

"Really? Because I heard what Lucrezia was saying."

He came over and wrapped his arms around me. I leaned against him, wishing it didn't feel so good. Could I walk away from this for his sake? For my own? I couldn't get Devon's accusation out of my head. Not even Lucen's magic was silencing my worries, although it was making it harder to care.

"She has a point," I murmured into Lucen's chest.

"Screw her point." He cupped my cheek and reached down to kiss me, slow and sweet. It was what I needed—or maybe what I didn't need—but a moan slid up my throat. Lucen's eyes glowed brighter with power as he pulled away, feeding on my desire. "Lucrezia doesn't know everything."

"But what about Dezzi?"

"Relax, Jess."

"I'm serious."

"So am I. Let me help you." With a slow smile, he slid his hands around my hips and unbuttoned my jeans. "Dezzi doesn't know everything either."

Gasping, I draped my arms around his neck, and his warm fingers skimmed over my underwear before slipping beneath. My thighs clenched around him, arousal seeping over his touch. "But I got you in trouble with her before."

"And it worked out before. So no worries." His breath was like fire on my ear, and when his lips tugged on my earlobe, I lost all ability to think. My body gave over to him, his fingers probing between my wet folds. My hands clenched into fists around his hair. He pressed me closer, playing my body with the skill of a maestro.

"You shouldn't...do this..." Hell, talking between breaths was hard. So was standing. "Someone could walk in."

One hand tightened its grip on my backside, while a finger on his other delved into me. I shuddered, clutching more of him to stay upright. "I don't care," Lucen whispered. "That's what you have to understand. Lucrezia, other people? They're not as important as this. This is what I want. You are what I want."

I tried to respond, but I couldn't. Longed to reach for his erection, hot and heavy against me through his jeans, but I couldn't do that either. I was lost, desperate and incoherent. And when he thrust a second slick finger in me to join the first, his thumb circling over my most sensitive spot, I couldn't do anything but muffle my moans in his T-shirt as I came, biting his chest. And still, he squeezed my ass tighter, holding me so close I could barely breathe until my shudders subsided.

God, he made that way, way too easy sometimes.

I sagged with disappointment, breathing hard, as he pulled his hand away at last. "Thank you for that. But now I really need to go back to work."

I loosened my grip on him but didn't let go. His cinnamon scent clung to me, and I wasn't ready to give up on him or his body. "I don't want to get you in trouble."

"You won't. You aren't." Lucen kissed me, decisively this time, as though that could stop my arguing, and he backed away before I could unfasten the button on his jeans. "Maybe just do me a favor? If you're going to go raid Purgatory or another of our businesses again, it would be really nice if you could give me a heads-up."

I closed my eyes, feeling my arousal sink like a lead weight. As fast as he could stoke my desire, he could also annoy me. It was impressive. I zipped my pants. "One, if you have nothing to hide, you shouldn't need warning. Two, Devon had no problem getting tipped off without my help. And three, that would be extremely unethical on my part."

"Four, it would nonetheless be a nice gesture, especially if you're truly unhappy about being forced into the Gryphons. It would go a long way toward convincing people, like Lucrezia, of that."

"Damn it. People are dead. Whether I wanted to help the Gryphons or not is irrelevant. I want the murderer found. If someone is tainting F, then I'm not about to help them get away with it."

Lucen flung the towel he'd used to dry his hands at the sink. "I don't care about random people. I care about you. About us. You say you're worried about getting me in trouble with Dezzi? I'm giving you ideas to help us make this work." He checked the time. "I'll see you in the apartment soon."

We would see about that.

I stared at the door after Lucen disappeared through it. *I care about you. About us.* But what about them? *Them* deserved consideration too.

But they wouldn't get it. Not from a pred. I knew that, and yet... And yet I was constantly trying to overlook it, wasn't I? Trying to do good with one hand, while my other covered my eyes from the evil I chose to associate with.

Not exactly a paragon of moral virtue. Just like Devon had said.

TEN

I SPENT THE NEXT FEW DAYS STEWING OVER MY ISSUES. THERE was no way to hide your turmoil from a pred, so Lucen had to be aware that I wasn't happy. More to the point, given his own foul mood, he must have been aware he was the source of at least some of my angst.

We silently agreed not to discuss it. It was familiar territory, and not something that could be solved by talking. He couldn't change his nature. I couldn't turn off my humanity. No relationship counselor was going to be able to talk us into a solution. All I could do was choose not to condone his behavior, but that meant leaving and probably ruining not just our weird relationship but also our ten-year friendship. The thought of that made me ill.

Besides our relationship, the other topic we didn't talk about was the Newton case. Andre and I were continuing to investigate the victims to see if we could find a motive. The Stacys' neighbors had been interviewed extensively to learn whether they'd seen or heard anything, and I was discovering more about the dreary tedium of detective work than I'd ever wanted to know.

Because of our lack of progress, the Gryphons were still counting on me to unlock the secrets of F from the satyrs, but I hadn't done a thing about it since my one conversation with Lucen. Bringing it up was sure to provoke a fight, and what I'd originally told the Gryphons was true enough. I really didn't know who else to ask.

That was, I didn't know who else to ask who might actually be willing to talk. I knew plenty of satyrs who *wouldn't* talk. I was living with one.

Thursday at noon—Steph's lunch hour—I got a chance to break out of my gloomy rut and do something I'd been looking forward to. Steph was taking me to meet her contact about cracking the encrypted files.

I hopped off the Green Line and crossed the street, heading away from one of Boston University's dorms. Above, the sun darted in and out of the clouds, and below, heat rose off the street like steam. It had been cool and rainy the last couple days, but summer had returned with a vengeance. I fanned the back of my neck with my ponytail and frowned at the street sign on the corner. None of the businesses down the road had readable signs. I passed more restaurants, a laundromat, and a used books and music store, but no computer repair place. I was about to cross the street when I heard my name.

Steph waved, and yes, she was on the other side of the road. Figured. I hurried over and glanced up at the dingy sign on the storefront over her head. Ye Olde Computer Shoppe. Nice.

The window was dirty and didn't contain much to look at. A smaller sign by the door advertised repairs, custom-built machines, and data recovery specialists.

"How's the apartment search going?" Steph asked.

With Lucen's help, I'd thrown myself into the effort. It was one of the few subjects we could agree on—I needed my own space. "Slowly. I checked out a new place yesterday, but it was very meh. So have you ever met this person?" I motioned toward the store.

Steph shook her head. She was dressed for work, which always amused me because the black chinos and collared blouses she wore were so not her. Dress codes were a bitch.

She crushed a cigarette beneath her spike-heeled boot. "I've only met him online, and I've told you all I know. You could be exposing all sorts of secrets by doing this. Are you sure you want to?"

"Positive. The Gryphons are blocking me from talking to Victor, so those files are all I have until I can figure out another plan." Preferably another plan that did not involve Tom Kassin. "I have a way to deal with the trust stuff. It'll be fine."

Steph finger-combed her hair using the store window as a mirror. "You and your plans. Just promise me this one doesn't include an imp swarm."

"No imps, no dragons, no charms even." I held up my empty hands.

"I'm holding you to that. Okay then. Let's do this." She pulled the door open.

The shop interior was every bit as dark and dingy as the window, and the place smelled like stale coffee. It was tiny too. Cramped. Computer parts and accessories littered the shelves, and the far wall was decorated with Bruins paraphernalia. Boston the band played on a stereo somewhere, but I didn't see any speakers.

A black curtain swung open beneath the most recent year's pennant, and a twenty-something guy emerged from a back room. His brown ringlets were pulled back in a ponytail, and he was a couple days late for a shave. "How can I help you?"

"Are you Ben?" Steph asked. "I'm the one who contacted you about some data recovery."

"Oh, right. My special recovery services." He grinned impishly and beckoned to the curtained-off room in the back. "Excellent. Come into my office, ladies."

Ladies? Steph threw me an I-told-you-so glance, and I whispered, "Geeks" at her, which earned me a smack on my ear.

We barely fit in Ben's back room. He had so many computers, they took up every available surface inch, and they all appeared to be on and functioning. It was also cold, the AC cranked, presumably because of the machines.

Ben turned down the music, which was playing from one of them. "So what do you have, and when do you need it by? I make no promises."

I took a flash drive from my pocket and set it on the table by him. I'd made a copy of the files, leaving the originals hidden in my apartment. "There are five files on it. I'm guessing they all have the same protections, so if you could start with the one labeled Jessica Moore first, I'd appreciate it."

"As you wish." Ben plugged the drive into one of the computers and opened the directory. Each file was labeled identically—a name, the word "Philadelphia" and a number one through five. He pointed to the screen. "Aubrey? Isn't he the sack of salamander shit the Gryphons arrested for those murders?"

"Yup."

Ben twisted around in his seat, his eyes suspicious and his gaze darting between me and Steph. "So you want to give me an idea of what I'm dealing with? Anyone who might be interested in why I have these files or where I got them?"

Steph crossed her arms. "I thought you didn't ask questions."

"Yeah, well, no one's ever given me an encrypted file with a serial killer's name in it before. This is a little different from what I'm used to dealing with. Do I get hazard pay?"

Ben had been jittery to begin with—the result of too much coffee, I expected—but his anxiety was rising. It was time to put my plan into action and hope it worked.

"Relax," I told him, pushing out with my gift on the second syllable. The magic wormed its way around him, and Ben's face drained of some of its tension. In its place came lust. I hated this part, hated making strangers yearn for me this way, but it left their minds malleable. I could take advantage of that, and my ability to do so had never failed me before. "No one is going to come looking for those files. No one is going to ask for those files."

"No?" His full attention was on me. I could taste his longing like chocolate ice cream, but I gave him credit for not being rude. Some people couldn't keep their hands off me once I worked my magic on them, which was partly why I loathed doing it. Ben, however, was a gentleman. A geeky gentleman, but a gentleman, and that was worth something.

"Nope, no one knows the files have been copied. And this is important —no one can ever know what's on them except for me." He was in a chair, so I lowered my head until we were face-to-face. Through the bond connecting us, I concentrated every drop of my power. I'd never tried something like this before. I'd convinced people to forget my face or forget that we'd met, but this was far more complicated. "You cannot tell anyone else about me, these files, or what you might find. Understand?"

His eyes were glassy but focused. "No one but you. I get it."

"Good." I broke the connection. Ben's glasses had slid down his nose while he'd fixated on me, and he pushed them up. "Now how much do I owe you for this?"

I wanted to keep his mind busy so he didn't figure out what I'd done. Usually, after bashing someone over the head with my gift, I got to hightail it away, but not this time. I had to make sure, as best I could, that my trick had worked.

Thankfully, Ben proved easily distractible, and after discussing a price —half of which I paid up front, the other half due if he could actually crack the encryption—Steph and I left.

I could sense a storm brewing in her, but I'd been too focused on talking with Ben to pay it much mind. Once we stepped outside and I decided the heat called for ice cream, I had Steph's cayenne anger flooding me instead. "What?"

"What? What, Jess?" Steph stuck her hands on her hips, her eyes wild. "Are you really asking that? You magically assaulted him. Don't think I can't recognize when you're using your gift. I've gone hunting with you enough times."

I gaped right back at her, then stepped off to the side to let a group of girls in sorority shirts walk by. "Yeah, you have. Exactly. What I did is no different than what I've done hundreds of times. So I'm not following your outrage."

Even dressed in her mundane work clothes, Steph could be kind of scary when she got angry. It had to be something about a woman of her height with a voice that deep. She pulled me by the arm onto an empty section of sidewalk. "You've done it to criminals."

"If he cracks those files, he is a criminal. I thought the whole point of you finding this guy was because we needed someone with flexible ethics."

Steph stuck her sunglasses on, sparing me from her glare. "You are missing the point by miles."

"Maybe you're not being clear enough then. I mean, Ben's not a violent criminal like the people I usually go after, but it's also not like I mind-fucked him to steal his soul. I just needed to put a suggestion on him so he wouldn't screw me over later. You were the one reminding me how risky it is to let anyone else see what's in those files."

Down the block, a train pulled up to the stop making a terrible racket. Damn. Now we'd have to wait for the next one.

Steph took out a cigarette. Her anger was fading, but she was on edge and most definitely unhappy with me. "Ben is doing something risky for you. Yes, you're paying him, but you want what he can do—that makes him one of the good guys. Yet you just treated him like he's one of the bad guys. Like there's no difference."

"Of course there's a difference. I'm not hurting him."

"But you are. It's coercion."

"It's minor. It doesn't affect him in any other way."

Steph turned away to blow her smoke downwind. "It's using your gift to bend another innocent human to your will. That's pred-like, Jess. You know it. Or have you been spending so much time in your other friends' company that you're starting to think like them?"

Her words were a slap to the face. A wrongly deserved slap, but a slap nonetheless. They stung. "That's not true."

"No?"

"No. I used to use my gift all the time to get us into clubs, or buy alcohol when we were underage. Remember that? So how is this different?"

Steph wet her lips and started toward the T stop. "I was younger and dumber. Same reason I used to do all kinds of illegal hacking before wising up. 'Sides, I was never exactly comfortable with you using your gift that way, and I was happy when you finally stopped. You decided it wasn't right, and you were only going to use your gift to help people. Do you remember that?"

I hung back at the edge of the crosswalk because more people had gathered for the train. I had said that once, hadn't I? "This was a one-time deal. Getting into those files is helpful, or might be. I'm not going to make a habit of this. I'm an almost-Gryphon now."

Steph took a long drag, assessing me through the smoke she exhaled. "Please don't. It creeps me the hell out when you do it for a good cause, but I let it go because I know your heart is in the right place. You're my best friend. I don't want my best friend acting like a pred."

She smiled, and I smiled back, but inside I felt vomitous. I was not acting like a pred. Of that I was confident. But what was I going to do if Steph found out that the reason I had the potential to act pred-like was because I really was part pred?

She and Lucen were all I had for confidantes these days. Suddenly, I was on the edge of losing them both.

MY MOOD WAS BAD WHEN I LEFT STEPH AND HEADED TO THE Gryphon's building. The upside to our argument was that I had a bottomless well of energy to draw from. Thus, I might not fall asleep during my meeting with Andre and Brian.

I set my coffee down, booted up my computer, and checked my email. After telling my meeting reminder to go away, I froze as I read the subject line on my sole message. It was from Anna.

BLOOD ANALYSIS: Jessica Moore results

Hadn't I just been worrying what Steph would do if she discovered the truth? I might be one step closer to her finding out. Her and *everyone* finding out.

Bracing myself, I clicked on the email, which was brief and not useful, then opened the attachment containing the actual analysis.

Here, alas, I was at a bit of a loss since I had only the barest idea how to read the graphs and numbers Anna had supplied. Fortunately, she'd written up her interpretation, and that's what I focused on, discovering two relevant paragraphs.

The first came at the beginning: *As you can see from the insoluble magic, JM's blood doesn't fit the typical human profile, although that was expected. The third and fourth lines on pages 5 - 7 are suggestive of a pred profile, most likely a satyr, but that's not a clear match either. (Not surprising!)*

Her ability to sense emotions... Here Anna went on about a bunch of technical stuff that didn't mean much to me.

Then there was this gem: *I'll search the database to see if we have anything similar on file, but recommend taking up Agent Kassin on his suggestion to obtain a sample from Aubrey for cross-reference once he's through withdrawal.*

My mouth went dry. My brain didn't know what to fixate on first, and my blood pressure didn't care. I could practically hear my blood thumping through my heart over the din of the AC.

On one hand, this was a relief. Anna could see a suggestion of satyr magic in my blood but couldn't actually pin me down as being part satyr. An older, more knowledgeable Gryphon might have come across a similar profile before and recognized the signs, but then again, perhaps not. I could only hope Gunthra was right when she'd told me how rare I was. I might not yet have my darkest, ugliest secret exposed.

But that brought me to the last paragraph. The Gryphons did have someone they could compare me to in the form of Victor, although I wasn't sure what good that would do anyone. Unless Victor knew he was part pred—assuming he was part pred, which I couldn't be sure of—then it only meant the Gryphons had two confusing blood analyses instead of one.

Yet there must be something to it, or why would Tom Kassin have suggested it? And for that matter… I checked the names listed at the top of the report. It had been sent to me, Olivia Lee, and Tom. Why the hell was he privy to my blood analysis? He was supposed to be here investigating the furies.

"So you ready for the meeting?" Andre smacked his hand against my cube wall, and I almost fell out of my seat.

I closed down the report. "Yeah, meeting."

He cocked his head to the side. "You all right?"

"Fine." I grabbed some paper and a pen, then remembered to snatch my mostly untouched coffee too. "Lost track of the time while reading my blood analysis."

"Ooh. So what does it say?"

"That I'm weird."

"Like we needed an analysis for that. What is Anna getting paid for if that's the best she can do?"

Frankly, I was quite happy the Gryphons were not paying her more to go digging any deeper. But that said, she might have some other answers for me, and I intended to ask.

Anna was part of our meeting, but I didn't have time to question her before it began. Brian started the discussion immediately once Andre and I arrived. We had to update him on everything we discovered—or didn't—since the weekend.

Andre did most of the talking since collecting that information was mostly his responsibility. I listened, but my attention was largely devoted to collecting my excuses for not having discovered who the satyrs' F dealers were yet.

Brian took copious notes while Andre talked and questioned both of us on what happened at Purgatory. "It's disappointing you didn't discover anything, but I'd have been surprised if you did. I wouldn't expect the satyrs' lieutenant to be sloppy. If Devon knows about the dealing going on there, he'd make sure it couldn't be traced back to him."

I coughed. "Isn't it possible that if dealers are using Purgatory, that it would be beneath Devon's notice? How much say or knowledge would he have in the F business to begin with?"

Andre quit biting his pen cap and turned to me. "No one making F in the area is doing it without their Dom knowing about it, and no one deals F without being protected by a satyr, so the deals can't be traced back to them. Anything a Dom knows, her lieutenant should know."

"So Devon should know." I sipped my coffee. I hadn't expected him to be clueless, but that gave me an idea. Maybe I had something to talk about after all.

As if reading my thoughts, Brian raised a finger in my direction. "Have you found us anything?"

I swallowed. "Nothing concrete, but I did overhear Dezzi's number two and number three talking about the F." Buying time, I took another sip of coffee and searched for the right words—ones that were accurate without giving away my part in the conversation. "They sounded concerned and said something about 'if the F supply was tainted.' It seems to be causing some worry on their end. I don't think they know what's going on either."

"You'd think they would by now," Anna said. "If they got wind of our suspicions, they'd know who makes F and would talk to that person."

"Exactly. Which suggests the F might be tampered with down the line."

"But they know who the dealers are. They'd be addicts."

"Right." I leaned forward in my seat because it seemed like we were getting somewhere. "So assume they were looking into it and didn't find out anything. What could it mean?"

No one had a good answer, and Andre and Brian tossed around a lot of speculation, including the idea that Lucen and Lucrezia were merely misinformed. I doubted it but kept my thoughts to myself. My opinion of Lucen's intellect was higher than their opinion, but it was also not something that needed to be revealed.

"Have you had any other leads with the satyrs?" Brian asked.

That was the specific question I'd hoped to avoid by sharing my overheard conversation. "No. Shockingly, working for the Gryphons means no one wants to talk to me anymore."

Andre chuckled. "First they protect you, now they won't speak to you."

"They think I'm betraying them, but really, most weren't happy about protecting me in the first place. I told you—I don't actually have a lot of contacts there."

"But you do have other contacts in Shadowtown," Brian pointed out. "You're probably not quite as despised as we are. Consider trying them."

It took me a second to catch his meaning. "Other contacts? You mean other preds? Would any of them necessarily know something?"

"It's possible. Shadowtown is insular, and yet everyone is going to be watching everyone one else because no one gets along. Some races are better at it than others."

"Goblins." Lucen had once explained to me that none of the pred races were truly friends, but satyrs and harpies had an agreement where they'd watch each other's backs. Goblins had the same arrangement with the sylphs. Which meant if you wanted someone willing to spill dirt on the satyrs, you went to one of the latter two races.

While the sylphs struck me as too self-centered to pay such close attention to other preds, goblins hoarded knowledge like they hoarded everything. Knowledge was power, and power was a commodity. If the goblins knew who made the satyrs' F, they might be willing to part with that information for a price. Unknown to the Gryphons, however, I was already in hock to the goblin Dom for an uncomfortable amount. If they wanted this information, they were going to have to cough up the payment. Assuming I could get anywhere by asking around.

I mentioned the price.

Andre rolled his eyes. "Yeah, we've dealt plenty with the goblins. The threat of prison has been acceptable in lieu of payment to them before. If you can find out whether they know something, we can find a way to put on some pressure. You don't have to worry about it."

"Good to know." How might my negotiations with Gunthra have gone down if I'd had the Gryphons at my back?

The meeting broke up, and I hung back at the end, hoping to corner Anna. As it turned out, she was the one who approached me as we left the conference room. "Did you see your report? Very interesting."

Anna, I'd already discovered, was way too bubbly for my cynical self's comfort. But her joy in discovering my weirdness felt practically demonic given my own feelings on the matter.

"Yeah, interesting is one word." Alarming would be another. "Can you tell me why Agent Kassin got a copy?"

Anna hit the elevator button. "He asked."

"So anyone who wants it can get a copy?" I wouldn't be surprised if I made the news in that case.

But Anna shook her head. "Anyone with the right clearance who wants a copy. Clearance is the key."

I bit my lip. "Did Tom say why he wanted a copy?"

"Not to me. I'm just a lowly analyst. What Kassin is working on is way above my own clearance."

Anna got in the elevator, and I checked the clock. Perhaps it was time to put aside my unease and have another conversation with Tom Kassin.

It was getting late, but I'd noticed the past few days that Tom frequently worked into the evening. I didn't know if it was because he was under pressure, or simply the result of being in a new city with no friends and thus not having much of a social life, but it worked for me. I found him in his office, the door half open.

I knocked, and it swung open farther. "Can I talk to you for a moment?"

Tom's head popped up from where he'd been hunching over some book. "Jessica, of course. Come in and have a seat."

He sounded far too happy to see me. Probably, he was hoping I was ready to spill some secrets to him. To make it clear that's not what this was about, I opted to remain standing. "I got my blood analysis from the lab, and I saw you also got a copy. I was wondering why."

His blond eyebrows shot up. "You're instrumental in the case against Aubrey, and the two of you—like it or not—share an unusual ability. The more we know, the better."

"But I didn't think you were directly involved in the Aubrey case. I thought you were investigating the furies."

Tom marked his page in the book and shut it. "The Aubrey case and the furies' behavior are related, tangentially if nothing else. I need to keep a broad perspective, consider all the evidence. You understand."

I didn't, and for the first time, I caught the slightest taste of Tom's emotions. Burnt toast. That was why I didn't understand.

He was lying.

I clasped my hands behind my back to hide my excited fidgeting. As interesting as this was, I had to be cautious. Tom would know I could feed off negativity, but I'd been careful to downplay my abilities. The taste of his lie was faint. That either meant it was minor or that he was covered in some serious protective magic—charms much stronger than what the average Gryphon was given. I was starting to suspect the latter, and if that was true, I shouldn't accuse him of lying. Not only would that be bad for my career, it could expose my gift far more than I cared for it to be known.

"So do you think the furies going after Victor, and then going after me, wasn't random?"

Tom regarded me, his baby face scrunched up in thought. "It's a possibility, one that suggests the furies were able to tell you both had unusual talents. What do you think?"

I thought Tom was much better at subtly digging for information than I was. "I don't know, but I think it's odd that the Gryphons have no record of anyone with our gifts before, yet both Victor and I were living in the same area. That suggests a connection."

"It does, which is also interesting and something I wish I had more time to study. I was hoping that's why you'd come here. Given our conversation the other day, maybe you'd thought of something."

I shook my head. I hadn't sensed a single outright lie from him since the original. Either I'd chosen to probe badly, or he was far more adept at this game and better magically protected than I could handle. Probably the latter.

"I was curious about the report, that's all." I forced a smile. "And you answered my question, so I need to get going. Sorry to bother you."

"No bother at all."

I turned my back on his smugness and returned to my desk. That had been enlightening, though as usual, the more I learned, the more questions I had. Possibly it was time to add another item to my to-do list: poke around Tom Kassin's office.

Add that to breaking into stolen Gryphon files, and the list of charges Olivia Lee could hit me with would soon approach treasonous levels. Yet something was up, and it was becoming more and more obvious the Gryphons—or some Gryphons—knew more than they were letting on.

Behind me, someone cleared their throat in an exaggerated fashion. Feeling guilty for planning my next crime spree, I spun around and discovered Andre.

His arm was draped over my partition wall, and he'd changed out of his uniform into a blue T-shirt and a pair of rumpled khakis. My eyes diverted course. Instead of landing on his face, they momentarily paused to be impressed by the size of his previously hidden biceps.

"So a few of us are heading out for drinks." He tapped his fingers against the wall. "You looked like you could use one, and I thought I might be able to induce you to be sociable and join us. What do you think?"

I laughed and absently picked up the pen on my desk. All of a sudden I was feeling self-conscious. Was it from being caught thinking about snooping through Tom's office, or from noticing the super-nice body Andre had previously hidden under his less-than-flattering uniform. Or was it...?

Yeah, that—I could detect a hint of lusty sweetness on my tongue. So there was more to Andre's invitation than friendliness. Had I missed that earlier, or was his interest in me something new?

Either way, it didn't matter. Andre was funny, apparently quite hot, and a Gryphon, but I had a satyr. Charming as Andre's smile might be, it would be wrong to not shoot him down quickly—before he could start thinking I might be interested or available.

Step one to that end: stop fidgeting with a pen like I was some high school girl. "Thanks for asking, and yes, I could use a drink. But today's not good. I already have plans."

"All right then." He stopped his tapping, but he wasn't upset. "Some other time then."

"Absolutely."

Not. Absolutely not. I cringed as Andre walked away. Crap. There was a fine line between being friendly and being encouraging, and I was pretty sure my enthusiastic "absolutely" crossed into encouraging territory.

This was why I was unsociable. It made life so much simpler.

ELEVEN

I HADN'T BEEN BLOWING ANDRE OFF WHEN I TOLD HIM I HAD plans. It had been a few days since I'd taken on Bee's case, and I needed to find a soul donor. My last outing had been fruitless, and I'd simply been too tired to try since. But I was awake enough this evening, and so this evening was it.

Steph declined to go with me, which wasn't surprising considering it was a work night, but I suspected she was relieved to have the excuse. Although I couldn't sense her emotions over the phone, I got the distinct impression she still wasn't comfortable with what happened with Ben earlier.

That weighed on my mind as I decided which of my usual scumbag-hunting spots to stake out. I needed Steph in my life as much as I needed Lucen. I didn't have many friends, but I had two good ones. Two people who knew—most of—my darkest secrets. For that, I counted myself lucky. At some point I'd have to make some serious decisions about what to tell Steph and what to do about my relationship with Lucen.

But not tonight. Donor-hunting gave me plenty to keep my mind occupied, and I was grateful for it.

Without Steph for company, it was a lonely task, yet going about it alone gave me greater flexibility. I could go wherever the mood struck and follow whichever potential targets caught my eye. Plus, being by myself made me a more enticing mark for the sort of creep I was hoping to snag. By eleven, I'd found my man. By midnight, I'd gotten his attention. And by one, I'd achieved my goal. His questionably legal blood donation tucked in my bag, I headed toward Shadowtown.

I didn't get to Lucen's until after two. Bypassing the bar, I climbed the stoop to Lucen's front door. The moment it shut behind me, I could tell something was different. Normally after closing down the bar, Lucen would make himself—and occasionally me—dinner. Sometimes while it cooked, he'd take Sweetpea for a walk.

Tonight, the kitchen and living room lights were on, but no dinner was in the oven and Lucen wasn't downstairs. Sweetpea was sleeping in his cage.

And there was a purple thong lying on the steps.

I blinked, and when I looked again, it remained—a purple freaking thong splat in the middle of the second step like a warning about the evil I'd invited into my life, a skull and crossbones on my bottle of chosen poison. I took a deep breath and backed into the kitchen. Thank dragons I couldn't actually hear any noises coming from upstairs, but merely knowing Lucen was up there with an addict was bad enough.

I did my best to suppress the hundred-and-one emotions flooding through me, well aware Lucen could sense them all, but it was no good. I grabbed my keys and darted outside once more.

The night, so inviting and enjoyable just minutes ago, was now dark and unfriendly. Whereas I'd formerly been Jess the vigilante soul-swapper, I was now Jess the pathetic human and part-time Gryphon. An outsider in Shadowtown. A dumbass who thought being part satyr gave her some sort of magical ability to carry on with a true satyr like such relationships were possible.

I should have known better. This wasn't the first time I'd walked in on Lucen and an addict. Yet I was supposed to be handling it because I was mature and reasonable and had gotten myself involved with my eyes open. We'd actually had discussions about this. We'd planned it so Lucen could arrange time with his addicts when I wouldn't be around and uncomfortable.

But I was around, and I was way beyond uncomfortable.

Hadn't I recently been berating myself for condoning his behavior? I didn't feel like I was condoning it now, although my anger had less to do with him hurting other people than it did with him hurting me.

I supposed that made me selfish as well as irrationally jealous, but was it too much to wish that the guy I'd fallen for didn't have to sleep with other people? Was it too much to want—with all my weird magical abilities—that I could have been gifted with the power to satisfy his needs on my own?

A spell to cure people of being preds—that was what I wanted. To be able to uncreate them the same way they were created. To undo my freakishness and to make Lucen all mine.

But even if such a cure existed, would he take it? Here I was full circle, wondering whether he'd chosen his current life.

I kicked a pebble down the sidewalk, wearing my scowl like a neon sign. A couple ghouls shrank into the shadows as I passed.

Buildings faded into buildings. The night and my dark mood made Shadowtown live up to its name, the scenery dissolving into dark blurs as I pushed my legs harder. At last, I paused next to a restaurant on a less familiar block and caught the scent of garlic and beer from the outdoor dining tables. Wandering away, I could hear a group of goblins discussing work.

That turned my thoughts to Andre and his invitation to join his group of friends earlier today. Andre with the warm eyes, friendly face, and laid-back personality. Andre the non-pred. Andre, whose behavior wouldn't require me to condone anything.

And now my mind drifted to those muscular arms of his. Bad Jess.

My scowl deepened. What was I chastising myself for? Where did this saintly voice in my head get off telling me it was wrong for me to consider Andre's positive qualities when the satyr I had a screwed-up relationship with was banging some other woman this very moment? Why did I have to be good and chaste when he couldn't be?

But it's different for you, annoying Saint Jessica whispered. *Lucen has to have sex with his addicts to survive.*

Which was true, but didn't I deserve the chance to have a non-fucked-up relationship? If Andre was interested in me, why should I run from that opportunity without seeing how it went? Sure, I didn't exactly have a great track record for dating humans, but Andre was different. He knew about my so-called unusual ability, and he obviously didn't have a big problem with it. It could work with him, maybe. Didn't I owe it to myself to find out? It wasn't as if Lucen and I could ever be exclusive. There was no reason not to try.

My phone buzzed in my pocket, and I pulled it out, guessing correctly who the text was from. Lucen wanted to know when I was returning to his place and if he should make me dinner.

I sighed because it wasn't fair. I had a sort-of boyfriend who wanted to make me dinner. It should have been a source of happiness, not angst.

Soon, I wrote back, and was proud of myself for refraining from asking whether purple-thong addict had left for the night.

Slipping the phone away, I took in my surroundings. I'd been strolling aimlessly, and that was a problem. Thirty feet in front of me was the fury bar into which I'd chased Victor a few weeks ago. That had not been one of my brightest ideas, but I'd stolen Misery from there, so something good had come of it.

Misery. My hand immediately went to my hip, but my knife was missing. Shit. Of course. I hadn't been able to take it into Gryphon Headquarters, so I'd left it at Lucen's place this morning. All this time I'd been wandering Shadowtown with no physical protection. It was definitely time to haul ass back to Lucen's.

Before I could do more than take a couple steps, however, the bar's door opened and three furies stepped out. Given their sloppy steps, they were probably drunk, but that might be worse. Furies fed off anger, but they thrived on violence and chaos. A drunk fury would be more prone to those things than a drunk human.

"Hey, girlie," one of them called out.

Gritting my teeth, I walked faster, ignoring them and hoping they didn't recognize me.

"I'm talking to you, satyr's girlie."

So much for hope. Had he said "satyr's girlie" or "satyr girlie"? His words slurred, and it was hard to tell. Possibly it didn't matter. Odds were slim that the furies knew about my half-breed status. Then again, the furies were more likely to know something was different about me than anyone else, seeing as I'd fed off a fury's power before.

Footsteps picked up the pace behind me. They were following. Damn it. I wasn't worried about a mental showdown, but if they wanted to pick a fight with their fists, I was in trouble.

The furies surrounded me before I could decide whether running would be wise. Two were male, one with strange horns near his ears and another with the bright red hair so many furies had. The female fury had violet eyes and matching hair, neither of which were likely the result of magic. At least not the magic that had transformed her. Those either came from a glamour spell or contact lenses and a bottle of Manic Panic.

Violet pursed her lips, and I had the craziest notion that between her and thong addict, this wasn't a good night for me and anything purple. "Scared of us, are you?"

"She's not so tough now," Horn-head said. "Not when she doesn't have a bunch of satyrs at her back."

These three must have sensed my spike of fear once I'd realized I didn't have my knife and had decided to take advantage of the situation. That meant to get rid of them, I had to show them that my fear had nothing to do with them.

Always easier said than done when dealing with people who could sense your emotions.

I rolled my eyes and pressed my lone, secret advantage. "Try me. If you're so big and scary, make a play for my soul. I dare you."

Horn-head laughed with the others. "Oh, she's brash. You want to challenge all three of us like that?"

"Like you said—I'm a satyr's girl. You think I can't handle three people at once? Besides, you're drunk. I think you've only got one decent play among you."

"Drunk is right," came a new voice. "Drunk and stupid."

I spun around. The fury I thought of as Mace-head, courtesy of his crazy spiked hair, bore down on his fellow preds. His black eyes were colder and harder than I remembered, but his temper was surprisingly not focused on me. The other three furies shrank back.

The redheaded fury threw me a disgusted glance. "She's that bitch who—"

"Yeah, I know who she is." Mace-head took another step closer. He was almost touching me, but I refused to back away like his friends. Or his not-friends, seeing how they were acting.

It was odd. I was used to each pred race acting as a united front in public. Behind closed doors they might argue or jockey for position, but they kept their disagreements private because they could be exploited by other pred races, Gryphons, or the magi. Most humans probably never thought about it, but each big, scary pred race was greatly outnumbered. And the preds themselves knew it.

Mace-head leered at me, but beneath his contempt was something more. I was pretty sure it wasn't fear, and it sure wasn't respect, but it was something in the tightness around his eyes. Something that explained why he was chasing off my would-be assailants.

If only I could read pred emotions like human ones. I'd had the thought a million times. But no. I was eternally, mentally cock-blocked.

Mace-head stood so close I could smell his leather jacket, yet no irrational anger touched me. Lucen kept telling me the furies were different, but apparently they weren't so different. I was as immune to their power as I was to the other races' mojo.

"Remember what Raj said?" Mace-head asked, referring to the furies' Dom. He glared at the others. "Now I suggest you get your drunk asses out of here before I tell him what you were doing."

With disgruntled faces and muttered curses, the three strange furies shambled away. Mace-head didn't move, and since he didn't, neither did I.

Once they were a sufficient distance down the street, I turned to him. "What did Raj say?"

He threw his head back and laughed sharply. "You got nerve asking about private business and strutting around this neighborhood like you have nothing to fear."

"Looks like I don't." I raised an eyebrow. "Raj has that covered, right?"

"I like you." Mace-head waved a finger in my face. He'd painted his nails black, and the many silver rings he wore flashed in the streetlamp's glow. "Girlie's got spunk. Too bad you got issues too."

I pulled hair off my neck. Mace-head might like his leather too much to give it up on a warm night, but I was sweaty. The adrenaline rush I'd gotten thanks to the furies hadn't helped. "Issues, huh?"

"Yeah, issues. I know what you did at the Match." He leaned in closer, blasting me with cigarette breath. "So does Raj."

"I'd think if Raj knew something, he'd be fine with his minions attacking me. So would you. Red-eye was your friend, wasn't he?"

I had no idea what the name of the red-eyed fury whose addiction bond I'd reversed was, but Mace-head caught my meaning fine. "Friends come and friends go."

He said it simply, but his meaning wasn't lost on me any more than mine had been on him. "Raj killed him." That would explain why the Gryphons hadn't been able to track him down and question him about Victor.

Mace-head pulled out a pack of cigarettes and offered me one. "You'd be better off concerning yourself with lives closer to home."

I waved off the nic sticks. "I am concerned. That's why I'm asking you what's up with Raj."

He grinned, lighting his smoke from an elaborate silver lighter. "Secrets, girlie. Secrets and plans. Raj is very interested in you."

"Peachy." As I didn't seem to be getting anything more useful out of him, I started toward Lucen's again.

"Speaking of friends," Mace-head yelled after me, "how be your friend Victor?"

My friend Victor? Sounded like a doll for budding serial killers. "I think your definition of friend needs some tweaking."

"I thought since you both shared a talent, you know." Mace-head spread his arms in an exaggerated shrug, a curl of smoke wafting around his spikes.

"Takes more than that to be a friend in my world."

"Then you won't miss him?"

That made me pause, and my heel snagged a crack in the sidewalk. I fought for balance, an ominous feeling growing in my gut. "Is he going somewhere?"

"It happens. Friends come and friends go." Mace-head winked. He stuck the cigarette in his mouth and made gun motions with his hands.

Great. Was that an idle threat? Was Mace-head screwing with me, or was it something I should take seriously? Victor was locked up in a maximum-security prison, awaiting trial. He should be safe. Not that I cared if he met an untimely end, but I needed information from him first. And to be fair, the families of his victims deserved closure.

Lost in this new train of thought, I forgot about why I'd left Lucen's in the first place until I made it back to his apartment. Two glasses of wine sat on the kitchen table, and I heard noises from the living room that suggested he was coaxing Sweetpea into his cage. Sighing, I sat and helped myself to one of the wineglasses. Damned if I didn't need it.

Lucen entered the room a moment later and hung up the harness he used to exercise his dragon. "I'm sorry, little siren. I didn't expect you'd be back until later, and I thought I could deal with Caroline before you got in."

I pushed the glass away. "See, part of the problem is the whole 'deal with her' thing. She's a person."

"Fine. Pardon the euphemism. I thought I could fuck her before you got in. Does that actually make you feel better? Because I doubt it."

"It's not like I don't know what you were doing."

He sat across from me. "I'm not sure you do, or can. I was feeding an addict so she can feed me."

"I get it."

Lucen ran his fingers through his hair. "Superficially, yes. But I'm not sure you can truly get it. It's not a shortcoming on your part. It's just a reality of you being human."

I kept my face neutral, but something inside me flinched. Lucen clearly noticed from the way his brow furrowed, but I wasn't about to explain. "You're right, fine. Maybe I can't. It is what it is, and we don't need to talk about it again."

"Are you sure? Because the silence that's been going on the past few days doesn't feel healthy."

"Yeah, well, I don't have anything new to say." Not yet. I picked up my wine but suddenly felt too tired to drink it. I just wanted to curl up in bed.

Lucen got up at last and pulled stray strands of hair out of my face. His touch felt so good, and I wished it didn't. "How did the meeting with Steph's hacker friend go?"

"Fine, I guess." I filled him in on my day, glossing over everything with the Gryphons, but dwelling on what happened with the furies. The only part I left out was Mace-head's insinuation that he and Raj knew what I'd done to Red-eye.

Lucen frowned. "It's not surprising Raj would be interested in you, but I don't like it."

"Me neither, and I don't get it. I'd think his interest would extend only so far as it meant my death."

"True." Lucen went to top off my glass, but I put my hand over it. "Furies are weird."

"Yeah, I know. Are they also powerful enough to breach a maximum-security prison and get to Victor?"

Lucen fell back into his chair, shaking his head. "No idea. I'm sure they're positioned to try, but that doesn't mean they'll be successful. You still determined to talk to him?"

"Yes, but I'm not sure how. I've been denied."

"You've been denied by the Gryphons." He smiled slyly. "I had a thought, and I have someone who owes me a favor."

I raised my head. "What are you talking about?"

"Just because pred prisoners are locked up separately from human prisoners doesn't mean it isn't to our advantage to have people throughout the system. Let me make a call tonight and see if I can't get you granted an interview."

"Really? You can do this?"

He reached out and took my hands. "Personally, no. But what I can't do myself, I know people who can."

In spite of my frustrations, I smiled. Lucen's touch—and probably the wine—were relaxing me. I might be able to sleep in his bed tonight without thinking about purple-thong Caroline.

He peered deeply into my face. "Say it."

"You're amazing."

Lucen kissed my knuckles. "I know."

He opened my hands, kissed my palms, then my wrists, and I shivered. Some guys were very hard to stay angry at.

TWELVE

I WASN'T SURE WHO LUCEN CALLED AFTER I WENT TO BED, AND I wasn't sure what strings his friend pulled, but I was sure I was happier that way. When I got up the next morning, he whispered, "Good luck" to me then fell back asleep. I discovered what that was about when I went downstairs.

On the kitchen table was a note, a student ID, and his car key. I turned the key around in my hand while I read his message. I could have ridden my Dragon'sWing down to South Walpole, but according to Lucen, the forecast called for severe thunderstorms. He must have known how much everything was bothering me and was trying to atone.

I skimmed the note a second time while I made coffee, beginning to wonder how the Gryphons managed to operate at all given the various and many unethical ways preds used their addicts. I'd always been vaguely aware of how many addicts abounded in the world, but only recently was I learning how strategic some preds were about whom they addicted. Sure, many—possibly most—addicts were nobodies, the equivalent of one-dollar bills in pred currency. But even a one-dollar bill could be useful when you needed to get something from a vending machine.

After I finished, I took the ID to the guestroom where I'd stored my belongings and got out one of my jars of an extremely potent magic. There were disguise charms, and then there were *disguise charms*. This stuff wasn't the relatively cheap spells you could buy at your average charm shop. This was a glamour that could fool your mother and as such was highly regulated. Or it was if it was obtained legally.

A harpy named Lei, who was a master charm maker, had concocted it for me while I was in hiding during the Victor fiasco, and I'd ended up only needing a small amount of the spell. Lucky me got to keep the rest as it was keyed to my body and thus no good for anyone else.

I took a dollop of the gloop onto my fingers and began working it through my hair—the easy part first. Fifteen minutes later, I no longer resembled myself but one Jennifer Coleman, a law student interning at the firm providing Victor's defense. I had her short, sleek blonde hair, most of her nose, and her full lips. Comparing myself to the ID, I figured I was passable. Who ever had a decent ID photo taken anyway?

I poked my head into Lucen's bedroom before I left. "Thank you."

He yawned, appraising my handiwork. "Not bad. Hope you find out something juicy."

"Me too."

It felt like forever navigating my way out of the city, or maybe it was nerves. I fiddled with Lucen's stereo until I found something good then cranked the volume.

Victor was being held at Walpole State, and the note Lucen had left for me had me down for an appointment with him at eleven. That was going to be tough.

By the time I arrived, it was thirty minutes past. I got out, wondering if I should have put on something more professional than jeans to play at being Jennifer, but it was too late to worry about such small details. I signed in, was given a set of instructions, and was eventually led beyond security checkpoints to a private visiting room.

"You sure you want to talk to this creep?" the guard asked. "No offense, but you look like the type he went after."

I tucked a strand of my fake blonde hair behind my ear. "Victor favored brunettes, but thanks for the concern. I need him to answer a few questions for the bosses."

The guard snorted, clearly not convinced it was appropriate for Cohn,

Donaldson, and Kleinfeld to have sent a young intern to do a hardened defense attorney's work. "Suit yourself, and remember the rules."

"Got 'em." I took out a pen and notepad, the only props I'd been able to scrounge on such short notice.

A minute or two later, a door at the other end of the room opened, and two guards escorted Victor in. He had his hands and ankles bound, but it wasn't his restraints that caught my attention. It was his face.

In the days since his capture, Victor appeared to have aged about ten years. His skin was pale and lined, shadows circled his eyes, and he twitched as he walked. There had always been something about him that looked off and creeped me out, even in photos. Now there was a recovering addict's withdrawal added to his unhealthy appearance.

Victor's eyes, however, were alert. His gaze drilled into me, and no matter how good my disguise, no matter what he'd been told, I could tell he knew who I was. How was that possible?

The guards ran over the instructions with him, then one nodded at me. "Someone will be watching from the window. You need us, you wave."

I nodded back.

The door shut, and Victor smiled. "Hi, Jennifer." His voice was raspier than I remembered, probably a withdrawal symptom, but I could remember him saying "Hi, Jessica" with the same lilting tone.

A chill slithered down my back, and I struggled to maintain my indifferent attitude. Considering his condition, I didn't know how strong Victor's ability to sense my emotions was, but I'd rather him not be aware of what I was feeling.

"Hi, Vicki. How's withdrawal?"

He chuckled, but only briefly. His laughter became a cough, became a moan, and he rubbed his hands across his arms. Scratches and abrasions covered his visible skin. He looked like he'd gotten into a fight with a dragon and lost. That was another symptom of the withdrawal. Addict magic itched as it left your veins. "That's an impressive spell. You look so different."

"Yeah, it is impressive. How did you know it's me?"

Victor clamped his lips tightly together.

"Come on, can you sense me? Am I different?" Lucen and Devon had both indicated at various points that they could pick me out of a crowd—or from beneath a disguise charm—as if I gave off some kind of emotional fingerprint. Such a skill was one of many pred abilities I lacked. It would be interesting to know if Victor had it.

But Victor defied me. He tilted his head back and stared at the ceiling as though bored.

Fine. Cataloguing Victor's skills wasn't why I was really here. Time to get down to business. "I know how proud you are of your pred-like talent. How much do you know about it?"

Victor narrowed his glassy eyes, still refusing to look at me. "My head hurts. What you did to me was so mean."

"What? Stop you from killing me? Yeah, I'm awful. Can you answer my question?"

"I can answer any question, Jennifer."

"Then do it."

He stopped craning his neck. "Maybe I don't want to. You wouldn't play with me when I gave you the chance. Why should I play with you now?"

I took a deep breath. Locked up or free. Addict or not. Either way he made me want to smack my head against something hard. "I thought you'd want to talk about your gift."

Victor winced. "The real lawyers already made me talk about it to the Gryphons. I get headaches. It hurts. That damn Nelson Gryphon says withdrawal hurts more because I have magical blood."

"If you're expecting sympathy, you've got the wrong woman."

"Of course I'm not expecting sympathy." Victor leaned forward sharply, color rushing to his face. "You like pain too."

I tapped my pen against my temple. "I can't feed off your physical pain. Can you feed off mine?"

"No. But you can tell I hurt. It's mental pain. So sweet. It's my favorite."

"I'm in a prison. Half the people here are miserable, as you must know. Your anguish isn't sticking out. Sorry. You're not that special."

He sat back. "We're special. Very special. Two of a kind."

"Actually, I'm not so sure." I set the pen down, pausing until I had his full attention. "I have reason to believe we might be five of a kind."

Victor shook his head slowly, then closed his eyes. More pain, I assumed. Or nausea. "There's no one else like us."

"You sure? Maybe you couldn't answer my question earlier because you don't know much about your gift after all. Were you ever in Philadelphia?"

"Philadelphia?" From his tone and the taste of cheap butterscotch candy in my mouth, I knew I'd confused him. "What's in Philadelphia?"

"You? Once? Am I right?"

Victor whined like a creaky hinge. "Yes, once. A long time ago." He dragged his nails across his bare arms.

"Why? When? Were you ever enrolled at one of the Gryphon Academies?"

He continued to scratch, and I swore he was stalling just to piss me off. If Victor had gone to an Academy, that made three of us with names in the Gryphon files who'd gone through the pre-training. And if Victor had been in Philadelphia at a Gryphon special summer institute, that made two of us. Possibly—probably—all of us.

I didn't know what that meant, but it had to mean something.

"Vicki?"

"Fine, yes. I went to the New York Academy. They invited me to a summer camp in Philadelphia one year because my gift was so strong. This bothers you. I can taste it. Why do you care? No one else does."

I swallowed. "It doesn't bother me. It intrigues me. Do you remember anything from when you were there? What you did? The year?"

My experience at the institute was a blur. I remembered arriving, leaving, and attending a few activities. But I'd gotten sick and spent a lot of time in the infirmary. My specific memories of that period had more holes than Swiss cheese.

"I don't know what year," Victor said at long last. "I was fifteen or sixteen. Do the math. I don't remember much. I went there. It must have been boring."

I froze. "You don't remember much?"

"Stop already. I don't know. I think I got sick. Why are you bugging me?"

"Wait, you got sick?" Just like I got sick? "Victor, focus. This is important."

He tilted his head back again, eyes closed. "It's not. I don't want to think. I'm done, Jessica. My head hurts." Victor waved to a guard.

"Damn it. Don't you care?" Oh, brilliant. I was asking a psychopath if he cared. I rephrased. "Don't you want to find out more about yourself?"

Victor didn't answer, and I got up as the guards came in to take him away. I couldn't believe this. I was so close I could almost grasp the answers in my sweaty hands. I wanted to shake Victor until he released them.

"That's all you've got? That's it?"

He grinned at me as the guards led him out of the room. "Bye, *Jennifer.*"

I was going to scream, and what was worse was that Victor was feeding off my anger. Bastard.

"You all right?" asked the guard who'd brought me in.

I must have looked as upset as I felt, and I took a second to compose myself. "Yeah, fine. Thanks."

"Time you got out of here." He opened the door into the hallway. "Get you some sunlight. Nothing good comes of talking to whack jobs like Aubrey."

Likely not, but sometimes something useful did. Regardless of his whiny defiance, Victor had confirmed one detail I'd wanted to know and given me something new to ponder. He'd been in Philadelphia, and like me, he'd gotten sick and didn't remember much. Though it made no sense, it was too much of a coincidence to write off.

If only I could talk to him more when he was feeling cooperative. Maybe after he finished going through withdrawal. Assuming he lived that long.

Back at the car, I got out my phone, recalling I had a reason to talk to Bridget.

"This is Agent Nelson."

I stuck Lucen's key in the ignition. "Bridget, it's Jess. Last night I ran into a fury, and he made a rather cryptic threat on Victor Aubrey's life. I thought I should pass it on."

"What were you doing talking to a fury?"

Lucen's car was black, making it hellishly hot inside. I picked at my clingy shirt. "I've been pounding the streets of Shadowtown, searching for leads on the case I'm working on."

"Oh, yeah. The Newton one." I heard her say, "One minute" to someone, then she returned to the phone. "We've gotten a lot of threats on Aubrey's life. He's well protected."

"Unlike all the vigilantes out there, the furies have a credible reason for wanting him dead. Do they have the means to carry it out?"

"Jess, he's in a supermax prison. No one is getting in or out unless they're allowed. Not even the furies. Besides all the mundane security, Walpole State has anti-magic security too. I appreciate the info about the furies though, and will make a note to be extra careful when he's transferred to the courthouse."

I caught my reflection in the window, or rather Jennifer Coleman's reflection. Anti-magic security, huh? Yeah, that had worked great at keeping me from doing anything shady.

I really hoped Bridget knew what she was talking about.

THIRTEEN

AFTER I GOT BACK TO BOSTON AND RETURNED LUCEN'S CAR, I stripped off the glamour and made some notes about what I'd learned from Victor. I had a lot of interesting threads, but none of them wove together in any sort of recognizable pattern.

Five names in an encrypted Gryphon file, plus Philadelphia. Me, Victor, a deceased high school teacher named Kyra McNaughton, and two others.

Two confirmed misery junkies. Are both of us part pred? If I'm part satyr, what's Victor?

Gunthra said most people with magical blood die during transformation. That makes us anomalies. What are the odds?

Was Kyra part pred too? Could be why she committed suicide.

Three of us—me, Vic, and Kyra—confirmed having gone to a Gryphon Academy. Did the other two?

Me and Victor went to the summer institute in Philadelphia. Both of us got sick— does that mean something? Must find out what year Victor went. He said he was fifteen or sixteen. Were the other two people in the files there too? Was Kyra? Way to find out?

I heard Lucen thumping around in the bedroom, so I saved my notes and shut down before he could see what I'd written about myself. Then I started a fresh pot of coffee. It was nearly done by the time he lumbered downstairs.

Lucen poured us each a mug. "Learn something?"

"Yeah, Victor's a baby who can't handle withdrawal." I gave Lucen a quick rundown of what Victor had said about attending the New York Academy and being in Philadelphia.

"Suspicious." He tossed a couple pieces of bread in the toaster. "Sounds like someone in the Gryphons knew there was something different about the two of you. Maybe you were invited there because of it."

"Someone knew something, but they sure didn't bother to pass it on."

He got out the jam. "Maybe the reason you got sick at the camp in Philadelphia was because they were trying to lift the curse."

"Curse?"

"You said a goblin told you that you'd been cursed."

"Oh, yeah." A goblin had, although apparently he'd been using a figure of speech. I hadn't known that when I'd mentioned it to Lucen, and I was content to let him continue thinking my weirdness was an actual curse. "But I'm wondering why none of the Gryphons would have bothered to tell me what was going on if they knew something."

Lucen gave me a long, thoughtful look. I was talking a fine line here. Not exactly lying, but definitely not being truthful. Could he tell?

Finally, he returned to his breakfast. "You know my opinion of the Gryphons."

"Uh-huh. Well aware. Watch out who you're talking to these days."

"Little siren, if you were putting half as much effort into your consulting job as you are into investigating yourself, then I'd be worried."

I smiled, though that didn't exactly make me feel better. More like guilty.

I spent the rest of the afternoon catching up on chores—mainly laundry and restocking Lucen's kitchen with food. Then I had an appointment with the orthopedist who announced I could ditch the brace on my wrist for good.

That upped my spirits considerably, and I decided my next move was to finish the deal for Bee. It was early in the evening, and I could probably catch Rik at the bakery and exchange the blood samples.

Lucen was busy opening The Lair, so I didn't see him as I got my vial and left again. The scent of sugar, coffee, and all things wonderful hit as soon as I stepped into The Shadowtown Bakery, and I breathed in deeply. Seriously, it challenged my brain to understand how a place run by people so evil could smell like so much heaven.

A glass case filled with croissants, muffins, and assorted pastries sat in the center of the large room, and preds circled around it, placing their to-go orders. Along the back wall was another case filled with cakes and cookies. That one was less crowded, fortunately, because behind it stood Rik.

I waved to him as I wove through the mismatched tables and chairs where a few goblins were eating their croissants and coffee.

Harpies tended to be tall and disturbingly thin, as though someone had stretched them on some medieval torture device, and they had fanciful colored feathers in place of hair. In that way, they resembled the magi, but their skinniness and more rainbow plumage differentiated them from the human-friendly bird-shifter race.

That, and if you were a normal person, the intense feelings of jealousy they aroused in you when you got too close.

Rik motioned for me to have a seat at one of the empty tables. I chose one next to the wall so I could keep my back to it.

He pulled up a chair, but his face was grim. "You still trading souls?"

"Yup, and you have one I want."

"Unfortunate for whomever you promised to help. I'm not trading."

My good mood evaporated, and a pit of dread opened in my stomach. "Why not?"

"You're a Gryphon. Everybody knows it."

For the love of dragons—had everybody heard about my new job? Just a few weeks ago, I didn't think most of Shadowtown even knew my name. I guessed fame was what happened when you nearly slit a fury's throat right in front of his Dom and a few hundred witnesses.

I slapped my hands against the table. "I'm supposed to be consulting for the Gryphons. It's not the same thing, and I didn't have much choice. It's still me. I'm still offering a commission."

That wouldn't mean as much to a harpy as it would to a goblin, but it was worth a shot. Money was money, right? Unless…

"Eyff's warned us to stay away from you."

Unless the harpies' Dom had slapped a Danger sign on me.

Oh, this was bad. I'd never failed to come through for a client, and I had no intention of starting today. Bee might not be the most deserving or blameless person I'd attempted to help, but I loathed the thought of a pred getting the soul of anyone who wasn't a seriously nasty person.

I struggled to keep my voice down. The bakery was loud, but I didn't want to yell. "Are you kidding me? The Gryphons ask for my help with one case, and I'm a damned pariah? I've been doing this crap for ten years."

Rik ruffled his feathers, which were a bold, robin's-egg blue. "It's nothing personal, but you can't expect to play both sides. We don't do business with Gryphons."

My hands had balled into fists, and I banged my knuckles impatiently against the Formica table. "This isn't Gryphon business. This is personal. Will you talk to Eyff? Ask for just one exception? I know you don't care, but I gave my word to someone. I won't take on any new cases until this gets straightened out. That's the best I can do."

Rubbing my eyes, I caught a glimpse of two horns peeking out of familiar black hair. Beneath it, a black shirt and black pants. Their owner's back was to me as he paid for his food, but it had to be Devon. I hoped I could sneak out without his notice when this conversation ended. He'd enjoy my frustration too much given the hassle I'd recently caused him.

A sylph approached the far counter where Rik had been working, and the harpy stood, raising one finger. "I've never had trouble with you, Ms. Moore. I'll talk to Eyff this once."

My muscles unclenched as I got up. "Thank you. I appreciate it."

I darted around the other side of the center case, trying to avoid Devon's line of sight as I left. A wall of hot air and the relative stink of the city slammed into me as I stepped outside. Swearing under my breath about uptight harpies, I fumbled for my phone as it rang.

"Jess, it's Andre."

I paused. Crap. Had I missed a meeting? "What's up?"

"Just wanted to check in. I didn't see you around today."

I took a few more steps down the sidewalk, pausing for shade under a spindly tree. "Yeah, I didn't come in. Had a doctor's appointment, then thought I'd do some work on the other side of things if you know what I mean."

I didn't specifically want to say "question preds" while surrounded by preds, not after recently pleading my case with Rik. And especially since I hadn't actually questioned anyone.

Andre was quick on the uptake though. "You in Shadowtown?"

"Right now, yup."

"Learn anything?"

"Not yet." Nor was I going to unless I did some of that purported questioning.

Andre made a sympathetic noise. "Be careful, and good luck."

"I will. Thanks." Hanging up, I found myself staring at Devon. So much for being sneaky.

He wore his usual smirk and had rolled up his sleeves, a small concession to the intense heat. "I didn't realize you worked more than one side, Jess. How lucky for Lucen."

I cringed, feeling my skin flush. "Funny. Too bad I'm not in a humorous mood."

"No, I can tell. Things didn't go down so well with Rik, did they?"

"Were you listening to my conversation?"

Devon took a long drink from his iced coffee. "Far too noisy in there to hear. But you were broadcasting your opinion to everyone, and given your side job, it wasn't difficult to figure out you weren't giving Rik an order for an elaborate birthday cake."

"Do preds even celebrate birthdays?" I asked, trying to change the subject as I started walking again.

"No. You realize no one is going to want to do business with you anymore. It's not only the harpies. You need to pick a side."

"A side? Seriously? I'm on the same side I've always been on. Team Human."

"Which we could overlook while you were part of the infantry. But lately you've been promoted to officer class. The situation's changed."

We turned left onto a main road, and two furies on enormous Harleys roared past. I had to wait before they ran a light until I could hear myself think again. "You're mixing your metaphors. I was going for sports, not war."

Devon gave me an admonishing look. "Sports are just simulated wars with uglier uniforms and less risk of dying. Besides, the last time I used a sports metaphor, you got angry at me for making light of the situation. Seriously, Jess, I'm offering you good advice."

"Shocking, all things considered."

"What can I say? I like you, and Lucen likes you. So I don't want you to get hurt."

"I'm touched."

"Not yet by me. Hence my concern with you getting hurt before I get my chance."

There it was again. That faintest, fleeting sensation of lust rippling through my body, reminding me that I might not be totally immune to pred power. I'd forgotten all about it until now. The last time it happened had been around Devon too, hadn't it?

Weirdly conscious of this fact, I stubbed my toes on an uneven section of sidewalk. "Hope you're patient."

He laughed, stopping beside one of the more ritzy apartment complexes in Shadowtown. "Oh, I am. It's one of my few virtues. See you later, Jess. It's always fun talking to you."

"Yeah, I bet."

Devon disappeared inside, and I pushed on to The Lair. I could use a place to ponder the dead ends I'd run into with both my jobs.

And a strong drink to wash down all that thinking.

LUCEN WAS SYMPATHETIC TO MY PLIGHT WITH THE HARPIES, but he basically agreed with Devon. This shit was not going to get better. I didn't have time to talk through it with him because it was Friday and The Lair was hopping.

I stuck it out for a while, nursing a shot of Jameson's, but eventually the stupid-human watching got on my last nerve. With the darkening sky, the satyrs and harpies flocked to the bar, driving the tipsy human clientele into doing more and more embarrassing things.

Up in Lucen's apartment, I kicked off my shoes and lay on the sofa. I could either nap so I'd be awake when Lucen closed the bar, or I could do something useful. The latter held more appeal, but I wasn't sure where to start. Maybe Brian had a point and the goblins could help, but the idea of seeking them out, particularly Gunthra, was not welcome.

Aimlessly, I flipped on the TV to see if I could catch a bit of the Red Sox game while I pondered. Then I shut it off before I even found the right channel.

Devon's comment about sports rang in my head, and there was my answer. I was going to go to Purgatory. Not as a Gryphon this time, but as an anonymous club-hopper. One who was interested in scoring some F. If I could get someone to sell it to me, it would be a start. I'd get a face, a person I could keep an eye on and see who they talked to. See if they spent time around any particular satyr. It might not be the world's greatest plan, but it was a plan. At the moment, that was all I cared about.

For the second time today, I hit up the jar of glamour I'd brought with me. Since I still had Jennifer Coleman's ID, I used her face as a model again, although this time I gave myself bright red hair and heavy eye makeup. On went my leather pants, combat boots, and the slinkiest black top I owned.

When I was done, I looked nothing like myself. I'd simply have to hope Devon would be too busy doing whatever it was he did to sense me in the crowd. The odds were in my favor. It was Friday. From experience, I knew the club would be even more packed than The Lair.

Finally feeling like I had chance of being useful, I headed out.

I NEVER STOOD IN LINE OR PAID COVER AT PURGATORY. Although Devon owned it, his staff was a mix of satyrs and humans, with the humans working the most public-facing jobs. One hit of my gift and the human bouncer was only too happy to let me jump the line, much to the annoyed squawking of the black-clad queue.

Stepping inside, it was hard to believe I'd been here a few days ago. The empty club in my memory was so different.

So much quieter.

My eyes adjusted to the dark and flashing lights before my ears adjusted to the industrial metal. The music wasn't bad, but I rather wished my eyes could have remained blind. Friday nights at Purgatory were known as Fetish Fridays. Although the club never tolerated men in preppy shirts or women in designer dresses, Fridays ratcheted up the weirdness by a couple degrees. What it took to get in was…interesting.

As a clothing choice, latex didn't do most of the world's population many favors. But the crowd here drove home an inconvenient fact. Namely, there were a lot of people I'd have paid good money to see covered in it as long it meant they were covered in *something*.

I meant, if dog collars and leashes were your thing, knock yourself out. Fishnet? Rock it. Women who wanted to go around with nothing but electrical tape over their nipples? I'd cringe when they danced, but I sure as hell didn't mind watching. However, the pasty guy in nothing but a leather thong and boots? My eyes—they bled.

I turned away from ball-bagger guy and circled the main room, swaying to the music and eyeing anyone who gave me a second glance. Lust, anger, and general angst were thick in the air, along with the reek of alcohol and sweat. Vinyl and latex, though stylish in some circles, were not the most breathable clothes for dancing.

When I'd made it back to the main bar, I wormed my way through the crowd and ordered a drink. I didn't need the alcohol, but a woman drinking was more likely to be approached than one who wasn't, and I needed to appear available and potentially interested to a dealer.

And approached I was, although not by dealers yet. First, it was by a woman whose hair reminded me of Mace-head's, then by a guy who wanted to show me what his tongue piercings could do for me.

I chatted up everyone who came my way and danced with a few people too, drawing energy from the potent buffet of unfulfilled desire that swirled around me like smoke from the machines. On the balcony, hired dancers set each other's nipples on fire, and on the dance floor, a woman in full dominatrix gear slung her whip salaciously over people, smacking the backsides of those who asked for it.

As ball-bagger guy inched his way toward me, I begged off another dance and headed toward the bar because I'd seen my target. A woman with a white-blonde pixie haircut was talking to group after group of people. She was a lust addict, and if she was approaching tables, there was good chance I'd found an F dealer.

The bar area had gotten crowded as the club's numbers swelled, and it was a struggle to get close. She was heading toward one of the stairwells that led to the balcony and the VIP room.

I signaled her with a wave of my finger. "Hey, you got something?"

"You alone?" Her gaze lingered on me, and I flung my hair around, trying to act like I was drunk.

I smiled coyly. "Yeah, but not looking to leave that way."

She ran a finger down my arm, her gaze ending lightly on my lips. As a lust addict, the only person who could satisfy her needs was the satyr who'd addicted her, yet she was simultaneously doomed to suffer from a hellacious sex drive. It was the satyrs' version of the double punch to the soul that all addicts had to live with. And it had to suck.

The dealer pulled herself together. "Twenty bucks will make two people happy."

"That's all I'm looking for."

"All right, then. I'm out. Hang around the bar and I'll find you soon."

"Okay." I melted back into the shadows as she climbed the stairs.

Once she reached the top, I followed. Unfortunately, as I suspected she might, she turned right, heading toward the VIP room. The bouncer obviously recognized her because he lifted the velvet rope without a word, and then she was gone down a dimly lit hallway.

Damn it. Leaning against the balcony, I reached out with my gift toward the bouncer. Under his stoic expression, he was bored and somewhat irritated. That was more than I needed to know. So long as he was a non-addict human and not a satyr in disguise, then this chase wasn't over yet.

I sauntered over to the guy with a flirty smile, and his I-get-this-from-a-hundred-girls-a-night-and-I'm-not-impressed scowl faded as I exhaled my gift on him. "You want to move the rope for me."

His eyelids drooped slightly and his brain emptied. A salty caramel sweetness washed over my tongue. All lust tasted good to me, but the particular type my gift could arouse was the best by far.

The bouncer lost most of his coordination as he reached for the rope. His eyes were plastered on my breasts. "Anything for you, doll."

I squeezed his arm in thanks as I slipped through, and he inhaled sharply.

Then another male voice stopped me cold. "Who are you?"

I glanced over my shoulder. A second bouncer had arrived.

One disadvantage of my gift, compared to a full-blooded pred's, was that I wasn't able to use my power to seduce more than one person at a time. Although in this case, I quickly realized it wasn't going to matter. As soon as I took a read on Bouncer Number Two, I discovered nothing. No emotions at all. Since he wasn't an addict, that meant one thing—he was a satyr, probably using a cheap disguise charm to hide his horns.

Shit. I wracked my brain for an explanation.

That, apparently, was also in vain. Satyr bouncer could tell I'd worked my gift on his coworker, and he scratched his head, looking between me and the human. "What did you do to him?"

"Uh, nothing?"

The hallway into the VIP room was lined with blue and purple lights like guide lines. I didn't suppose making a run for it would help. My F dealer was probably talking to her contact this second, and I was missing everything.

Cautiously, I took a step farther inside. "Do you mind?"

"Actually, I do." That voice was familiar—a faint British accent tinged with cocky sarcasm.

Double shit.

Giving up, I turned all the way around, taking in the two new people who'd joined the satyr bouncer. One was unknown to me. The other was Devon.

He too, was wearing a charm to disguise his horns. But unlike the others, he didn't seem the slightest bit confused about what I'd done to the first bouncer. No surprise. It didn't take a genius to figure out who the human with the satyr's power had to be even if she was flaunting someone else's face.

Devon wore the expression of an exasperated parent staring down an unruly child. "Jess, nice hair. Now, kindly release my employee from your thrall, and next time, if you're going to work your way into the pants of anyone here, feel free to start with mine."

"I'll keep that in mind." I cut the bond that attached me to the human bouncer, and he shook himself.

"What the...?" The guy stepped away from me, his caramel lust evaporating, replaced by tangerine fear. As though I were the biggest threat here. It was almost funny.

Devon whispered something to his companion, and the other satyr disappeared. "You'll be fine," he said to the human bouncer. "Jess, come with me."

"That's okay. I'm leaving."

"I said, come with me." Devon's tone, and the way the satyr bouncer moved closer, made my decision easy.

"Right. Happy to."

Devon took my arm, although I didn't think he was afraid of me dashing toward the exit. With Devon, it was all part of the game—outwardly friendly but asserting control.

"What am I going to do with you?" he mused as the elevator took us to the third, and private, floor.

"Well, to start, you could tell me everything I need to know to crack the case I'm working on. I'd stop bothering you then."

He laughed once. "No, really. Finding you snooping about my club is becoming old. This is the third time in how many weeks?"

"I was being serious."

The elevator door opened, dumping us in his office. To the left, the wall of one-way glass provided a sweeping view of the crowded main dance floor. The rest of the office was more businesslike, with several sofas and a large ornate desk.

Lucrezia sat at the desk, doing something on the computer. "Was wondering where you'd gone to. We need to finish that conversation about the—" She finally deigned to look our way. "Who is that?"

Devon let go of my arm. "It's Jess."

I faked a grin. "Hi."

"What are you doing here?" Lucrezia pursed her bright red lips. "And why the disguise?"

"Good question." Since it was no longer useful, I began removing the glamour from my face. I kind of liked the red hair, though, and decided to leave it a bit longer. "Why am I here, Devon?"

Devon sat on one of the sofa arms. "That's what you should be telling us. You and your Gryphon friends already did a thorough search of this place, if you'll recall."

"Can't a girl want to go dancing?"

Their expressions said "no" quite clearly.

Lucrezia slipped off the chair and joined Devon on the sofa. Tucked away in the office, she hadn't bothered hiding her horns, and her bright skirt and strappy heels made her look as out of place around the club as I felt. At least Devon was dressed in all black. Side by side, though, Dezzi's number one and two were formidable. I needed to talk myself out of this somehow. Not only had I lost my best lead, I might be pushing my luck entirely.

Lucrezia crossed her legs. "Well, pet? Would someone please explain to me what's going on?"

I stalled, strolling over to the window. Lying would get me nowhere. There had to be a way of bending the truth enough that they wouldn't detect my deception and I wouldn't spill my actual plan. After all, I maintained hope of trying again. Next time with Andre to watch my back.

"What's that?" I shifted a couple steps to the right, squinting for a better look. Some sort of commotion had broken out on the far edge of the dance floor. My angle sucked, and the flashing light show didn't help, but I could see that the problem was spreading. People had gathered around, and the mob shifted and swayed. Then a woman shoved her way through the chaos, clearly shouting though her words were lost on me in Devon's soundproof room.

Devon silently joined me, his face alarmed.

"Is that a fight?" All the times I'd come here, I'd never seen a fight break out. Purgatory attracted a less than mainstream crowd, but not a violent one.

Lucrezia was also at the window now, frowning. As I watched, relieved for the distraction, several bouncers worked their way across the floor.

People scattered, revealing that the actual source of the commotion wasn't on the dance floor at all, but off to the side. Seconds passed. The backs of the bouncers were swallowed in the mass of gawkers. Then, finally, they emerged from the melee. Each was manhandling one person; each squirming person only half dressed.

My first impression was that the bouncers were hurting the people, but I quickly changed my mind. Those people weren't struggling. If anything, they were trying to hump the bouncers. Or each other. Or anything else unlucky enough to get close to them.

What the hell?

From what I could see, the bouncers were as confused as I was and distressed too. They were having a hard time containing the humans despite the woman in the group being drastically smaller than the man who held her. She and the others writhed like people possessed.

Concentrating over the distance between us, I stretched out my gift toward the woman because she was the easiest to focus on. No sooner than I'd touched her mind, her lust and anguish rocked me so hard I almost fell backward.

Damn. And that was with all the satyrs in the club who were sucking up the strongest emotions before I could.

This wasn't just weird. This was freaky. If my read of the woman was correct, then she was desperately craving sex even though she didn't want it. Even though she was tired and unhappy, and embarrassed to be caught this way in public.

Yet she was unable to stop.

This wasn't a matter of being overpowered by satyr magic. This was more like bad drugs—the sort whose charming effects I'd witnessed the aftermath of before. In Newton.

FOURTEEN

I SPUN TOWARD DEVON, AND HE CAUGHT MY EYE. JUDGING from the panic I saw there, he'd had the same epiphany.

His face tightened. He'd gotten on the phone with his security staff and was finishing up the conversation. "Put them in the Blue Room and tie them down if you have to."

"What is wrong with them?" Lucrezia asked.

"It's the F," I said. "It's probably the same thing that happened in Newton. You want to give me some more BS about how you know nothing?"

Devon hung up and strode over to the elevator. "If people are taking F while they're here, it's none of my business or my responsibility."

"And if four people end up dead here, then what?"

"Then nothing. We make sure that doesn't happen." He stepped into the elevator. "Coming?"

I wasn't sure if he was asking me or Lucrezia, but I jumped in with her.

The Blue Room turned out to be a private lounge located next to the VIP room, so called because it was painted blue. A large table, laden down with partially eaten food and half-empty glasses of champagne, had been pushed against the wall. The occupants had been kicked out by the time we arrived.

New occupants had replaced them. The bouncers had taken Devon's instructions literally, although I supposed they hadn't seen many other options. The four people—three men and the one woman—had each been tied to one table leg where they struggled helplessly, less in anger than in pain. As far as I could sense, they were lost in that erotically excruciating point between pleasure and torture. The one that's bliss for a little while before climax but would become unbearable if you were left there for too long. Like an itch left unscratched.

I could feel their suffering along with their lust, and with two such strong and potent emotions, it was difficult for me to control myself. My head and muscles buzzed with energy. I longed to be able to turn off my gift like never before.

Even Devon and Lucrezia looked queasy, as though they were being force-fed a meal that was too rich and too plentiful.

"What do we do now?" one of the bouncers asked, wiping sweat from his forehead. He was the same satyr who'd stopped me from entering the VIP room.

Devon threw a glance my way. "If it's F, they'll come off it soon enough. Keep them hydrated until they do. I don't need them exhausting themselves and dying of heart failure."

"I need to get a blood sample from them," I said. "And there's got to be more that can be done to help them. Something to counteract the effects. A sleep charm or a sedative or something."

Devon ran his hands through his hair. "I don't exactly carry those sorts of thing around with me, Jess. It's a club, not an infirmary."

I reached into my waistband for my phone. "You don't have to. I'm calling for help."

Lucrezia snatched my wrist. "Oh no, you're not."

I yanked my arm away, so jacked up on all the heavy emotions I sent her flying a couple steps backward with the force. "The Gryphons are going to find out about this one way or another. I am not letting any more people die."

I was so intent on facing down Lucrezia that I didn't notice Devon come up behind me until it was too late. I held my phone in a loose grip, and he pried it away easily.

He dodged me just as smoothly when I lunged for it. "Jess, stop a second. Lucrezia, take a couple people and go calm everybody down. Free drinks or whatever you have to do to help them get over it."

"Whatever you have to do? You're going to put compulsions on everyone, aren't you?" I grabbed fruitlessly for my phone.

Lucrezia pointed at me. "What about her? I think I should—"

"I think you'll do what I ordered you to do," he snapped.

Lucrezia's eyes flashed, but Devon outranked her, so she vented her annoyance by barking orders at the bouncers.

I started to protest again, and Devon grabbed my arm. "Jess, we're going back to my office."

He dragged me into the elevator, and I huddled against the opposite wall when he released me. Devon sagged slightly. I'd never seen him so frazzled. Not even during the middle of the crisis with the sylphs.

He caught me looking. "There can be too much of a good thing. Even for us."

"This isn't a good thing." I held out my hand for my phone, but he ignored the gesture. The elevator doors opened, and I stormed after him into his office. "Lucrezia's going to put compulsions on everyone, isn't she?"

"No, she's not. That kind of spell requires far too much preparation. She's probably going to do exactly what I said, hand out free drinks and try to convince people it was part of an act." He stuck my phone in his pocket. "You can have this back later when I know you're not going to do anything I'll regret."

I stuck my hands on my hips. "If you want to make this difficult, I can make it difficult. Who do you think the Gryphons are going to believe if I file charges against you?"

"You're not going to do that because if you want to get to the bottom of this, you need our cooperation."

I laughed. "What cooperation? I want blood samples from those people, and I want the Gryphons here to help them. You don't know if the drug wearing off will be enough. The drug itself could be what kills them."

"If this has something to do with F, then this is my business. Not yours. Not the Gryphons. If you want credit for solving the problem with the Gryphons when we work it out, it can be arranged. But you need to let us handle the problem so you don't get hurt."

"You know, this is the second time you said that today. Are you concerned, or are you threatening me?"

"I'm warning you. As a friend."

"Warn someone who cares. I'm not afraid of you or any pred."

Devon stared at me a second, his brow furrowed, then the next thing I knew he pinned me against the desk. I swallowed. His eyes were as bright as Lucen's could get when he was angry, and power leaked off him the same way. I could feel it spilling over my skin and rousing my nerve endings, just as I could feel Devon probing about in my head.

I breathed in, ready for a fight. Devon's satyr pheromones smelled of cloves. Why hadn't I ever noticed that before? My body awakened with desire, skin alight, and mouth tingling. I could stretch forward and touch my lips to his, imagine their salty taste, the scratch of his day-old stubble on my chin.

Never mind that whole fight-or-flight response. With satyrs, it was totally a fight-or-fuck response. And damn, I knew which one I wanted. I slid my hands around Devon's waist, down his hips, into his pockets, pulling him closer.

His body responded easily. I could feel his desire pressing against me, see the heavy rise and fall of his chest. He leaned in closer, his gaze so intense I was surprised I wasn't starting to steam. Every breath he exhaled brushed my skin like a caress, urging my eyes to close and my lips to part.

Then he backed away, confusion replacing his smoldering look, and the poking in my head stopped. My own lust evaporated. Being stared at like a lab rat must have that effect on a person.

"No, you're not afraid," he said. "But you used to be. What changed?"

What *had* changed? I wished I knew. Why was his power affecting me when no one else's did except for Lucen's?

But that wasn't what Devon had been asking, and I wasn't about to explain how I no longer feared addiction. So in response, I simply dialed the Gryphons' emergency number with the phone I'd retrieved from his pocket.

Devon's mouth fell open, and instead of trying to swipe the phone from me again, he backed farther away with an incredulous laugh.

"A lot of things seem to have changed," I told him. And wasn't that the truth?

I'D BEEN ON MY FEET WAY TOO LONG, AND THEY WERE LETTING me know it. Though I'd like to assume the nurses were giving me odd looks simply because I'd hobbled by their station carrying my third cup of coffee, being dressed in leather pants and a barely there tank top probably had more to do with it.

"It's impolite to judge," I muttered to myself, savoring the coffee aroma.

Andre tucked his phone away as I approached. "You say something?"

I handed him one of the two cups I was carrying. "I think the nurses are wondering what a stripper is doing hanging out with a bunch of Gryphons."

He snorted. "They're jealous. You won't sue me for sexual harassment if I say those pants look damn good on you, will you?"

"Might depend on how you say it. If it's sarcastically, I make no promises."

Andre yawned. "It's one in the morning. I'm too tired for sarcasm."

The Gryphons had descended upon Purgatory in record time. I swore, they must concoct some magic in their labs that could make Boston traffic poof into smoke when they wanted it to.

Alas, their unnatural speed aside, since I had no power to order people around or secure the scene or whatever it was an authorized Gryphon could have done in my place, I wasn't sure how much useful evidence they found by the time they arrived.

What I did know was this: The four drugged humans had been taken to the nearest hospital where they were met by Gryphons who specialized in healing magic and doctors who could monitor their vitals. Other Gryphons had been left to deal with the situation at Purgatory. And Andre and I had headed to the hospital as soon as we'd gotten word the victims had stabilized.

Also, while I didn't know it for sure, it was a pretty safe bet that I was in deep shit with the satyrs. Naturally, Devon was giving the Gryphons polite lip service, but he'd called the group's lawyer faster than I could say "addict."

The Gryphon healer came out of the hospital room, rubbing bloodshot eyes. Obviously I was the only one around here used to such late nights. "You're fine to go talk to her. The magic from the F appears to be almost entirely out of her system."

"Wait, does that suggest she's got magic other than F in her?" I asked.

The healer shrugged. "Girl's got a veritable charm lab in her blood. A lot of it's probably nothing more than the effect of being around satyrs at the club. Other than that, I can't tell you without a full scan. She's exhausted, but should be okay for questioning."

"Who isn't exhausted?" Andre said. "You'll have those blood samples sent to the lab?"

"Attention Anna Scott, yeah, I can handle that." The other Gryphon eyed our coffee, his emotions salty with jealousy. "Go do your detective thing. I've got three other patients to check on."

Andre motioned to me. "After you, stripper girl."

Our first and only female victim sat on the bed with her knees pulled to her chest. The pink hair she'd sported at the club must have been a wig because she tucked black hair behind her ears as we entered the room. Considering her complexion, I doubted that was her natural color either.

She didn't look healthy, although I had no clue whether the tainted F was the cause. Her eyes were a pale gray, her pallor ghostly white, and she sported a bunch of minor cuts and scratches from her ordeal. At least she had pants again though. She hadn't had any on when the bouncers had gotten to her at Purgatory, but someone must have retrieved her clothes. Not that they covered much.

And not that I was in a position to talk.

Andre double-checked the driver's license we'd found on her. "You are Natalie English of Marblehead, Mass?"

She nibbled at a fingernail. "Am I in trouble?"

"I don't know. Are you?" Andre sat on one of the two chairs and pulled the other closer for me. "We know you took F at the club tonight. What can you tell me about it?"

Natalie groaned and rubbed the exposed skin on her hip. I thought she was massaging another cut, but on closer inspection it appeared to be some faded tribal tattoo. "You're gonna bust me for F?"

"No, actually." Andre suppressed a yawn. "Right now I don't care if you indulge in F to celebrate Fridays. I want to know where you got the F you had tonight. You remember what happened after you took it?"

Natalie made a funny face. "Sort of, but not really. It was intense—way too intense—but a lot of it's blurry."

She should probably be thankful for that. Although given that what went down was likely to show up online by tomorrow—if it hadn't already—she wasn't going to be allowed to forget.

"I don't usually do F," Natalie said, her twitchy hands now playing with her shirt. "It's not like this is a regular thing for me, I swear. Jake thought it'd be kind of fun tonight 'cause he had some extra cash, and... Shit."

Andre cleared his throat as he made some notes. "Like I said, I don't care that you did F. I care about what was in the F you bought. You heard about those people who died in Newton last Friday? Someone put something in their F too, or so we think. You could have been this week's them. Understood?"

Natalie's eyes opened wide. "Oh, shit. For real? The dead people? I am never listening to Jake again."

"For real. So Jake bought the F?"

She nodded.

"Were you with him?"

Another nod.

"Do you remember how the sale went down?"

"Yeah, course."

A dull pause filled the room. I pressed the coffee cup to my forehead, willing greater potency to it. "Will you enlighten us?"

"Oh, yeah, right." Natalie rested her head against the pillows. "Um, a dealer approached us and asked if we wanted to buy some. That's pretty much all. We didn't have to search anyone out or nothing."

"Can you describe the dealer?" Andre asked.

"Yeah, sure..." Her mouth hung open, then she snapped her jaw shut. "It's just... That's weird, I totally could have until you asked. Now it's like a blank. There's nothing there."

My eyes closed in anger and frustration, and I held my tongue, which was loaded with curses and the taste of Andre's emotions. They matched my own foul ones.

Someone had gotten to Natalie and screwed with her head. No doubt that accounted for part of the magic the Gryphon healer had noticed in her blood. So much for Devon's assertion about how compulsions took time. Damn him.

"I should have stayed with her." I shoved my empty coffee cup in the trash after we left Natalie's room, wanting to punch something. "As soon as I saw what was going on, I should have stayed. Instead I let Devon drag me out of the room, and someone came in and put a charm on her."

"You can't blame yourself." Andre sighed. "For all we know, that compulsion was put on her before the drug took effect. You remember what I told you about how F dealers operate. The compulsion spell might even have been in the drug itself. There's a hundred ways it could have happened."

"But what if I could have stopped it?"

"If you could have stopped it, then the only person we can be certain didn't put it on her was Devon. But since we can't be sure you could have stopped it, then we know nothing. You can't beat yourself up over could haves, Jess. That's one of the hardest things to learn about this job."

I dug my nails into my palms. My life was like the world's most pathetic collection of "could haves," but I tried to put on a resigned face for Andre.

He gave my arm a friendly shake, although he felt as defeated as I did. "Come on, let's go interview this sleazy Jake and the rest of the Scooby gang."

Not surprisingly, Jake couldn't tell us any more than Natalie could. Neither could their friends. The one thing we did learn wasn't good news —Jake had bought enough F just for the four of them. We'd been hoping for a larger sample that Anna could analyze, but there was nothing left over to send to the lab.

Which meant that in one week we'd had two attacks, and we were no closer to uncovering the culprit. On that happy note, I left Boston and the case behind for a weekend guaranteed to be almost as painful.

It was time—the first time since my name had been linked to Victor Aubrey—to come face-to-face with my mother.

FIFTEEN

DON'T GET ME WRONG. I LOVED MY MOTHER. I EVEN LIKED MY mother. In fact, I was convinced I'd won the parental lottery. She'd always been fair and generous, and she'd passed down to me not only her dark hair and green eyes, but her love for mysteries and thrillers.

But there were some areas of my life that had to be shut off from the woman who'd once changed my diapers and literally knew my dirtiest secrets.

My father had been a Gryphon who'd died in the line of duty. The day the Gryphons had told me my gift wasn't going to develop and I'd had to fight back my tears in public, my mother had probably let out the world's biggest sigh of relief. She'd had the sense not to do it in front of me, but I'd heard it anyway.

Thus, starting at age eighteen, I'd been denied the ability to talk to her about large pieces of my life. From the truth about my gift, to befriending a satyr, to discovering I wasn't entirely human, my mother had to remain in the dark.

As such, every visit became the same. My mother didn't understand how someone as smart as I was could be satisfied with a waitressing job, or why someone as nice and pretty as me didn't date more. And there was no way to explain because she couldn't know about my vigilante side work or how awkward it was to have a relationship with someone whose suffering made you feel good.

It was bad enough she knew I'd been instrumental in helping the Gryphons catch Victor Aubrey. While the worst of the details were a carefully guarded secret, or would be until they'd undoubtedly be spilled during Victor's trial, she nonetheless knew she could have lost her only child. That was enough.

As I eased my bike down the long, winding driveway, I once again had to shake my head at whatever had possessed my mother to move so far away from the city after my father died. I supposed people needed a change after a dramatic event like that, but I'd hoped it would be a temporary one.

No such luck. When she'd married Nick several years later, she and my new stepfather had picked out an even more secluded house than the first. Victor could have buried bodies in the woods around my parents' house and no one would have known because you could barely see the neighbors. Plus, there was an overabundance of mosquitoes and ticks hanging around all those trees. At least with preds, the creatures that wanted to feed off me could verbalize their intent.

The driveway was crowded with the cars of everyone who'd come over for my stepbrothers' birthday party. I squeezed my bike between Nick's truck and a towering birch, and checked the front door. Country security remained the same. The door swung open, and I tucked the key I had for emergencies back in my pocket, unused.

Everyone was already in the backyard, the party well underway. Adding my gift to the pile in the dining room, I adjusted my best everything-is-awesome smile. Then I stepped onto the back patio and flashed that grin in my mom's direction.

She set her drink down and pulled me into a rib-crushing hug. "Jess, my baby, you look…" She cupped my chin and tilted my head side to side as she examined my face for bruises that had long faded.

"Healed?" I suggested.

"Healed, mostly. Hmm." Never mind that my mother was a physician's assistant for a neurologist, not an ER doc. She was going to be hypercritical of my wound treatment since she hadn't been there to supervise.

I opened my arms wide. "Babe, I'm fine."

"Did you call your mother 'babe'?" Nick asked from where he tended the grill.

"She started it." I grabbed a beer from the cooler, thinking coffee might have been a better choice. I was beat.

Last night, I'd managed to avoid Lucen's questions by feigning exhaustion, and as such, had gotten into bed with less hassle than I'd expected. Unfortunately, being in bed didn't mean I'd slept. All night, I kept reliving what I'd witnessed at Purgatory, guilt for being unable to do anything about it eating away at me.

Beer was a poor substitute for coffee, but it worked far more efficiently to keep me pleasant as I answered—or dodged as necessary—everyone's questions. My stepbrothers had no interest in anything but the food, the cake, and eventually the new video game console my parents had gotten them for their birthday. But my mother and Nick had invited over a few of their friends, and along with my extended stepfamily, I had plenty of adults pestering me for information on what happened with Victor.

Thank dragons there wasn't only beer but strong sangria to go with the cake.

Nick shook his graying head sadly as I passed him a plastic fork to replace the one he'd dropped. "Ever consider leaving the city? After everything you went through, do you really want to stay?"

We were sitting around a loose collection of tiny patio tables, and a couple of step-aunts chimed in with their agreement.

I swallowed my bite of cake, conscious of being the center of attention while my teeth were coated in blue icing. "I like the city. You have all this green stuff here. It makes me sneeze."

"The city has preds," one of the aunts said.

"Preds don't make me sneeze."

They stared at me. Okay, jokes about preds did not go over well with this crowd. Noted.

While I talked, I mixed different colors of icing around on my plate to see what hideous combination they'd make. "Actually, I have a new job, indirectly thanks to preds and Victor Aubrey, so I need to stay where I am."

My mother glanced up sharply, and the plate she'd balanced on her lap almost toppled over. "You never told me you got a new job."

Yeah, there'd been a reason. Damn beer and sangria loosening my tongue.

"What kind of job has to do indirectly with preds?" Nick asked.

I could taste my mother's minty anxiety, and it went awful with chocolate cake and fruity sangria. For ten years, she'd thought she'd gotten a reprieve, but she'd always feared the worst for my safety. And with good reason. I was about to confirm her nightmares. "I, uh, am consulting for the Gryphons."

That spurred a round of congratulations mixed with another round of twenty questions, although these questions I could answer more truthfully. Eventually, though, even with the booze, I had too much of the third degree and excused myself to go make coffee.

My mother and Nick stored the coffee in the fridge, a terrible habit I'd tried to cure them of to no avail. After some digging through bowls of leftover potato salad and the wrapped plate of extra burgers, I found the bag. I opted for a full pot, figuring if no one else wanted it, I could probably down the whole thing over the rest of the afternoon and evening.

When I put the bag back, I discovered a photo of myself attached to the freezer with a magnet. Curious where it had come from, I pulled it off and moved closer to the window for better light. I must have been about twelve or thirteen in it, and I was standing on a rock on some mountain. Behind me, the ground fell away into a valley.

I recognized the gray bandana I wore because I still had it, but otherwise the photo jarred precious few memories. Yes, I'd gone camping several times in the White Mountains with my mother, and if I thought hard about it, I could remember the scent of the white pines in the forest, and the aches in my feet from climbing, and the beautiful vistas that could have been found on any number of mountaintops.

But specifics? I had nothing, and that seemed odd. For that matter, I didn't even remember wearing glasses when I was younger, and yet I was clearly wearing glasses in this photo. How could I forget a detail like that?

Goose pimples rose on my arms as I thought of the way Natalie's memories had flown last night. But this was different. I had a feeling my memory had vanished longer ago than that. I simply had never noticed before.

The coffee maker gurgled as it neared the end of the brew, and I stuck the photo back on the fridge.

My mother entered the kitchen, carrying a pile of dirty plates. "Too many questions out there?"

"No. I mean, yeah, but it's not that exactly." I poured a mug and stuck the carafe back on the burner. "I get that people are curious and concerned about me, but it's all so removed up here. Everybody has the luxury of distance. After a while, it starts to feel sensationalistic explaining it, and numbing too. I don't want to be numb to it. That's a luxury I shouldn't have."

There was more to it that I couldn't tell her, such as how the normality around here was getting under my skin like imp stings. My mother, my extended stepfamily, their friends—they were all normal people who went to normal jobs. Had normal lives. Me and my life, just the few pieces they knew, had to be very weird to them.

In Boston, I was insulated from that. My most normal friend, Steph, didn't even have a normal life, in part thanks to me, and in part because of the crap she had to deal with on a daily basis because she was transgender.

What it all meant was that weird had become my normal. No matter how strange I thought my life was, I had no idea just how bizarre it truly was until I came to quiet, peaceful, normal New Hampshire.

It bugged me, and I wasn't sure why.

My mother brushed hair out of my face. "My poor baby, you've been through a lot lately, and you're putting yourself in a position to go through more."

"Because I'm working with the Gryphons?"

She nodded, filling a mug of her own. "Don't get me wrong. I'm happy for you, really. I know it's what you always wanted to do. But you have to understand why I worry."

"I do understand, and honestly, this wasn't exactly what I wanted anymore. It was just something I had to do." Because I was being blackmailed. Piece number seventy-eight of Jess's life that my mother couldn't know about.

"It's a calling." She poured a splash of milk into her coffee. "I get it. That's what your father said."

So it was. One I'd been cured of due to recent events, but she could go on believing it.

"Just be careful," my mother continued. "But on a happier note, now that you have a good thing going career-wise, perhaps you could expend some energy in other areas."

I narrowed my eyes at her. "Other areas?"

She made an innocent face. "Seeing anyone?"

Yes, and he was tall, blond, and horny—in every sense. I buried my face in my mug. "I've been kind of busy lately."

"That excuse is getting old."

"And so are my ovaries?"

"That's not what I was suggesting. I want you to be happy."

Plenty of people were happy single, but I didn't go there because that wasn't the issue. What my mother wanted—more so than the possibility of grandchildren, which I suspected my freakish biology rendered impossible—was for me to be normal.

Relationships were normal. I didn't think she cared about a house in the suburbs, a dog, and a 401(k) plan. Merely showing up at a family gathering one day with a date would probably make her ecstatic.

A human date. Like Andre. What would that be like—having a normal boyfriend? Maybe I'd feel less like a freak at these shindigs. Much as all this normality weirded me out, there was something appealing about it too. "There's a certain Gryphon who might be on my radar. Let's leave it there."

"Oh, yeah?" She smiled.

It made me happy to see her happy. Take that, my misery-loving satyr half.

I pointed to the photo. "Where did that come from?"

My mother plucked it off the fridge for closer inspection. "This? I found it a few weeks ago. I was going through some stuff in the basement. This was from one of our camping trips."

"I figured. This is going to sound like a strange question, but when did I stop wearing glasses?"

She gave me a funny look of surprise. "You don't remember?"

"Not entirely, no." I hazarded a guess to make my question appear less odd. "It was when I was a teenager."

"Yes, you were about sixteen, I think." She sipped her coffee, pondering. "I can't recall your precise age, but I'm surprised you don't remember. Your eyesight changed so rapidly. Puberty can do that, although it usually changes your vision for the worse. But I remember because it happened that one summer you went to the Gryphon camp."

I almost dropped my mug. "That summer? You're sure?"

"Positive. Why?"

"My memory is kind of hazy. I'd forgotten I used to wear glasses." Carefully, I set my mug on the counter. My hands shook. So did my insides.

"Oh, that's probably because you hardly wore them. You hated them, so you preferred to walk around blind."

"Yeah, probably."

Yet wearing glasses didn't seem like the kind of thing normal people forgot. And that my eyesight changed around the summer I'd gone to the Gryphon institute—could it be a coincidence? Sure, my mother was right. It could have been puberty, but I doubted it very much.

Ben, the hacker extraordinaire, had better be able to get into those stolen files. I wondered what other memories I might be missing, and whether they were contained within.

And Victor—what else did he know? It would be risky going back to the prison for a second interview, but there was no way I could leave this alone.

I LET MY MOTHER BELIEVE I WAS FEELING NOSTALGIC, AND WE spent the evening going through my belongings that she'd stored for when I "move to a grownup place." I didn't bother to point out that in Boston, living with roommates was a grownup thing to do because of the rents.

Some of my anxiety dissipated as we poked through photo albums, old books, and elementary school art projects that proved there had never been a time during which I'd been a budding Michelangelo. Most of my memories were there. They simply required a bit of jarring to shake loose.

Yet odd gaps remained that I had to cover up, and eventually I discovered a pattern to them. Everything I couldn't recall had to do with personal details—the glasses, how I'd played viola in the Academy's orchestra in fifth through eighth grades, that I used to be allergic to all forms of tree nuts.

It made no sense.

On Sunday morning, my mother prepared an elaborate breakfast feast in honor of my presence. The scent of real maple syrup, coffee, and bacon filled the house, and my stomach rumbled as I got dressed.

I pulled my hair back in a ponytail and grabbed my phone, thinking I'd check my email before heading to the kitchen. The phone rang in my hand, startling me. It was Bridget. Warily, I answered because there could be no good reason why Bridget was calling me on a Sunday before noon.

"Hi, Jess." She sounded beat. "I figured I'd give you a heads-up before you saw what happened on the news. Victor Aubrey is dead."

I grasped the cheap guest room bureau for support. "What? When?"

"Last night. He was murdered. Keep it to yourself for now because we don't know anything official, but it's looking like you were right. We've found traces of fury magic in the guards who did it, but we have no idea how it could have happened yet."

I took a deep breath, wishing my stomach would settle. "Great."

"Yeah, well, I don't expect anyone's going to be torn up about it, least of all you. But he was our strongest lead on finding the furies responsible."

I nodded dully, as if she could hear my brain rattling. "Yeah, I know. This sucks."

In so, so many ways.

When Bridget hung up, I flopped back on the bed, no longer in the mood for pancakes and bacon. Possibly my best hope for finding out more about myself was dead, as was the Gryphons' chance to bring justice down on the furies.

No wonder they'd taken out Victor, but how was I supposed to get my answers now?

SIXTEEN

I DROVE BACK TO BOSTON IN A BAD MOOD AND STAYED THAT way over the next couple days. Without Victor, there would be no trial and no closure for the families of the victims. All the work Bridget and the others had accomplished was for nothing. I wasn't the only one frustrated by far. Every time I entered the Gryphon's building, the power of everyone's unhappiness was overwhelming.

I held tight to my one consolation—without a trial, I wouldn't have to take the witness stand. All the secrets I'd dreaded being exposed on national news would be safe. They weren't exactly secret anymore since the Gryphons knew most of them, but at least there'd be no talking head on CNN discussing whether my gift's similarities to Victor's meant I should be preemptively locked up. And my mother could continue getting a few hours of sleep each night, blissfully unaware of all the nastiness I'd been keeping from her.

But my ordeal wasn't over yet. Since I'd told Bridget that the furies were up to something, I was grilled repeatedly about it. Who was the fury who'd warned me? How did I know him? What did he look like? Could I come with a team to Shadowtown to find him?

I took them to the bar where I'd twice run into Mace-head, but he wasn't there.

To make matters more irritating, without Victor around, I was considered the next best lead for finding the fury responsible for addicting Victor and turning him into their pawn. Based on what Mace-head had told me, I figured it was a futile effort. Red-eye was likely dead.

That suggested the furies' Dom knew what Red-eye had been up to, but good luck to the Gryphons getting that information out of him. Raj looked like a Syfy channel version of the devil, and I had no doubt his forked tongue spewed lies every bit as smoothly as the devil was alleged to do. Charms could encourage truth-telling in humans, but using magic on preds was something else entirely. Possible, but sure not as easy.

Nevertheless, it didn't stop everyone from hounding me with questions about the furies, and every one of these interviews took place in the presence of Tom Kassin. He rarely asked questions, but he took copious notes, and I didn't appreciate the way he looked at me. As soon as I had the chance, he was the next person I wanted to investigate. I just hoped he didn't end up dead afterward like Victor.

And then there was the actual case I was supposed to be working on.

A familiar pattern of knocks on my cube wall had me bolting upright. "Hey."

Andre laughed. "You could use some sleep."

"Yeah, that wouldn't be a bad idea."

"It's seven o'clock, and Bridget has left the building, so I don't think you're going to be further interrogated about Aubrey today. How about instead, you start with dinner, then you go home and get that sleep? There's a pizza place not far from here, lots of beer on tap. Good company?" His smile was hopelessly endearing.

I double-checked the time. Getting out of here didn't sound like a bad plan. But with Andre?

Well, why not? I'd rationalized this all before. My relationship with Lucen was doomed to failure. As I got more deeply involved in the F case, that became clear. It would be nice to try for a normal one. Visiting my mother had made that clear. In fact, maybe this was why the normality of her life in New Hampshire bugged me—it was a reminder of everything I always thought I couldn't have.

But everything was changing. Besides, it wasn't like Lucen could get upset about me going to dinner with a coworker when he had a handful of other people he had to screw on a regular basis.

I returned Andre's smile. "Pizza, beer, and company sounds good to me."

MY WORKLOAD DIDN'T RELENT THE NEXT DAY, BUT I WAS IN A better mood. Andre and I had hung out at the pizza place for several hours, talking about subjects other than work and watching the Sox game. I wasn't sure if the experience counted as a date or simply two people getting food together, but it was fun. I rarely did things like that with anyone besides Steph.

When I asked myself if I wanted it to be a date, I wasn't sure.

My phone rang as I walked up the massive stone steps to Gryphon Headquarters, cutting off these thoughts. The number calling me was unfamiliar. "Hello?"

"Is this Jessica? This is Ben, from the computer store."

"Oh!" Surprise left me exceedingly articulate. "Hold on a sec."

Ever since word about Victor's death broke, the building had been packed. Even four days later, there was a news van out front, for what purpose I couldn't imagine. It wasn't as though there was anything to update people on.

I edged away from the crowded stairs and stood in the shadow of one of the granite gryphon statues out front. "You have news?"

"Sort of. This is some real world-class encryption here, I gotta say."

"That doesn't surprise me." It was the Gryphons. I'd have been horrified if their files were easy to break into.

Ben coughed. "Me neither, but it means it's taking me a bit. But I'm determined, and I had a small breakthrough the other day. I'm not in the files exactly, but I got some information to send you. It's not in English, so I have no idea what it says."

I frowned. "Not in English? Okay, yeah. Go ahead and send. Thanks."

"Coming now. It's a screenshot. There's a bunch of technical stuff I can explain later if you want."

"Right, thanks." I hung up, and Ben's message arrived a second after.

I covered the screen with my hand as I opened the photo. Even in the shade it was difficult to read the text with the late-morning sun overhead.

Ben wasn't kidding about the technical crap, but Steph could probably explain what all those numbers and abbreviations meant. What concerned me was the non-English phrase. My eyes homed in on it, and my blood went cold in spite of the heat. That much, I didn't need someone to translate.

Le Confrérie de l'Aile. The Brotherhood of the Wing.

Actually, the entire phrase read: *These files are the property of the Brotherhood of the Wing*. But it was only the last phrase that had my attention. This was the group Tom belonged to.

Suddenly, every question he'd asked me and every meeting he'd sat in on over the last few days took on a far more sinister overtone. I didn't like him and had been meaning to pry into his life ever since he'd attempted to pry into mine. The time had come to put that plan into action.

Victor might be dead, but my search for answers was on.

ONE OF THE BIGGEST PERKS ABOUT CONSULTING FOR THE Gryphons was access to their private library. If I was going to learn more about this mysterious Brotherhood, that was the place to start.

The library wasn't contained in a large space, nor was it a large collection, but it had books on Gryphon history unavailable elsewhere. I got straight to work, assuming I might be here a while.

After an hour of fruitless searching, that didn't look so likely anymore. There was no librarian around, so I was on my own for research, and so far I'd found only two references to the Brotherhood—or *le Confrérie*, since I searched for it in both languages.

The one reference was extremely cryptic and not helpful. The second reference explained it was a private, invitation-only group within the Gryphons that had existed in one form or another since the eighteenth century. Although it was called the Brotherhood, women had started being admitted in the mid-nineteen hundreds as they rose to positions of power within the Gryphons.

And there my quest ended. Or should have.

I put the last book away and swore. Tom had lots of books in his office, and although I wasn't averse to snooping, that couldn't happen until he left for the day. Which left me hanging in the meantime, unless...

I bounded out of the room, struck by an idea. I might not have a librarian here who could help, but I knew a librarian who considered himself an expert on, well, basically everything. And if he didn't know something, he took pride in knowing where to find out.

Twenty minutes later I stood in front of The Feathers' branch of the Boston Public Library. Like Shadowtown was pred territory, The Feathers was magi territory. In this neighborhood, the bird shifters outnumbered humans, and the shops, restaurants, and housing catered to them with foul-sounding food and apartments that boasted of their private rooftop perches rather than, say, their laundry facilities.

Unlike preds, however, magi were friendly. Or most of them were. I'd had a run-in with a politically powerful magi not too long ago whose wings I wouldn't mind clipping for being an asshole. In general, however, I certainly didn't mind magi, and magi didn't mind Gryphons. The groups' alliance went way back, a fact I was counting on.

Pleased I wore practical boots instead of sandals today, I dodged a suspicious puddle on the sidewalk and entered the library. The AC blast hit hard. I wrapped my arms around myself, passing the checkout desk and the rows of computers, and hoping Olef was working so I hadn't made the trip for nothing.

I found him near the children's section, pushing a cart of returned books.

"Ms. Moore." His owlish ears perked up in greeting. "What a nice surprise. I don't believe I've seen you here before. Are you on Gryphon business?"

"Wow, news travels fast. But no, I'm not." I sucked on my lip, rethinking the truthfulness of that statement. "Actually, I am. Sort of, I suppose."

"Sort of?"

"It is about the Gryphons, but it's not official Gryphon business. I have a history question and was hoping you might be able to help."

Olef gestured to an empty table by a window, and I sat across from him. "What do you need to know?"

"I was wondering if you'd ever heard of a group within the Gryphons known as the Brotherhood of the Wing or *Le Confrérie de l'Aile?*"

The white feathers around Olef's eyes constricted, and he thought for a while. Finally, he raised his four-fingered hands in defeat. "I'm afraid that's not an organization I've come across. You have a record of stumping me, Ms. Moore. It bothers me greatly."

"Sorry." He looked put out, so I hid my own disappointment. I'd been certain that if anyone would know something, it would be Olef.

"It's not your fault. It's my failing." Olef pulled a pen from the pocket of his tweed jacket and grabbed a piece of scrap paper from the table. "Would you spell the French for me? I'll do some research for you if I may."

"I'd appreciate it." I wrote the name, in English and in French, and added my cell number.

Olef tucked the paper in his pocket. "Do you mind if I ask what spurred your curiosity?"

"There's a new guy in town who's a member, and he was sent here to investigate the furies and the stuff with Victor Aubrey. I'm being nosy."

Olef's feathers ruffled at Victor's name. "Awful what happened with Aubrey. Such a lack of closure for everyone."

"That it is." And much more. "Thanks, Olef."

"Of course. And, Ms. Moore, do be careful."

For the second time today, I got the chills. The last time I'd heard those words from Olef, bad shit had followed soon after. "Why?"

He smoothed his jacket nervously. "You remember that vision I told you about?"

"The one about the purple smoke and the salamander fires? Yeah, not likely to forget." Olef had shared that lovely scenario with me during the hunt for Victor.

"I might have been mistaken in my interpretation." He frowned. Mistake was a dirty word to Olef.

Yet I didn't understand. "How could you have been mistaken? It came true. The furies set salamander fires on the city."

"I thought so too, at the time. But once an event occurs, a vision should pass. This one hasn't, suggesting what I saw was unrelated to the fires here. That it's still to come, and more."

I rubbed my cold bare arms. "More?"

"It's not only Boston I see these days. It's many cities. I couldn't tell you which ones, but several. In the middle of them all…" His brown eyes were apologetic. "In the middle of them all, I see you. Somehow, I am quite certain you will be at the center of whatever will happen."

I gaped at him, and the hairs on the back of my neck rose. Magi visions weren't to be taken lightly, and for once I couldn't summon a sarcastic response.

I RETURNED TO LUCEN'S A FEW HOURS LATER TO FRET ABOUT Olef and plan my attack on Tom. I was determined to break into his office tonight, but I wanted to be smart about it. Quick, efficient, and productive. And uncaught—that most of all.

Tom frequently hung around the building until eight in the evening, so I had one or more hours to kill before I made my move. I debated taking a nap, but there was no way my eyes would shut. I was wired on adrenaline and nerves, and fairly sure a good chunk of those had to do with my conversation with Olef.

So instead, I sent Steph the screenshot Ben had sent me, along with a message asking her to explain what the gobbledygook it included, meaning in non-geek speak. She called me a few minutes later to oblige. But although Steph's explanation was clear, she was convinced that nothing there was of use to me. Since I didn't know enough to argue, I took her at her word and explained to her what I found out about the Brotherhood.

"So this secret fraternity created the files on you and Victor?"

I stretched out on the sofa, watching Sweetpea sharpen his claws on the stones in his cage. Why on earth Lucen aided this habit of his, I couldn't imagine. Who needed a more dangerous dragon? "Looks like it."

"I've seen this movie, Jess. Nothing good ever comes of people who go after secret societies. Why don't you wait until Ben gets in the files before making a move?"

"Because I'm impatient, frustrated, angry, curious—take your pick?"

Steph made a tsk noise. "Just don't add 'dead' to that list. You owe me too many favors, and it would be just like you to croak before I can to collect."

"You are the best friend a girl could ever want. You know that?"

"Don't trifle with my emotions, bitch. I heard too much sarcasm in there."

I laughed, and Lucen entered the living room as I hung up the phone.

"This is the third day in a row you haven't stopped at The Lair when you got home. I've barely seen you since last Thursday—a whole week. That's impressive since you're living out of my spare bedroom. Have you developed an aversion to alcohol or to me?" His tone was light, but the expression on his face wasn't. Naturally, the latter was what I reacted to, and I tensed.

"Work, family, and more work." I regretted my shortness as soon as I spoke, but I was on edge. Must have been something about preparing to break into a colleague's office and being told you were associated with what sounded like the end of the world. "Speaking of which, don't you have a bar to run?"

Lucen sat on the coffee table so that our knees touched. "Slow night. Besides, that's why I have employees. Jess?"

"Yeah?"

"Are you avoiding me again?"

I'd been staring at the screenshot from Ben, and I glanced up. "No. I'm here, aren't I?"

Lucen reached over and put his hands on my legs. "Are you? I see you so infrequently, and you don't seem entirely present mentally."

"I told you—I'm busy." I put my phone down. "Like tonight? I have to go back to work. I'm breaking into Tom Kassin's office."

Lucen had been sliding his hands up my thighs, and he paused. "This is the Gryphon who's been acting weird?"

"Yup."

Sighing, he let go of me. "Does it have to be tonight?"

"Kind of, yeah. I discovered something new, and I can't take what's going on anymore. I need answers and he might have them."

"That's too bad. I was hoping since it was a slow night, we could spend some time together."

I tucked my hair behind my ears, chewing on my internal conflict. Spending time with Lucen might be great stress relief, but was it such a good idea? As usual, my body didn't care. And if it didn't care, and Lucen didn't care...

But I cared. Both about Lucen and my conflict.

Still. I swallowed, letting my eyes feast on the satyr before me. He wore one of his usual tight T-shirts, and he looked so sweet. So tempting, like a satyr should. It didn't hurt either that I could see his concern for me in his eyes, as well as his desire.

"Yeah, I suppose," I mumbled. "I've got a couple hours..."

Lucen was at my side before I could talk myself out of it, laying me down on the sofa. "A couple hours isn't going to leave much time when I've been deprived of you for so long."

I arched up to meet his lips, wrapping my hand around his neck. It was hard, even for me with my reduced awareness of his magic, to control my body around him. Without trying, he could push me over the edge too quickly. But tonight I wanted this to go slowly and gently. To fool my body into believing we weren't as different as we were.

Yet his comment made me think of his addicts. He might have been deprived of me, but I'd bet my life only one of us had been celibate these past few days.

"Jess?"

"Nothing. Just nerves." I pressed closer. "Make me forget everything else."

HE SUCCEEDED. I'D HAD NO DOUBTS HE COULD. BUT THE moment he pulled out of me, it was as though I had a void inside, and it filled once more with questions and angst—over what I'd done and what I was about to do.

"What is it?" Lucen sat at the end of the battered sofa, his chest rising and falling hard as he ran a finger down my leg. I hadn't moved.

"What is what?"

"You're hiding stuff and it bothers you. I can sense it."

The last of my post-sex relaxation evaporated. I sat up and busied myself with putting on my clothes. "I've had a busy day. I can regale you with what I found out about the Gryphon files and my meeting with Olef if you want."

"No, see, that's what I'm talking about." He pushed hair out his face but didn't budge from his spot. "Even when we're in the same room, you're avoiding me. Yes, tell me about what you discovered. Please. But there's something else you're hiding. I didn't notice it before, but I do now that Devon pointed it out. It's so present on your mind that I can't believe I missed it before."

My shirt was stuck half over my head, and I yanked it down. "You're talking to Devon about me?"

"Devon talked to *me* about *you*. Over the weekend at Dezzi's council meeting. Apparently you two had an interesting exchange Friday night when you were at Purgatory and called the Gryphons on him." Lucen got up at last and grabbed his pants.

"Okay, first, I didn't call the Gryphons on him. That's a load of salamander shit. Second, if you're referring to me telling him I'm not afraid of him, why is it so interesting? Do you want me to be afraid?"

"No, but you used to be. That's what's interesting." He held his balled-up T-shirt like a weapon. "You used to be afraid of all of us. Remember? It's why I had to fight so hard to get you to trust me, and I thought I'd finally succeeded."

I threw cushions back on the sofa, not looking at him. "You did succeed. I'm here."

"But being here has nothing to do with you trusting me, does it?"

"Of course it has to do with trusting you. I do trust you. I don't trust

Devon. But that doesn't mean I have to be afraid of Devon. And just because I trust you doesn't mean I'm ready to spill all my secrets. Hell, I trust my mom and Steph too, and there's plenty I'm not ready to share with them either." Thanks to my anxiety I was worked up, unable to silence my tongue. Lucen had come too close to the truth, and so had Devon, although he was less aware of it. "Let's face it, it's not like you're sharing everything about yourself with me. You have a whole, hugely long life I know almost nothing about."

He put his shirt on with a wry expression. "There's far less to talk about there than you're thinking, and that's not what I'm referring to anyway. I'm talking about recent events. Something about you changed since Victor Aubrey's murders. You know, the same time our relationship changed? The timing suggests that, one way or another, it involves me. Am I wrong?"

"Not exactly."

"But you won't tell me what it is."

I hurled the last of the poor, undeserving throw cushions at the couch. "You going to tell me which satyr is responsible for producing and selling a drug that's killing humans?"

"The drugs are a completely different issue."

I glared at him. "I disagree. People are dead, more people almost died, and it all comes back to your race doing something bad and you not caring."

"I care about you."

"And sometimes that's not good enough for me. I care about other people, other humans. It bothers me that you don't."

Lucen turned his head toward the ceiling in obvious exasperation. "I don't like innocent people dying. I'd expect you'd know this by now, but I have other obligations. Ones that trump the lives of strangers. We're investigating the F situation ourselves, and I wish you'd trust about it."

I let out a small scream. He wasn't the only one exasperated. "I trust you, and I trust the satyrs have a strong interest in protecting their own asses so you will do what you can on your side to fix things. If someone's selling tainted F, you'll stop it. But stopping it doesn't mean there will be justice. See the difference?"

"What I see is that you have a hard time doing anything but assuming the worst possible motives about us."

"What reasons have I ever been given to see any others?"

The moment the words tumbled from my lips, I wanted to take them back. I'd gone too far and I knew it. Lucen's whole body tensed, and he stomped into the kitchen. I couldn't blame him. He had a right to be pissed off after all he had done for me.

But he was the exception. Our relationship was an anomaly.

I sank against the sofa arm. On the plus side, I'd sure derailed his question about what I was hiding. Yay? "I'm sorry. I didn't mean you."

"I know what you meant, little siren." He sounded as defeated as I felt.

Tears welled up and pressed against the back of my skull. There was a reason preds and humans kept their distance. Beyond that whole predator-prey issue, there was a serious conflict of interest between our races. They wanted to protect themselves as much we did.

Correction: as much as humans did.

Although I wasn't sure what good being a quasi-satyr did in this regard. I felt pretty damn human.

I rubbed my eyes. Whatever my concern about condoning Lucen's behavior, the truth was always going to be that I wanted him in my life. I just wasn't sure if it was possible, and it sounded like he was starting to wonder the same.

SEVENTEEN

Lucen went back to work. I moped and attacked the ice cream in the freezer, which wasn't my usual style when moping, but I needed to snoop later with a clear head. So that ruled out whiskey.

When I couldn't take being alone with my thoughts any longer, or the sick feeling in my stomach from indulging in ice cream, I gathered some supplies and left.

The air was humid but pleasant. I got off the subway one stop too far away and walked the rest of the distance trying to burn off the ice cream and my mood. Deep in downtown, surrounded by steel and concrete, the night hummed with energy. I breathed it in and relished it.

It couldn't possibly be as healthy for me as the fragrant, woodsy air near my mother's house, but my blood didn't buzz in the country. There was something about the tall buildings and ceaseless movement of the city —not to mention the occasional dragon darting through traffic—that made me feel alive.

Or maybe it was simply the relentless hit I got from the thousands of nearby, ever-suffering people. A power source I only noticed when it was absent. After all, that was why preds lived in cities, and I was...

Shut up, Jess.

It was ten o'clock by the time I entered Gryphon Headquarters and made my best attempt to judge how many people were around by the emotions within. The building officially closed at eleven, but Gryphons could come and go whenever they pleased, and many worked late since preds were nocturnal. Plus, security would be roaming.

My first stop was my desk. Going there enabled me to scout out a large swath of the floor and get a better read on who was around. I'd also stashed a few supplies in there earlier.

Once I was certain I had a good shot at breaking into Tom's office unnoticed, I gathered my remaining tools and hurried down the hall. There were cameras at various points around the building, but I was trusting no one would notice what I'd done and would therefore have no reason to scan the security footage later.

Using a magic-detection charm I'd borrowed from a supply room, I checked Tom's lock for magical supplements and found none. I hadn't expected any, but I breathed a sigh of relief anyway. I could probably break a ward if it had existed, but doing so could have alerted Tom to what had happened. Then footage would definitely be checked, and I'd be busted.

The lock on the door was an old-fashioned, easily pickable—if you knew what you were doing—cheap deadbolt like all the office doors had. I was inside within a minute, and I shut the door behind me. Switching on the light, I took a deep breath. Where to begin?

Tom had done more unpacking since I'd last been in here, and a few of the new items sitting on his bookshelves and desk snared my attention. The salamander fire-forged swords for starters. Holy hell.

He had two, each shaped vaguely like a katana. Elaborate glyphs had been worked into the perfectly black blades, and more glyphs covered the silver guards. Carefully, I ran my finger over one of the edges. They were beautiful, but they were most assuredly working blades. They'd slice a human as easily as a pred.

They weren't the only weapons I discovered either. Tom had unpacked a veritable arsenal—knives, daggers, and something I'd never seen before. Shell casings forged in salamander fire.

I swore as I held up the box for closer inspection. He didn't have many, three rows of four, but it was enough to make me shudder. The danger in fighting preds had always been the need to get close enough to them to land a killing blow since only the salamander steel could cause a lethal wound. But getting that close meant a pred could work their magic on you or simply fight back physically.

If you took that problem away... If you created a bullet wound they couldn't heal...

I snapped the lid shut, my stomach revolting at the memory of Lucen bleeding out on his sofa. Even a poor shot could be a kill shot with one of these, and I didn't want to think about that.

What I wanted to think about was why—why did Tom have so many weapons, and so many rare ones? These were not tools issued lightly or in great number. The box the casings were stored in suggested how rare they were. It was highly polished wood with a fancy catch. More like something you'd display rather than use for day-to-day storage.

I attempted to rationalize it as I turned to his books. Tom had been sent here by World to investigate the furies. They must have thought he could get into trouble, but that didn't truly explain anything. All Gryphons were issued their own salamander-forged blade.

Blade singular. So what did one Gryphon need with multiple swords and daggers? It wasn't like he could use them all at once. Besides, Tom was supposed to be investigating. Not heading into a fury war zone. It didn't make sense.

Creepier and creepier. Something was not right about Tom Kassin or his fraternity.

On that note, maybe there was something in these books about the Brotherhood. That was why I'd come here after all. Not so I could drool over his weapons.

All the books he'd brought were old. In some cases, so old I felt nervous touching them. Whispery paper rustled between my fingers as I paged through the first one I picked up. It appeared to be a spell book, but the language inside was—unsurprisingly—as ancient as the pages themselves. It was English, but it made me think of the painful experience I'd had in school of trying to decipher whatever Chaucer had been going on about in *The Canterbury Tales*. There were too many Es and Ys in places they didn't belong, and a good half of the words could have been Latin for all I recognized of them.

The second book I paged through was probably in Latin. This one had interesting drawings in it though. I wasted a few minutes taking in particularly fearsome sketches of furies and goblins, my thumb finally coming to rest on one of the last pages and at a picture that made my jaw drop.

This drawing featured another goblin, only it wasn't a true goblin. The artist had neglected to include certain details, such as the goblin's eyes. Generally, goblin eyes varied in shape and size much like human eyes did, but they were always bigger and rounder, distinctly nonhuman in appearance. But not the ones in this sketch. The artist had given the goblin human-shaped eyes. Also, ears that were a cross between goblin and human, and hands with shorter, stubbier fingers than a goblin should have.

In short, the creature looked like a hybrid. Like a part-goblin.

Unbidden, my free hand rubbed the top of my head as though feeling for stunted satyr horns.

Stop it, I told myself for the second time tonight. If I had any half-formed horns, I'd have noticed by now. Right?

Right. My skull felt as un-knobby as ever. Anyway, this was missing the point. Or was it?

For someone who was supposed to be investigating the furies, Tom seemed awfully interested in me at times. Plus with the Brotherhood and the files... Could he actually be investigating me too? I'd told the Gryphons a lot about myself because I'd had no choice, but I hadn't told them what I truly was, or how I could use my gift on people like weak satyr magic. Did Tom suspect there was more to it?

"It's just one drawing in one old book." I snapped the cover shut then cringed when I remembered its age.

Gently returning it to where I found it, I moved on. I would have to page through several more books before I began to believe this was anything more than a coincidence.

Alas, most of Tom's books were as unenlightening as the first, although some were more intelligible. I spent the most time reading a thin volume that contained notes on the most obscure charms I'd ever seen. Judging by the writing, it was a couple hundred years old, and among the other tidbits, it detailed methods for warding entire villages against preds, something I wouldn't have thought possible.

Sticking that book back on the shelf, I reassessed Tom's office. I had yet to discover anything illuminating about the Brotherhood or about Tom's alleged investigation, and my hopes were sinking fast.

I took to his desk next, pulling open each drawer and mostly finding the sorts of items I'd expect—pens, paperclips, sticky notes. He had a thin file on me and one on Victor, but nothing worth noting in either. I already knew he'd obtained a copy of my blood analysis, and the other papers in the file were copies of statements I'd given to Director Lee. Victor's file was just as sparse. Anything important I'd bet was on Tom's computer, but I hadn't thought of trying to get into it, and I didn't foresee my chance of guessing his password to be high.

His laptop bag sat on the floor. I gave it a cursory search, not expecting to find anything, but my hand encountered another book. When I pulled it out, I discovered Tom had bookmarked a page.

My lips spread into a tentative smile. Maybe I hadn't taken this risk for nothing. The book—journal to be more precise—wasn't as old as the others, although the plain leather cover was quite beaten up. Before opening it straight to Tom's bookmark, I checked the front for identifying information, but there was none. Most of the books he had didn't contain any. Shrugging it off, I pulled the pages open to where the gold ribbon had marked them.

He'd left off in the middle of a long passage, and I ended up turning back a page to see where it started. The page contained a date, 2 April, but no year. Following it, in a tight, neat hand, the writer had recorded a magi's vision.

I began by skimming because the writer's syntax was difficult to follow, as if English wasn't his first language, but my pace slowed as it became clearer what the vision described—nothing short of the end of the world.

Or, as the writer referred to it, "the death of civilized days."

The demons shall rise…freed by fire…humanity enslaved…rivers of blood…Hell on Earth. Pleasant stuff. And then there were some things the writer called the Others and the Firsts, which were lost on me.

Gee, no wonder Tom had bookmarked this. Nothing like a little light reading.

I flipped back the pages, trying to figure out who these Others and Firsts were, but I couldn't find anything that explained. One interesting note, however, was that the writer called this passage a "prophecy" and not a vision. Subtle difference, but did he mean the same thing? Magi visions could be vague, or misinterpreted as Olef had apparently done, but they almost always came to pass.

Olef. Cities burning, purple smoke...

I dropped the book on Tom's desk as though burned. Not buying it. Besides, I had enough problems to deal with. This so-called prophecy was at least one hundred years old. There couldn't be a connection with what Olef saw, but I was so busy looking for links between myself and whatever Tom was up to that I was jumping to all sorts of weird assumptions.

Anyway, Tom was here about the furies, or me, or both of us, and the Gryphons dealt with magical law enforcement, not doomsday prophecies and the end of the world. Tom probably just had some twisted imagination. Lots of people got off on that shit, and Tom was plenty weird enough to be one of them.

My cell rang as I stuck the journal back in his bag, and my heart skipped a beat. I should have set it to vibrate. Hurriedly, I picked up before someone in the hall might hear.

"Jess, it's Andre. I hope you're not busy tonight because we've probably got two more victims."

I swore. "Again?"

"Again." Andre's breaths were heavy. He sounded almost like he was jogging. "We got a call from the cops. They're waiting on us. How fast can you get down to the Wonderland T station?"

My heart had found its rhythm once more, and it pounded in my chest in anger and despair. "I'm downtown, so however long that will take."

"I'll meet you there. I'm on my way too."

I hung up and inspected Tom's office to make sure I'd put everything back as I found it. Satisfied that I had, I snuck back into the hallway, returned the magic-detector and lock-picking tools to my desk, and grabbed my official jacket from the back of the chair.

This was turning out to be one crappy night.

―――――――――

WONDERLAND WAS THE LAST STOP ON THE BLUE LINE. THERE'D be no getting there fast, but I decided a car was my best option.

By the time my driver dropped me off, the police were out in force, and as much of the busy station as they could block off had been demarcated with yellow police tape. A crowd of gawkers hung around, pointing and taking photos. There was even a news van already on the scene.

I put on my Gryphon windbreaker and dove into the melee. With a flash of my ID, I got beyond the crowd and found Andre waving to me from the train's outbound platform. Anna was with him and so were a couple Gryphons I knew only by sight.

Andre introduced the others briefly, saying they were the first to arrive on the scene when the police called. "So what happened was this: guy gets off the train, sees a couple kids—his description—going at it on the platform. He yells at them to knock it off, and they don't listen, so he's disgusted and calls the cops. As you can imagine, this isn't high on their priority list, so they say they'll send someone around."

As he talked, Andre led me toward the victims. I couldn't see them yet because of the cops hovering around them, and I was thankful.

"Half an hour later, the cops get another call about two people acting *inappropriately*—" Andre made air quotes around the phrase, "—on the platform. This time it's a mother whose kids saw what was going on, and she's livid. So the complaint gets bumped up in priority. When the cop gets here, the victims are clearly exhausted and ill, but he can't get them to stop. They ignore him, and as soon as he intervenes, they're back at it although the male can barely stand. So the officer calls for an ambulance, assuming they're on some kind of drugs."

"Which they are," I interject.

Andre nods. "As far as we know. Only by the time the ambulance arrives, it's too late. They're already dead. That's when someone makes a connection to the Newton case and calls us. We got lucky."

"How is this lucky exactly?"

"It's not for the victims, but if someone had assumed they were on meth or any normal street drug, they'd have taken the bodies and done a regular toxicology analysis. By the time they realized that didn't explain it and called us, it could be too late for us to do our own analysis. Whatever's tainting this F has a damn fast half-life."

In confirmation of this, Anna popped out of the group of officers surrounding the victims, holding two vials of blood. "I've got what I need. I'm taking these into the lab so the analysis can start right away."

The group of officers shuffled as she left, their attention shifting to the people from the coroner's office who'd shown up. I caught a glimpse of the two bodies—victims—in the light, and clasped a hand over my mouth. Aside from the scenery, this was exactly like the Newton case.

Had the two died simultaneously or one before the other? I didn't know why I cared other than the idea of lying with a dead person added to the horror of the whole thing.

The man and woman both appeared to be in their twenties. She'd passed out on top of her partner, her head landing crookedly on his chest. He must have pulled her dress up at one point because it remained in a heap around her hips, but his arms had long since fallen to the ground. Except for their lifeless stares, they almost appeared comfortable. Sleeping.

I winced, partly in sympathy and partly from the creepiness. At least no one was making jokes this time. I supposed these two deaths felt a bit more tragic than the unusual show in Newton. I could taste the soup of emotions all around me, everyone a different flavor of unhappy, but I could deal with that.

Bad jokes about going out with a smile? Not so much.

"Hey." I nudged Andre's arm as I noticed something on the male victim's right leg. "Can I get a closer look?"

"Yeah." He was distracted, watching a couple cops, then he snapped out of it. "Yeah, of course. That's why I wanted you here—for your insight. Come on."

The remaining cops and the two Gryphons moved aside so I could kneel next to the bodies.

Andre squatted next to me. "You find something?"

"That." I pointed to a tattoo on the guy's thigh. His leg hair obscured it, but I was certain I'd seen it before. "That woman from the club—what was her name, Natalie?—I think she had the same one. I thought it was some tribal thing or a kanji, but what if it's not?"

Andre rubbed his chin. "If you're thinking it could be a glyph, I've got to say it doesn't look like any glyph I've seen before. But then, I'm not an expert."

Neither was I, and my memory could be totally wrong. But if it wasn't?

What had I been lecturing myself about an hour ago? Making connections where none existed? I could be leading us down a completely irrelevant path. I did have a strong motivation for not wanting the satyrs to be responsible for this after all.

I stood, biting my lip with apprehension. "Can we check and see if she has one too?"

"Yeah, can't hurt." Andre beckoned the other Gryphons over for their opinions.

We checked her legs first, and there it was. It was also difficult to see —this time because of her darker skin—but it was clearly the same symbol.

"Could be matching tattoos," one of the younger Gryphons said.

I stuffed my hands in my pocket. "Could be. One way to find out. If that Natalie person from Purgatory has one, we'll have a better idea."

"Tomorrow," Andre said. "We'll track down Natalie tomorrow."

NATALIE ENGLISH, AGE TWENTY-ONE, WAS AN UNDERGRAD AT Harvard. Go figure. Andre found this out when he called the phone number associated with the address on her driver's license. Natalie's mother had answered.

Since she wasn't aware of what had happened to her daughter, she was less than pleased to have a Gryphon call and was highly alarmed. So Natalie and I had something in common besides our love for dark music and a preference for black underwear—we liked to keep our mothers sheltered.

Andre assured Mrs. English that he'd remind Natalie it was nice to keep her parents informed about her life.

"I wouldn't," I said as Andre snagged the first spot we found in relative walking distance to Harvard's campus. "There are reasons a girl might want to keep her family clueless about certain aspects of her personal life."

"Know this from experience, do you?" Andre laughed as he locked the SUV.

"If my mother knew half of what I'd gotten into, her blood pressure would be as high as mine gets when you drive."

"Oh, please. I have a perfect driving record."

I rolled my eyes. "Sure you do. What cop is going to ticket a Gryphon?"

Even in the summer, the paths around the university were swollen with undergrads taking summer courses and grad students slaving away without a break. We crossed the tree-filled campus, an oasis of green in the middle of congested Cambridge. Andre had gotten directions to Natalie's dorm, and we managed to find it with minimal confusion.

Natalie, however, was more of challenge. Her roommate told us she was in the library, and finally we cornered her after much searching.

"A tat on my hip?" Natalie repeated several minutes later when we were standing in the sun near the library. "Which side?"

I motioned on my own hip to the general area. "Left. About this big."

She wore a pair of low-cut jeans, and she pulled the waistband down even farther without a care in the world. And here I'd worried she was going to be horrified when videos of her half naked showed up online.

Good for her that she wasn't modest, but not good for us. There was nothing there. Her skin was pale and pristine.

"You sure I had something?" She squinted at her hip.

Andre peered at me over his sunglasses. "I second the question."

"Yeah, I'm sure," I said, biting down a curse. "Glyphs wear off."

"It hasn't been a week. They usually last longer than that."

"Wouldn't it depend on what the glyph was made of?"

Andre acknowledged the point with a shrug. "Possibly. And also how fast the magic in it got used up."

Natalie chewed on a particularly ragged fingernail. "So you're saying it wasn't the F making me act crazy, but something someone drew on me?"

"We're saying it's possible," Andre replied. "Do you remember anyone doing that?"

"Dude, I still have like almost no memories of that night from the time Jake decided to score F until I came to in the hospital. It's a blur."

Andre gave her his card for a second time after ascertaining she'd lost the one given to her at the hospital. "If you get any memories back, call me immediately."

"You think she will?" I asked as we returned to the car.

"Unlikely. If there was a compulsion put on her, they're probably gone for good. But then again, sometimes preds screw up. That's how we busted a satyr producing F down in Austin a few years ago. The guy in charge made a mistake or got lazy, and some people started getting their memories back. We figured out how to put the pieces together."

The SUV was like an oven. Silly Gryphons and their black cars. "Now what?"

"Now we might as well check out the other victims from Purgatory. If what you saw really was a glyph, they'd have them too, and there's a chance not all of them would have faded yet." Andre adjusted the mirrors and scowled at the traffic. "We can also pull the reports from Newton and see if the autopsies mentioned any tattoos."

"I hope I'm not leading you on some pointless chase."

"Eh." Andre smiled at me. "It's not like we have much else to go on."

WE MANAGED TO TRACK DOWN TWO OF THE THREE GUYS involved at the club, but it was for nothing. Neither of them remembered getting a glyph, temporary tattoo, or simply someone drawing on them with a pen that night. And neither had noticed any unusual marks on their skin. We asked them to check again while we waited, but their answers didn't change. Barring requiring them to strip so we could check ourselves, we had to take their word for it. Under the circumstances, odds were there truly was nothing on them. Not anymore.

After that, we returned to the office. Andre had another case he had to check in on, so I went over the Newton autopsy reports. It didn't make pleasant reading. Less so because, once again, I discovered nothing.

I kicked my chair away from my desk and rested my head on the back. I was so close; I could feel it. The more I thought about it, the more convinced I became that this was the answer. Somehow this glyph was interacting with the F in such a way as to make people insatiably and uncontrollably horny. F already stimulated sexual desire, so this was like a stimulant on steroids. A curse that overrode the body's ability to stop even in the face of deadly exhaustion.

Remembering I'd seen books on glyphs and charm-making, I headed to the library for more research. Unfortunately, I had no way to search for a specific symbol, and frustration set in quickly. I had to rely on possible meanings to pick out the glyphs, then compare the books' symbols to the crude re-creation I'd drawn of the one in question.

With a sigh, I put my head down on the table. This was going nowhere. I needed a new idea for my new idea.

Rolling over, I gazed blankly at the ceiling and found myself staring straight into one of the security cameras. That was it. Devon had security cameras around Purgatory. What if they'd caught something—either a shot of Natalie's hip, or better yet, someone drawing the glyph on her and her friends in the first place. Devon had claimed the club's cameras were for real-time surveillance only, but I wondered. With the secrets he hid in the club's basement, I'd be surprised if he didn't record and more. And if I explained my new theory and the glyph, he might be willing to cooperate.

Of course, there were legal means the Gryphons could use if he wasn't willing, but it would be best to keep this relatively friendly. Assuming Devon was willing to talk *to* me, and not just *about* me at this point.

I called Lucen, half expecting he wouldn't pick up because he was angry about yesterday evening, but he did. "I was hoping you could give me Devon's number. I need to track him down."

There was a pause filled with suspicion. "I could. Why?"

I drummed my fingers against the table in annoyance. "Nothing bad. I had a new theory about the F case, and I wanted to talk to him."

"Little siren, you remember when the Gryphons first called you in? You were furious. You considered it blackmail."

I lowered my voice, but the library was as dead today as it had been yesterday. "I still do. That doesn't mean I don't want to help people too. Look, I'm not going to interrogate Devon or anything. I have a couple questions he might be able to help me with. He was a witness to what happened last Friday, and I need a witness." Or his security footage.

"All right." Lucen sounded skeptical. "But I don't know if you'll get a hold of him. He's at Purgatory, I think."

"Perfect. That's where I want to meet him. Wait—why is he there so early?"

"That's where he meets his addicts."

Peachy. I groaned and Lucen laughed. "Then I'll be sure to call before I start banging on the door so he knows to put on some pants."

EIGHTEEN

When Devon let me into Purgatory, not only was he fully clothed, he looked as put together as ever. His joy at seeing me, however, didn't seem as strong as it used to be.

"Hope I'm not interrupting anything," I said, stepping inside.

"Just work."

"I see. Is that what sex is for you?"

Devon shut the heavy door behind me. "Not in a long time, although I'm concerned about you and Lucen if that's what jumped to your mind when I said work."

I flipped him off. "Lucen suggested you were coming here to meet an addict. I thought maybe that was considered work."

"I did, but no. Sorry you missed it if you were curious about the difference between the two."

"Not curious, but sad for your addict given how quick it must have been."

His lips twitched. "Sadly, there are days when all you have time for is fast food."

Nice. I made a disgusted face, which was surely his goal. "That's very unhealthy."

"I'm touched that you care."

"I meant for your addict."

Devon clutched his chest. "You know that hurts." He took out his phone and began typing.

Pausing in the entry to the club proper, I sighed. In the empty room with its high ceilings and hard floor, the noise sounded louder. More piercing. "You know, it's rude when people text instead of paying attention to the conversation they're having with the person right in front of them."

"Actually, you're at my side," he said without glancing up. "Not in front. And I'm not texting. I'm making a note. 'Jess doesn't like quickies.' Could be useful someday."

"I didn't say that. I believe in variety."

"Aha."

"Now what?"

He smirked. "In the past, your first response has always been to say something like 'you wish.' This time your first thought was to correct me. Interesting."

Damn it. He was right. I felt blood rush to my cheeks. "You wish."

"Too late."

I glowered at him. He was being more infuriating than usual. "Whatever. I came here for a reason. Can we talk about that?"

"Yes, and yes. You have a new theory. I'm curious." He tucked the phone away and headed toward the main bar's seating area.

"Did Lucen call to warn you?" I scuffed my boot against the smooth dance floor in frustration.

"Yes, but that's all he said. Also, now you know the real reason I rushed my addict out of here. I'd hate to make you uncomfortable."

"I wish you hated to piss me off."

"That's not going to happen. You're very entertaining when you're angry."

I put my head in my hands and took a deep breath. "And you're very good at being infuriating."

"Not a coincidence." Devon pulled a chair around from one of the bar tables. I didn't move. "Oh, come on. Admit you like me in spite of everything, I'll admit I like you in spite of everything, and tell me your new theory. I'm sure Lucen's explained that we want to clear this up as much as you do."

I sat but admitted nothing. "Something like that." There was no need to relive the same argument I had with Lucen with Devon as well. I had enough futility in my life.

"So?" Devon prodded.

"So I have an idea." I explained to him about the marks we'd found on the Wonderland victims, and the mark I thought I'd seen on Natalie.

Devon tapped his fingers together, his impishness appearing to have succumbed to the serious business at hand. "But there were no marks on the first set of victims noted in their autopsies, and nothing on the other people who were affected here?"

"No, but glyphs fade. Hours had passed by the time the Newton people were found."

"Glyphs don't generally fade that fast."

"Generally." I scanned the bar area and the ceiling for hidden cameras. "You have security cameras. All the victims from the club were exposing a lot of skin at one point or another. If we could go through the…"

I paused because Devon was shaking his head. "I told you and your friends last week—we have cameras, but we don't record or keep footage of anything inside. It's for real-time monitoring only."

"I just thought with—"

"I know what you thought, Jess. You thought I was lying. I'm not, sorry. For liability reasons, I would never record."

I swore. Maybe that was true. Especially since the satyrs—or a satyr— regularly dealt F here. "I don't suppose you remember seeing anything like I described, do you?"

"I can't say I remember it, no. Do you remember what the symbol looked like? I might be able to help identify it."

"Sort of." I'd brought my drawing with me on the off chance I'd have something to compare it to, and I passed it to Devon.

He smoothed out the folded paper on the black bar table and examined it from different angles. "Interesting. Parts of it are similar to a very generic glyph for endurance, but then other parts… I don't know what they could be."

Endurance. Of all the symbols I'd looked up in the library earlier, that was one I hadn't thought of. "It could be my lousy memory or lack of artistic talent."

"I'd blame your memory over your skill, but it could be neither. That's the problem."

"What do you mean?"

Devon slid the paper back to me. "How much do you know about glyphs?"

"Only the basics. Lucen's taught me a bit, and I learned a little at the Academy, but that was years ago."

He sat back in his chair. "Glyphs are like all magic in that they depend highly on the skill and sensitivity to power of the person creating them. Even beginners can make basic ones, but it's possible for someone who's highly skilled and experienced to create their own—either from scratch, or more often from combining glyphs of known power into something new. How they get put together will determine their effect as much as the spell ingredients used to draw them."

I closed my eyes in frustration. "So what you're saying is—I have nothing."

"You're always the pessimist. No, not nothing. I can't tell you if this glyph is causing the deaths, but if it is, that tells you a lot."

"Such as?"

Devon got up and opened a fridge behind the bar. He took out two beers and handed me one. "If you're going to make me do all the work, I should be the Gryphon consultant."

"Excuse me for not having proper training in any of this shit. The Gryphons kicked me out, and I'm not a..." I twisted the cap off the bottle. "I don't have a Dom teaching me Intro to Magic."

Devon chuckled into his beer. "Now that's a good visual of Dezzi. Can't you picture her in front of a chalkboard?"

"No one uses chalkboards these days."

"Really? Well, what do you want? I'm old."

I paused with the bottle pressed to my lip. Devon was dragging this conversation a long way off track, but I couldn't help myself. "How old?"

I wasn't sure how long the average pred lived other than that it was far longer than humans. Their magic made them fairly indestructible and resistant to human diseases, but they could be cut down by the right weapons or curses, and isolation from humans could kill them too. They had multiple ways of starving to death.

Historically, I didn't think many preds died of natural causes. Something—or someone—always got to them first. It was why they'd started to live in such tightly organized, hierarchical communities. For protection.

But that was then. Now, although they still lived in those communities, they'd wormed their way into human and magi civilization.

Devon's blue eyes filled with humor. Any coldness he'd felt toward me when I'd arrived was clearly long gone. Possibly, he'd never been truly upset with me, or he'd simply amused himself long enough at my expense to let it go. "I'm old enough that I shouldn't be here anymore. Let's leave it there, and let me answer the question you really want the answer to."

"What the glyph tells us?"

"Yes, and what the glyph tells us is—assuming it's responsible—the person behind it is very magically skilled. That will narrow down your search considerably."

I frowned. "If you're implicating a human, yeah. But not if it's a pred." I was careful to say pred instead of satyr, although odds were it was a satyr. From Devon's point of view, though, life would be much sweeter if it wasn't, and I wanted to be on his good side.

For that matter, it would be better for me too.

"Either way. Many preds—" Devon said the word with the same distaste Lucen did, "—are better at magic than Gryphons because we have a greater sensitivity to it, but most don't use it on a regular basis. It's like any other skill. The more you practice, the better you get. Most preds don't use it and wouldn't be able to create their own glyphs. Whoever did is either a very powerful pred or a master charm-maker."

I sipped my beer thoughtfully. If he was telling the truth, that would definitely narrow down the suspect list. Assuming I was on the right track with any of this. "I guess that's something."

"It is. Sorry I couldn't be more help, Jess."

I made a wry face. "I'm sure you are."

"It's the truth. Part of my job is to minimize the damage this could do to me and mine, and I don't like to see collateral damage either."

"Meaning?"

"You and Lucen." I opened my mouth to object, but he cut me off. "You being a Gryphon, working on a case that on the surface involves us— it's harsh. I get why the Gryphons wanted your help. Very slick of the Director there. And I'm going to guess none of your coworkers actually understand your tenuous connection to us or know about your relationship with Lucen. But it can't be fun for you. I'd say this is about as unhealthy for a relationship as fast food."

"This time I'm touched by your concern."

Devon shoved his empty beer bottle aside. "You can lay off the sarcasm every now and then. I'm being serious."

That was debatable. In my experience, a serious Devon was a pissed-off Devon.

"I just don't like talking about this sort of thing." Particularly with someone I couldn't trust. "Don't take it personally."

"Fair enough." He grinned. "Should I make a note of that too? 'Doesn't like to talk.'"

I punched his arm. "You know, this is why you're impossible to take seriously."

"I'm very serious. If you give me the chance, I'll show you just how serious I'm willing to take you." He draped the arm I'd punched around my shoulders.

My muscles tensed, not in fear but in anticipation as I breathed in his clove scent. Damn traitorous body. I scooted out from his grip, annoyed at myself. "Ha-ha."

Before Devon could say or do anything else to mess with me, the sound of heels clicking and clacking echoed off the walls and ceiling. Lucrezia appeared around the partition that separated the long entry hall from the main club. Her bright red lips formed an "O" as she noticed me.

"Ah, Crezi, you're here." Devon turned his shit-kicking grin on her.

Lucrezia glared at him with the disdain she usually reserved for me. "Do not ever call me that again." She tossed her long auburn waves over her shoulder and narrowed her eyes at me. "What are you doing here, pet?"

I took a few steps away from Devon. "I had to ask Devon some questions about the case."

Lucrezia clucked her tongue. "Honestly, hasn't Dezzi made her feelings on your questioning quite clear?"

"Actually, Dezzi hasn't said anything to me at all."

"Really?" She climbed the steps up to the bar. "Perhaps that's not so surprising. I hope her lieutenant has risen to the occasion then."

Devon cleared his throat in an exaggerated manner. "Jess, in case you haven't figured it out, we don't like you questioning us."

"Honestly." Lucrezia crossed her arms, scolding him with her eyes before turning to me. "We're looking into this ourselves. Believe us as depraved as you want, but we're not killers or furies. We don't enjoy death and destruction, and dead humans don't do us any good."

Lucen had once said something similar to me, back when the bodies of Victor Aubrey's victims had started piling up. "I know that."

"I like Jess's new idea," Devon said. "Jess, explain it to her."

I wasn't sure what good it would do, but for the second time in the last hour, I summed up my theory.

Lucrezia picked up my drawing of the glyph with a dubious expression. "That doesn't look like a glyph so much as someone pretending to write Chinese."

"But the idea has promise," Devon said. "If it's not the F that killed those people, then anyone could be doing it."

Lucrezia set the paper back on the table. "It's a nice idea for our sake, but I disagree. Two lovers at a train station with matching tattoos isn't so shocking. Nor is people buying very temporary charms at Purgatory."

Devon acknowledged the point with a shrug, but I snatched my drawing back, confused. "People buy charms at Purgatory? Since when?"

"Since always, pet. Cheap disguise charms to make themselves look different, or charms to make themselves appear more attractive, or energy boosters—they're for sale if you know where to look."

"But drawn on as glyphs? Those sorts of charms are usually sold in vials."

Lucrezia inspected her nails, seemingly bored with my ignorance. "One vial can contain a lot of magic. If you only want something to last the night, you could have someone paint it on you for much cheaper."

Devon pushed his hair behind his ears. "Fair point. But I still like the glyph idea, for what it's worth."

"Damn it. I thought I'd been onto something."

"You might be." Lucrezia didn't sound convinced. "Find more victims with markings on them and you'll know."

"I'd rather not find more victims."

She yawned. "Understandable. Personally, I'd rather not be here so early in the day, but since I am, can we get to work already?"

"Yeah, yeah. I guess you're being kicked out, Jess," Devon said. "Crezi and I have a complicated task ahead of us before the club opens in a few hours. Too bad Jess cut my snack short. I hope I have enough energy to get through it."

Lucrezia frowned at him. "You'd better after dragging me out of my apartment before the sun set. I'm not even sure what we're doing is necessary. The wards seem plenty strong to me."

I folded my drawing and stuck it in my pocket. "Wards?"

Lucrezia walked away, making a show of ignoring me.

"Yeah." Devon drew the word out. "The most restricted areas of the club are secured through wards rather than a typical security system. I have it on good authority that someone breached one of those wards in the basement recently. So we're going to check and strengthen them all."

"It's a waste of time," Lucrezia said without glancing back. "I told you. It's not possible. There was no way anyone who wasn't a satyr got through there."

Devon slipped his arm around my shoulders again and lowered his head to mine. "So she keeps saying."

I kept my face carefully neutral, but inside, my heartbeat stuttered, and it wasn't from lust. Busting through the club's wards like I'd done had obviously been weird, but the full implication of how weird hadn't dawned on me before. Judging by Devon's current behavior, though, weird was an understatement. And he wasn't over it. No wonder he was talking to Lucen about me.

Also, just as interestingly, he must not have told Lucrezia about the incident. Who else hadn't he told? And what, if anything, did he suspect?

"One of you must be wrong then," I said when my breath returned.

"Possibly." He let go of me, and my shoulders sagged. Lucrezia had disappeared into the bowels of the club, and Devon walked me to the door. "Or possibly the human who managed this incredible act is more fascinating than I'd originally given her credit for. What do you think?"

A sense of relief washed over me as I crossed the threshold into the late-afternoon air. "I think I'm out of my depth. Have fun."

Then I took a lesson from Lucrezia and hurried away without a backward glance.

NINETEEN

"RIK LEFT A MESSAGE FOR YOU." LUCEN SLID THE WORDS across The Lair's bar like the shot of Jameson's he'd poured me. I'd planned to ask for coffee, but since he'd poured without asking, what the hell. Liquid courage wasn't a bad idea. "He said if you stop by around eleven, he'll be available to trade."

I let out the breath I'd been holding for the past week. "Awesome. Thank you, Eyff, for not being a total birdbrain."

Lucen held on to my hand as I reached for my drink. "You look nice."

He sounded more curious than complimentary, but hey, someone noticed. I wasn't sure if that was good or bad, just as I wasn't sure whether this evening counted as a date with Andre or not. Just in case, however, I'd figured ditching my usual jeans and a T-shirt for something less casual was prudent.

I gave his fingers a squeeze. "Thanks. I'm doing something I don't usually do—being sociable."

"I find you very sociable, little siren." He released my hand, and I swished the ice around the glass. "And you socialize with Steph. Is that what you're up to?"

"True, but no. I'm meeting up with a coworker."

"A coworker? A Gryphon?"

I sipped my drink, wondering if it was normal to feel nervous about hanging out with a coworker. Or slightly guilty. "Yeah. I thought it might be a good idea to socialize with humans other than Steph for a change. It's been a while."

"Sounds very...normal. Are you feeling well?" He put his hand to my forehead.

I playfully smacked him away. "Normal is the idea. We'll see if I can pull it off."

"I'm sure of it. Is it this Bridget person you've mentioned before?"

"No, I'm not sure Bridget socializes any more than I do." I finished my drink and spun the glass around on its pool of condensation. "His name's Andre. He's my partner on the case."

"Ah...*your partner.* The dressing up makes more sense." Lucen swept my glass away before I could drain the melted ice.

Yeah, and... But Lucen didn't give me the chance to retort. He was suddenly busy at the other end of the bar, and it was Paulius who asked if I wanted another.

I told him no thanks and left, wondering what that was about or if I'd imagined something. There'd been less mischievous teasing in Lucen's comment than there'd been crankiness. Very unlike him.

That made two of us not acting like ourselves tonight.

I met up with Andre, and then we met up with two couples at a pub called Molly's Tavern in Cambridge. The pub boasted authentic Irish cooking, and on Saturdays, Irish music too. I was down with the live music, but I hoped the menu didn't include things like corned beef and cabbage. I'd been forced to choke down enough of my mother's authentic cooking for too much of my childhood, and I infinitely preferred Irish drinks to Irish food.

Andre introduced me to the other Gryphons, both of whom were there with their non-Gryphon partners—one who worked for the fire department, the other who was finishing up a PhD at Tufts.

Kendra and Sara, the unmarried couple, were talking about neighborhoods since they were looking to move in together. "Jess, where do you live and do you recommend it?" Kendra asked.

I took a long draw from my Guinness. "I'm kind of not living anywhere right now. My roommates got spooked by my involvement in the Victor Aubrey thing, so I'm staying with a friend."

"That's not fair." Kendra was the Gryphon, and I had vague memories of her being one of the ones who'd tried to arrest me not long ago. That meant she'd probably seen me hit one of her colleagues with a chair.

Truly, it was amazing any of these people were willing to talk to me.

"So you're apartment-hunting too?" Sara asked.

"Yeah, although I think I found a place this afternoon, or so I'm hoping." Given the weirdness of my relationship with Lucen, hoping was an understatement. The apartment was small, but I didn't need a lot of space, and the rent couldn't be beat. I only needed the landlord—one of Dezzi's satyrs—to be willing to give it to me. At the moment, I considered that no sure thing.

"Where is it?" Sara asked.

I wished the band would hurry up and start so I didn't have to answer, but they were still setting up. "Shadowtown," I said at last.

Kendra's brown eyes bugged out over her beer. "You think it's a good idea for a Gryphon to live in Shadowtown?"

"Is it a good idea for anyone to live in Shadowtown?" Sara asked.

So much for normal. I'd ruined any chance of pretending. "Technically, I'm not a Gryphon."

"You are to them."

Kendra had a point, but I shrugged it off. "I can afford it, and I can handle myself around them. Beats nervous roommates."

Andre laughed. "You're wild, Jess. That's why I like you."

I supposed if I couldn't fake normal, then finding a normal guy who liked wild was the next best thing. The only question was—how much did I want Andre to like my style of wild?

The question occupied my thoughts over the next hour as the band started to play and we all moved on to our second or third beers. If only all the secrets I hid didn't make this so awkward, I could have had fun. But even with the beer fuzzing my brain, I couldn't shake the feeling that I didn't fit in with these people and we all knew it.

To drive home the point, my phone buzzed with the alarm I'd set to remind myself when ten o'clock rolled around. The others at our table bopped to a particularly raucous jig as I leaned over to Andre. "I need to sneak out. I'm so sorry."

He lowered his head to mine, the table's candlelight reflecting in his warm eyes. It was almost enough to distract me from the disappointment he was feeling. "Everything okay?"

"Yeah, before I left I got word that a contact in Shadowtown was willing to talk if I stopped by around eleven." He'd assume this was work on our case, and though I felt bad letting him believe it, it really was work of a sort.

Andre nodded. "You getting somewhere then? Good."

"We'll see."

"Good luck. I'll see you on Monday."

I slipped away from the table, trying to ignore the confusing mix of emotions he stirred up. Although he hadn't tried to kiss me good night, I could sense he'd thought about it. If I hadn't needed to leave early, who knew what might have happened. As awkward as this evening had been, maybe I'd spared myself more awkwardness by leaving early.

Then again, maybe I'd have had more fun if it were just the two of us. It didn't matter because I wasn't finding out.

Before I left, I hit up the restroom because, you know, beer. As I passed the main bar on my way, the back of a blond head caught my attention. A familiar, unwelcome, blond head.

Tom was here? Could this be a coincidence?

He was deep in conversation with a man I didn't recognize, so I took the farthest path I could manage to bypass him, but it was too late. Tom must have seen me in the mirror behind the bar. I was ten feet from the restroom alcove when he called my name.

I wiped the wince off my face as I turned around. Tom had left his friend at the bar, but not his beer, which he looked too young to be drinking.

"I see you're here with a couple other Gryphons." He smiled in that annoyingly smug way, made all the more so by the stupid banality of his statement.

"Yeah. Sorry we didn't know you were here."

Tom checked over his shoulder at his friend. "I'm glad to see you're making an effort to fit in. I have to say, with your abilities I wasn't surprised to discover you spend a lot of time in Shadowtown."

How did he know that?

I bit my lip. "I wouldn't say I spend a lot of time there. I used to do business there, as you know. That's all."

"Yes, but I have to assume you made some friendly business associates, like you're making here."

Once again I felt like I was being probed, ever so gently, for damning information. "Preds aren't exactly friendly."

"Not to us, but I imagine some satyrs probably treat you that way because of your gift."

I said nothing. Merely stared blankly at him.

"You're wise not to assume they'd mean it," he continued, unflustered by my lack of response. "As your current case shows, they aren't friends to humanity, regardless of what face they put on. It's a good thing to keep in mind since I can see how it might be tempting to identify with them."

Was that some kind of warning? Like I might identify with a pred?

"Thanks for the tip, but I'm well aware of what preds are and what they can do. A bunch nearly got me killed if you'll recall." I motioned toward the bathrooms. "Excuse me."

I didn't see Tom when I left the pub five minutes later, but I didn't spend any time looking. His being there, I told myself again and again, was only a coincidence. But that conversation was weird. I ran it through my head on the train back to Shadowtown, but couldn't figure out Tom's motivations. Not unless being a condescending prick was one of them.

Fortunately, my meeting with Rik went smoothly, and I was able to put aside my confused musings. I handed over the blood I'd obtained, and he destroyed Bee's with only minimal admonishments about my choice of new occupations and dire warnings from Eyff about not allowing any further trades if I kept this up. I even bought two chocolate croissants from him to have as a Sunday breakfast treat with Lucen. The whole exchange felt normal, and that bugged me because there was nothing normal about it.

I left the croissants on the counter when I got to Lucen's and kicked off my shoes. My satyr was obviously still at work, Saturday being The Lair's busiest night. I collapsed on the sofa and turned on the TV, thinking to take advantage of Lucen's Netflix subscription. I needed a break from reality. Preferably one with explosions.

I didn't get the break, although I might have gotten the explosions. Lucen entered the living room soon after, and the tightness in his jaw didn't bode well.

I turned down the volume. "Shouldn't you be working?"

"We've been over this. I take breaks." He crossed the room and sat next to me, but didn't touch me. "How was your date?"

"I'm not sure it qualified as a date."

"Good. It better not."

Did I hear that correctly? "Sorry? Why do you have an opinion?"

"Because…I don't know. I thought we had a thing?" He tilted his head to the side, regarding me like a child. "Or was I wrong about that? I guess we never actually discussed it, so I could be."

Okay, TV off. I was not awake enough for this conversation as it was. "Yeah, it would seem we have a thing, but I don't know what that thing is. And whatever it is, it's not an exclusive thing."

"It's not?"

"How could it be?" I got off the sofa, too irritated to continue sitting. "It can't be an exclusive thing as you like to make clear all the time. At the very least you have to have your addicts. If you can do that, I don't see why I can't go out on a date if I want."

He looked at me like I'd lost my mind, and unlike Andre's look, it wasn't endearing. "It's not the same thing. At all."

"No? I'm failing to understand here. You can screw whoever you like, and that's okay. But I can't even go out for drinks with someone without you suddenly acting like a harpy's addict?"

"Sex is different." He rested his head in his hands, then sighed a sigh that suggested he thought I was being obtuse on purpose. "Look, Jess, I don't care if you want to get naked with your coworker. Hell, I don't care if you fuck every guy on the Red Sox. What I care about, despite my better sense and Dezzi's lectures, is you. Going on dates suggests you're willing to get emotionally and romantically attached to other people. That's what I don't want."

"Emotional attachment." I guessed now was not the time to bring up wanting a normal relationship. Not unless I really was in the mood to deal with explosions. Which I wasn't. "So I have to put up with you and your addicts, which bothers me but is normal for you, but I'm not allowed to do anything that's normal for me."

Lucen closed his eyes. "Why is it so wrong to not want you forming emotional attachments to people who would not be okay with our relationship and who will try to take you away from me?"

"Because I feel like there's a double standard here."

"It's not. That's what you need to get over. The only one acting like a harpy's addict is you. I'm a satyr. I feed on sex to live, and it can't just be with you even if you were my addict. You need to stop seeing my addicts as some kind of betrayal."

"The mere fact that you have addicts is a betrayal. Not to me, but to my race. Just thinking about what you and your people do to humans makes me ill. So I try very hard not to." I fell back onto the sofa, helpless tears stinging my eyes as I held them in. I'd known this couldn't work for long, hadn't I? But it seemed like it was falling apart faster and faster these days. "I'm not like you, and sometimes I want to be normal. To have normal things."

Lucen put a hand on my knee. "You need to stop trying to be normal for a human, little siren. Because you aren't."

"Thanks for the reminder."

Lucen stood, his face haggard. Funny, because all the misery this conversation had induced left me wired. More proof, as he said, that I wasn't normal. "We can talk more later."

I nodded and he left. Later was only putting off the inevitable—the collapse of whatever thing I had with Lucen. The ruin of any façade of normal I put on in front of Andre and the Gryphons.

The end of hoping I could ever be anything but a freak.

TWENTY

I ATE MY CHOCOLATE CROISSANT ALONE THE NEXT MORNING while Lucen slept. Never had I been so glad for an impulsive purchase. I was sore and anxious from last night's conversation, had slept badly because of it, and therefore needed chocolate with my coffee.

Since I didn't have to go into work, I caught up on chores, doing my best to stay busy so I had less time to dwell on my negativity. I got home from food shopping around three to find Lucen in the kitchen eating the other croissant. The Lair was closed today, so I didn't know what his plans were. Torturing me with another conversation seemed likely.

"Can I?" I pointed to the coffeepot, which had another mug's worth left in it.

He nodded and set down his phone. "Dezzi stopped by last night after I returned to work."

Yup, here came the metaphorical hot pokers. She probably told him to kick me out of his apartment, among other things. "And?"

"She likes your new theory about the murder victims." Lucen waited for me to acknowledge his comment as I poured the coffee. I did, after my surprise wore off. "Devon mentioned it to her," he explained.

"Ah. Of course she likes it."

Lucen broke up the last of his croissant. "It's more complicated than what you're thinking. But the good news for you is that Dezzi is willing to believe someone might have it in for the F maker. Your theory, if correct, could indicate that."

"I suppose it could. Why would someone have it in for this person though?"

"Long story. I'll have to fill you in on some of the details before you meet with her, but Dezzi is going to allow it."

I set my mug down sharply, and it made an unpleasant racket against the granite counter. "I get to meet this mysterious person at long last?"

"With precautions taken, yes."

"Precautions meaning?"

Lucen put his empty mug in the dishwasher and gave me a sideways glance. "Dezzi's going to want to put a compulsion on you so you can't share what goes on."

"Great, so if I learn anything useful, it's actually still useless."

"Not necessarily. Dezzi can create some pretty clever spells. It is why she's Dom. On the other hand..." He appraised me. "You're apparently capable of breaking some strong compulsions. But if Dezzi's willing to risk it, that's her decision."

I sipped my coffee, watching him head into the living room. "Talking to Devon again, were you?"

He glanced at me over his shoulder, his eyes twinkling. Considering our conversation last night, he was in a surprisingly good mood. "Your ability to get by his wards was impressive. Not to mention completely unheard of. I thought they must have gotten weak for you to slip past at Purgatory that time, but he just reworked them with Lucrezia and he said no. Devon is no slacker himself when it comes to creating wards and compulsions. His skills are good enough he could be a Dom. Probably should be by now."

Cradling my coffee mug, I followed Lucen into the living room. "Really? So why isn't he? Who decides these things anyway?" I was curious, but more than that—I wanted to change the topic.

"The Upper Council." Lucen took Sweetpea's harness down. "They're the ones who decide how many new people we're allowed to turn, and when or if to set up a new domus in an area."

I leaned against the fireplace, digesting this. "So if this council decided they wanted to establish a satyr domus in, I don't know, my hometown back in New Hampshire, they'd pick a Dom from a high-ranking satyr in an established group?"

"Basically."

"So if Devon's overdue, why hasn't he gotten asked yet?"

Lucen adjusted his gloves and opened Sweetpea's cage. The dragon made a mad dash to get by, but he was no match. Lucen stayed silent a minute, wrestling his scaly pet into its harness. "There's not a lot of new groups forming these days. We need to be near humans, remember? And while the human population is increasing, the Upper Council is picky about locations."

"So that must be frustrating for Devon, right? To have all that power but be stuck?"

"You'll have to ask Devon yourself."

"Yeah, I think I'll take a pass on that."

I stayed behind while Lucen took Sweetpea for his walk. Pleased as I was that our first conversation of the day hadn't resulted in resuming last night's discussion, I saw no need to risk it. Besides, Lucen had given me a few things to consider. I should be prepared to talk to the F maker today.

THEY WERE COMING BY AROUND SEVEN—DEZZI AND THE mystery woman. As usual, The Lair was serving as the satyrs' unofficial meeting space.

"Things you need to know about Dezzi and Angelia," Lucen said. We were back in his kitchen, waiting for the call that would tell us they'd arrived. I wouldn't be permitted in the bar until Dezzi had worked her mojo on me.

"That's her name—Angelia?" Seemed ironic for a creature once considered a demon by most people.

"Yes." Lucen sounded utterly serious and oblivious to the irony, so I forced the smirk off my face. "She and Dezzi go way back, and Dezzi is very protective of her."

I checked the clock. "Dezzi seems very protective of all of you."

"She's supposed to be, but Angelia more so. Like I said, they go way back. And Angelia, well, you'll see." He tapped his phone on the table, seemingly twitchy. "Angelia's blind. That's why."

I had to take a few seconds to think about this. "I've never seen a satyr with any kind of disability before." Nor, when I considered it, any pred.

The sorts of physical or cognitive ailments that humans had to contend with were, as far as I knew, unheard of in preds. Sure, I'd seen some goblins and certainly some furies sporting pretty bad battle scars, but this was altogether different. Their own magic protected them from most injuries, meaning it took a nasty curse—or a salamander fire-forged blade —to truly hurt or disfigure them permanently.

Lucen shifted uneasily in his chair. "She wasn't born that way, and if she'd lost her sight while human, she'd never have been turned. All I know of the story is that Angelia was attacked by a bunch of humans many years ago. She's a very gentle person. She probably wasn't armed, and there were too many for her to subdue with her magic. The humans had a knife like yours. They used it on her. They took her eyes."

I put my hand over my mouth. "Oh, God. That's awful." Pred or not, no one deserved that.

"Yeah." Lucen seemed to realize he was playing with his phone and stopped. "Her domus healed her before she died of her wounds, but her vision obviously couldn't be restored. And since that made her defective, once she'd healed as best she could, her Dom let her go."

My fingers curled into a ball. "Wait? Defective? Let her go?"

"It's not a word I use lightly, and it's not the word I'd use myself, but it's the word that gets used by others. There's a strong bias among satyrs and sylphs for physical perfection." Lucen made an apologetic face. "It's not always nice. Without her sight, and with her empty eye sockets, Angelia didn't fit what a satyr was supposed to be. Her Dom was within his rights to kick her out. It happens, and as a result Angelia became a lone satyr, or she was until Dezzi found out what happened and took her in."

"And you're okay with that?"

"With Dezzi taking her in or with her old Dom kicking her out?"

"Either. You're way too 'whatever' about all of this. Like it's no big deal that she got kicked out of her home for being wounded and disabled."

"I like Angelia. I'm glad she's here."

Which didn't exactly answer my question, so I continued to stare at him.

Lucen got up. "Things change for you when you change, Jess. On the inside and the outside. And no one tells you most of the risks. I accept certain things as normal."

I started to ask why no one explained how screwed up pred society must be and what he meant by "change," but his phone finally buzzed. "They're here. Be right back."

Convenient. One day I would have to ask Lucen how he became a satyr and why, and the hundred other uncomfortable questions that I didn't even know enough about to form yet. But not while things were so shaky between us.

And while I had more pressing issues to ponder.

I drummed my nails against the table. So Dezzi had taken in a physically "defective" satyr, which was apparently some sort of satyr taboo. My first thought was this made me like satyrs less than I already did, which was sad because I still disliked them the least of all the pred races. But on the other hand, I respected Dezzi more.

My second thought was I now understood why Dezzi figured it was possible for someone to have it in for Angelia. One of the Boston satyrs didn't care to have an imperfect satyr in their domus and was trying to frame her for murder. Perhaps it was a touch farfetched, but I'd been framed for murder for a far more batshit idea.

I tucked these musings away as the sound of footsteps coming up the back stairs grew louder. Lucen opened the door with Dezzi following behind him.

The satyr's Dom took a deep breath when she saw me. I hadn't spoken yet and she was weary. Peachy. "My number three has explained my generosity in allowing this conversation?"

Number three meant Lucen. Generosity meant what—her self-interest?

Still, there was only one answer if I wanted to talk to Angelia. "Yes.

But if I learn anything useful from Angelia, I need to be able to follow up on it."

Dezzi closed her eyes briefly, giving me a good view of her long, thick lashes. "You will follow up with me. Together we will decide what you can share with the Gryphons. Fair?"

"Enough." In theory anyway. I suspected there'd be a whole lot less of me and a whole lot more of Dezzi going into that decision.

But with that agreed upon, it didn't take Dezzi long to put a compulsion spell on me. I didn't even know she'd started until she pronounced it done.

"That's it?"

"That is it." Dezzi whipped out her phone, typing as she wandered to the door. "You're free to talk about whatever here. I have a meeting with the harpies."

Lucen gestured for me to follow, and we made our way down to The Lair. Dezzi left after a quick word to the three people in the bar's main room. Two of them appeared to be on some sort of guard duty. For Angelia, I assumed. They reminded me of the satyrs Dezzi had assigned to watch over me when the sylphs had been out for my blood.

That left the third person to be Angelia. She sat at a central table, her legs delicately crossed, her head turned in my direction. Despite not being able to see me, she could sense my emotions—and hence my presence—as well as any pred. And my emotions were, well, surprised.

Angelia's silky brown hair spilled down her shoulders in loose curls, her lips were a perfect bow, and her body was what you might call a pinnacle of feminine perfection. Soft, slim, and extremely curvy. She was Aphrodite personified, or satyr-ified, given her horns.

It boggled the mind to imagine that someone could consider her imperfect, although the evidence of her physical suffering was clear. Angelia wore a satiny black scarf tied around her head over where her eyes should be. Yet even that looked like a carefully chosen accessory, designed to be as seductive as it was practical. She could have been a model on one of Val's erotic romance novels.

Eh, satyrs. Everything was about seduction.

Lucen introduced us, and as if they'd been waiting for the cue, the two brawny satyrs with Angelia strolled outside. Apparently they weren't permitted to take part in the conversation.

Angelia held out her hands to me, beaming a smile that was the stuff of an adolescent boy's wet dreams. "So you're the mysterious human woman with a satyr's power I've heard so much about. I'm thrilled to finally meet you."

I had to stifle a laugh since I'd kept thinking of Angelia as the mysterious F maker. All at once, and in spite of everything that had led me here, I took a liking to her. "People seem to be talking about me a lot. I feel famous." I cast a wry glance at Lucen.

"Infamous," he retorted.

"You certainly intrigue people," Angelia said. Her hands remained extended, so although I usually tried to avoid touching preds—even my new immunity was weakened through direct skin contact with their magic —I took them.

Immediately, I was overwhelmed by the hyacinth scent of Angelia's pheromones. The flowery fragrance was almost too much as she clasped my hands. Her skin was as smooth as it looked, and my burnt-out, magic-detecting nerve endings were pleasantly awakened by her touch.

Despite Lucen's nearby presence, I found myself wondering if her full lips were as soft to kiss as they appeared.

Next to her, Lucen smirked, sensing my desire.

I dropped my hands back to my sides quickly when Angelia released them, and was pleased my body returned to normal. No offense to Angelia, but since Devon's magic was starting to have an effect on me, I was growing worried that my immunity was wearing off. There was no way I'd want to rent an apartment in Shadowtown if it were.

Angelia brushed her hair behind her neck. "You have to believe me. I have nothing to do with those deaths. I think it's awful. Violence and murder…" She shuddered. "I'm sure you don't approve of what I do, but I make F because it's about pleasure and sensuality and enjoyment. It's the opposite of what someone is using it for."

I chewed on my lip. I didn't know if it was because of what Lucen had told me about Angelia's past, or if I just wanted my own theory about the glyph to be correct, but I believed her. Hell, if she were lying, she was the best actress I'd ever met. Everything about her, from her figure to her sweetly sultry voice, screamed, *I am the opposite of violence.*

That said, I couldn't let her protests stand without challenge. "The murders aside, you do realize how often F is used to commit rape?"

She sighed. "I'm aware of it. Actually, I've been tinkering with ways to adjust the magic, to make it impossible to use my version that way."

"You've been changing the spell around?"

Angelia seized on the implication. "Yes, but I haven't sold any of the altered version. It's purely experimental so far. It couldn't be what's caused these deaths."

Maybe or maybe not. I wished I'd been allowed to take notes. "Dezzi mentioned you might have enemies."

"No. I used to have many, but not anymore. They're all dead by now or far away." She waved her hand carelessly.

I wasn't sure how to bring up what Lucen had told me without sounding totally crass, so I turned toward him for help.

In response, he grimaced. "Dezzi suggested some people might not have appreciated her bringing you here."

"Oh, yes. Naturally. You mean because of this." Angelia touched her blindfold. "I'm sure that's true, but no one's said anything about it to me. It would be particularly stupid of them to openly challenge Dezzi's decisions."

"What if they weren't up for openly challenging them?" I asked. "How hard is it to make F? Could someone be trying to set you up?"

Angelia traced a finger over her pink lips in thought. "It's not especially hard, but there would be differences in the magical signatures between my F and someone else's F. You could figure it out."

"We could if we had enough of the killer F to run analyses on, but I'll keep that in mind." I stretched out in my chair, getting antsy. "Could any of your dealers be tampering with it?"

"No, not my ladies." Angelia's voice was firm. "But to be sure, I questioned them all when this first came to light. I'd know if they were lying. I can't say it doesn't happen farther down the line, after it leaves their hands. It could always be resold. I've told Dezzi that."

"Your ladies? They're all addicts?"

"Naturally."

Naturally. Andre had told me they would be.

I took out my phone. Friday, after I'd met with Devon, it had occurred to me to ask whether anyone had gotten a photograph of the mark—or glyph—on the Wonderland victims' legs.

Yesterday, Andre had sent me one, along with a note informing me that the real mark on the victim's leg had vanished. It was both good and bad news. It bolstered my theory that the glyph was related to the murders since glyphs didn't typically disappear so quickly. But as a result, this photo was now all we had as evidence of its existence.

I brought up the photo on my phone to show Angelia, then realized my colossal mistake. Embarrassed, I handed the phone to Lucen instead since he hadn't seen it yet. "I'm sure Dezzi told you my theory about how there might be more to this than tainted F. Do you recognize this mark?"

Lucen inspected the photo. "That could be something to do with endurance or perseverance. But it's heavily mixed with other glyphs."

"Devon said endurance too. Confirmation is good."

"Someone else's magic is tampering with my F?" Angelia crossed her arms. She sounded indignant. "Show me the glyph."

I hesitated, unsure what to say or do, but Lucen understood. Angelia held out her palm, and he drew the glyph on her with his finger. Clever, but it turned out not to be so helpful. Angelia was as perplexed as the rest of us.

I asked a few more questions, probing for theories on whether tampering with the F could work that way or who might have the skills and the means to do it, but I came up short on anything I could work with. Angelia's information was enlightening and potentially useful in the long run, but it didn't give me much to go on. If I could share it all with Andre, he might have ideas...but I couldn't.

"Lucen?" Angelia twirled a curl around her finger. "Would you let me talk to Jess alone for a minute?"

Lucen raised his eyebrows in surprise. "I suppose I could. I'll be upstairs."

Watching him leave, I wondered what was on Angelia's mind that she didn't want to share it in front of him.

Angelia was silent until the door shut. "You like him a lot. I can sense it in you."

I pulled my knees in, hoping she also sensed how uncomfortable it made me to have my emotions blasted to all and sundry. "Yeah, most of the time."

"He cares a lot about you."

What was all this satyr interest in my relationship with Lucen about? First Devon, which was weird but at least understandable since he was Lucen's friend. Now Angelia who I'd met only ten minutes ago? "This can't be what you wanted to talk to me about."

"Actually it is."

"Seriously?"

"When you mentioned this—" Angelia pointed to her blindfold, "—and brought up Dezzi taking me in, it made me think. You're absolutely right that there are probably satyrs around here who don't approve of what she did. But Dezzi is special and amazing, and she cares about me and was willing to risk the turmoil bringing me here might have caused." Angelia's voice was sweet and wistful. She talked like a woman in love.

Like *any* woman in love, and in that moment she struck me as more human than not. I'd never heard a satyr—or any pred—speak in such a voice. Lucen told me he cared about me, and he always sounded sincere, but cared was the extent of it. I wasn't sure he was capable of anything more. Until recently, I hadn't been entirely convinced he was capable of that much.

"I'm telling you this…" Angelia leaned forward, her voice hushed, "… because I want you to accept that we can feel very deeply. I'm not sure you believe it because it's a side of us you'd never usually see. But what Lucen feels for you—I can't say I see it in his face or sense it in his emotions— but it's in his actions. This relationship he has with you—it's a risk. It's like Dezzi taking me in. You're different than most humans, but you're not one of us. There are satyrs who I'm sure don't approve, or wouldn't if they knew. Dezzi allows it because she knows, because of me."

Angelia's speech left me bereft of words. Some of what she said, about Dezzi's approval of our relationship mattering, I'd already suspected. But mostly, Angelia caught me off guard.

I picked through my thoughts, searching for something to say, but it was useless. So I said nothing. Let Angelia discern the intricacies of my emotions. She was probably better at it. I spent too much time denying them.

Angelia smiled. "I stunned you. It's okay. And I'm talking out of turn. It's not my business. I just wanted to let you know we can form strong bonds. So just because you don't understand Lucen, don't assume he's incapable of it." She patted my hand, and this time I was so out of it I didn't feel the fragrant lust.

"I appreciate the lecture," I finally managed. "I think."

"Good." She got up perkily as if my comment had made her day. "I should go. Do let me know if I can help. I don't want any more people to die."

My head didn't feel stuck on correctly as I stood too. "Thanks. That makes two of us."

Angelia left, and through The Lair's window I could see the shadowy figures of her bodyguards leaving with her. Slowly, I climbed the stairs to Lucen's apartment. I'd been doing fine until Angelia decided to play relationship counselor. Now I felt like I knew less about everything than I had when I started the day.

TWENTY-ONE

Monday afternoon our investigation team had another meeting with Brian. Entering the conference room, I gripped my coffee chest-high as though it were a shield. Although I was convinced of Angelia's innocence, I didn't need a magi's clairvoyance to foresee that convincing anyone else was not going to go over well.

"So." Brian bustled in the room and dropped a file on the table. "What's new?"

Andre went first. He'd been busy without me, tracking down leads, searching for connections between the victims, trying to find out if the latest victims had ever been to Purgatory. When he got to the part about my theory on the glyph, I tightened my grip on my coffee cup.

Andre tucked his pen behind his ear, an especially dorky look on a guy who was built like a professional athlete. "I've asked around, but no one can identify the mark or say positively what combination of glyphs it might be. If it is glyphs, at all."

I forced my fingers to relax before I crushed my cup. "I showed it to a couple magically skilled satyrs, and they both suggested endurance might be part of it, which fits with how the victims died."

Brian frowned at me. "You showed it to satyrs? Why?"

"Well, it made sense to me that if someone was drawing glyphs on people that either killed them directly or worked in concert with F, they might know something useful. It might also mean someone is trying to set them up and make them—or the F maker—look like a murderer."

"What did they say to that?" Andre asked.

"They liked the idea."

Brian snorted. "Of course they did. Did you learn anything useful since you're sharing things you really shouldn't be sharing?"

I shouldn't have been sharing? It would be nice if someone told me this crap. But I bit my tongue because arguing I'd been blackmailed into this job without being given sufficient training wasn't going to get me anywhere. I needed their buy-in on my theory so I had to play nice. "I think there's a good possibility that my theory is exactly what's happening —someone is trying to frame the F maker. I don't think she's intentionally putting out tainted F."

"She?" Two pairs of eyebrows shot upward, and my own rose with them. I hadn't realized just how little they knew.

"You got a name?" Brian asked.

My jaw clenched beyond my control. "Yes."

"And?"

"I can't tell you. Dezzi allowed me to talk to her only after she put a compulsion on me."

As expected, what Dezzi had decided I could share with the Gryphons was not much, and my rational arguments for greater leeway had been shot down. "Tell them your theory first and see what they say," she'd told me. "We can release details as they need to know."

I'd argued that it wouldn't work. Sometimes getting to say I told you so was not worth the gloating.

Brian swore, but Andre chuckled in some sort of amused annoyance. "Of course she did. Dezzi's no fool."

"Fine." Brian raised his hands in defeat. "This person's convinced you she's innocent and someone might want to frame her. Why?"

I took a deep breath, not sure how much of my response would come out. "She might have enemies among the satyrs."

To Brian's increasing frustration and Andre's decreasing humor, I couldn't answer their questions about the reason for those enemies in much detail.

"Look." I shoved my coffee cup aside. "Dezzi is willing to admit there might be satyr involvement here. This is big. She's been trying to protect her F maker. If we follow up on this, we could have her cooperation. Doesn't that mean something?"

"It means shit, Jess." Brian stood up, apparently so he could glare down at me. "It's a cute theory. Maybe Dezzi buys it, maybe she doesn't. I can think of a lot of reasons she might be willing to go along with it, including to sacrifice a satyr who's gotten on her nerves, someone she'd like to kick out anyway. Then she can do what Doms always prefer to do—handle the real problem themselves. She'll cover it up and dole out her own so-called punishments, and the real culprit will never see justice for what they did."

Beneath the table, I dug my nails into my palms. "There are legit reasons to think someone might have it in for…" I tripped over Angelia's name, "…the F maker."

"So you say." Brian shook his head. "It's not good enough. I need to know the motive if nothing else. We all need to know it so we can consider it. If you can't share it with me, then all I've got is your word, or the word of some satyrs, and a symbol that may or may not be a glyph. There's nothing we can act on. Unless you bring me back something to lend credence to this—frankly outlandish—theory, then it's a nonstarter. Get me a motive or I can't take it seriously."

I dropped my head to the table. Well, that went about as well I'd warned Dezzi it would.

My day didn't improve after the meeting broke up. I was back to work with Andre, helping him gather information about the Wonderland victims. It was dreary and dull, and made all the more so because I didn't believe it was actually getting us any closer to solving the case.

For his part, Andre wasn't unsympathetic to my theory. But on a practical level, he agreed with Brian. Me vouching for the F maker's innocence and suspicion about enemies was nothing they could use.

"Get us a motive," he said, echoing Brian. "If we have a motive, we can find suspects. If we can find suspects, we can bring them in for questioning."

Unfortunately, I had a motive, but it was vague and I couldn't share it unless Dezzi gave me permission and lifted that part of the compulsion. I'd send her a message, but I wasn't hopeful. Alas, this just meant if anyone was going to follow up and try to uncover who might have it in for Angelia, it would have to be me and it would have to be on my free time since I wasn't permitted to chase "frankly outlandish" theories on the Gryphons' dime.

On Wednesday, things got weirder. I was packing up after another pointless day spent with the unpleasant task of talking to friends of the deceased, and a slightly less unpleasant task of learning about magical blood analyses from Anna, when Tom appeared at my cube.

"I don't suppose you remember our conversation from the weekend?" he asked.

No, I didn't, and I stuck my water bottle in my bag unconcerned about it. "Conversation?"

"At the pub."

Oh, that. I hadn't thought we'd talked long enough to consider it a conversation. "Yes, I remember. What's up?"

"Just that I hear you're pronouncing the satyrs innocent of the recent string of F-related deaths. True?"

My computer finished shutting down, so I swung my bag onto my shoulder. Tom wasn't part of what I was getting paid to do. I felt no need to hang around late because he wanted to be creepy and invasive. "Not quite. I don't think the F is tainted. That's all."

"But you're willing to trust the satyrs." He started toward the elevator with me.

"I'm trusting my own judgment. How do you know so much about this case anyway? Don't you have furies to investigate?"

"With preds, more is connected than you might imagine. I thought perhaps you needed another reminder that it's unwise to put your faith in the satyrs, regardless of your friendships."

I jabbed the elevator button. "I don't have faith in anything or anyone. But if I need a life coach, I'll find you. I know what I'm doing."

"I hope so."

Smug, condescending, nosy, paranoid bastard. I hopped into the elevator without a word. When I got the chance, I should totally take a second peek around his office. Just on the principle that he pissed me off, and I wanted to be as nosy right back.

But not tonight. Having finally gotten to do my exchange with Rik, I had plans to meet with Bee and finish our deal. It had dragged on long enough, and I was sure I wasn't the only person eager to complete the transaction.

I met her at the amphitheater again, after stopping at home to pick up my knife and my scarf. Traces of blue still streaked across the sky as I sat on a bench looking out onto the Charles. Normally I waited until full dark for this sort of business, but I'd been forced to wake up early the last couple days, and I needed to continue my questioning in Shadowtown later. I couldn't keep nocturnal hours.

With my hair wrapped in a scarf and sunglasses covering my eyes, I felt comfortable enough. Besides, all I had to do was tell Bee it was done, accept some money, and be gone. It was my last deal, and I'd no longer have evidence of me doing anything illegal.

I should have known something would go wrong.

I waved to Bee when I saw her, and she approached cautiously at first. I had to pat the bench to get her to sit. She was dressed much like last time—leggings, ballet flats, an unflattering dress. It was so not my style, but nonetheless I felt very mannish next to her in my jeans and sneakers.

"Is it done?" she whispered.

I handed her the piece of tape with her name on it. "It's done."

"Oh, my God." The tape trembled, stuck to her fingers.

Then she burst into tears.

Dragon shit on toast. I did not do well with crying. All I wanted was to get my money and get out of here, go to The Lair, and continue my private investigation of Angelia's potential enemies. Yet even I had the social graces not to ask a crying woman to discuss payment.

Not immediately anyway. So I sat there uncomfortably until she collected herself, trying not to fidget.

"You have no idea…" She gazed at the tape like it was a thing of magic, then tore it into pieces. "I haven't been able to sleep or eat."

Given how tiny she already was, that couldn't be healthy. "Well, it's over, and you'll never do that again, so lesson learned."

Bee moaned. "But it's not over. I have to live with myself, knowing what I did. I'm an awful human being."

Oh, brother. I was glad for the sunglasses because she couldn't see me roll my eyes. "Look, you feel bad. Trust me when I say that puts you ahead of ninety percent of the people who have been in your situation. Awfulness is relative. You got jealous, you cursed a rival. It happens."

"But she was innocent. She's not even a rival. I don't dislike her and I did this anyway." Bee pulled out a tissue and sniffed into it.

"Wait, I thought you cursed another dancer who was your director's undeserved favorite?"

She crumpled the tissue. "I did, but it wasn't because I hate her. It was because I hate *him*. I wanted her to screw up her big performance and teach him a lesson. He knows she's not as good, but he favors her because he wants her to sleep with him."

I propped my elbows on my knees, contemplating. "So you cursed the dancer to take down the director instead of cursing him directly. Why not curse him directly?"

"Because I wanted to humiliate him, not hurt him. I thought it would serve him right to have to answer for her failure. I wanted to be there for it, to watch him squirm when the Board confronted him. I hoped they'd fire him." The venom in her voice suggested her guilt didn't extend as far as the director's well-being.

"That's actually kind of brilliant. No one would suspect you had something against the dancer because you get along, so if someone got suspicious about a curse, it wouldn't be as likely to get traced back to you. They wouldn't see who your real target was. They'd assume the curse was planted by a jealous rival and miss the real motive entirely."

Bee's eyes widened. "I never thought of that."

I snapped my jaw shut, realizing I'd been rambling. "Probably not, but it gives me an idea. You've been very helpful."

"I have?"

"Yup." I bounded up, my urge to get back to Shadowtown twice as strong. "Let's call that your fee. That, and no more cursing if you can't live with the consequences because I'm officially no longer in the soul-swapping business."

"Oh?" Bee gasped, her tissue clasped to her mouth.

I have no idea how long she gawked at me because I was off and running to the nearest T stop. I needed to have a conversation with Lucen stat.

TWENTY-TWO

MISERY'S SHEATH SMACKED MY THIGH AS I JOGGED DOWN THE street to The Lair. Cursing, I shifted it to a better position. If only it weren't so practical to carry a knife around. I missed my old life, the one that didn't make me feel vulnerable when I was unarmed.

Only a couple satyrs sat outside The Lair, smoking nasty-smelling cigars. I hurried by, trying not to breathe. As I entered the bar, Aerosmith greeted my ears, and it occurred to me that I hadn't noticed the background music in a long time. Usually it was too crowded.

Too bad it wasn't tonight. I preferred the cover all those extra voices provided.

I took my favorite stool at the far end, two seats down from a couple harpies. Fortunately, they were deep in their own conversation and didn't pay me any mind. Paulius appeared in front of me a moment later.

I ordered coffee and asked him to turn one of the TVs to the Sox game. They were playing in Seattle, so it was just about to start. "Where's Lucen?"

"Taking a break. I'm guessing he'll be down soon once he realizes you're here."

I took a large sip and burnt my tongue. "Do my emotions really stand out that much?"

Paulius chuckled. "Not to me. You're just another human."

"So how come Lucen can pick me out of a crowd? Devon too?" I added, remembering that he'd been able to recognize me through various disguise charms.

Paulius took his time answering but seemed to be giving it some thought. He kept an eye on me as he refilled drinks for the harpies. "Could be a few reasons," he said when he returned. He rested his arms on the bar, leaning in close. "Lucen and Devon have a lot of power. They might be better at that sort of thing. Or it might be because they've spent a lot of time with you."

"I've hardly spent a lot of time with Devon."

The bartender grinned. "Then it could also be because they both like you. We notice things about the people we like that we don't notice about others."

Paulius got called away, leaving me to ponder. His first explanation sounded the most likely. For Devon anyway. I supposed any of them could apply to Lucen.

As predicted, he entered the bar soon after my conversation with Paulius ended. "Any more luck convincing the Gryphons?"

"Nope. But I had a meeting with my client before I came here, and she inadvertently gave me an idea." I lowered my voice. "What if Angelia isn't the target? I mean, what if someone's trying to frame her, but it's nothing personal? What if Dezzi is the real target?"

Lucen stole a sip of my coffee. "How would that work?"

I explained my client's twisted motive for buying a curse. "If someone has a grudge against Dezzi and knows she's close to Angelia, maybe they'd go after Angelia to hurt her? Dezzi's a Dom. It would take a lot of power or some serious balls to make a direct play at her."

"True. It would be hard to hurt Dezzi, but then why bother framing Angelia? Why not just kill her?"

"I don't know."

Lucen started to say something else, but someone behind me caught his attention. I twisted around in my seat and saw Devon and Lucrezia weaving through the tables. Devon grabbed an empty booth, but Lucrezia came our way.

"Lucen, can you send our usuals over, then join us a moment? Devon and I would like to have a brief meeting." She absently spun a silver bracelet around her wrist as she eyed me. "Here again, pet? You're always underfoot these days."

"Better get used to it. I'm moving in down the street." I'd gotten the message from the landlord on my way to The Lair. He'd approved me for the apartment.

Lucrezia's red lips parted in surprise. "We're letting Gryphons move in? This neighborhood is really going downhill. No offense, pet."

"Yeah, I'm sure you meant none. And I'm not a Gryphon."

Lucrezia didn't look convinced, and she returned to Devon. Lucen, however, slid an arm around me. "This is a good thing for us, right?"

I nodded since it was impossible to hide my anxiety. Not living with Lucen meant not seeing his addicts. Not seeing his addicts meant I could ignore the problem.

Now was that the best way to handle things? Undoubtedly not. It would have to do, though, until we had a better solution or until I could face the possibility of breaking up.

When I thought about it, I also thought about what Angelia had told me. If Lucen was taking such risks to be with me, I owed it to him—to us—to find another way. I just didn't know what would make me okay with everything.

Lucen wandered over to Devon and Lucrezia, and I drank my coffee, watched the game, and considered his very valid question about my new theory. A small mirror behind the bar advertised vodka, and every now and then I caught their table in the reflection.

So this was Dezzi's inner triad. I couldn't hear their conversation, but Lucrezia, I was pleased to note, acted as haughty with the men as she did with me. Still, she had to be pretty damn powerful to have made the group. They all had to be, and yet there was so little I knew about any of them. Even Lucen. Maybe that was where I needed to start with our relationship. Talk to him. Really talk to him. Not about the superficial topics or work-related crap like we usually did, but about his past and about the things that mattered.

In other words, all those topics he frequently tried to avoid even as he teased me for my ignorance about his life and what it meant to be a satyr.

We could start too, by him explaining how powerful he really was and what the point of the triad was versus the entire council. I was sick of living in the dark. How many addicts did he have? How had he gotten on Dezzi's council? Did he want to be a Dom someday?"

Huh. Did he want to be a Dom?

I pressed my fingertips together, replaying the question in my head. Lucen was only a third. High-ranking, but he had a ways to go. But what about Devon?

A light clicked on in my brain. I pulled my phone out so I could make some notes as I worked through this idea.

Lucen returned a few minutes later, and I put the phone away. "Everything okay?"

"Oh yeah, you know." He shrugged, but didn't look happy. "Satyr business. You're excited about something."

"I had a thought about your question."

"Yeah? So did I." He grabbed the stool next to me. "You might be onto something. Doms have a lot of enemies, and we in particular have a lot of enemies at the moment because of what happened with Victor. Something is going on within the furies—that's what we were meeting about. It's something big, but no one knows what. Plus, we've got the sylphs seriously pissed off for related reasons. But if this is about revenge on us—either to get to Dezzi or to make us all look bad—then it's going to be a lot of work to track down who's responsible."

I lowered my head because Devon and Lucrezia were still here. "True, and that would be bad. But I had a different thought that might be easier to investigate. What if the threat to Dezzi is internal?"

Lucen looked at me askew. "If it's an internal threat, little siren, I think it's more likely someone's after Angelia. Your original theory."

"But this someone could have both. Maybe Angelia is the cause and the means."

"Explain."

I braced myself for inevitable objections. "It sounds like Dezzi might be making some decisions that aren't popular. She lets Angelia in. She backs you when you put me under your protection during the Victor shit. She gives the okay for me to move in although I'm consulting for the Gryphons. Someone might think she's making all the satyrs appear weak."

"It's possible." The lines around his eyes suggested it was more. He'd probably heard grumblings of the sort.

"Okay, so our murderer goes after Angelia for two reasons. One, if she's framed and arrested or killed as a result, then one of the image problems you have is removed. Two, her alleged guilt reflects badly on Dezzi. Killing Angelia wouldn't have that effect. But framing her—now Dezzi didn't just let a damaged satyr into your group. She let in a damaged satyr who turned out to be a murderer. Bad, incompetent Dezzi. At that point, could she lose her position as Dom?"

Lucen exhaled heavily. "The Upper Council would probably take note, yeah, especially if someone here petitioned them to do so. It wouldn't be good for her. Where are you going with this? You have someone in mind. I can tell."

I clamped my mouth shut as I saw the very person I was thinking of approach in the mirror.

"Lucrezia's going to drive me mad one day." Devon dropped his glass off at the bar. "I'm going to work so I can have some peace and quiet."

"I thought the club was closed tonight," Lucen said.

"It is, hence the peace and quiet. Plus, I've got stuff to do." Devon winked at me. "How come you don't stop by my bar this often, Jess?"

I forced a smile. "Too many wards."

"Funny, I didn't think they bothered you." With that, he left.

From the corner of my eye, I caught Lucrezia watching him. Her typical sour face was unusually contemplative. "Devon," I said to Lucen.

"What about him?"

I played with my empty beer glass. Saying his name aloud made my mouth dry. I guessed some part of me had liked him because I felt sad accusing him. "That's who I have in mind for being behind everything."

"No way."

I grabbed his wrist to prevent him from leaving so fast. "Think about it. Devon owns Purgatory. We can tie two of the three sets of victims there. It's a major hangout for people buying and selling F, and people get temporary charms there all the time—a fact he very conveniently forgot to mention when I asked him about the glyph—and therefore it would be real easy for him to draw a curse on someone instead."

"Lots of satyrs go to Purgatory, little siren."

"But not lots of satyrs stand to directly benefit if Dezzi is no longer Dom. You're the one who told me Devon is as powerful as she is, and that he's overdue for his own domus. Wouldn't he step into her place if she got booted?"

Lucen removed himself from my grasp and walked to the other side of the bar. He set two shot glasses down and poured us each a drink. "He would, but you're going down the wrong path. I promise you."

"How can you be sure?"

"Because Devon is extremely loyal to Dezzi. She's the one who turned him. When Dezzi was promoted to take over the Boston domus, he followed her all the way from England. There's no way."

I downed the drink, hoping it would relax my stomach. "People's loyalties change. The more you trust and respect someone, the more deeply you might feel their betrayal if they start doing things that you believe are wrong."

"Not this, Jess. You have some good ideas, but this... I don't buy it."

I sighed. Of course he didn't. Devon was his friend, and Lucen was also loyal. But I knew someone who would hear me out. Someone with whom I finally had a theory and a motive that I could share. "Okay, fine. But I think I'm onto something. I need some fresh air and a walk so I can think more."

Lucen kissed my hand. "Be careful."

"Always." I patted my knife, but I had a feeling his comment was in reference to what I was pondering, not where I was going.

WHEN I STEPPED OUTSIDE, THE CIGAR-SMOKERS HAD GONE. Thank dragons for fresh air. I paused on the steps to street level, getting out my phone, and was passed by Lucrezia who was doing the same. She murmured "Underfoot" as she walked around me.

I murmured "Bitch" back.

Andre picked up on the third ring, and I leaned against a lamppost about fifty feet from The Lair. A couple pred restaurants nearby had outdoor seating, leaving no good spot for a private conversation. In retrospect, I should have gone upstairs to Lucen's for this call. Since it was too late now, I simply hoped the traffic would suffice for cover.

"Jess, what's up?"

I swatted at a few imps, adjusting the phone to my ear. "I had an idea. It's not too late to call, is it?"

"Not for you, and not if it's about the case. I've been cozying up with my TV. Go for it."

"All right, you need a motive. I think I have one, and a suspect." I still couldn't share the specifics about why Angelia might be a target, but Dezzi's compulsion had no effect on the rest of my theory. I laid it out for Andre, keeping a careful eye on the imps.

He was silent for a moment after I finished talking. "There's something to that. I had no idea you were on such good terms with some satyrs."

Alas, because I couldn't give specifics about Angelia, in order to lend credence to my theory, I'd felt the need to share what I could about my role in potentially ruining the satyrs' reputation. "It's a long, weird story. But you think the idea has merit?"

"It's a new lead and something we can work with. We're stuck unless we can prove there's something to those marks you found, but I don't see why we can't bring Devon in for questioning. Even if it's not him, doing that might light a fire under the satyrs and get us some more cooperation. You up for it?"

"What, now?"

Andre laughed. "Normally I'd say first thing tomorrow morning, but this is tomorrow morning when you're dealing with preds. They're nocturnal, so we are too. Come on—you have something better to do at ten o'clock on a Wednesday night?"

"Not anymore."

"That's the spirit. See? You're a natural at this Gryphon stuff. Twenty-four hours a day, seven days a week—it's the job that never ends, and I wouldn't want it any other way."

I was glad he couldn't see my face. Once, I'd have agreed, but that ship had sailed and sunk. "Devon said he was heading to Purgatory to do some work. The club's closed."

"Perfect. I'll meet you there. Give me about forty-five minutes."

"Do we need backup?"

"For this? Nah. I know about Devon. He'll come quietly then sic his high-powered addict lawyer on us. Won't be the first time."

I laughed once, not amused. "Great. See you then."

After Andre hung up, I ran into Lucen's apartment and grabbed a light jacket. On my way out, my phone rang. Assuming it was Andre, I picked up without looking as I hurried toward the Shadowtown T station.

It wasn't Andre. "Is this Jessica? It's Ben from the computer store."

"Ben! Yeah, this is Jess. Hold on a sec." A train pulled out of the station going in the wrong direction. Once the noise died down, I checked to see who was around, but I was alone. "Did you find anything else?"

Ben coughed. "Sort of. Here's where I confess that I didn't see their protections coming."

"What do you mean?"

"They had some kind of fail-safe. I finally got into the files through brute force, and that triggered it. I got that strange French message I sent you earlier. Then the files, kind of, uh, self-destructed. But all is not lost, I swear. I am as good as advertised."

Light shown down the track, and I closed my eyes in despair. "What's not lost, and can you make this quick? My train's about to arrive."

"Yeah, sure. Bottom lining it—I restored what I could, and it's some freaky shit. I'm going to email it all to you. I think you'll find what's there interesting."

My shoulders relaxed. I was certain I would, and wished I had the chance to go check my email. But the Gryphons' secrets would have to wait. What annoying timing. "Great, thanks, Ben."

Stuffing my phone away, I hopped on the train. It was an agonizing trip. All I wanted to do was take the phone right back out again and open Ben's email, but that would be a bad idea. I didn't know what I'd find in those files, but "freaky shit" probably covered it. It wasn't something I should read in public, particularly before I was about to meet with a

Gryphon to do the extremely uncomfortable task of bringing Devon in for questioning. I needed my head on straight, my brain focused.

That was a lot easier said than done.

Although Purgatory was closed, several other clubs up and down the strip were open. The train had filled as we approached the right stop, and I got off with a group of dolled-up twenty-somethings. I wondered who these people were who didn't have to worry about going into work hungover the next day. They definitely weren't Purgatory's crowd. There was a serious lack of vinyl and fishnet, and far too many designer shoes and preppy pants.

I outpaced the trendy club-hoppers, several of whom were drenched in perfume and cologne, and soon stood outside Purgatory's locked doors. A lone light illuminated the entrance, and Andre was nowhere in sight. Thudding bass from a club across the street pounded in my head.

Giving in to temptation at last, I took out my phone. I would not check my email, just the time.

And my voicemail. My phone must have rung on the train, and I hadn't heard it.

I punched in the number, and Andre's voice appeared in my ear. Quickly, I scurried around the corner of the club so I could hear better.

"Jess, I'm on my way, running late, sorry. I had someone at Headquarters check on a few things for me. Apparently, Devon is one very trusted lieutenant. Dezzi frequently sends him to take care of business with us on her behalf. Most Doms are loath to do that sort of thing, so it's interesting, but I don't know what it means. Second point—you brought up Devon being the owner of Purgatory. Actually, he's only listed as the co-owner, for what that's worth. He owns the business jointly with Dezzi's second, Lucrezia. Anyway, no need to call me back. It's ten thirty now. I should be there in another twenty."

I hung up. So that's what Lucrezia did for a living. I'd often wondered. One mystery solved, just not the one that needed solving.

I gazed wistfully at my email, then checked the clock. If he was accurate, Andre should be here in another ten minutes. That was a long time to make myself behave and not open Ben's message.

Or it would have been. With no warning, something cold and hard that felt suspiciously like a gun barrel pressed against my back. I guessed I no longer had to worry about losing focus.

My heart missed a beat, even as my brain rejoiced that I must have been correct about my theory. This was definitely not the time for gloating.

"Hands in the air," said a gruff male voice. He grabbed the phone from me and nudged me with the gun. "Back door. Move."

I peeked around my shoulder because this guy was clearly not Devon. "Yes, sir," I muttered, probably because my assailant looked military. He was only an inch or two taller than me with buzzed, graying hair. But damn was he thick. He wore a tight green shirt that proudly displayed a barrel chest and bulging biceps.

He was also a lust addict. Not a shocker.

The addict poked me harder with the gun. I started walking, not sure where I was supposed to go, but figuring the back of the building was a good start.

My pounding heart replaced the incessant bass from across the street as the loudest noise in my head. Shit.

Think, Jess.

I'd taught self-defense courses. I'd beaten the crap out of Victor Aubrey not even a month ago. I carried a damn salamander-forged knife I'd stolen from a fucked-up fury bar. For the love of dragons, I should be able to take care of myself.

Except no one had ever held me at gunpoint before. I knew what I taught others to do in this situation, but I was not feeling badass at the moment. Self-defense rule number one was always the same—pay attention to your surroundings so you're less likely to put yourself in situations where you'll get in trouble.

Oops.

I wet my lips, hoping it wasn't too late to atone for my lack of awareness. I still had Misery at my hip, but I wasn't stupid enough to make a go for it. Don't bring a knife to a gunfight—not just a rule, but a cliché.

My attacker moved silently behind me, his feet scarcely making a sound as we traipsed over the gravel-strewn asphalt. No wonder I hadn't heard him sneak up on me. This guy was good. Maybe a professional.

Eyes open wide, I pushed the panic inside deep into my gut. Strong fear provided an excellent high, but combining it with my own adrenaline could be too much. It could make me reckless, and I couldn't afford that.

Finally, we turned the corner around the back of the club. A single, sleek sports car was parked there, but I didn't recognize it. Farther down the lot, a foul stench rose from the dumpsters, and empty liquor cartons sat in a pile. A shadow flickered around one of them, and a flash of orange light illuminated a disturbingly large dragon. It sneezed a second time, producing an even weaker flame, and disappeared behind the trash.

To my right was the club and a narrow, utilitarian deck that ran along the back. Halfway down the deck, a door opened and another lust addict stepped out. He must have flicked on a light switch because suddenly the back of the building lit up.

"Hurry up," the second guy said. He was built a lot like the first, and as I was forced up the stairs onto the deck, I realized he looked a lot like the first too.

Interesting, but really not what I should be paying attention to at this point.

"Go," the gun guy said.

"I'm moving as fast as I can," I lied.

He grunted in response.

As we reached the door, guy number two stole Misery from its sheath. I gritted my teeth.

"Inside." He was also armed, a large gun sticking out of a shoulder holster. I didn't know anything about guns, but it looked mean. Then again, so did he. I hadn't been too optimistic about my chances of devising a brilliant escape before, but I was far less optimistic now.

I took a couple steps inside the building and discovered I was in the club's kitchen. Stainless steel and white walls blinded me after so much time in the darkness outside.

Guy number two shut the back door and turned off the switch by it. His companion never wavered, the gun barrel still pressing into me.

My stomach was in knots, but I did my best to hide the fear in my voice. "Is that really necessary? It's not like I'm going to run."

Neither of them answered. Apparently I was dealing with the strong, silent type.

"Fine. Now what?" I asked.

Guy number two motioned with my knife. "Into the main room. Let's go."

I had no idea where to go, but he led the way. After a few turns through a side of Purgatory I had yet to explore, we entered the main bar. Every footfall echoed off the walls and ceiling. The club's lights were on but dim, and a red haze hung over the dance floor. Someone had created mood lighting. Swell.

Scowling, I stretched my neck, searching the bar area for Devon since the floor was empty.

I didn't find him. I found someone else.

"I warned you earlier. You really do get underfoot, pet."

TWENTY-THREE

Lucrezia emerged from around the far side of the bar. For once, she didn't look like she was sucking a lemon. She looked pleased.

Figured it would have to be at my expense.

She waved one manicured finger at the men, and the gun barrel stopped poking me in the spine. Guy number two handed my knife and phone to Lucrezia, while number one holstered his weapon.

She turned off my phone and tossed both objects on a table. "Adorable, aren't they? John and Jay—they're brothers, ex-special forces and my personal security detail when needed. There's a delicious wickedness to having them both, sometimes at once. I love a man in uniform unless it's Gryphon black. Don't you, pet?"

"Can't say I care one way or another." The longer Lucrezia droned on about her magically stolen love life, the longer I had to find a way out of this disaster. My gaze roamed over the empty club, but scanning the area and finding an idea weren't the same thing at all.

"No, that's true. You like satyrs. Powerful ones."

If I grabbed a chair or knocked a table over and made a lunge at Lucrezia, would her addict goons actually shoot me? The fact that she hadn't had them do it yet suggested not. On the other hand, I wasn't sure

I wanted to risk it. Not while I had questions, and not while my fate was uncertain.

"Only one satyr," I said, trying to pretend as though I wasn't contemplating methods for bashing her head in.

She laughed. "I don't think so. There's something different about you —you and your weird satyr-like gift—and they're all fascinated by it. Personally, I don't understand, but I've always been hopelessly mainstream about what attracts me." She ran a nail down Guy One's biceps to illustrate the point.

The enthralled look on her addict's face made my already unhappy gut twist in disgust. "Stop playing with your food. Where's Devon?"

Lucrezia perched on the edge of a table. "Devon's not here. When I heard that you planned on coming by, I asked him to run an errand for me and told him I'd handle the paperwork he had to do. It's just the four of us, pet. For now."

"What do you mean for now?"

Lucrezia clucked her tongue. "A bit late to be playing coy, don't you think?"

"I'm not playing." It was the truth, mostly. My brain was piecing everything together, but I had missing chunks. Besides, getting Lucrezia to talk was keeping me alive. "The four people who succumbed to the curse here—obviously you drew the glyphs on them at the club. The ones who died in Newton—I'm guessing you were the surprise we were told was supposed to be at the party. You stopped by the victims' house to put glyphs on everyone."

"Yes, and the same with the last two. It was so very easy, in case you were wondering."

Her careless tone disgusted me as much as it fed my anger. "What about Devon? Was he working with you to frame Angelia, or was it you alone?"

"Just me." She pursed her lips, examining me from head to toe. If I wasn't so insensitive to most pred magic these days, I'd probably be able to feel her power probing my soul. "You can thank your boyfriend for this. Lucen mentioned your latest theory about Angelia being framed during our talk at The Lair tonight. I knew you weren't entirely stupid given how you put together the way what's-his-face Aubrey framed you, but I figured it was mostly luck. You're annoyingly lucky."

I hoped she could sense how stupid I thought her comment was. "Yeah, so lucky I'm stuck here with you at gunpoint. How did you know I was coming here?"

"Honestly, pet. You've seen my work with the glyphs and how they interact with F. You should know I'm wicked good at magic. A nice little distraction charm on me while you were on the phone with your Gryphon partner, and you never noticed how close I stood during the call. Speaking of which..." She pointed at Guy One. "Her partner should be arriving any moment. Go keep watch and bring him to me as soon as he gets here."

My heart sank. That must have been what Lucrezia meant by us being alone "for now." Not only had my stupidity gotten me in trouble, it was going to get Andre in trouble too. And possibly dead.

"Poor you." Lucrezia smirked, clearly getting a read on my despair and guilt. "So upset. Don't worry, I'll let you give your partner the best last hour of his life any man could hope for."

I bit down my surge of rage because Lucrezia wasn't the only one picking up on my thoughts. Guy Two must have noticed me getting squirrelly. His hand hovered by his holster.

Taking a deep breath, I inched to the right. My best shot was now, without Guy One in the room. If I could get close enough to my knife, it might be worth the risk to make a go for Lucrezia.

"So why?" I asked, aiming to distract them both. "I get why Devon might want Dezzi gone, but not you."

"But that's the thing, pet. Devon doesn't want Dezzi gone. He doesn't mind being her lieutenant, and she gives him enough authority that he doesn't care about getting more power. He's pathetically loyal to her in spite of the poor decisions she's made. But someone had to step in and put a stop to it."

I slid a hairsbreadth closer to the table. The addict watched me like a hawk. "Is this because of Angelia?"

"You, Angelia, you again. Mostly you, to be honest. First she drags us into conflict with the sylphs because of you. Now she's letting you run around with Lucen after the Gryphons claimed you. It makes us appear vulnerable, and it makes us vulnerable in truth."

"Wow, and all this time I thought the reason you disliked me so much was because you couldn't stand not being the prettiest woman in the room." I inched a little closer to my goal.

Lucrezia rolled her eyes. "Honestly, pet. You really can't control your tongue, can you?"

"Nope. Some people like that about me."

"Some people would." Lucrezia motioned to her goon, and he stepped between me and the table. Dragon shit on toast. She must have sensed I was up to something. "There's dissension within our domus, and at the same time the furies are up to no good. We don't know what their aim is, but we don't have time for Dezzi to play at being a benevolent den mother. We need a Dom who's watching out for us and going on the offensive. And let me tell you, if Devon won't be the leader we need to do that, then I'll petition the Upper Council for the position myself."

"Consider me shocked by your kindness. The way you care for your fellow satyrs is touching. And to think, you only had to kill a dozen humans to do it."

Lucrezia slipped off the table. "A dozen plus two. Our company has arrived."

Wincing, I glanced over my shoulder. Guy One must have successfully gotten the jump on Andre like he had on me.

"Jess, you okay?" Andre had his arms raised, the same gun at his back that had been at mine. He wasn't wearing his uniform, so Lucrezia had either given her goon his description or there weren't a whole lot of guys wandering around a closed club this time of night.

"Yeah." I sighed. Was this the time to start offering apologies, or was it better etiquette to wait until our fates were officially announced? "I'm fine."

"That doesn't look like Devon," Andre said with a weak smile.

Lucrezia left Guy Two at my side and walked over to Andre. "You're so observant. And so pretty." She ran a finger down Andre's cheek, and I could taste revulsion beneath the lust she naturally invoked. It was like eating ice cream made from spoiled milk, rich and sweet with an undercurrent of something gag-inducing.

Lucrezia took her time searching Andre's pockets until she'd satisfactorily molested him and seized his phone, badge, and salamander-forged knife. Andre kept his face impassive, but the only people he was fooling with his stoicism were the addicts. I could tell he didn't blame me for our predicament, although that wasn't much consolation since he should have been blaming me.

"It's a shame to kill the pretty ones," Lucrezia said, setting his belongings on the table next to mine. "But I don't have much choice this time. With two Gryphons dead by Angelia's F, and evidence planted on you both that leads them straight to her, the organization will react swiftly and deadly. She'll be gone, and Dezzi will be in big trouble with the Gryphons and the Upper Council. And finally we'll gain some real leadership around here."

I wanted to challenge her, do the whole "you'll never succeed because..." spiel that always seemed to work in the movies. But alas, she had already succeeded. I couldn't think of a reason why she wouldn't continue to get her way after I was dead, and I couldn't think of a way to prevent my dying.

Yet some part of me refused to give up. So long as I breathed, I wasn't going to get all teary and sentimental and wish I'd done things differently. So long as I breathed, I was going to spend my energy fighting. All the reasons to get teary and sentimental were the same reasons worth fighting for—Lucen, my mom, Steph. Not to mention finding out what was in that damn file Ben had sent me.

I'd start fighting with something brilliant any minute now. I had a ton of energy flowing through me, a massive hit of fear and anger. My own and Andre's. There was no way I couldn't channel this into a plan.

Any damn second.

Lucrezia tapped her finger against her lips. "I think it'll be too messy if I leave you down here to die. Up to the Blue Room then. Darlings, get them moving."

"Yeah, you know blood's a real bitch to clean off vinyl," Andre said, as we were nudged forward at gunpoint once more. "You might prefer to do this elsewhere and spare your business."

Whatever he had in mind for a plan, it didn't matter. Lucrezia laughed lightly. "Blood's not what I'm concerned about. Although if you get bloody, that could be entertaining. Jess probably is the sort who likes it rough."

I clenched my jaw. "She's going to kill us like the other F victims."

"Oh. Great. No offense, Jess."

"None taken."

Lucrezia unhooked the velvet rope at the bottom of the stairs. "You both are so cute. Jess, just think—if you'd stuck to humans, I might not have needed to resort to such drastic measures. In a way, this is all your fault."

"Whatever it takes to clear your conscience, Crezi." It was a small satisfaction, but satisfaction nonetheless, to see the smirk fall off her face at the hated nickname.

The addict goons marched us up to the Blue Room, the same room where Devon had once stored the people who'd fallen victim to Lucrezia's schemes that one Friday. When we were all huddled inside, Lucrezia pulled two items from the bag she was carrying.

Andre coughed, and as I glanced at him, he nodded almost imperceptibly. So this was it. If Lucrezia was going to kill us, we would go down fighting. It made sense to do it here. The room was too small for the addicts to risk shooting.

I nodded back at Andre, then steeled myself.

Lucrezia must have noticed the change in our emotional states. She barely had time to yell "Don't!" before Andre went on the offensive.

He fell backward into the closest addict, knocking them both into the wall. That was the last I saw of him because I took advantage of the momentary confusion to slam my foot into the knee of the guy who was holding me. Spinning around, I lunged for his arm and for the gun. Mostly, I wanted to make sure he didn't shoot by accident. Lucrezia had said they were both ex-special forces, so theoretically they shouldn't be twitchy, but who knew. They were also addicts.

Of course, addict or not, ex-special forces also meant they knew how to fight. I wasn't facing Victor Aubrey here. I might have been able to hold my own against an untrained sadist, but all other things being equal, the guy with the leverage and strength had a big advantage.

That wasn't me.

"Pin him down!" Lucrezia screamed. She sounded seriously pissed off, but she must have been referring to Andre. My partner was nothing but a pile of limbs in my peripheral vision.

Guy Two dropped his gun and grabbed for my arms. White-hot pain shot through my recently healed wrist, his fingers crushing me. I deflected his attempt to snatch my other arm but succeeded in losing my balance in the process. My leg crossed with his, and down we went. My tailbone smacked the floor, and the addict and I cursed in unison as he landed on me.

Then something wet hit me in the face. All at once, my world turned upside down. The floor seemed to fall away beneath me, and the worst vertigo I'd ever experienced turned my insides to vomit. Vaguely, I was aware of the addict climbing off me, but although I was free, I could do nothing. The room spun in wild circles, color and form streaking together. Closing my eyes only made the falling sensation worse, but I did it anyway, and I curled into a fetal position, grasping at the cold tiles beneath me.

So this was what it felt like to be hit with a disorientation curse. Fuck.

"Move," I heard Lucrezia say. "You'd better hold them down while I do this."

Oh so slowly, I shuffled left and cracked my eyelids. Andre was down for the count too, lying on his back with his arms draped over his face.

Powerful hands grabbed me from behind, and I almost lost it on the floor. Only the sheer determination not to die covered in vomit helped me keep my lips together. The addict shoved me into a sitting position. My eyelids fluttered, and I groaned as my head flopped to the side.

Smooth fingers forced my mouth open. Lucrezia. I opened my eyes the rest of the way, and she stuffed something sweet on my tongue. I wanted to spit it out, but she held my jaw shut and it dissolved quickly.

"Just the F, pet. You'll like it." Then she was gone, doing the same to Andre. When she returned, she pushed up my shirtsleeve and drew a mark on my upper arm. My weak struggle merely resulted in her addict squeezing me harder.

I breathed deeply when she moved over to Andre for his glyph. Already my head was starting to clear, the curse's effects wearing off. But it was too late. She'd gotten the F into me. The glyph was drawn.

I slumped against the wall as the addict let go of me, unable to stand. Above me, Lucrezia wiped her hands together. "The drug should kick in around the time the curse has fully worn off. As fun as this might be to watch, I need to go do that paperwork I promised Devon or he'll get suspicious. Enjoy yourselves, pets. I'll be back in a few hours, but you should be dead by then."

As she shut the door on us, I heard her tell one of her addicts to wait outside.

Andre, who seemed to be reeling worse from the disorientation curse than I was, struggled to sit up. "This is why I should have known better than to laugh at any of those stiff jokes the Newton cops were throwing around." He inhaled sharply and closed his eyes. "Bad karma."

I rubbed my arm where Lucrezia had drawn her cursed glyph, but the mark stuck to me like a bad tattoo. The magic ink didn't even smudge.

"It doesn't work that way," Andre said.

"Yeah, I know. A girl can't help trying though."

"Hey, please try. Try anything you can think of." He rested his head against the wall. "How are you feeling? Still dizzy?"

I quit the useless rubbing and assessed myself. The floor didn't feel solid and everything blurred if I moved too fast, but the nausea was gone. I could probably stand if I tried, but for how long? I was in no state to attempt to overpower the guard Lucrezia had left. "I'm getting better."

Or maybe worse. Already I could sense my body reacting to the F, and possibly the curse. I was getting warm, and my skin was increasingly aware of the feel of my clothes. Rough denim dug into my thighs. My bra scraped at my all-too-sensitive nipples. I held still, focusing on my breaths, searching within me for something grounding. Something to drive away the sensations. Something to fight for.

Like Lucen.

Okay, not Lucen. Bad idea. Thoughts about him weren't helping, but oh, I wanted nothing more than to think of him.

"It's hitting you too, isn't it?" Andre's voice was thick, and he slid to the floor, lying on his back. "You're staring into space."

"I am?" I blinked and tried to focus on Andre, but that was also a mistake. My partner looked really good right now. Really good. Why hadn't I ever noticed how good before? Those warm eyes. That smooth, tan skin. He had cheekbones sharp as knives. I'd never dated a guy who shaved his head before, and I wanted to know what it would feel like to run my fingers over his scalp.

Then keep them running right on down his body, over his broad chest, down his abs... Shit.

Andre was staring at me too. I could see the desire in his face but could barely taste it. Either the F or Lucrezia's glyph had to be interfering with my gift.

"Jess, we've got to think."

"I am thinking." Just of all the wrong things. I dug my nails into my palms. Pain usually snapped me out of any stupor, but it wasn't helping this time. Even pain felt good. "How long did it take for Natalie and her friends to come off this?"

It took Andre a while to answer. "Hours, and the medics gave them sedatives on the way to the hospital."

"Oh. Damn." I'd forgotten the sedatives part.

I was starting to forget everything in fact. My brain felt like it was getting duller and duller. I didn't want to think. I wanted to feel, and I knew just what I wanted to feel. If Andre and I weren't resisting as best we could, I was certain I'd already be laying on top of him.

"Rope," I muttered, forcing my thoughts out of the gutter. "How come we don't have anything like that in here?" The room was barren except for a long banquet-style table and a few chairs.

"Rope, huh?"

"Not for that. But if we could tie ourselves down, maybe we could wait it out."

"I'm not sure that would work, but I don't see any rope anyway."

I gave up and collapsed to the floor. My body was starting to hurt with repressed longing. It built inside me, triggering memories of Natalie's frantic behavior. Merely observing and sensing her unfulfilled lust had been unpleasant for me. I didn't want to live it myself, but it was coming whether I was ready or not, slowly taking control of my body.

I swore I could smell Andre's skin—no cinnamon, no cloves, just something manly, human, and hot. A fine sheen of sweat glistened on his face and arms, and his chest rose and fell heavily. I had to touch him. Needed to touch him. Was going to explode if I didn't.

"Oh, God, Jess." His voice was so soft and thick I could barely hear him. "This is getting bad. I'm sorry."

"Me too."

"I don't know how much longer I can fight it."

"Me neither."

I wasn't sure if I said the words or only thought I did. I wasn't sure what happened next at all. Who moved? Who initiated? Who could tell? The fog hung so thickly over my brain, and my world dissolved into nothing but Andre. Andre, and the pain of a burning desire that I knew from experience couldn't be satiated.

But we'd try. Oh, we were trying.

I was on top of him, straddling his waist. My lips were on his, his tongue exploring my mouth. Every time I breathed in his scent and every touch of his lips sent me further over the edge. His warm hands slipped under my shirt, and as I sat up to pull it off the rest of the way, he flipped me over.

Pinned to the floor, I moaned as he ran his tongue down my chin, my neck, onto my breasts. Andre whispered my name, nudging my breast from my bra. Grasping fingers clawed at the lace. Greedy lips sucked on my nipple, too hard to feel good, yet not hard enough to satisfy me. Andre's touch was neither gentle nor sexily rough. He was driven by this mad hunger. Consumed by this artificial fire that couldn't be quenched.

So was I.

Desperate for more of him, I pushed his face deeper into my body, crying out as his teeth skimmed my sensitive skin. I strained to reach his arms and tug off his shirt, to rub his bare chest against my own. His hardness grazed my legs as he kissed me lower and lower. My hands balled into fists at my sides, unable to reach him as he ripped open my jeans button. My hips arched to meet his mouth.

Stop it, Jess!

I squeezed my eyes shut, wishing I could kill the voice of reason inside my head, but it wouldn't shut up. Even as Andre finally tossed his shirt aside, even as my hands tore at the button on his jeans, something inside me hadn't fully succumbed to the lethal combination of magic I'd been given.

I hated that something. It was the voice screaming, *You're part satyr. Feed off this energy. Control it.*

But I didn't want to control it, and even if I did want to, I couldn't. I'd tried.

I yanked Andre's jeans and boxers down his legs, and my body wailed as he emerged glistening with sweat and ripe and ready before me. If I couldn't feel him inside me soon, I'd go mad.

No, you'll live. Fight it.

Instead my fingers trailed along his thighs and curled around his cock. Andre moaned. I struggled to sit, to bring my lips to him and feast on my prize.

Fight it. Why can't you do this? Why can't you feed off this energy?

I didn't know. Whatever was in this magic had killed my gift as easily as it had killed my ability to feel anything but senseless lust, and I was going to die because of it.

No, I was going to die if Andre didn't fuck me soon. I couldn't stand this need anymore. The ache between my legs had become a howling pain. Damn you, Lucrezia.

Anger, spicy and harsh, ran through me like an electric shock. With it came power. With the power came some control and awareness.

But my lips were already closing over the tip of Andre's erection. His hands pulled me closer, fingers delving into my wetness and burrowing inside me. My body was alive and screaming, my hips thrusting in time with his hand.

Kill Lucrezia. I scarcely could manage the single thought, but I grasped it with what little willpower I had. *Kill Lucrezia. Kill her. Kill.*

My anger rose again. I couldn't stop the lust, not entirely, but I could overpower it, push it down, bury it in my gut.

Gasping, I removed my lips from Andre and pulled his hand away from me, though I reeled from the empty coldness that took over. Unfortunately, he used the opportunity to press me back on the floor. With him hovering above me, I had to close my eyes to roll out of the way. Looking at him made it too difficult. The rage gave me some strength, but I was holding on to my self-control by an imp's wing. It was fragile, barely there. Easily broken.

"Jess, come back." Andre landed on the floor without me.

I moved quickly. He'd reach me soon. He'd push me back down, and I'd let him because my body ached for him. So I had to act while I could. My fingers found the leg of the closest chair, and I winced in anticipation. "I'm so sorry."

Then I yanked the chair closer and brought as much of it as I could down on Andre's head.

I didn't hit him quite right. Part of me didn't want to hurt him, and I couldn't get a good angle. Andre grunted in pain and gawked at me like I'd lost it, which in fairness, I had. But so had he. Luckily, the F left him so out of it that he couldn't react. I sat up, gained a better grip on the chair and hit him again.

Focus. Anger. Lucrezia. Stop.

I had seconds before Andre regained his wits. I'd stunned him, nothing more. Crawling over his body, far too conscious of the warmth of his skin, I grabbed his T-shirt and tied his wrists together behind his back and around a table leg. "I am so, so sorry."

I just hoped he'd thank me later.

A trickle of blood ran down his temple, and his eyes fluttered open. "Jess?"

I pulled my pants and shirt on, and clenched my jaw. Though the worst of my lust was buried, I could tell it was only temporary. My skin was super sensitive. My clothes irritated.

Hate. Kill. Lucrezia.

"Jess, come back." Andre writhed on the floor, his moans morphing into screams as he fought the table. "Jess!"

"Hold tight. I'm taking down Lucrezia."

Some understanding flashed over his face. A single bead of sweat ran down his forehead. "God, yes. Do that. Please."

"I will." As soon as I formed a plan.

Who was I kidding? I could hardly walk straight. Partly because of the lusty pain, partly because my body didn't want to cooperate. Which was also because of the lust.

I cracked the door an inch, doing my best to tune out Andre, who seemed to have already forgotten the plan and was begging me to come back. Naked and tied up, and looking good enough to lick every inch of— my body shivered with longing for him. My knuckles whitened as I gripped the doorframe. It killed me not to answer his pleas.

Get out. Kill Lucrezia.

Her addict was gone, if he'd ever been there in the first place. I opened the door wider and stuck my head outside.

The coast was clear. If Lucrezia was actually here doing work, she was probably on the top floor in the office—a room that had a view down onto the rest of the club. The only way up there was via the locked elevator. Attacking her, therefore, was out of the question.

On hands and knees, I crawled to the edge of the balcony before realizing I was directly under the office here. Lucrezia couldn't see me. I got up, my knees shaky. I needed a plan and I needed it fast. The ball of magic I'd created was coming unwound even now. When I couldn't hold it together any longer, that power was going to explode in me all at once. I'd start humping anything that moved. Or maybe anything that didn't. I was pretty sure I wouldn't be picky.

I grasped the balcony rail, and my gaze settled on the bar area at the far side of the floor beneath me. My phone was there, and so was my knife. Lucrezia had left them on a table. It wasn't much of a plan, but it was all I had.

Staying low, I took the stairs one trembling step at a time because my body fought every movement. The ache was delicious torture, the longing enough to make my eyes tear up. I couldn't decide which was worse. Everything was too intense—alternately pleasure and agony.

It took forever to reach the bottom, and the dance floor stretched out before me. I could keep up the stealthy creep, or I could make a dash for the bar. The addict goons were nowhere in sight, and I suspected Lucrezia was keeping them close by in the office. Possibly, she had them on watch duty up there. If that was the case, then running was my best option because they'd see me any second.

I gritted my teeth, channeling my fury at Lucrezia. I needed the speed, but more than that—this was going to chafe. My uber-aroused inner thigh area was not going to appreciate running.

Go. Now.

I sprinted across the floor and up the few stairs to the bar table where my belongings waited. My fingers fumbled over my phone, and only belatedly did it occur to me to wonder who to call. I might not get more than one shot at this.

I crashed to the floor, sucking a breath through my teeth, and chose.

"Jess?" Lucen picked up on the second ring. If The Lair had been busy, it might have gone to voicemail. I wasn't sure why I chose him when I knew I should have called the Gryphons. I could only assume it was because when my body was alive with desire, Lucen was the person who sprang to mind.

Alas, his voice alone was enough to melt me. My grip on the curse slipped another fraction. "I need help. Get to Purgatory. Lucrezia's the one, not Devon. Hurry."

"Jess, you okay?"

I groaned, grasping blindly over my head until my hand found my knife. "No. Hurry."

I could hear footsteps, but I couldn't see who was coming. No matter. It had to be one of the addicts, who were as interchangeable to me as they appeared to be to Lucrezia. I shoved the phone aside, hoping Lucen understood, and pulled Misery from the sheath.

Don't bring a knife to a gunfight. Oh well.

Back on my hands and knees, I crawled away from the table. I needed to buy time until Lucen could get here, and that meant I needed to go somewhere I'd be safe. I could scramble for the exit, but I'd already been captured once that way and I didn't relish the idea of running around in public in my current state. I was liable to assault someone.

So what I needed then was to get someplace where Lucrezia's goons couldn't reach me. The basement. Once I was beyond the wards designed to keep out pesky humans, I'd be safe. Lucrezia could get to me, but she'd have to make the effort herself. It would take time, and unless she wanted to shoot me, she'd have a problem. As long as I had my knife, she'd be extra careful about getting close.

Somewhere behind me, the footsteps grew louder. Holding my breath, I tucked myself into a nook behind the bar. The floor was gritty and the tile worn, the confinement most unpleasant.

"Where are you?" the addict muttered. His feet were close. I could smell him—smoke and beer, like a walking bar. In my cursed state, the combination didn't rankle as much as it normally would have. Give me enough time and nothing would. I'd be like the Newton or Wonderland victims—willing to screw a corpse.

Stop Lucrezia. Focus. Fight.

And there he was. I sprung before the addict could react and threw myself into him. We tumbled backward, but this guy was well trained, and I was pathetically uncoordinated thanks to the curse. He deflected my arm with the knife easily. I tried to jerk out of his grip, a move that should have been simple, but he was too strong and too ready. Instead, I wrestled with him, which didn't work so well for me.

He didn't smell as good as Andre, or look as good as Andre, but to my drugged-out, cursed-out body, those were minor details. His arms were wrapped around me, trying to hold me and force me to drop the knife. All those hard muscles rubbing me were a distraction. I fought my urges as much as I did him. No surprise, I didn't fare well against both opponents at once, but I had a couple advantages—I had a knife, and he had balls. He couldn't dodge my weapon and my knee at the same time.

As soon as he went down, I raced for the door that led into the basement. It was off the main room in a darkened bar. Light seeped around the entryway, but I banged my leg on a chair nonetheless. Surprisingly, the pain helped me focus. Apparently there was nothing erotic about a throbbing shin, not even while strung out on F.

But although that was a good thing to learn, I realized my mistake as I crashed into the storage room door. Last time, it had been locked.

Cursing in desperation, I yanked on the handle anyway and the door flew back. So did I since I hadn't been expecting it. Maybe the door was unlocked because the club was closed. Maybe I'd finally caught a lucky break. I didn't care so long as I was in.

I turned on the light and darted down the winding stairs behind the shelves. Just like last time, an eerie blue glow lit the way and the humidity rose as I descended. I could feel the wards and compulsions that Devon and Lucrezia set creeping over me. My skin tingled with power. Two pairs of invisible hands seemed to grasp hold of me, one squeezing my mind, the other pushing me back the way I'd come.

Last time I'd fought the magic, it had been a struggle. This time, it was much easier. It was as if the magic recognized me. I'd been down here before, and if I'd managed it once, then I'd been accepted. With a pop, like a change in air pressure, the compulsion released me.

I stumbled deeper into the basement and caught my breath. My body raged with Lucrezia's curse and the F, but for the moment I had time to breathe and fight it back down. The ball of power burned in my stomach, tendrils of magic escaping. One wormed its way into my groin—an unpleasantly arousing reminder of what was to come when I no longer had the energy to hold the worst of this at bay.

Meanwhile, above, heavy feet clunked around on the landing. I froze, waiting and watching the stairs.

It sounded like the addict kicked something, and he cursed. "Where the fuck did you go?"

Another bang rang out, then the footsteps disappeared. It was almost as though he couldn't actually see the stairs. Interesting. Maybe the compulsion worked that way.

I crumpled to the concrete floor in the shadow of the sarcophagus farthest from the elevator. My whole body trembled, and beneath the painfully unfulfilled erotic energy in me, I detected the stirrings of a headache. Whatever magic I possessed, I was using a lot of it to fight Lucrezia's curse.

My reprieve down here was only temporary too. I had as long as it took the addict to admit defeat, find Lucrezia, and for her to figure out where I was. Rubbing my temples, I wished I hadn't dropped my phone during the struggle upstairs, and I wished I knew how Andre was faring.

Seconds passed like minutes. In the dark and quiet, my mind raced. Had Lucen understood my message? Was help really coming? Or were Andre and I destined to die here, one way or another? I was out of ideas and overmatched. My ability to resist Lucrezia's curse would take her by surprise, but she maintained the advantage. I was too weak to fight much more.

As I waited for my doom, my gaze fell on the nearby sarcophagus. Inside the cocoon-like shell it held, a human was dying and a satyr was being born. Had I gone through that process? And was my part-satyrness the reason Lucrezia's magic wasn't working as effectively as it should?

My freakishness had both gotten me into trouble then saved my life with Victor. The scales were even. But if it was helping me resist Lucrezia's curse, I'd have to admit it was useful, and I didn't like that.

But maybe I was getting ahead of myself. I hadn't survived yet.

The elevator opened, and I tensed. Climbing to a better position, I adjusted my grip on the knife and peered out from around the sarcophagus. Lucrezia strolled into the room, carrying a gun.

Puzzlement spread across her beautifully evil features as she approached. "How, pet? How do you do it? I should have known when Devon told me someone got past the wards that he was referring to you, and here you go again after I just strengthened them, and you're resisting my spells. What is wrong with you?"

"What is wrong with *you*?"

"Cute. You know this is nothing personal. I'm trying to save my people."

I didn't say anything. I couldn't. The closer Lucrezia got, the harder it became to keep my control over the curse. It had to be her satyr power—it was affecting me the way satyr magic used to, before I became numb to it. It was somehow mixing with the F and pitching my arousal to an even higher level. I should have expected as much.

I backed away, keeping low to the floor. My fingers were perfectly positioned around the knife, and I was ready to spring. I would only have one chance. Lucrezia's gun aside, being close enough to hurt her was going to push me into no-return territory. Even now, the fingers on my empty hand opened and closed, rubbing against my leg. If I wasn't touched soon, if this itch wasn't scratched, I was going to have a breakdown. It fucking hurt.

Lucrezia realized my dilemma. "Is this what it's going to take, pet? Am I going to have to watch you and that Gryphon screw to death to make it happen? You have no idea how unpleasant it is for me to be around that much lust. It's like gorging on sweets. It makes me ill. But if that's what must be done…"

She pointed the gun at me and motioned for me to get up, but I didn't move. "Go ahead. If you're going to kill me, I want it over with faster."

Lucrezia flinched. I'd called her bluff, and she wasn't sure what to do. Shooting me ruined her ability to use my death as another strike against Angelia.

In the silence that followed her hesitation, someone shouted upstairs. "Crezi, where are you?"

Devon was here.

TWENTY-FOUR

Lucrezia swore, but I tried not to get my hopes up. "You're lucky I left the disorientation curse in my office or I'd hit you with it. Don't even think about yelling or going up there, pet. John is waiting at the top of those steps. He has orders to shoot you if necessary, although I hope it doesn't come to that. I have other ways of making you cooperate."

She took off upstairs, and I loosened my grip on the knife as her footfalls vanished. Don't even think about it—yeah, right. The addict who was supposed to have been guarding me and Andre in the Blue Room hadn't done a very good job. So like I wouldn't test her this time?

There was only one way to find out if she was lying. I was going after her.

Just not yet. First, I needed to recover. The effects of her magic lingered in my blood, and I didn't have the strength to call out to Devon.

Although I worked to push the curse away once more, this time even less obeyed my will. More tendrils of magic slipped out, entwining themselves around my body. It was hard to breathe, and I grasped the edge of the closest sarcophagus as my knees weakened. Oh, God. I wanted nothing more than to collapse to the floor.

My eyes closed, and I focused on my breathing. Anger. I needed anger or some other negative emotion to boost my power, but I couldn't summon enough. Nor could I focus for long. My mind wandered to Lucen. I wanted him here so badly. Where was he? Why was Devon here instead?

I must have spaced out again, like I had with Andre. Next thing I knew, someone was pounding down the stairs. A moment later Devon appeared around the corner.

"Jess!"

I turned to him, sensing his clove-tinged magic sweep over me. *Don't come any closer*, my brain screamed. But my mouth wouldn't obey. It didn't want to.

Not that he would have listened.

Air caught in my throat, and I moaned before he touched me. I couldn't hold it together any longer. He was too close, and even without the F, his magic had affected me for unknown reasons.

As Devon knelt in front of me, the curse unleashed all at once. I grabbed fistfuls of his shirt and pulled him closer. He lost his balance, falling into me where I was pressed against the sarcophagus. His body was so warm, so what I needed. I stretched my neck, straining to reach his lips. The tension in me grew more intense by the second. I needed more. I needed it now.

Devon didn't fight me. The scruff on his chin scraped my skin as he kissed me back. His lips were as insistent as mine, and he tasted so good. He'd regained his balance, and his one hand pressed against my cheek, gliding his thumb over my skin. With his other, he squeezed my hip. The pressure from his fingers seemed to send shock waves straight to my groin. Wrapping my legs around him, I arched my back to get closer.

Then he stopped abruptly and pulled away, breathing heavily. "Jess, you're making it very difficult to help you."

I struggled to find a better position while my hand slid down to where his erection strained against his pants. More heat spread between my legs, encouraged by my discovery. So much for his protesting. The restraint he was exercising couldn't hide the raw desire on his face or the way his body throbbed beneath my hand. "Please, I need you. This is helping."

This was all that was helping anymore. Lucrezia was a distant memory, so unreal. All that mattered was satisfying this craving. Every nerve ending had ignited. I was going to scream, and the pain wasn't the good sort. Any real pleasure had fled. My body was on fire, and I needed him to put it out.

Devon took my hands and flattened me against the sarcophagus. Not the best move on his part because I could feel his arousal pushing into me, and it worsened my own. His eyes burned, their normal pale blue almost silver in the basement's creepy lighting. "I can help you, but you have to hold still for a minute."

"I can't. Please."

"Yes, you can." He adjusted his arms, pinning both of mine with one of his own. Then he kissed me again. Harder. His mouth tugging on my lips as though trying to fight mine into submission. His power was all I could breathe. My body shook and my eyes watered. But it wasn't enough. Nothing would be.

Cool glass touched my cheek. Once more, Devon pulled away and I whimpered. "You need to drink this." He held up a small vial filled with pinkish liquid.

"What is it?"

"Something Azria cooked up," he said, referring to one of the satyrs who acted as their healer. "After the first incident here, you gave me the idea that it would be smart to find a counter-charm in case it ever happened again. She's been looking into remedies for me."

"Are you sure it works?"

Devon smiled grimly. "To be honest, I'm not sure it won't kill you, but I'm sure you'll die if it doesn't work. So bottoms up. Be a good girl and take your medicine." He twisted the cap off with his thumb and forefinger. With his other arm, he continued to hold me down.

I nodded. Devon flicked the cap to the floor, and I let him pour the contents in my mouth. I gagged. It tasted awful, reminiscent of cough syrup, but I forced myself to swallow.

"That good, was it?" He watched me with a wary expression but didn't ease up.

"You tasted better."

"That should be stating the obvious. How are you feeling?"

I shrugged but the motion didn't get me very far. Devon was stronger than he appeared, and I couldn't move. "How long should it take?"

"No idea. I'm afraid you're the guinea pig."

"Great." Yet as I spoke, it dawned on me that the counter-charm must be working. I'd managed something like an actual conversation with Devon. I'd focused. Plus, I could feel the cold, rough stone of the sarcophagus digging into my back, the unpleasant way my knees were twisted beneath me, and the headache slowly kicking up a fuss in my brain.

Incredibly strong lust still raged within, but the pain of it—the overstimulation that had been driving me mad—was subsiding. I was no longer so desperate for sex that I'd have done anything, or anyone, to get it.

No, now I merely wanted the guy in front of me with his clove-scented pheromones and the surprisingly sweet concern on his face. It was an expression I'd never seen on Devon before, and damned if it didn't turn his attractively average face into something undeniably hot.

"You can let go," I said, although part of me would much rather he not. "I have control again."

Devon seemed to consider, no doubt assessing my emotions for himself, then he removed his arm. "What do you know? I've got to give Azria more credit, assuming you don't drop dead in the next few minutes. Glad I stopped by her place after leaving The Lair."

I slumped against the sarcophagus and stretched my aching legs. Without Devon touching me, more of the lust lifted. My brain was clearing too. I could think straight again, although that didn't feel like such a great thing at the moment.

Blood rushed to my face as I realized what I'd done. "Oh, shit. I am so sorry about what just happened."

Devon smirked. "No need for that. I'm happy to have you tear my clothes off, Jess. Didn't I once tell you it was inevitable? Just next time don't be dying while you're doing it."

"Don't get ahead of yourself. Dying and desperate is the only way it could happen. And, oh—Andre and Lucrezia!" In spite of my soreness, I climbed to my feet. Fury returned with a vengeance. I wanted to hunt Lucrezia down and drive my knife through her. But first, I had to make sure Andre was okay. "You don't have any more of that stuff, do you?"

Devon capped the empty vial and pocketed it. "I have two others. Your partner is alive. I can sense him up there."

"We need to give him the counter-charm too." I raced to the stairs. "And what about Lucrezia? Do you know—?"

"Jess!" Devon stood by the elevator and beckoned me over. "This way, and I wouldn't worry about Lucrezia. I got everything out of her."

I hurried over as the elevator opened. "Where is she? She has armed addicts running around."

"I don't know where she went, but don't worry about the addicts. They've gone with her, and she won't get far."

ANDRE WAS WORSE OFF THAN I WAS. IT WASN'T A SURPRISE, but it was awful to witness regardless. It took a concerted effort between Devon and myself to hold him down and force him to drink the counter-charm, and the potion itself took longer to work on him. After he'd calmed down, we untied him and let him recover in peace. He was barely coherent, and I hoped he was spacey only as a result of the curse's lingering effects and not because I'd knocked him on the head. His wrists were raw and bloody from the restraints, and more blood stained his head and his back. He must have banged his body against the table trying to get free.

I stepped out onto the balcony and frowned down at the empty club. "I should call an ambulance. Andre needs medical help."

I figured Devon would protest like he had last time, but he didn't. "The counter-charm should be enough to treat the magic. That's why I asked Azria to work on one. But your partner has other injuries, so go ahead."

"And Lucrezia?" I paused at the top of the steps.

Devon took out his phone and offered it to me. "As I said, she fled with her addicts. My first concern was getting to you. I had to let her go."

"How did you know what was going on?"

"Lucen called me after you called him. I was close by, so I got here first, but he should be on his way. As for Lucrezia?" He grimaced, and I noticed he wasn't using his nickname for her. "It's not as though she could hide what was going on when I could sense you and your partner losing your minds. She tried to convince me to go along with her, but when I made it clear I didn't approve, she ran."

So that explained it. My fingers hovered over the phone's keypad, but I felt Devon staring at me. "What?"

"Is it true you came here expecting to bust me for cursing those people?"

I bit my lip sheepishly. "You were a logical suspect."

Devon stuffed his hands in his pockets, but he appeared more amused than angry. "I'm hurt, Jess. I think you owe me an apology, and while I'm at it, a thank you for saving your life would be nice."

"I'm sorry, and thank you?"

He inhaled deeply, feigning pain. "I don't know. You don't sound very sure of yourself, and words are so meaningless. If you wanted to pick up where we left off downstairs though…"

"Dying and desperate, remember?"

He took a step closer and pushed my knotted hair behind my ear. "Not even you believe that, do you?"

I backed away, not knowing a good answer. There had to be a reason why Devon's magic affected me more than anyone else's. Besides Lucen's, that was. I just preferred to ignore the more obvious possibilities. One satyr was more than enough for a part-human.

A door opened below us, sparing me from a weak rebuttal. Voices filled the club, and Devon darted down the stairs to the main room. I stayed where I was, tired and unsure I wanted to be a part of the commotion.

Lucen entered the main room with Lucrezia. He had her arms bound behind her, and it was a toss-up as to which of them looked more pissed off.

Lucen's face softened, however, when he saw me. Unlike Lucrezia's. "Jess, are you all right?"

"I'm fine." I tightened my grip on the balcony railing.

"Lucrezia dosed her up well," Devon said. He explained to Lucen what had been going on when he arrived.

Lucen's face hardened a second time.

"I was trying to protect us all," Lucrezia said through clenched teeth. "Do you care more about your human pet than you do us?"

"What they care about isn't your concern." A new voice—Dezzi's voice—cut through the club. I held my breath, and Lucrezia fell silent. Her eyes opened wide as her Dom strode into the room. Dezzi's attitude was regal as always, but murder lined her face. "This is how you thought to protect this domus? By framing one of your own for murder? By turning the Gryphons on us? You care nothing about us, just your own ambition, and you'd stomp on whoever got in your way, even your own people. It's vile."

Lucrezia tossed her hair. "Your disregard is what's vile. You going to kick me out for this? You'll take in a freak like Angelia, but kick me out?"

Dezzi turned her back on her—presumably—former number two. "No. It was Jessica who figured out what was going on, and Jessica who was willing to work within the Gryphons to minimize the damage to us."

That wasn't entirely true or exactly what happened, but who was I to correct Dezzi?

The Dom stared up at me. "I think it is only appropriate in this case to let Jessica deal with you. I'm therefore relinquishing my privilege as Dom to punish you, Lucrezia. The Gryphons can have you and put you on trial instead."

Lucrezia gaped at Dezzi, and so did I. That was most unexpected, but after a moment's thought, I realized it was also smart. Dezzi's move would go a long way toward placating the Gryphons' unhappiness with the satyrs, and by treating Lucrezia like she was beneath her, Dezzi sent a powerful message to any other satyrs who might have backed her former number two. Undermine your Dom and face the most serious of consequences—be kicked out of the domus.

I'd anticipated a fight over Lucrezia's fate, but this would make the next few hours a lot easier. On that note, I remembered I had Devon's phone, and I dialed the Gryphons' emergency line.

TWENTY-FIVE

How did I escape Lucrezia's curse? How did I keep getting past the compulsion and wards on the basement? Those were the answers Lucen, Devon, and Dezzi wanted to know as we waited for the Gryphons to officially arrest Lucrezia and an ambulance to take away Andre.

"You know my gift is weird," I told them. It was the truth, just not the whole truth, and it was evident from their expressions that it was getting thin.

"You're human," Devon mused. "It should work regardless."

I said nothing to that, and was thrilled when the Gryphons arrived. I hadn't been feeling like I needed their healers to check me out, but letting them do so meant a faster escape from the satyrs' questions.

Once we got to the hospital, I asked around and found out Andre had a minor concussion. The nurse who informed me didn't attribute it to a chair, but I knew it was probably my fault. One more thing to add to what would—no doubt—be some serious awkwardness between us.

Unsurprisingly, the Gryphon healers pronounced me fine, magically speaking. I didn't feel so fine, however. Now that the adrenaline had worn off, I had a massive headache and every muscle was sore. The nurses gave me painkillers, and the healers told me to drink lots of juice and eat crackers to help me ground my gift. While I nibbled and drank, I had to fill Brian in on what transpired. Only after that was I allowed to leave.

Before I did, I stopped by Andre's room. Judging by the expression on his face and the mortification I could sense rolling off him, I suspected that he wished he'd been pretending to sleep when I arrived.

"Hey, Jess. You all right?" Genuine concern laced his voice, but his gaze roamed everywhere—the empty wall, the curtained window, the ugly ceiling. Everywhere but me.

I chose to stare at my shoes, not so much out of my own embarrassment, but because I thought it might alleviate some of his. "Yeah, I'm fine. Sorry about your head."

"Yeah." He snorted. "You hit me with a chair. If I recall, they're your weapon of choice against Gryphons."

"They are handy that way. I am really sorry."

Andre held up a hand to cut me off. "You saved my life. No need to be sorry."

"Well, I am. You stuck here?"

"Yeah. Docs want to keep me overnight for observation—the head and all. And Brian was kind enough to leave me with this—" he tapped a laptop on the bedside table, "—so I could get started on my report in order to pass the time. So you know." He brought the laptop onto the bed.

It was clearly a sign he wanted me to go. Just as well. "I'll see you soon then."

But I wondered if I would. I suspected any chance I had at a normal relationship with Andre was ruined. I was more sad that this probably meant I wouldn't get to work with him in the future than I was at the loss of anything else. He was a great guy, but he wasn't Lucen, and I wanted Lucen.

On that thought, I returned to his apartment and promptly passed out as soon as I hit my borrowed bed.

When I woke up the next morning, Lucen was sleeping, so I crept downstairs. I hadn't seen him since leaving Purgatory last night. No doubt he'd been sucked into a satyr council meeting to discuss the Lucrezia situation. Although I was extremely curious about what the fallout from that would entail, there was something else occupying my thoughts.

The clock on the coffeemaker declared it to be noon. Taking an extra-large mug to the table, I turned on my laptop and finally checked the email Ben had sent.

I scrolled past the note he'd written and went straight for the good stuff—the files, particularly the one with my name on it. My coffee grew cold as I read. And read. And read.

After a while, I turned cold too.

Much of the data was corrupted and read like gibberish, and in some places information was clearly lost. But on the whole, enough was available to figure out what was going on. This file contained my life, every detail from when I'd been enrolled at the New England Academy for the Magically Gifted.

Most of it was normal—the file had my grades, teacher notes, and test scores. All the usual academic stuff. Then there were my yearly blood screenings and notes on magical aptitude. Also normal for Gryphons. Where it started to get weird was the personality assessments. Over the years, someone had kept a running commentary on my behavior. I was described, among other ways, as having "a stubborn streak and determination that was borderline reckless."

And finally, there was a different sort of running note. This first one was written when I was thirteen years old—by a Gryphon I had no recollection of ever meeting—and it described me as a good candidate for a "special service project." A year later, this candidacy was formalized into a recommendation for something called the Philadelphia Project. Following that was a third note, signed by the same person. It only mentioned my candidacy hadn't worked out and called me a failed test subject. Then, at last, on my eighteenth birthday, another note appeared. This one suggested that my transformation might not have taken because my gift wasn't strong enough after all.

My transformation.

My fucking transformation?

I stared at the file, specifically at these last notes, for forever. My coffee was forgotten. Everything was forgotten. Bile churned in my stomach as I read and reread the words on the screen. There was no way.

Yet I knew better. With trembling fingers, I opened Victor's file. It was less complete than mine, but we shared significant similarities in the information it contained, and very similar magical profiles and notes. Victor's "transformation" had failed too.

I opened the next, and the next, and the next. With each file, I hoped beyond hope that I'd find something in the corrupted data to make my suspicions fade. After what I'd gone through last night, I couldn't possibly be fully functioning. I was tired and sore. I was reeling from the aftereffects of serious magic.

But I wasn't stupid, as le Confrérie had kindly noted in several places.

I checked the dates on the notes and did the math in my head. The Philadelphia Project coincided with the summer I'd attended a Gryphon-sponsored summer institute there. A summer institute at which I'd allegedly had the flu and couldn't recall what I'd done. And no coincidence, that was right around the time *all* my childhood memories became hazy, like they belonged to a different person.

I swallowed, unable for another moment to take my eyes off the file while I debated what to do. Truthfully though, there wasn't much to debate. Right there in my file it said everything that made my decision inevitable—I was stubborn, borderline reckless.

That did it. I tore my gaze away from the computer and grabbed my keys. It was time to get wholeheartedly reckless all over Gryphon fucking Headquarters.

ACTUALLY STORMING A BUILDING WHEN YOU HAD EVERY RIGHT to be there, and in fact were expected to be there so you could write a report on your recent activities was anticlimactic. I breezed through security, the dark expression I could sense on my face not bothering anyone. But no matter. One person in this building wasn't expecting me, and to him, I could damn well storm.

I threw open the door to Tom Kassin's office. He was on the phone, and he gave me a very annoyed *what are you doing?* look until he read my face. I imagined I looked a lot like Dezzi had last night—filled with a barely controlled murderous rage.

"I'll have to call you back." Tom hung up, and it pleased me to no end to sense that I'd unnerved him. Finally. "What brings you here, Jessica? I heard you had a late but productive night yesterday. I'm glad you're okay."

I shut the door behind me. "Yeah, I bet you are. Wouldn't want your precious experiment to get herself dead, would you?"

Surprise passed over Tom's face and settled in my mouth like ice. "Whatever you think you know—"

"Everything. You did this to me, didn't you? It was your people. Your Gryphon fraternity."

To his credit, Tom didn't deny it. Then again, he ought to know I could detect lies. "You need to calm down."

"Calm down?" I slammed my hands on his desk. "Are you kidding me? You ruined my life! You screwed with my gift. You made me some kind of misery-sucking freak. I trusted this organization, and you betrayed me."

Tom picked a book off his shelves and dropped it on the desk by my hands. It was one of the ones I'd browsed through while sneaking into his office. The one that contained the weird prophecy crap. "You have no idea what we're up against. The fraternity didn't have a choice. It wasn't a decision anyone in it wanted to make, but that's the responsibility that comes with being selected for it. Sometimes we have to make regrettable choices and live with them."

"Regrettable choices? You did experiments on kids. You're sick!"

"They weren't experiments with life-or-death consequences. We knew you would survive. We simply didn't know if the magic would take." He fell back into his chair. "How much do you know?"

I crossed my arms. "I told you—everything."

"Really? How do you know so much?"

Because I stole your files? At this point, I didn't actually care whether Tom learned the truth, but I didn't want to derail the conversation or risk getting Steph and Ben in trouble. The focus was supposed to be on Tom's misdeeds. "I know you tried to transform me, and I know what happens when you try to make a pred out of a human with magical blood. It either doesn't work and the person dies, or they become…"

"You." Tom raised an eyebrow. "It did work on you, didn't it? The experiment didn't fail like the Brotherhood thought."

"You had no right." My voice quivered. Magic danced along my skin, and every hair on my body stood at attention. This much power was a head rush, yet I was so full of rage, I thought I might explode. For the second time in twenty-four hours, I felt on the verge of losing my mind. Once this nightmare was all over, I wanted to find a beach, the sort of drink that comes with an umbrella, and a good book. I needed to relax.

But first, I kind of needed to kill.

Tom shoved the book my way. He should have been afraid of me, but what I tasted from him was a spicy anger, and his eyes shone with an intensity I'd seen before but couldn't place. "There is a war coming, Jessica. A war the magi foresaw a long time ago. If we're going to survive, we need people on our side who fight preds like we've never had to do before. That is the Brotherhood's mission. That has always been its mission. And despite the urgency of what we had to do, you were never in any danger. The organization worked for over a century perfecting the spells involved, figuring out why gifted humans couldn't be transformed under normal circumstances. We knew you and the others like you would survive, but until recently, we thought we'd failed anyway. Your gifts vanished. But then you showed up, and Victor Aubrey, and we learned we were wrong."

"Oh yeah, you were wrong. You were wrong in so many ways I can't even count them." I paced in front of his desk, my hands clenching and unclenching into fists. "Is this why you've been so in my face about me spending time in Shadowtown? Why you were so afraid of me being around satyrs? Did you think I might relate to them, or that they might discover what I was?"

Tom got up, and I backed away from him. If he got too close, I might deck him yet. "You can spend time there because you're invulnerable to their power, aren't you? You can take it. You'll be what they fear—our secret weapon."

"I am nothing to you except the woman who'll hit you if you come any closer. And to answer your question—no. Most of my life I've been as affected by their power as anyone."

"But something happened recently to change that." Tom almost smiled. "Something to do with Victor Aubrey?"

A zealot—that's what I was dealing with. His half smile was the proof. He was as insane as Victor, only in a different way. "You created me. You tell me. I'm just your lab rat."

"Don't be absurd. We made you better. Stronger. The Brotherhood toiled for ages to perfect what we did for you and for the human race. That's why I'm here. As soon as we got an inkling of what you might be capable of, I was flown to Boston to investigate."

"You didn't make me better. You made me into a freak and an outcast. You made me miserable. You made me so it was impossible for me to have a normal life. And all the while you agonized over your own fucking choice, you never gave *me* one."

Tom picked up the book again and pressed it on me. "Read this. I know you're upset, but read it. See for yourself what's coming. You'll understand. You have to."

I tossed the book away. "I understand nothing except that I've never been so disgusted in my entire life." Then I spun around, aiming for the door.

The sound of a blade scraping against a scabbard stopped me, and I couldn't help but look behind me. Tom had removed yet another sword—one I hadn't seen before—from its sheath. A jolt of fear ran through my blood, but it was nothing. A pinprick overwhelmed by my fury. My hands balled into fists.

Let him try.

The blade's deathly black sheen cut a line across Tom's pale face. Holding the hilt in a loose but confident grip, he flipped the sword to make sure I could see the glyphs etched on both sides of the blade. Once he was certain he had my attention, he slid it back into the scabbard. "Your disgust and your anger won't change anything, Jessica. What's coming is coming, and when it does you will need us as much as we will need you. Go ahead and walk out that door. When you've calmed down and walk back in, I'll be here." He flipped the sword around, holding the scabbard and presenting the hilt for me to take.

As if he could buy my forgiveness.

My hands remained in fists at my side. "Don't count on it. I used to want nothing more than to be a Gryphon. Now I want nothing to do with you, or this organization, ever again."

I charged out of his office, unable to take any more of this conversation. At the end of the hallway, I clutched the wall, fighting for control of my breaths. Tears pricked at my eyes. Reading those files and putting it all together had been one thing. Hearing Tom admit to everything, and without remorse, made it real.

The Gryphons had done this to me. The people I trusted—the people humans everywhere trusted—to protect us from preds and curses and evil magic had turned that magic on me. Had betrayed me in a way I'd never imagined possible.

Thank dragons my Gryphon father was dead. He hadn't been a member of this secret group, and I hoped he hadn't known and would never have allowed them to do this to me. For the first time in my life, I was glad he wasn't around so I couldn't confront him about it.

When I got my wits together at last and no longer felt as though I was going to hurl, I headed toward the stairwell. Plowing down the fifth-floor hallway, I ignored everyone who acknowledged me, including Olivia Lee's secretary.

The woman flagged me down as I opened the director's door. "You can't barge in…"

But I could because I had. Because I no longer cared.

Like Tom had been, the director was on the phone. Maybe she was on with him and he was warning her that a crazy woman was in the building. That would certainly be ironic given my new opinion of Tom.

Olivia hung up right as I threw my Gryphon windbreaker at her face. "I quit."

"Jessica—"

"You can threaten me with all the prison time in the world, but I promise you this—if I'm arrested, I will take everything I know about *Le Confrérie de l'Aile* public. I will tell the world about the secret experiments they conducted on me, Victor Aubrey, and at least three other people that I'm aware of, when we were children. I have proof, and I don't care about all the good your precious Order does for humanity. It doesn't make you above the law or give you a moral blank check to cash in as you please. So I'm done. Call my bluff if you want, but you'll regret it."

Olivia set the jacket neatly on her desk. "I don't know what you're talking about."

"Ask Agent Kassin then. I'm sure he'd love to fill you in on how the end of the world is coming." Then I spun around and left, and my world spun with me.

TWENTY-SIX

LUCEN WAS AWAKE WHEN I GOT BACK TO HIS PLACE. HE SAT ON the sofa, my laptop in front of him. I'd never shut it down when I left, and the files must have been open.

Before I could explain, he ran over to me. "Little siren."

I wrapped my arms around him. Maybe it was because I was so distraught, or because of the aftereffects of last night's magical cocktails, but for the first time all I felt was comfort in his arms. He held me tightly, silently, and I buried my head against his chest, listening to him breathe. We stood there for a while.

I never wanted to let go, but I'd had thoughts on the way here. Many thoughts. Many painful thoughts. Lucen had obviously read through my file and drawn the same conclusions I had, so it was time to get those thoughts off my mind. "You read it all?"

Lucen let go of me. "Everything. It's sure interesting reading. Jess, this wasn't a curse that warped your gift."

"Oh, I know." I flopped on the sofa. "I've known that for a while. I just didn't know it was the Gryphons behind it all."

Lucen paused. "You knew you weren't cursed? Since when?"

"Long story." He would certainly freak out if I told him I'd made a bargain with the goblin's Dom for the information, so it was best to gloss over that part for the moment. "Bottom line is I found out I was part satyr about a month ago. It kind of explains everything about the compulsions at Purgatory, huh? I wasn't trying to lie last night when I didn't tell you. I just hadn't found the right time."

He sat next to me and took my hand. "Fair enough, I guess. But little siren, you're not part satyr. You're *all* satyr."

I entwined my fingers through his and didn't say anything for a moment. All satyr? No way. Gunthra had called me a hybrid, and I'd been clinging to the fact that I didn't have horns and didn't need to feed on addicts as proof I was somewhat human. "I can't be. There are so many ways I'm not like you. I'm a hybrid, maybe."

"I'd say more like a different subspecies. Transformed is transformed. If you're not dead, you're no longer human. There's no hybrid or part. Do you even know if you could survive on your own, cut off from humanity?"

I rested my head in my hands. "No, I don't."

Much as I hated to admit it, Lucen's description sounded more accurate than Gunthra's. And I had to face the facts—in the end, it didn't matter. Addicts, no, I didn't need those. But I chose to live in an urban area. I chose to be around lots of people. I had no idea how well I'd fare without that constant source of misery to fuel me. Maybe I wasn't as unlike him as I pretended.

"Jess." Lucen put a hand on my back.

"I'm okay. There's a few more things I need to tell you."

He kissed my forehead. "If there's more, I need a drink. I think you do too."

"I won't argue. It's been a hell of a couple days. Speaking of, what's happening with the Lucrezia aftermath? What did I miss last night?" I was curious, but more than that, I wasn't looking forward to my next confession.

Lucen returned to the living room with two cocktail glasses and a bottle of bourbon. "Never mind Lucrezia. What else is going on with you? That's what I care about. I need to know you're okay with all of this."

I downed the first shot he poured me. Alcohol burned my throat, and my muscles relaxed. "I'm fine, really. Can't you tell?"

"I admit, you are calmer than I'd have expected."

"Well, you missed my ragey wrath. I left for the Gryphons before you were up, and the stuff about what I was—as I said, I already knew. I vented all my anger on the Gryphons earlier."

"Ah, right. So what else is there that I should know?"

This was the difficult part. Gunthra had called me an abomination. While I didn't think—very much hoped—that Lucen wouldn't share her view, telling him about the most interesting part of my abilities made me nervous. "Did you ever figure out what happened between me and that fury who addicted me when we took down Victor?"

"Figured it out? He released you quickly. Was there more?"

"Yeah, actually. The reason he released me so fast is because I'm an abomination." I made air quotes around the word and forced a smile, although I wasn't fooling Lucen. "People like me aren't supposed to be able to survive the transformation, but when we do, we have unique abilities."

"So much is clear."

I wet my lips. "I flipped the bond between myself and the fury. I can't create a bond with another pred, but if they create one with me, I can addict *them*. The fury cut me loose because I was stealing all his power."

After a moment of staring at me, Lucen grabbed the bourbon and poured us both another drink. "Wow. You are full of surprises. I've never heard of such a thing."

"I don't think many people have." I watched his face for a moment. It was curiously blank as he stared into his drink.

Finally, he set it down, untouched. "So the truth comes out at long last. It's never been about whether you trust me. This is the reason you're not afraid around us anymore."

"I wasn't lying when I said I trusted you. But others? No. This makes me less vulnerable though. I feel less like a piece of cattle around this place. More like an abomination."

He squeezed my hand. "You are not an abomination."

"Oh, I don't know. To some I am, and I'm okay with it, I guess. So long as I'm not to you, that's what counts."

"Never." He pulled me closer. "To me, you are the reckless-but-fascinating, beautiful-but-infuriating woman who's burrowed her way into my dark, depraved heart over the last ten years."

I curled up, half on his lap, and placed my hand over that heart. "Good thing I like dark and depraved. But you should also know that I'm supposed to be the Gryphons' savior."

"You're fairly amazing, little siren, but savior might be taking it a bit too far."

"Uh-huh." I didn't touch my second drink until I filled Lucen in on everything Tom had told me. "My life keeps getting crazier and crazier."

"It does." He scratched his chin, lost in thought. "What the Gryphons did to you is horrible, and much as I want to say I told you so, have you considered that there might be something to this prophecy?"

I took his empty glass from him and set it on the table. "No, and if you're considering it, you've had enough to drink. I quit the Gryphons. I told Olivia Lee where she could shove her job and that I'd go public with everything if they arrested me."

"Really?" Whatever thought Lucen had given to the bullshit prophecy vanished. His face brightened with a beautiful grin. "Now you're talking sense."

"I figured you'd agree." I climbed the rest of the way on top of him and draped my arms around his neck. "Here's the wrap-up. I've been thinking —I've tried to be a good Gryphon and a good human, and this was what I got for my efforts. So I'm done. I want to be a good satyr, hybrid, subspecies, whatever. I want to be good to us, and I'm ready to embrace what I really am to make that happen."

I'd barely finished speaking when Lucen caught my lips with his own and stole the rest of my breath. His hands reached under my hair, pulling me closer, and I sank deeper into him, relishing that cinnamon scent of his and reveling in the way my body came alive. Blissfully this time. Perfectly.

He ran his teeth over my lips, and I held my breath. Then his mouth nibbled and licked its way down my throat, and I moaned with anticipation. Sliding my fingers through his hair, I pressed against him. Tighter and closer. Longing to envelop him. I could feel him growing harder, and my body answered in kind. Desire welled in me and pooled between my legs, and my body writhed with the building heat.

If I couldn't be human, I was going to enjoy learning to be a satyr.

He pulled away then, but his hands slipped under my shirt and unclasped my bra. "I want you to know, little siren, I fully support this idea and will do all I can to help."

"Shocking."

He grinned and in one swift motion tugged my shirt over my head. My bra followed it to the floor. Then his fingers cupped my breasts, and his lips caressed my nipple, his tongue swirling around it, teasing and tugging until it was so hard I seethed with the ache.

He turned from the left to the right as I ran my nails against his back, clawing at him for more. When he raised his head and wet his lips, I lifted his shirt, desperate for the touch of his skin, to feel the hard ridges of his muscles undulating beneath my body. His hands seemed to brush every inch of me at once, stoking my desire something fierce.

Gasping, he pushed me back, firm hands squeezing my breasts, his gaze on me like a weight. He was so beautiful already, but more so with that hungry expression on his face. The one that didn't just seem to look at me, but into me. "You have no idea how happy this makes me. You're mine, Jess. Just tell me you trust me, that you give yourself over to me, and we can make this work."

I wanted to scream it, but I could barely manage to whisper, "Yours." So I took his cheeks in my hands, letting my lips and my tongue be my answer, feasting on his flesh while offering up my soul.

He grabbed my ass, pushing my pants and underwear down as he did. My body sang with need for him as his fingers stroked my most sensitive areas, an ache stronger and hotter than anything Lucrezia's foul magic could conjure, until I was tearing at his pants, panting for the touch of his cock. And when he finally slid inside me, I cried out with that desire, every nerve ablaze.

But as Lucen's hands guided the rhythm of my hips, two errant memories flitted through my mind, destroying the brutal ecstasy that should have engulfed me. One was of Steph, chastising me for acting too pred-like. The other was of Olef, telling me about his new visions of cities burning and me at the center of it all.

Something like guilt and fear nipped at my conscience.

"You okay?" Lucen asked.

I tightened my arms around his neck, taking him as far into me as he could go, and he sucked in a sharp breath.

"Way better than okay." I entwined his hair around my fingers. "So much better than okay." I bent my head lower so I could suck the cinnamon salt from his skin.

Lucen's groan of pleasure sent shocks through me, and he thrust deeper, driving away my annoying thoughts of the rest of the world. Squeezing him tighter between my legs, I closed my eyes and concentrated on him—the only thing I wanted to matter.

Thank you for reading! Did you enjoy? Please add your review because nothing helps an author more and encourages readers to take a chance on a book than a review.

And don't miss more in the Miss Misery series with book three, MISERY LOVES COMPANY, available now. Turn the page for a sneak peek!

Also be sure to sign up for the City Owl Press newsletter to receive notice of all book releases!

SNEAK PEEK OF MISERY LOVES COMPANY

In retrospect, choosing to live near a sylph who could wield a straight razor might not have been one of my best decisions.

True, the sylphs hadn't done more than shoot me dirty glances during the past few weeks, and also true, razors were essential tools in a barbershop. But neither of these things made me feel better. Sylphs plus razors plus an apartment building reeked of a bad idea.

Or maybe I was just nervous about living on my own. For the first twenty-eight years of my life, I'd always had to share space with people, be they family or roommates. What if I discovered the hair in the shower drain had been mine all along? What if the peanut butter got moldy because no one was sneaking spoonfuls of it behind my back? What if the glorious peace and quiet drove me insane?

"Jess, I'm not holding this door forever."

What if my satyr-with-benefits was getting impatient while I rambled about stupid shit?

I snapped my gaze away from the sylph-owned barbershop on the bottom floor of my new apartment building, and let it fall on Lucen. Six feet of mischief-eyed, blond-haired, and sweetly muscled satyr adjusted the box he was holding and motioned impatiently.

Who was I kidding? I would never have peace and quiet as long as I had him in my life, and for that I was grateful.

I picked up my suitcase and hurried over to where Lucen had the building door propped open with his back. "Coming. I'm coming."

He let the door swing shut behind him as he followed me into the dimly lit lobby. There were four mailboxes on the right, an ancient art deco-style chandelier dangling from the ceiling, and a wide set of stairs in front of us. Cozy.

"Second floor," I told Lucen, and led the way.

The wood steps had been polished to a dull sheen by years of shoes, and they were slippery as a result. But the beige walls, unpainted wainscoting, and warm light gave the building a homey feel. Not bad for a place that, by Boston standards, was dirt cheap.

Thank dragons for Shadowtown rents. The only humans who lived in this neighborhood were crazy or desperate, and the preds owned more buildings than they could fill with their own kind.

Technically, their own kind included me since I'd recently discovered that I was a strange subspecies of satyr. It was a fact I was slowly learning to accept, although most people—human and pred alike—had no idea about my true biological makeup. They both believed I was just a reckless human freak.

One of these days I would have to enlighten some of them. Sooner rather than later if Lucen had his way.

The old brick building contained only two tenants per floor, with the second and third floors given over to apartments. I stopped on the second-floor landing, setting my suitcase down once more to fish my key from my jeans pocket.

The lock gave way and I grabbed the suitcase before pushing open the heavy door with a flourish. "Welcome to my new apartment. Much nicer than my old one. And roommate-free, to boot."

"I'm glad you're so proud of yourself." Lucen smirked. "Welcome to adulthood."

I stuck my tongue out at him and dropped my suitcase in what would become a combined living room and dining room space.

Lucen followed suit with the box and circled around. "Do I get a tour?"

"It'll be the briefest tour in history." I walked him over to the picture window that overlooked the street and pointed straight to the back of the apartment. "You can see everything from here except the bathroom."

Frowning, Lucen crossed his arms. "So you can. It's...quaint."

Fine. So the apartment wasn't much, but even so, it was more than I could currently afford. I'd signed the lease the same day I unexpectedly quit my consulting job with the Gryphons. Which meant I was temporarily unemployed. Again.

Like the last time I had found myself jobless, Lucen had offered me a waitressing position at his bar, The Lair. He'd even offered to pay me more this time, but that was no surprise. I could actually work, seeing as I didn't have a sprained wrist. Plus, Lucen was probably so thrilled that I no longer associated with the Gryphons that he'd do anything to prevent me from missing the generous hourly wage they'd paid me.

Then again, it could have been Devon's fault that he was willing to pay me more. Devon was Lucen's best friend, lieutenant to the satyrs' Dom, and now—thanks in part to me—the sole owner of the strangest nightclub in Boston. He'd also offered me a job as a cocktail waitress.

Kind as it might be for both of them to keep me gainfully employed, I didn't really want to return to my pre-Gryphon life as a server. Ever since I'd been forced into finding the guy who'd framed me for murder, schlepping drinks and food didn't have as much appeal. My short stint working for the Gryphons had driven that point home.

Alas, there was no way I was going back to the Gryphons, but there had to be another job out there that let me use my brain to help people and that paid me better than the satyrs were offering. No offense to Lucen or Devon.

I had time to figure it out. My first three months' rent had been paid upon signing.

"It might be small, but it's all I need," I told Lucen.

It was the truth. Behind the living room was a narrow galley-style kitchen, and behind that was the bedroom. Another door in the bedroom led into the narrow bathroom that ran parallel to the kitchen. There wasn't much space to fill, but I didn't own much stuff.

While Lucen went to check out the kitchen, my phone rang. Pulling it out of my pocket, I scowled. The number on the caller ID had become very familiar to me over the last week.

It was Olivia Lee, director of the Boston Regional Office of the Angelic Order of the Gryphon. The woman who, a few weeks ago, had blackmailed me into working for her as a consultant, and as a result had almost gotten me killed on my first case.

Okay, I suppose *I* had almost gotten me killed, or Lucrezia—the satyr I'd busted had almost killed me—but it was Olivia's fault I'd been sucked into the mess.

She wasn't pleased that I'd quit afterward, though it had nothing to do with her or the case and everything to do with a Gryphon named Tom Kassin and his damned Gryphon fraternity, *Le Confrérie de l'Aile*, aka the Brotherhood of the Wing.

The Brotherhood were the ones who'd made me the satyr-ish freak that I was, and they had done so when I was a teenager, without my consent or even my knowledge. When I'd discovered the truth, I'd had a good rant at Tom, and had then told Olivia she could shove her consulting gig she-knew-where.

I hadn't heard from Tom since. Olivia, on the other hand, was more persistent. So far, she hadn't followed through on her original threat to have me arrested if I refused to work for her, but I didn't know why. Especially seeing as she wouldn't leave me alone. I could only assume Tom or the Brotherhood had something to do with her hands-off approach, but that didn't exactly reassure me. The Brotherhood had to count some damn powerful Gryphons as its members, both in the magical and political senses.

I was still frowning at the phone when Lucen emerged from his self-guided tour. "Nice, new stove in there. Too bad it will be wasted on your cooking skills. Was that the evil winged-one calling again?"

Distracted by Olivia's call, I let the slight on my culinary achievements slide. "Yeah, only this time she left a message."

That was unusual. Olivia had left a voicemail the first time she'd called me, but none since.

Lucen yawned. He'd gotten up early to help me move. "Well, you going to play that message for my amusement?"

"Sure, if this is what you really find entertaining."

"Oh, you know what I find really entertaining." He grinned. "But we've got to finish unloading my car first. So give me a quickie with this."

"I'd rather give you a quickie with something else, but if you insist on listening to my voicemail..." I pressed my body against his, wrapping my free arm around his back. It was hot outside, and hotter inside with the apartment's stagnant air, and a thin sheen of sweat glistened on his skin. The scent of his cinnamon-tinged pheromones was stronger because of it, and I breathed him in deeply. My muscles, achy from loading his car this morning, decided they didn't ache as badly as my need for him.

Lucen was easily the most gorgeous person I'd ever met, and he would have been hard enough to resist if he were human. With his satyr magic, he was damn near impossible.

Sensing my desire, he leaned down into me and pressed his lips against mine. I let him for a second, grazing my teeth over his bottom lip and sliding my tongue gently over his skin. With a sharp breath he yanked me closer so that my chest pressed into his hard muscles.

I pulled away. My body whined at me for it, but I loved watching the fierce heat on his face when I teased him like this. I was probably the only person who could. Pred power—be it satyr lust, goblin greed, fury rage, harpy jealousy, or sylph insecurity—barely registered with me if I noticed it at all.

But Lucen was the exception. Well, Devon too, but it made me uneasy thinking about him.

Still, I had way more resistance to Lucen's power than I should, and it drove him crazy when I did resist because he wasn't used to it.

"You said you wanted the message now?" I reminded him innocently.

Putting the phone on speaker, I played Olivia's voicemail, which turned out to be far less exciting than the foreplay. Big surprise.

"Jessica, this is Olivia Lee, but I assume you know that and that's why you're not picking up. Whatever your issue with Agent Kassin, it does not concern me, and I want to remind you of the agreement we struck. I expect you to return my call at your earliest convenience, or I will be forced to arrange a meeting using methods you won't like."

I hung up. "Damn. Sounds like Olivia's getting bored with playing nice."

"That didn't take long, and she's calling on the weekend too. Did she forget your threat?"

When I'd told Olivia our deal was off, I'd also told her that if she arrested me, all the dirt I had on *Le Confrérie*—and the Gryphon organization as a whole by association—would go public. "Maybe. Or she's calling my bluff."

Or she didn't know exactly what dirt I had and thus didn't understand the magnitude of my threat. She'd been confused by my quitting, and now that my rage had blown over, it had crossed my mind that Olivia was probably ignorant of what the Brotherhood had done to me and at least four other children.

Ignorant, and perhaps as likely to be appalled by it as I was.

But I wasn't going back, even if that were true. They were all guilty by association in my mind.

Nonetheless, Lucen must have picked up on some of my internal conflict. "If Olivia is going to get on your case and put you on the outs with the Gryphons again, you know what you should do."

I lifted my ponytail and fanned the back of my neck. "Let me guess. You mean tell Dezzi the truth."

"You don't have to make it sound like a death sentence."

"How do we know it's not?"

Lucen didn't bother to respond to my question verbally. He just gave me a quit-being-stupid look.

Fair enough. It wouldn't be a death sentence. Not literally. In fact, Dezzi, the satyr's Dom, was very pleased with me since I'd exposed the plot by Lucrezia to oust her.

Yet telling Dezzi about my quasi-satyr status was a death sentence in one very important way. In my mind, coming out of the pred closet meant the death of my ruse. My entire self-concept. Despite having lived with the truth about myself for a few weeks, I still thought of myself as mostly human. So long as only a handful of people knew otherwise, it was easier to cling to that illusion. Once Dezzi knew, all the satyrs would know, and soon enough, all of Shadowtown would too. I was certain.

I wasn't sure I was ready for that, and for what felt like the hundredth time, I explained my thoughts to Lucen.

"You can't conceal this forever, little siren." He sighed. "I have obligations to Dezzi. If you don't tell her, at some point, I should."

"Then why don't you?" I asked, suddenly irritable. I blamed it on the heat, but the truth was, my satyr status was growing to be a touchy subject between us.

"It should be you. I don't understand why you don't want to do it. As unfair as what the Gryphons did to you was, it's got to be a relief to finally know the truth."

I picked at my T-shirt. It was one Steph had gotten me for my last birthday, black with the words "Bite me" in blue glitter. "It is a relief for me to know, but other people knowing is something else."

"Dezzi will be happy. The domus owes you a thanks for catching Lucrezia. Besides." He came up behind me and put his hands on my arms. I held my breath as his mouth brushed my ear, and sweetly cinnamon lust drove away my irritation. "You're supposed to be embracing your satyrness. Part of that should mean owning up to it."

He had a point, but I didn't like it. "I'm working on it. On every part," I added before he could interject.

The other part I was supposed to be working on was coming to terms with the fact that monogamy was impossible where he was concerned. Lucen was a satyr, and like all preds, he needed to addict humans to his magic to live. For a satyr, that meant he needed to occasionally have sex with those addicts so they remained healthy. I didn't particularly like it, but as far as I knew, there was nothing I could do about it.

Because Lucen understood that I linked sex and emotional attachment, his grand plan was to break my association. And he believed the best way to uncouple them was for me to have lots of mindless sex. We weren't even talking one-night stands. More like one-hour stands. Preferably with people whose names I never bothered to catch. If I did it enough, Lucen was convinced I would separate my feelings for him from my lusty urges.

No surprise, this was easier said than done. We'd had a conversation about it a week ago, and I hadn't done a damn thing since. Merely thinking about it bugged me. Satyr or human, I'd never been the sort of person who felt interested in hopping from one person's bed to another. Lucen's insistence that it was no big deal was a potent reminder that although I wasn't truly human, I also wasn't a normal satyr.

Lucen tugged on my earlobe with his lips, his arms locked around me from behind. I closed my eyes, not for the first time wishing for a magical solution to the problem we faced. But though I didn't know much about magic, one thing I did know was that it wasn't a solution for all problems.

"We should finish unloading," I reminded him.

"I think I changed my mind. Now might be a good time for a break, after all." Hot breath fell on my neck, followed moments later by his lips nibbling their way to my collarbone.

I breathed deeply, trying to be strong. "This place is a dusty mess. There's no furniture and no drapes over the windows yet."

"Satyrs aren't modest."

I twisted around in his arms. "I'm not a normal satyr, and I don't need to give the people at the pizza place across the street a dinner show."

Lucen laughed. "Fine. If you insist." He kissed me hard, as though to remind me what I was delaying, then let me go.

It took another hour of carting boxes and bags, but we finally headed downstairs for the last load. While packing this morning, I'd been impressed that I could fit my entire life into two trips in Lucen's midsize sedan. Now, on further reflection, I felt the serious need to do some furniture shopping lest I eat all my meals off cardboard boxes.

Sweat rolled down my neck and I massaged my throbbing hand. Getting my damn futon frame up the stairs had resulted in minor scrapes and bruises for both of us. Lucen's healed almost instantly, but being the abnormal pred that I was, I healed more like a human. Slowly and painfully.

Outside, Shadowtown was coming alive. Though I'd joked about giving the pizza place a show, they were only now opening for business. As was the chain drugstore next to it, and the barbershop and magic-supply shop on the ground floor of my apartment building.

Waving politely at the satyr who owned the magical-supply shop, I turned down the alley next to the building where Lucen had illegally parked his car. In Shadowtown, no one had to worry about tickets. The Gryphons, who policed all magical matters, had more pressing responsibilities, and so did the preds, who policed themselves for pred-on-pred offenses.

Lucen grabbed the last box, which contained my pots and pans, and I grabbed my comforter. "You owe me for this, little siren. You owe me so much."

"I'm looking forward to it."

"Oh, no." Lucen was grinning again as he shook his head. "Not that way. I'm repainting my apartment this fall. I hope you know how to use a roller."

I banged my hip against the building door to open it. "Your apartment is gorgeous. What does it need repainting for?"

"It doesn't. I just want to watch you work."

I called him a few names as I climbed the stairs, but my laughter faded when I reached the top. Lucen smacked me in the back with the box, and I jumped out of his way.

His brow furrowed as he noticed what I was staring at. "Where did that come from?"

"No idea, but someone was sneaky." And fast. Lucen and I couldn't have been outside for more than a couple minutes.

I pushed the gift basket aside with my toe so I could open the apartment door. After I dumped the comforter on the partially assembled futon, I stuck my head back outside and scanned the landing and stairwell. They were both empty. Not exactly surprising. I didn't see a reason why whoever had left the basket would hang around to watch me take it. Yet its presence left me with a bad feeling.

Lucen had been moving my kitchen boxes around on the scant counter space, and he opened the fridge and took out the two beers we'd stuck in there earlier. I put the gift basket down in the spot he'd freed. Wrapped in cellophane was a bottle of wine, some cheese, crackers, and nuts.

"That's a harpy-owned shop that sent it." He must have recognized the logo on the envelope. With a nod, Lucen handed me one of the beers. "So who's it from?"

The beer hadn't chilled enough, but it was better than nothing. I took a swig and contemplated. "Dezzi?" I couldn't think of anyone else who might send me a welcome basket.

"I wouldn't count on it. What about your family?"

"I wouldn't count on it. They wouldn't contact a pred-owned business."

"The suspense is killing me. Open the damn thing." Lucen made to grab for the envelope, but I snatched it away and tore into it for the card. Almost immediately, I wished I hadn't.

Miss Moore, welcome to the neighborhood. I request that you grant me the honor of your presence at four o'clock tomorrow for tea.

Best wishes, Gunthra

I swallowed and reached for more beer. Shit. My gut had been right to be wary.

Lucen grabbed the card from my hand. "What does the goblins' Dom want with you?"

Since I suspected the answer and knew it wouldn't please him, I opted to say nothing. During the week when I'd been framed for murder, I'd made a bargain with Gunthra. She'd known what I was, and in desperation, believing knowing the truth about myself could help save me, I'd made a deal with her. The truth about my gift in return for an unspecified future favor.

I'd been right to a degree. Gunthra's information had probably kept me alive. But now I'd bet she was ready to collect. I'd also bet that I wasn't going to like upholding my end of the deal.

Welcome to the neighborhood, indeed.

Don't stop now. Keep reading with your copy of MISERY LOVES COMPANY

And find more from Tracey Martin at www.tracey-martin.com

Don't miss book three, MISERY LOVES COMPANY, coming soon, and discover more from Tracey Martin at www.tracey-martin.com

---

When it comes to magic, more isn't always merrier.

Keep letting the Gryphons blackmail her —or join a goblin for tea? Jess must make some choices.

Furious at the Gryphons' betrayal, former vigilante Jessica Moore is determined to cut the law enforcement agency from her life—and hopes doing so will solidify her rocky relationship with Lucen. But when a friend's soul is sucked dry by a goblin, Jess finds it's not so easy to let go of her past. Unwilling to let down someone who needs help, she puts aside her anger to work with the Gryphons and solve the case.

But a stolen soul isn't her only problem. Boston's goblin leader is calling in the debt Jess owes. To find the soul and pay off her debt, Jess must unearth information about a magic she never knew existed, all the while testing Lucen's patience and stirring the wrath of old enemies.

What she discovers will reveal the terrifying truth behind the Gryphons' treachery, and force her to choose where her loyalty—and her heart —truly lie.

Escape Your World. Get Lost in Ours! City Owl Press at www.cityowlpress.com.

ACKNOWLEDGMENTS

Thank you to Danielle DeVor, Vanessa Wotjanowski, and all the staff at City Owl Press for making this book happen. And, as always, thank you to my family, friends, and writing groups for for supporting me on this journey.

ABOUT THE AUTHOR

TRACEY MARTIN lives in New England where she collects pen names, tattoos, and hoodies in shades of gray and black. Under the name Alanna Martin, she's the author of the *Hearts of Alaska* contemporary romance series. If you can't find her online, it's because she's lost in the woods. Send help.

www.tracey-martin.com

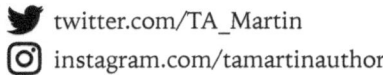 twitter.com/TA_Martin
instagram.com/tamartinauthor

ABOUT THE PUBLISHER

City Owl Press is a cutting edge indie publishing company, bringing the world of romance and speculative fiction to discerning readers.

Escape Your World. Get Lost in Ours!

www.cityowlpress.com

facebook.com/YourCityOwlPress
twitter.com/cityowlpress
instagram.com/cityowlbooks
pinterest.com/cityowlpress